DEUS EX MEC

Ryann Fletcner

To my fearless pirate captain, queen of my heart. This book wouldn't exist without you.

CHAPTER ONE

"FUCK," ALICE SAID UNDER her breath, as a small gear rolled under the boiler she was fixing for the third time this month. That gear was tiny, but mighty: without it, there's no way the boiler would function properly. If only the Coalition would update their merchant ships as often as their military ships, she wouldn't have to spend as much time crawling around on the floor of the ship, trying to dig out tiny pieces that came loose during a turbulent flight. She mused on the laughable impossibility of the Coalition updating a merchant ship, especially when she was able to make it run smooth. If they updated these systems, she'd be out of a job. She bent down with her standard issue, hand crank kinetic flashlight in her hand. She squinted and peered under the boiler.

"I'm too tall for this shit," she muttered, blowing the cobwebs and dust away.

Her radio crackled to life as she located the gear and hauled herself upright. "Bridge to boiler, how are we looking down there?"

Alice crossed the room, wiping her hands on her gray Coalition standard coveralls. These were her oldest, most worn out pair, with threadbare patches on the elbows and knees, and a brass pocket zipper that wouldn't stay zipped.

With the small radio in her hand, she responded, "Boiler to bridge, almost set down here. The damn valve came loose again, we should have enough steam to start the engines in about twenty minutes."

The radio fell silent, and Alice shook her head. She'd been flying with Captain Augustus Allen for decades now, ever since their first ship assignment long ago. He was a man of few words, but loyal to Alice; he always requested her to be his mechanic when he changed ships, and loyalty seemed to be in short supply lately.

Alice sat down on a nearby overturned apple crate and sighed, checking her watch. "The sooner we get out of this system, the better," she said, this time to herself. This area was thick with rebels and marauders, and this was the largest trade ship that traveled the nearby systems. Though this ship was staffed with Coalition military, most of them were recruits, and still green.

She didn't want to think would happen if they were faced with a full on attack; then again, most rebels wouldn't dare attack a ship of this size out in the open.

"You talking to yourself again, gorgeous?" Barnaby, Alice's oldest friend, confidently strode into the room, deftly stepping around the greasy puddles that had gathered near the boilers.

Alice turned and smiled, rolling her eyes. "As if you could talk, old man."

"Old man!" Barnaby exclaimed incredulously, chuckling, "How dare you? We were born in the same year!"

"Maybe, but I don't look it," Alice said, "All those dodgy trade deals have taken their toll on your face."

"Yes, I suppose hiding in boiler rooms and cargo holds would indeed shield one's face from any hint of sunlight," Barnaby countered, and after a beat added, "Or fun." He leaned against a large anti-gravity unit and tilted his head towards Alice. "You'd be hot property if you'd wear something other than those old coveralls and goggles, you know."

Alice pushed her long silver braids over her shoulders and looked at Barnaby, laughing, "As if you have any clue what would or wouldn't make me *hot property*."

Barnaby stood up straight and puffed out his chest with his hands on his hips. "I may prefer my lovers more masculine, my dear Alice, but I still have *eyes*."

She snorted with a laugh and stood up, towering over Barnaby. She pushed up her goggles to rest on her pale, grease smeared forehead and looked towards the main boiler. "These things always break at the least opportune moment. I just fixed this one last week." She weakly kicked at the boiler with a scuffed tan boot.

Barnaby poked through a nearby box of steam droids, all of them lifeless without their solar powered battery cores. "How long until we're ready to go? With all this equipment and provisions on board, we're sitting ducks for the local wildlife." He picked up one of the droids and held it up to the dim light. "And by wildlife, I mean pirates," he added. "What are these doing down here, anyway? Did one of the new recruits forget where the cargo hold is?"

"It's currently being occupied by crates of land mines," she replied. "We haven't been back to the base on Gamma 3 to drop them off yet, so we're flying through space with a wondrous eclectic assortment of fruits, vegetables, and mass casualty weapons." She kicked her boot against the box of droids, and one weakly lit up, using the last vestiges of its stored solar power. "I don't care where they put it, so long as they don't start storing this crap in my bunk."

"Bridge to boiler," the radio called again, "Are we clear to power up the main thruster? Over."

Alice raised the radio to her chin and replied, "Just a few more moments, Captain."

Once again the radio fell silent, and Barnaby added into the silence, "He's always been such a personable fellow, hasn't he?"

Alice crossed to the boiler to inspect the pressure gauge. "He's a good man, Barnaby. Better than you." She turned and smirked at her friend, who was still looking through the box of small robots.

"You can't be a good man *and* be a good merchant, Al." Barnaby's suit was a testament to his success: it was well tailored using the finest fabrics and buttery leather. Next to Alice's shabby coveralls, he looked like the picture of success. "I do what I must. Because I can."

Alice tapped the pressure gauge and furrowed her brow. "You do what you do because you like money," she replied. She looked sideways at Barnaby, "And you like the kind of men that tend to follow that money. What was the last one's name again, Barns? *Chad*, was it?"

"And what kind of women tend to follow engine grease, then?" he retorted, gesturing at the oily patch on her left elbow.

Alice ignored his question, turning her attention to the misbehaving boiler instead. "Looks like the pressure gauge is faulty. Probably won't last another flight, but I think I have a replacement down here."

Barnaby looked around at the mountains of stacked boxes, bemused. "And how would you even know where to start looking?"

Alice shot him a look. "I have a very meticulous filing system, thank you very much." She turned to push a pile of metal instruments out of the way. "Just because you're not intelligent enough to grok it, doesn't mean it doesn't exist." She bent and reached her arm behind a mound of copper wiring. "Aha!" She shouted triumphantly, "I knew I had one!" Barnaby watched her as she crossed the room to her workbench, poking at the gadget with tiny screwdrivers. "Anyway, I'm far too busy keeping this hunk of junk ship together to think about love," she said defiantly.

"Hunk of junk?" Barnaby said incredulously. "This is the fastest merchant ship in the entire Coalition fleet."

Alice turned to him and grinned, "Yes, and I'm the only reason why it's the fastest. Why do you think this ship outperforms newer models by twenty percent?"

Barnaby held a droid aloft, examining the tiny robot. "Your modesty is astounding, Alice."

"What can I say," Alice smirked, "I learned from the best." She rummaged through a pile of sprockets and wrenches, and pulled out a tiny pair of pliers with a red rubber handle, perfect for handling electrical equipment.

"Well you'd better hope that false humility isn't misplaced," Barnaby grumbled. "Just last week a merchant ship was attacked by pirates, not too far from here. They say there were no survivors."

Alice let out a laugh. "Give me a break, Barnaby, you sound ridiculous," she chuckled, adding, "No survivors. Did they have to walk the plank too?" She bent over the pressure gauge in front of her, tapping on the glass and poking it with the pliers. "Anyway, this is a Coalition military staffed vessel. No rebels, or pirates, or bogeymen would be stupid enough to attack it. Not without a death wish, anyway."

She straightened her back and yawned, stretching her arms out over her head.

"BRIDGE TO BOILER: PREPARE FOR IMPACT!" the radio suddenly screeched.

CHAPTER TWO

ALICE WAS THROWN INTO her workbench, tiny gears, copper wiring, and the tiny pliers flying in every direction.

Barnaby fell backwards into the pile of boxes, tiny droids sailing through the air and smashing onto the floor, disintegrating into millions of tiny pieces. The shelving against the wall started to tip over, boxes of tools sliding off of the shelves and crashing onto the ship floor. Crates that were stacked to the ceiling were cascading down in slow motion, their contents spilling out and collecting into small mountains of disarray. Alice braced against the workbench, scanning the wreckage for Barnaby. She saw him pinned under a crate of heavy bronze tubing, struggling to push the crate off of his left leg.

"Argh, what the bloody hell was that?" Barnaby grunted, using his other leg as leverage to free himself. He stood up and dusted himself off, examining his suit for any damage.

"Don't worry Barns, you look as dapper as ever." Alice looked around, surveying the damage. She dug under a pile of aluminum scrap metal and pulled out the radio. Half the electrics were missing, and it snapped and crackled with a garbled message from the captain.

"Brid——ler. Pi——tacked. Prep-—to be—." The radio gave one last pop and the display faded to nothing, leaving a useless, blank screen.

"Goddammit," Alice muttered. "Barns, I have to head to the bridge to see what's going on. Try not to break anything," she smirked.

"Hands up and stay where you are!" a voice yelled.

Alice spun around and was faced with a small group, led by a woman who was even shorter than Barnaby. She wore a tan leather waistcoat layered on top of a green shirt with matching trousers, tucked into tall black lace up boots. Her tight curls were tied up, her dark brown skin shining with sweat. A long scar crossed her face from her left eye, across her nose, ending just below the right side of her chin. It gave her a malevolent, threatening look. Alice's breath caught in her chest – was this a pirate raid?

"Who the hell are you?" Alice demanded, her hands in the air. She was tall, a woman to be reckoned with, but she was not a fighter, especially not to protect a bunch of now-broken equipment.

The woman arched an eyebrow and looked Alice up and down. "You mean you've not heard of me? I'm told that I'm infamous."

"I assure you, I don't have the slightest clue who you are, other than someone who is holding me at gunpoint." Alice shifted in place, trying not to stare.

"Well I know who you are, Alice. I'm told you're the best mechanic in the whole of the Coalition. My name is Captain Violet. I'm here to confiscate the goods you carry on this ship."

"Well you're welcome to steal whatever you like, I won't stop you," Alice responded confidently. "Most of it is broken anyway."

Violet stepped forward to inspect an overturned crate and sighed. "Yes, it would seem we damaged some of the electrical equipment with our little ship. I didn't anticipate that there would be so many crates in the boiler room, that's why we attacked on this side." She straightened and grinned at Alice with a twinkle in her deep brown eyes. "Still, I'll get what I came for. Your captain and the rest of the crew are otherwise engaged, probably still hiding in cupboards from the reprogrammed solar droids I set loose on the bridge."

Alice looked at Violet suspiciously. "Clever to reprogram the droids," she said, "but how did you do it? There are safety protocols that prevent tampering."

"Well I'm not about to give away my best kept secret, am I?" Violet smirked.

Alice frowned. "Well what is it you're here for?"

Violet stepped closer and looked up at Alice. "I'm here for all of it, Mechanic. We're taking everything, from the produce, to the metal scrap and computer components. Stand aside so my crew can expedite this process."

Alice shrugged and stepped to the side as she called to Barnaby, "Barns, you alright? Just let them take what they want. Neither of us are exactly warriors, eh?"

Her oldest friend shot an angry look at the pirates before sitting on an overturned crate in the corner. "The Coalition will never let you get away with this, you know," he muttered. "You're fools if you think you can ransack the largest trading ship in the near systems."

From across the room, one of the other pirates yelled, "Some more platinum scrap over here, Captain!"

Violet turned to face her second in command, a petite, sinewy woman half her age dressed entirely in black. "Thank you Kady, see that it makes it onto the ship. I'm sure that will prove useful in your recent experiments." She faced Alice again and raised an eyebrow, looking her up and down. Alice knew that her height and burn scarred arms made her look more threatening than she really was, and the silver braids that were draped over her shoulders were evidence of her practicality. She wondered how long it would take for Captain Allen to save the day and get them back on course.

"Ned, keep an eye on that one in the corner," the captain said loudly to a tall, burly man behind her. He had tattoos covering his arms and a generous ginger beard, his long fiery locks tied up into a bun that sat loosely on top of his head.

Ned strode across the boiler room, surprisingly graceful amongst all the debris. He stopped in front of Barnaby and crossed his arms threateningly, the tiniest flicker of recognition flashing across his face.

"I suppose *Ned* is just here to serve as muscle then," Barnaby hissed. "How utterly predictable that a pirate would rely on brute force to get what she wants." He squinted and looked at Ned, the very picture of masculinity. His glare softened and he raised an eyebrow. "I bet you don't even speak. Your types are rarely a paragon of intellect."

Ned laughed a deep, hearty laugh, throwing his head back and slapping his knee. "Actually," Violet said, "Ned is my best navigator. He just doesn't enjoy speaking to slimy Coalition traders."

Barnaby frowned, but fell silent.

They heard a deep scream and a series of thuds from the above deck, a Coalition crew member fighting off one of Violet's reprogrammed droids with a mop. Violet laughed, and Ned began his throaty laugh anew. "Who knew that these would cause quite so much ruckus?" Violet asked Ned, laughing.

"Well, Kady obviously thought they were a good idea," he responded, "though I imagine their batteries won't last much longer with their current programming. We should get a move on, Boss."

Violet scanned the room, looking for more valuable loot to relocate to her ship. "Soon, Ned," she reassured him, "But we need to finish what we came for first." She turned to Alice. "You can put your arms down if you wish. You would have attacked me already if you had the spine for it."

Alice lowered her arms, glaring. "I have the spine for plenty of things, but risking my hide for a bunch of broken down droids isn't one of them." Alice leaned against a nearby cooling unit, her coveralls soaking up the condensation of the machine. After this tense encounter, the cold water was a welcome refreshment. She closed her eyes briefly as she enjoyed the cool dampness of the condensation, and wondered if she could use this experience to leverage her way to a pay raise. She could do with a few more credits every month.

Kady entered and picked up another large crate. "Anything else in particular, Captain? Our cargo hold still has plenty of space if you have your heart set on something."

Violet glanced at Alice out of the corner of her eye, but the large mechanic had no intention of bolting. "Make sure you get those droids, Kady," she said, "You can reprogram those as well for future endeavors." Kady gave a terse nod and exited the room with her crate of scrap metal, her long stride disappearing around a corner, her steps all but silent.

A radio on Violet's belt crackled to life. "Captain, anything else from the cargo hold you want? We're about ready to wrap up here."

Violet paused to think, and then responded, "Make sure you get all the peaches." She looked at the tall mechanic. "They're my favorite, and I've not had a ripe, juicy fruit lately."

Alice noted that their radios were somehow getting around the scramblers they had on board, and wondered if Kady had reprogrammed those, too. Another thing to fix when this was all over – though Alice was more of a mechanic than a programmer, if she was being honest with herself.

"Roger that, Captain, we'll make sure those make it onto the ship. Over."

Violet clipped her radio back onto her belt and turned to Alice's workbench, left in disarray by the impact. The captain tutted at the mess, and Alice felt irritation and annoyance flare in her gut. Sure, tools and screws were strewn all over the floor, scattered with gears and valves, but it wasn't her fault that her carefully stacked piles had been thrown across the room. Decades of equipment, some obsolete in the eyes of her superiors, mixed in with new tech in a hideous, disorganized heap.

"Do you have any idea how long that's going to take me to clean up?" Alice asked, noticing Violet's interest in her workbench. "It took me years to get that exactly how I wanted it. I probably won't even live long enough to return it to order," she said with a tinge of anger.

Violet smiled and looked at Alice, bemused. "Why are you more concerned about your workbench than the theft in progress?" Violet asked.

"Because while I work for the Coalition, their equipment getting stolen won't affect how many credits I take home. I'm a mechanic, not the head of security." Alice kicked a screw across the floor. "How long are you going to hold us up here, anyway? Thanks to you and your band of merry pirates, I get to add at least a dozen jobs to my to-do list." The condensation had soaked through the right arm over her coveralls by now, and instead of feeling refreshed, she just felt vaguely damp. Alice stood up straight and brushed the dust off of her knees. "As if I didn't have enough to do around here."

"Well, I sincerely apologize for adding to your workload," Violet replied with a mocking deep bow. "I guess a mechanic's work is never done."

"Not when pirates make a mess of my workbench," Alice muttered.

"Oh please, Alice, it always looks like that," Barnaby quipped, still sitting in Ned's enormous shadow. "I don't know how you ever find anything down here."

"I told you, I have a very specific filing system—"

BANG.

All the lights went out, and the electrical equipment flashed "0000000" and shut down.

"What the hell was that?" Barnaby yelled.

The only light left came from the pilot light on the boiler, which cast long shadows on Alice and Violet, leaving the men in darkness.

"FUCK! We need to move, Ned!" shouted Violet. "They used an electro-magnetic pulse to disable the droids, but they fucked the lights, too!"

Alice laughed at the chaos: no doubt it was the plucky new navigation assistant, fresh from the academy, that had initiated the pulse. He'd hate himself in about twenty minutes when Captain Augustus Allen was demoting him to cleaning crew for destroying the navigation system along with Violet's droids. Augustus was a man of few words, but his wrath was obvious and devastating to a promising new career. These confident newbies were hotshots in class, but they have a thing or two to learn about how Coalition ships actually functioned. Alice squinted in the dim light, but couldn't make out much. Her vision wasn't the greatest in broad daylight, and in the dark she may as well be blind.

Violet's radio beeped to signify that the power was on its way back. The equipment slowly and quietly started to reboot, and one by one the overhead lights flickered on. Alice knew that while she could get the core systems running in a few minutes, the ruined navigation system would take days to repair.

"This is Captain Augustus Allen," Violet's radio boomed at full volume. "Prepare to be arrested."

The pulse had reset the pirates' radios and removed whatever programming they had been using to get around the scrambler. Now the only frequency that was working was the Coalition's.

"In here!" Captain Allen shouted, and a group of young Coalition initiates streamed into the room with their weapons drawn. Some held Coalition standard pistols, while others were using steam powered heat guns, and others had random pieces of scrap metal they had salvaged from the destruction. Alice knew from looking at them that they hadn't yet retrieved their standard issue rifles from the armory, and so had improvised. Captain Allen was a man of sturdy stock, with wide shoulders and an ageing face, dressed in an impeccably pressed Coalition uniform.

Alice glanced at Barnaby, to offer a reassuring look. This was all going to be over soon. She was startled to see him staring at Ned quizzically, looking him up and down.

"Pirates," Captain Allen said. "Why am I not surprised?" He took a step towards Violet. "*Captain* Violet, I presume? I've heard how you target merchant ships for petty thievery. Fruits, vegetables, scrap metal. It hardly seems worth the effort. It's a shame you never learned how to apply yourself as a real Coalition officer."

Violet narrowed her eyes, and in a flash raised her gun and pointed it at Alice. "Pleased to meet you, Captain Allen. Let's negotiate. I'll even let you make your demands first."

"Leave my ship immediately, and I won't kill you myself," he began. "Though I can't promise you that the Coalition won't track you down, arrest you, and give you the death penalty for your crimes." He raised his chin at Violet, squinting his eyes. "I don't think you know who you're up against."

Violet laughed, staring at Captain Allen. "Hmm, let me see," she countered, "Captain Allen, renowned captain and pilot for the Coalition with a thirty five year track record and more awards and titles than any other living captain. You've been known to defeat whole pirate fleets single handedly, though that was a long time ago. *Sir.* Being relegated to crewing trade vessels is hardly evidence that you've continued to move up in the ranks, now is it?" She leaned towards Alice, gun still drawn.

Alice shrank back against the cooling unit, her damp coveralls soaking in more of the warm stagnant water. She hadn't anticipated being collateral damage today, and this wasn't how she wanted things to end.

Violet continued, "Let us board our ship, and I won't kill the best mechanic in the Coalition, leaving you stranded in the most pirate-infested stretch of space in all the nearby systems. After all, not all pirate crews are as polite as mine."

Alice stumbled against the machine, surprised: how the hell did Violet know that she was the best mechanic, and why did she care? Surely a pirate captain has better things to do than to research Coalition employees.

Captain Allen stared silently at Violet, seething with rage. He had never let a known pirate out of his sight before, and Alice knew he surely wouldn't be starting now. "I have more guns trained on you and your crew. Surely even *you* can understand that the odds aren't in your favor." He stepped towards Violet again, who flushed with fear before steeling herself and cocked the hammer on her silver revolver.

"Don't test me, Captain, I'm sure you know my track record," she boasted. "The deadliest in all the systems, no? I think you know I'm not bluffing."

Alice locked eyes with her captain, she knew that he wouldn't fail her, or he'd never forgive himself. The Coalition probably wouldn't forgive him, either. They weren't known for leniency, even when deciding the fate of decorated senior commanders like Captain Allen.

"Ready your weapons, crew," he stated boldly. "This *captain* has boarded the wrong ship." The crew raised their weapons, and all at one they cocked their pistols, started up their heat guns, and choked up their grips on their improvised weapons. Alice closed her eyes: whatever was about to happen, she didn't want to witness it. She'd been in proximity to enough carnage in her life, and she didn't need to have a front row seat to her own death. Violet stood straight and looked coolly at Allen, her eyes narrowed.

"Well, Captain, I highly recommend that you don't turn around, then."

Allen turned, and saw Kady sitting atop a support beam, with a menacing looking little droid in each hand. They flashed red, making angry little beeps and whirrs. "I think you already met my other creations, Captain. Perhaps now you'd like to meet the upgraded versions? They are programmed to target anyone with an implanted Coalition chip, which as employees and crew members, you all have, I'm sure you know." The color drained from Allen's face as his crew began to lower their weapons. "One blast by my little pretties here, and your heart stops dead."

Alice instinctively rubbed her left bicep where her Coalition chip had been implanted decades earlier. She knew droids like these could potentially cause chaos in the nearby systems, though at this rate she doubted she would even make it through today, much less another few months. Alice braced herself for whatever might come next, barely breathing at all. The room was silent when Allen made his decision, with barely a heartbeat to be heard.

"Get off my ship." Allen glared at Violet, his stare full of impotent rage.

Violet gave a triumphant laugh and gestured to Ned and Kady. "Round up the rest of the goods, Ned," she said victoriously. "Another successful pillage."

Ned hefted a box of droids and tilted his head towards Barnaby. "I'm sure we'll meet again," he said in a deep voice. "Perhaps the next time we raid your ship and steal all your ill-gotten goods."

Alice looked sideways at Barnaby, who sat on an old wooden crate in a silent tantrum. He was glaring at the tall, broad man who stood in front of him, who laughed and gave a mischievous wink before he turned and walked towards the center of the room. She couldn't help but wonder how much force it would take to disarm a man like Ned.

Kady walked backwards across the beam, still holding her angry little robots in her hands. She was astonishingly graceful, full of poise and balance, holding lives in the palms of her hands. "Ready when you are, Captain," she said as she perched at the end of the beam.

Violet looked at Alice apologetically, her revolver still pointed at her chest. "I'm sorry, Alice, but you're going to have to come with us," she said. From the corner of her eye, she saw Barnaby shift uncomfortably in his seat and flick his gaze back and forth between each member of her crew, possibly sizing them up.

"Over my dead body," Allen said angrily. "You're not taking her as a hostage. You goddamned pirates think that you can just do whatever you—"

"I'm going to interrupt you there, Captain," Kady interjected. "I think you'll agree that we still hold all the cards. It may be noble to sacrifice yourself, but is it wise to sacrifice the lives of your entire crew?" She gestured towards the Coalition crew members with the droids. "Or perhaps I should just drop these now and be done with it, and we can just strip this entire ship?"

"Alright Kady," Violet said, "I think he gets the picture." She turned to Captain Allen. "So, Captain, do we have an agreement? The goods and the mechanic for your life and the lives of your crew?"

Allen stared silently and left a long, angry pause. His voice poised with razor sharp, quiet rage, he said, "We'll find you, I hope you realize that. And you won't be exiting that exchange alive."

Violet grinned at him, her dark eyes sparkling. "I look forward to it, Captain." Her gun still trained on Alice, she backed out of the room, pulling her by the elbow. When she reached the door, she mock saluted Captain Allen with her revolver and motioned to Kady, who silently leapt down from the beam, droids in hand.

"Farewell, *Captain*," Kady said with a smirk.

The door began to close, the hydraulics wheezing and grunting with the weight of the heavy steel. Alice watched as her crew, her captain, and her best friend all stood with their heads hung in shame, silently watching her be taken away, maybe forever.

CHAPTER THREE

"CLOSE THE DOOR AND let's get the hell out of here!" Violet yelled, pulling Alice backwards up a ramp onto her ship. "As soon as those systems are back online, they'll be calling for backup. We don't want to be anywhere near here when that happens."

Alice wrenched her arm away and spun to face Violet.

"Get your goddamned hands off of me!" she roared. "I don't take *kindly* to people who hold a gun to me. Whatever you're after, I'll make sure you never get it. Return me to my ship immediately! How dare you! Release me immediately! I swear, I'll...I'll..."

"You'll do nothing of the sort," Violet said coolly. "Ned, chart a course for our next stop, and make sure you conserve as much energy as possible. We don't want to be left stranded with the Coalition on our tail." The ship began to come to life, with lights flickering on above them and the sound of the boilers beginning to heat the water into steam.

"Are you the worst pirate in history?" Alice asked, pointing at her left arm. "They'll be able to track you by the chip in my arm. You might as well stay put for all the good it's going to do you." She put her hands on her hips, towering over Violet.

Violet looked up at Alice defiantly, only realizing the mechanic's height for the first time. She was a tall, broad, attractive woman, the sort that Violet might have pursued if circumstances were different. "Stand still," she said with a firm voice.

"If you think I'm just going to stand here and – ouch!" Alice whirled around, rubbing her bicep. Kady stood next to her with a small gun in her hand. It was smaller than a tea cup and had a dull shine along the rounded barrel.

"It's a tiny electromagnetic pulse. Not enough to damage any outside equipment, but enough to disable the chip. No one is going to be tracking us, so you can just pipe down and behave." Kady snapped the minuscule gun back onto her belt. "We're the best pirate fleet in the nearby systems, we're not going to take a tracked hostage."

Violet reflexively rubbed her arm, glad that she wasn't subject to anything so underhanded as a Coalition tracking chip. Every employee of the Coalition had one implanted on their first day of service, meant to discourage both kidnappers and desertion.

"Kady developed that gun to help Coalition deserters," Violet said. "The penalty for defection from a corrupt institution shouldn't be death. They pay us in information, and we disable their chips for them. As you can see, it also comes in handy for...other endeavors."

Alice raised an eyebrow at Violet. "So why am I here, then?" she asked. "You already had them on their knees with those death droids you have, so why take a hostage?"

Violet sighed and holstered her revolver. "Come with me," she said, resigned. "I'll show you why you're a...well, why you're here."

They walked down a long corridor lined with metal doors and the cold blue lights flickered weakly overhead. The ship was powering up, the engines beginning to turn, preparing to disembark. Violet knew that it would be at least six hours before the nearest Coalition ship would be able to help Captain Allen, but hopefully they would be long gone by then. Violet looked sideways at Alice, who shivered in the cool ship, no doubt chilled by her damp coveralls.

They came to the end of the corridor, which forked into two hallways. "We'll finish preparing the ship for launch and see you on the bridge, Captain," Kady said as she and Ned took the hallway to the right, which led to the cockpit of the ship and the navigation boards. Violet led Alice down the left hallway, down towards the cargo hold and the boiler room. They entered the boiler room, which she knew was structurally similar to the C.S. Stronghold, and hoped Alice would feel comfortable working on their equipment, even if it predated the Coalition's technology by at least a decade. One thing was for sure, their boiler room was a far sight tidier than the disaster Violet had seen on the Stronghold. No cluttered workbench or boxes of scrap metal here, just an empty room with some cobwebs in the corner.

Alice looked at a large puddle of rusty water on the floor in the middle of the room and sighed. "You don't have a mechanic on this ship?" she asked. "These boilers and systems need near constant attention even on state of the art Coalition ships. How have you not just fallen out of the sky yet?" Alice turned towards Violet, who shuffled her feet and looked down at the floor.

"Our mechanic was a good man. We lost him a few months back."

"He died in one of your pillage raids, I presume," Alice said with acid in her tone.

Violet looked up at her, fire in her eyes and her right hand on the revolver on her belt. "He died because, when he was bringing food to his family, the Coalition sprung a trap and killed him. They were starving out his wife and children because they knew he'd come back for them. He was one of the best men I've ever known, and they murdered him without a thought."

Alice gasped quietly and looked down at the floor. Violet couldn't help but feel annoyed at the mechanic's indifference to the Coalition's crimes. How could a woman so talented and intelligent be comfortable working for such an institution? She drew in a deep breath to steady herself.

"I'm sorry," Alice said to Violet, her voice low. "It's never easy to lose someone, no matter the circumstances." She examined a boiler, tapping the temperature gauge. A moment of silence passed before Violet spoke again.

"As I'm sure you have figured out by now, I need you to fix and service these systems. One of the main boilers isn't reaching full pressure, which has impacted our ability to get to cruising speed. Once you are finished, you'll be free to go. We will drop you on the nearest terraformed base, and you can catch a transport back to your ship." She turned on the heel of her boot and sharply marched up the steps out of the boiler room, and back towards the bridge of the ship.

• • • •

ALICE WAS LEFT ALONE with boilers and machines, which gave her an old, familiar sense of safety. Systems like these could never surprise her, she knew them inside and out. She could predict any fault and repair any valve or gasket. The only thing that varied was how long a job could take; looking at these systems, she realized it wouldn't take more than a few days to get it all back into excellent condition. She sighed and looked around for the tools she would need to complete the job. Whoever Violet's last mechanic was, he certainly took a more minimalist approach to maintaining a ship, despite the neatness of his station.

She spied a small metal box underneath a table across the room. She crossed the room and dragged it out, the steel scraping across the floor. There was a rusty padlock on the clasp; that mechanic valued his tools just like Alice valued her own. Still, she couldn't break into the toolbox with her bare hands, and the empty boiler room wasn't offering her any alternative means to remove the lock. Alice stood up and wiped her hands on her damp and dusty coveralls. She would have to go looking for a key.

Alice purposefully climbed the steps out of the boiler room and peered down the long corridor. The lights no longer flickered, and cast deep shadows into the dark corners. She tried the first door she came to, but it was locked. The second door opened into a storage closet filled with cleaning supplies, with a dusty mop propped against the far wall. "I guess cleaning isn't a priority for pirates," she mused to herself.

She closed the door behind her and continued down the hall. One door after another was locked or useless, and she began to see why they had left her unsupervised. There was nothing she could use for an attack or to escape, unless she managed to devise a plan involving moth eaten bed sheets and vinegar. She was a brilliant mechanic and an accomplished engineer, but there were limits to her intellect and ingenuity.

She sighed. "Only one door left," she thought. If she couldn't find something to open that padlock, she would have to ask for Violet's help. After their last interaction, she didn't relish the idea of attempting conversation with her again.

Alice couldn't quite understand why she cared about Violet's opinion of her anyway, she was a *pirate*, and had taken her hostage besides. Alice gently nudged the door with her foot, and to her surprise it swung open several inches.

"Well someone forgot to lock their quarters," Alice muttered to herself as she pushed the door open, and cringed at the loud creak from the hinge. She looked around the room. It was a standard sleeping quarters, but with colorful fabric, perhaps made of old silk scarves, draped on the walls. It was much larger than Alice's quarters back on her ship, and contained a private bath off to the side. The bed jutted into the center of the room, covered in deep emerald green blankets and large purple pillows. There was a desk against the left wall, littered with stacks of papers and old photographs. Above the desk was a map on the wall, speckled with pins marking locations across all of the nearby systems. There was a large plush green chair in the corner, sitting next to a pile of books that were stacked a bit too high to remain stable.

Alice quietly crossed the room to check the desk for a key or a tool to remove the lock on the toolbox. A photograph sitting at the top of the pile of papers caught Alice's eye. The photograph was of three young women, dark skinned and freckled with huge grins and bright, smiling eyes. One had close cropped hair, one was wearing a knitted hat, and one had tight dark curls tied up. Violet's face was unmistakable, even though the photo was decades old.

"This must be Violet's desk," she muttered. Alice wondered if the women in the picture were Violet's friends, or perhaps sisters. Alice picked up the photo and flipped it over. There was a note:

"Violet, Rose, and Acacia: at Violet's flight school graduation."

Alice leaned in closer to examine the photograph for a hint of the calculating, stern woman she met just a few hours prior. Violet was young and carefree in this photo, and there was no trace of the scar she now wore across her face. "I wonder what happened to you," Alice whispered.

"The Coalition happened to me," Violet responded, and Alice jumped. Violet had crept up behind her, not making a single sound as she crossed the room.

"I, uh, I'm sorry, I was looking for a key, or a tool, or—" Alice stammered.

"And you thought you'd find that by rifling through my personal effects?" Violet snapped, snatching the photograph from Alice's hand. She put the photograph inside a desk drawer and angrily closed it. "If you needed something to assist your task to repair and service my ship, you should have come directly to me instead of sneaking around. I assume after decades serving on ships, you know how to navigate yourself to the bridge?" She glared at Alice, fire in her dark eyes.

"I didn't want to bother you," Alice replied meekly after a moment. "I thought I'd find what I needed in one of these rooms, I didn't know it was yours."

Violet stared at her a moment, then softened almost imperceptibly. "So you meant to poke through someone else's private quarters? Maybe you're a pirate after all," she challenged.

Alice shifted her feet and looked down at the ground.

"People don't generally keep bolt cutters in their desks, do they?" Violet asked. "Follow me," she sighed, "I'll get you what you need." They exited the room, Violet making sure to lock the door and jiggle the doorknob, and they turned back down the corridor. She unclipped the radio from her belt and said, "Captain to bridge: can someone please meet me in the boiler room with a pair of bolt cutters?"

The reply came a moment later: "Roger that, Boss, I'll be right down."

Alice and Violet walked through the ship with no sound other than their boots on the cold metal floor. Alice felt sheepish and embarrassed, while Violet looked angry at her loss of privacy. Alice felt a flash of annoyance with herself for feeling embarrassed at all; she was a prisoner, not a guest. They reached the boiler room, and to Alice's surprise, Ned was waiting with a pair of bolt cutters. He leaned easily against the wall, tapping the tool against a nearby cooling unit.

"Got lost, eh?" He chuckled. "I don't recommend sneaking around the boss' private affairs. She's got a sky high body count, and I'd hate to see you added to that list," he added with a wink. He stepped forward and gave the tool to Alice, glancing at Violet. "Alright, Boss?"

Violet nodded, and Ned stepped around them and disappeared up the stairs.

Alice picked up the tool box and placed it on the nearby table. She easily snapped the lock and removed it. She could feel the captain's eyes on her back as she worked, and hoped that she looked at least a little bit intimidating. She'd need to keep her respect if she was going to make it out of this alive.

"I think I've got everything I need," Alice said confidently. "The job should take a couple of days to get your systems back in order. Some patches, new gaskets, maybe a valve. It's nothing serious, but probably too complex for most baseline crew members."

"See that you finish promptly," Violet replied sternly. "We have a schedule I'd like to keep to. I trust I don't have to worry about a sabotage?"

"No point in that," Alice reassured her captor. "If I strand us out here, I'll never get back to my ship. May as well do the job so I can return to my post. You left my ship in quite a state, if you remember, and it's going to take months to restore it to full working order. Not to mention the reorganization of my tools, which will probably take me years." Alice frowned.

"I'm sure you can handle it," Violet mused, "From what I hear, no repair is too complicated for you." She paused. "You've quite a reputation, you know."

Alice looked up from the tools she had laid out on the work bench. "I wasn't aware most people cared that much about an engineer. I've just been around a long time, that's all."

"I met a few travelers in taverns recently who swear you saved their lives. Repairing a punctured main boiler in deep space, surrounded by rebels? That's impressive stuff."

Alice blushed, looking down at her scuffed boots. "It...it wasn't punctured. It was just leaking. And I was just in the right place at the right time. I don't go out of my way to be a hero, I just didn't want civilians to get caught in the crossfire between rebels and the Coalition. It's not their fight to die for."

Violet surveyed the empty room, and landed her gaze on Alice. "Well what about you? Is it your fight to die for? Why stay with the Coalition if you don't believe in their cause?"

Alice paused and looked across the room at Violet. "It's a job, Captain. I've been flying with Augustus Allen for decades. It's comfortable, it's a pay check. I make friends, like Barnaby. I'm good at what I do, but it's separate from any kind of righteous cause. I try to avoid political discussions when possible, if I'm honest."

Violet narrowed her eyes at Alice. "You're an intelligent woman, Alice. Surely you see how the world is now, how people are suffering. How can you turn away from that? How can you be so apathetic? Don't you remember what happened during the last revolution?"

Alice just shrugged and looked at the floor.

"I guess you just have the privilege of not caring," Violet quipped, "the rest of us have to live in the world that the Coalition controls."

Alice didn't respond, and bent to pick up a stray screw off the floor. She wasn't interested in having this argument with a woman she'd hopefully never see again in 48 hours. Violet glared, her stare still fixed on the tall, broad mechanic.

"Do you even pay attention to the world around you, or are you happy to remain neutral while children starve?" Violet pressed.

Alice straightened and looked at Violet. "I tend to work better without an audience," she said, instead of answering Violet's question. "I presume someone will show me to my cell this evening."

Violet smoothed a frizzy curl back behind her ear. "I'll send Kady down to fetch you for dinner, and then she will show you to your quarters. I may be a pirate, Alice, but I'm not going to keep my mechanic in a cell." She turned on her heel and silently stalked out of the room.

Alice sighed angrily. What did Violet expect her to do, anyway? Even if she'd had political or rebellious inclinations, which she did not, there was little she could accomplish as a Coalition mechanic on a trade ship. She wasn't anybody important, and aside from her chilly working relationship with Captain Allen, she wasn't particularly well connected, either. Besides, Alice remembered the violence during the last wide scale revolution when she was young, and she had no desire to return to the days when civilians fought each other with broken bottles and scavenged iron pipes over scraps of food.

She was lucky, because her parents had sent her and her brother north to distant relatives who lived in a rural area, and Alice hadn't seen much violence first hand. She grew up in the relative safety of a quiet farming village, unlike many her age. She'd never seen her parents again, though. They'd vanished during the fighting. Alice knew that they had probably died, but no one could ever confirm it. She'd been sent away at such a young age, she barely remembered her parents. The people that raised her hadn't been warm, but they had kept her and her brother fed, and that was more than most got then.

Alice squinted at the top of the boiler and leaned forward, pulling her goggles down over her eyes. Most mechanics would use a modified step ladder to examine the top of these steam boilers, but Alice's remarkable height allowed her to see and fix problems without one. It was a good thing, too; she couldn't see any ladders in the boiler room, modified or not. Her goggles steamed with the moist heat at the top of the boiler and she pressed a small button on top and the lenses cleared immediately, using their steam sensing technology. She saw it now, the safety valve was bent nearly in half.

"No wonder this old thing won't reach proper pressure," she muttered to the empty room. "The safety protocols are preventing it." If a boiler of this size reached pressure without a safety valve, there was a chance it could explode and blow a huge hole in the side of the ship. It would set off a deadly chain reaction. That kind of explosion would take out the other boilers, the backup generators, and the main directional control too. Perhaps it was a design flaw to have the main components in the same room, but technology couldn't yet support the systems being built into different areas of the ship. Steam and solar were still the primary sources of energy on Earth and on the nearby planets, too.

Alice peered into the toolbox and chose a large pair of pliers and a small blowtorch. She'd have to heat the safety valve first to make the metal pliable, or she would risk snapping it off when she tried to straighten it. She doubted there was a spare safety valve anywhere in this empty room, and it was always better to fix old components than to install new ones. They didn't make valves the way they used to, with heavy bronze and cast iron; lately all Alice could find was thin stainless steel. The logic was that safety valves are rarely in use, and so using the heavy, expensive materials to manufacture them wasn't necessary. She had seen enough malfunctions in her years as a mechanic to know that "rarely" wasn't "never."

She turned her head and took one more deep breath of cool air. The next several hours were going to be hot and exhausting. Alice adjusted her goggles, pushed her braid over her shoulder, and got to work.

CHAPTER FOUR

"HEY. HEY!" KADY SHOUTED, hands on her hips as she glared at Alice, who had been working on the boiler since Ned opened the toolbox for her.

Alice turned and saw the wiry second in command, who was looking less than welcoming. She flipped a switch on the blowtorch and the flame extinguished. "Sorry, I didn't hear you," Alice shouted, her ears ringing from hours of working with the loud equipment. These days, it seemed like her ears never stopped ringing.

"The captain sent me to escort you to dinner. She doesn't want you getting lost and pawing through her stuff again." Kady looked at the mechanic, who was covered in grease and ash. "And we'll stop by the powder room so that you won't nauseate us all with your appearance."

Alice pushed her goggles up to rest on the top of her forehead. "The, uh, powder room...?" she questioned, trying not to yell even though she could barely hear herself think after all those hours with the blowtorch.

"It's a sink. If you're lucky I'll give you some soap." Kady glanced around at the room, and Alice felt self-conscious about her messy workstation. "Follow me," Kady continued. She turned gracefully, and it was almost a pirouette. She was the most graceful person Alice had ever seen, and it was obvious that she had trained in dance from a young age, even if her interests had given way to science as she'd become an adult.

They walked down another long corridor, Alice's boots sharply thudding on the metal grate flooring. Kady's steps were remarkably silent as she moved through the ship like a swan through a calm pond. Alice looked around, trying to place the make and model of the ship. It looked like an old Federation build, a format that had been abandoned when larger ships became necessary to transport all the goods garnered through the Coalition's trade agreements.

"Looks stolen," Alice said, trying to fill the silence. "And stolen 20 years ago, by the looks of it."

Kady ignored her. Alice's boots dragged along the floor, her legs too tired from hours of stretching and crouching under the boiler to pick up her feet as she walked. Her back felt stiff and sore, and Alice wondered how long she could keep working as a mechanic. She certainly wasn't young any more, but she loved her work, even if the work happened to be on a pirate ship, under the forced employ of one of the fiercest marauders in the sky.

"Here," Kady said, gesturing to a rusted sink inside a small closet. "I'll wait." She leaned against the wall of the corridor, arms folded across her chest.

Alice ducked into the small closet, hunching over the old sink. She spied some dried out soap on a shelf, and she wondered if any crew members ever used this room, or if it was reserved for their captors. She lathered up her arms with the dusty soap and orange, rusted water. She winced when the cool water ran over a fresh burn on her left forearm. She had underestimated how hot that safety valve was when she stretched past it to examine another component, and seared her arm. It was raised red and angry, an L shaped welt. She allowed the water to run over her hands and arms, scrubbing away the dirt and grease. Her stomach made a loud rumble. She was much hungrier than she had realized, and she looked forward to what she was sure would be meager rations. Still, a little food was better than nothing, and at least Violet had promised her a real bed to sleep in.

She turned off the tap and wiped her hands on her coveralls. Her stomach rumbled again and she grimaced from the sharp pang of hunger. She needed food and a good night's sleep if she was going to finish that boiler the next day. She bent her head to fit through the doorway and saw Kady, artfully balanced on one leg and waiting in the corridor.

"Let's go, they're waiting for you," Kady said coldly. She began to lead Alice down another corridor, this one lined with maps on the walls, covered with scrawled notes in the margins. They were maps of Gamma-3, once known as Earth a long time ago. There were highlighted portions indicating the established Coalition bases. Alice gazed at them as she walked behind Kady. She slowed to study one of the maps; it was a map of her hometown, a Coalition city in the northern territories called Aarq. There were angry red lines through areas where fighting had taken place when she was young. The map was old and yellowed around the edges, the tiny writing faded and difficult to read.

Alice felt compelled to stop and lean in.

"Come on, hurry up!" Kady barked from further down the hall, having realized that the mechanic was no longer behind her. "And don't even think about looking for intel about our enterprises. These maps are all decades old. We aren't stupid enough to leave information out when a Coalition drone is on the ship."

Alice's brow furrowed. There was a green circle around the house she had grown up in. According to the map key, a green circle indicated a safe house for the rebels during that revolution. "What is this map?" she asked, turning towards Kady. "Why is there a green circle around my house? My parents weren't rebels."

"What? I have no idea, that rebellion was before my time," Kady replied dismissively. "You can ask the captain, but reopening that wound isn't a good idea for someone like you."

Alice walked towards Kady and continued into a large room with tables and benches, filled with the smell of something hot and delicious. She could hear chattering from the other crew members, and followed Kady around a corner. The rest of the crew was sitting around mismatched square and rectangular tables, piled high with steaming bread, cauldrons of thick orange soup, and plates of crispy fried tofu. She didn't know who the cook was on this ship, but this looked like a much nicer spread than she usually got on Coalition ships. Her meals there usually consisted of day old bread rations and dried protein supplements. Alice's stomach grumbled again, and she was glad when Kady gestured for her to sit and eat. She was less pleased when she realized that her seat was right next to Violet. She just wanted to eat, not debate politics or think about strange old maps lining a corridor on a pirate ship she was desperate to get off of.

Violet nodded to the crew. "Alright then, dig in everyone. And let's all thank Ned for cooking this fabulous meal."

There was a smattering of appreciative applause and enthusiastic praise. As the crew began to pass around plates and deep bowls of soup, Alice looked across the table at the rugged, bearded man who had acted as Violet's muscle on the raid this morning.

"You cooked this feast?" she asked Ned. "Brawn *and* cooking skills, that's not something you see every day."

Ned dumped a huge fist full of tofu into his soup. "The boss encourages us to explore our passions," he said with a grin. "And besides, we don't have the resources for someone to only be responsible for cooking. And nobody particularly liked Kady's culinary exploits." The crew stifled chuckles as Kady glowered at Ned.

"I'm a scientist, not a domestic servant," she spat. "And you never complained when I was in charge of the food."

Ned's eyes crinkled as he laughed. "Aw, Kady, calm down. You know we're just teasing."

Kady's glare softened, and she cracked a smile as she picked up her spoon and gestured at Ned. "Just don't come asking me for my recipes," she laughed.

"Don't think there's any danger of that!" Ned replied, chuckling.

Alice ripped a chunk of fluffy, steaming bread in half and dipped it into the soup. She shoved it in her mouth eagerly and groaned with happiness. "Ned, this is the best thing I've ever eaten. What is it?"

"Roasted red pepper and squash soup, from the produce that we liberated from your ship. I'll give you the recipe before you leave, so you can inform your Coalition cook!" Ned said brightly. Though his size initially made him look intimidating, he now seemed less threatening than even a teddy bear.

"Oh, we don't eat like this on Coalition ships," Alice replied with a tinge of regret. "We get basic rations unless we opt to use our credits for fresh produce. I'm but a lowly mechanic, so I save my credits for when I'm too old to keep crawling under boilers." She took another bite, savouring the flavor and the texture of the fresh food. "In fact, I'm surprised that pirates eat so well."

"It's not usually like this," Violet said between mouthfuls. "We tend to take all of the liberated produce to rebellion bases, or into the cities when we can be sure we'll avoid detection. Kady organizes those missions at least once a week; we're eating well tonight because we have enough to feed us and give extra to our next supply drop location."

"What, so you're like contemporary Robin Hoods?" Alice asked. "Some band of merry men you have here, holding mechanics at gunpoint."

Violet put down her bread and turned to look Alice in the eye. "Yes, but I think you'll agree your treatment has been more than fair for a prisoner, no? After all, you're eating well and sleeping in a bed tonight, and not on the floor of the brig. How are Coalition prisoners treated?"

Alice looked down at her bowl, filled with hunks of bread and tofu. "I'm not in charge of prisoners," she muttered, "And there's not much I can do about Coalition policy, either. I'm a mechanic, not a politician or an officer." Once again, the talk was turning to politics and rebellions, and Alice felt annoyed. She just wanted to fix this boiler and go back to her ship, where things felt predictable and manageable.

The table was quiet, except for the sounds of spoons clinking at the bottom of empty bowls and heavy, satisfied sighs from the crew. There was barely a crumb left on the table; no one would dare waste food on this ship.

"Thank you, Ned," said another crew member as she stood to clear her dishes. She wore a bright orange jacket with an upturned collar, and the name Hyun was embroidered in silver thread across the breast pocket. Alice hadn't seen her on the ship yet, and she wondered what her role was. "Come on, you lot," she chirped with an edge of authority, "Let's get this cleaned up so we can head to quarters. I've got a freshly made bed with my name on it." Her dark hair was braided in an elaborate coil on top of her head, complementing her dark eyes and sharp cheekbones. The other crew members cleared their plates and bowls, leaving Violet and Alice alone at the table.

Alice swallowed the last bite of bread. "So, I found the problems with your boiler. I should be able to finish up by tomorrow evening, provided I don't run into any problems with reassembly tomorrow. I'll do some more work before I sleep tonight."

"Don't be ridiculous," Violet said incredulously. "You're allowed to have a good night's sleep. Just because you were dragged here against your will doesn't mean I'm going to treat you like a prisoner."

Alice shifted in her seat and looked towards the far wall, hung with shelves full of canned food, each shelf bearing the name of a known rebel settlement: Red Top, Far River, Bright Forest. The names were vague enough to cause confusion in the beginning, but were now bastions of rebel forces planning the new rebellion.

"I suppose that means you'll be paying me, then?" Alice challenged, inspecting her plate for forgotten crumbs. "Where shall I send the bill?"

Violet stared at Alice, her eyes fixed on the mechanic's thick silver hair and her round, pale face. "Well, what do you want?" Violet asked when Alice stared at her, too surprised to answer. "I may not have much, but I consider myself to be a fair woman."

Alice let the silence hang for a long moment. She couldn't think of anything she wanted from Violet, but she didn't like the thought of being just a captive, either. She studied the shelves, piled high with food, and wondered why a pirate cared so much about these rebels. She'd have much more for herself and her crew if she kept the ship away from political conflicts. She thought about the old map in the corridor, and frowned.

"Why do you have that map of Aarq in the hallway? It looks old; many of those landmarks were destroyed in the last rebellion." Alice turned and was startled to see Violet's gaze fixed on her.

"Why do you want to know? That was a long time ago. And besides, whatever I tell you will undoubtedly make it back to the Coalition anyway. You're a fine mechanic, Alice, and I'm no fool." She brushed a tight, wiry curl from her face and produced a pin from her sleeve, pinning it out of the way.

"I may be a Coalition mechanic, but I have no political aims," Alice said with a shrug. "I don't want to get involved. It was just a question, and I'm just your prisoner."

Violet sighed. "Maybe I'll tell you what the map is for when you finish the job I brought you here for."

"Do you always abduct mechanics, or was I just lucky? Do you kidnap people to do your laundry, too?"

"Why do you think we chose your ship, Alice?" Violet asked. "Why your ship, and why you as our mechanic?"

"Wrong place, wrong time?" Alice guessed. She straightened in her chair so that she towered over Violet, even from a seated position.

"We chose your ship because you were on it." Violet sat back in her chair and looked very much like a captain, with her self-assured gaze and strong, quiet demeanor.

Alice squinted at Violet. "Because I was on it? What is that supposed to mean?"

"It means that you're the finest mechanic in the Coalition, and everyone knows it. I had a ship that needed repairs, and I needed a steady pair of hands. I met those travelers in a tavern last week, so I knew your ship wouldn't be too far away. It doesn't take a genius to track a merchant ship that large." Violet leaned forward and lowered her voice. "The food was just a nice bonus. I wanted a mechanic more than I wanted boxes of broken droids and a few crates of vegetables."

Alice shifted uncomfortably in her seat, suddenly realizing that she wanted nothing more than to be home on her ship, the C.S. Stronghold, in her drafty, too-small bed. She wasn't a rebel, or a pirate, and she wanted nothing to do with the radical aims of this captain. She began to worry that this wasn't going to be a temporary stay, no matter what Violet had said so far. Still, if Violet was a woman of her word, and it seemed she was, Alice had to hope she had nothing to worry about.

Violet leaned back in her chair and stretched out her legs.

"The Cricket needed repairs. I needed a mechanic, and I'm not a woman who settles for anything less than the best."

Violet's piercing gaze made Alice uncomfortable, and she turned away from the captain. "The Cricket?" Alice asked. "Why name your ship that?"

"Sometimes it makes a chirping sound," Violet said, shrugging. "Our previous mechanic, may he rest in peace, said it was something minor, nothing to worry about. The nickname just stuck," Violet explained.

"Sounds like you've got a loose coil in your cooling system," Alice said. "If it degrades, that coil can really tear up your filters. I can fix that as well before I leave, if you like."

"Thank you." Violet placed her hands on the table and looked towards the kitchen. "Can I offer you something to drink?" she offered.

Alice arched an eyebrow. "Are we talking water, or are we talking something more adventurous than that?"

"You've had quite a day," Violet smirked, pulling a flask from inside her waistcoat, "and I might have the right antidote for a day of abducting mechanics and fixing old steam boilers." She waved the silver flask in the air: it was engraved with one word: "JUSTICE," in all capital letters, carved with a florid script.

Alice reached for the flask. "Contraband swill, I presume?" Alcohol was prohibited in most territories, but everyone knew someone who could get some, but for a steep price.

Violet grinned and passed her the flask, the long healed scar shining against her dark skin in the dim light. "It's not rum, if that's what you're thinking," she said, "I may be a pirate, but I have a very particular palette. It's whiskey, distilled by an old friend of mine. Very rare stuff. Captain's hoard only. You should feel honored, Mechanic."

Alice unscrewed the flask and took a long drink. The whiskey warmed her mouth and her stomach, and she felt grateful for it. "It's been at least a decade since I've had swill as good as that. It almost tastes like old times." Alice sighed and settled into the subtle twinkling haze brought on by very strong whiskey.

"There's more were that came from, if you're interested, though the quality isn't quite up to my standards," Violet offered, standing up. "I have a bottle of inferior swill hidden inside an empty coffee can in the kitchen."

Alice leaned back into the chair. "And no one ever looks for coffee in the mornings? Do you only allow early birds to serve on your crew?"

Violet peeked her head out of the kitchen with a tall can in her hand. "I hide it inside the decaffeinated coffee can."

Alice laughed, in spite of herself. She found herself wondering if Violet's other captives were treated as amicably, or if she was genuinely this friendly.

Violet returned with two dusty mugs and a large unlabelled bottle full of amber liquid. She poured generously into both mugs, and raised hers to Alice. "To a successful abduction!"

Alice smiled and shook her head. "You're like no pirate I've ever met, Captain."

"Call me Violet. And just how many pirates *have* you met?"

Alice took a swig from her mug. "Admittedly, very few. Most were missing teeth. And none as attractive as you." Alice immediately blushed – why had she said that? The whiskey was strong, but she was a substantial woman who could hold her liquor. She quickly looked away from Violet, examining her mug instead. An awkward, silent moment passed. She picked up Violet's flask and ran her thumb over the inscription. "Justice?" She questioned.

"My mother gave it to me a long time ago," Violet responded. "She always said that what's right is rarely what's easy, and justice is rarely an easy goal." Violet reached forward and took the flask from Alice, flipping it upside down. "See here, on the bottom? Those were her initials. She died a long time ago now."

"Was she a rebel too?" Alice asked.

Violet laughed loudly, "Oh gods no. She was a meek woman, but she did what she could to help the rebellion, and then the revolution. She hid people, but quietly. She wasn't a fighter."

"Sounds brave to me." Alice took another sip of the whiskey. "Sounds like what a rebel would do."

"I'm never sure whether we're being brave, or stupid," Violet said, taking a long drink from her mug. "Sometimes it's a very fine line. Like when we kidnap a Coalition mechanic." She smiled and looked at Alice sideways. "And yet, here we are, drinking whiskey. What a life, don't you think, Alice?"

"It's certainly more excitement than I've had in awhile," Alice responded. "Life as a mechanic isn't quite the adrenaline rush that you might think," she added, a smile playing at her lips. She drained her mug and set it down on the table. Violet reached over and poured her more whiskey, and then added some to her own.

"Did you never think about working as a mechanic on a military vessel?" Violet asked as she put one boot up on the table. "It would pay more, at least."

"I don't relish the idea of being shot out of the sky," Alice said, "And besides, once I had my first assignment with Captain Allen, I just stayed on whatever ship he was commanding. It was just easier that way."

"Decades with the same captain? You must be close." Violet swirled the whiskey in her mug.

"No, we don't talk much. He's not a man of many words, at least not with mechanics or general crew. He always requested me on assignments so I guess that's as much a compliment as anything. He's a good man." Alice tucked a stray piece of silver hair back into her braid and adjusted the goggles on her head.

"Is he?" Violet pressed. "A good man? What makes him good?"

"He's a good captain, fair to his crew. He's loyal to people who do their work and do it well."

"And how often does he eat regular rations?" Violet asked. "How many times have you eaten with the captain of the C.S. Stronghold?" Her tone was too sharp, and Alice winced at the barb, even though it was directed at Captain Allen, not her.

"It doesn't mean he's not a good man, it just means that captains get paid more. I'd eat better if I had the spare credits for it, too." Alice felt defensive, adding, "And besides, it's not like stealing food makes you some kind of hero."

A moment of uneasy silence passed.

"So, the map," Violet ventured, "you were asking about the map."

Alice looked up from her mug and met Violet's gaze. "You have a map of where I grew up. A map of Aarq."

"I've not looked at that map in years," Violet responded. "I almost forgot it was still hanging in the corridor. That was a long time ago. The map was already outdated and old by the time I was using it, anyway."

"There's a green circle around my parents' house. Why?"

"Green circles would denote safe houses for members of the rebellion. They could go there for food, shelter, rudimentary medical care. The residents would protect them, hide them, and send them on their way. My mother was the one who organized many of these safe houses."

"My parents weren't rebels," Alice said, her temper flaring. "They were just civilians caught up in a conflict. They sent my brother and I away to keep us safe."

"If you say so," Violet shrugged. "I wouldn't know. I had that map because it was my mother's, and because some of those safe houses still exist. Not many, but some."

Alice felt conflicted. *Were* her parents rebels? She might never know for sure. She held out her mug for Violet to refill it.

"Listen," Violet said, pouring more whiskey into Alice's mug, "It's best not to get too wound up about what our parents did or didn't do. It was a tough time, and most of them had more secrets than we can imagine. They did what they had to keep their kids safe, or for what they thought was right." She put down the flask and reached over to Alice, "And besides, there was probably a reason they didn't want you to know those secrets." She patted Alice's arm, and Alice flinched away.

"Oh, watch it there, Captain," Alice exclaimed, "Got a burn from a hot hunk of metal today. Still pretty tender."

"Why didn't you ask for medical care?" Violet asked. "We have a medic on the ship, you saw her at dinner. Hyun, with the elaborately braided hair. Chirpy. Face like a sunny morning, but don't let it fool you. She's the best medic I've ever had on my crew."

"Oh yes, her," Alice said, "but it's not a big deal. Burns are a workplace hazard for me. Got burn scars all over the place."

"Let me see," Violet said, reaching out. She took Alice's wrist gently and turned her arm to examine the burn. It was red and angry, probably a second degree burn. "At least let me clean it properly," Violet said as she stood up from the table and wandered into the kitchen.

"It's no trouble, really," Alice called to Violet. "I'm fine, I promise."

She heard a crashing sound from the kitchen.

"I know it's in here somewhere!" Violet yelled. "Ah yes, here it is!" She reappeared in the doorway of the kitchen with an old aluminum medical kit, emblazoned with a large red X on the top of the tin. It was dusty and obviously hadn't been touched for years. Violet tossed the kit onto the table. "Alright, let's see it then," she said, gently pulling Alice's wrist towards her.

Alice knew she wasn't going to win this fight, and she was grateful for the medical attention anyway. An infection would only slow her down. She relaxed her arm as Violet began to gently dab at the sides of the burn with some antiseptic. She might be a captain, but her touch was so gentle and intuitive, like she knew exactly where the most tender parts of the burn were. Maybe it was just the whiskey, but Violet's touch felt like butterflies in her stomach.

Violet cracked the seal on a fresh tube of burn gel and proceeded to gently apply the slimy blue substance to Alice's arm using the tips of her fingers. The angry red burn would take weeks to properly heal, but at least the gel would make it less painful.

"Thank you," Alice said softly. The medicated ointment was already helping cool the burn and ease the pain, and she was grateful to her captor.

Violet traced the faded scars on Alice's arms. "I suppose these are workplace hazards, too?" she asked, following one scar from the mechanic's wrist to her elbow.

"In a manner of speaking. That one was from a brush with marauders about ten years ago. I was on a different ship then, the C.S Navigator, an exploration and supplies vessel that was meant to trade with the outer systems. We were ambushed before we got there, and I was welding at the time. Tried to use the blowtorch to defend myself, and burned the hell out of my arm in the process."

"Defend yourself?" Violet asked.

"Not all pirates are as polite as you, Captain," Alice replied. "You merely held me at gunpoint, they wanted to throw me off the ship."

Violet looked up at Alice. "And have you ever been held at gunpoint before?"

"A handful of times, yes. I was never taken as a hostage and asked to fix a boiler before, though. That, Captain, is a brand new experience for a lowly mechanic like me. When I return to my ship, I shall write of how well I was treated on the pirate ship Cricket."

"And do you always keep detailed accounts of your days aboard enemy vessels?" Violet laughed.

"No, but I do keep a journal with a log of all the repairs I do. I'll just write it in there for posterity." Alice pulled her arm away and sighed. "You know, you really should get a new mechanic. These systems will need consistent ongoing maintenance."

Violet shifted in her seat."You could...stay, if you wanted. Provided the crew doesn't object."

Alice guffawed. "And what, become a pirate? A fugitive?"

The captain frowned. "Of sorts." Violet sat back in her chair and studied Alice's face. "But no one will force you to stay. I'm a woman of my word, after all."

"I don't think that's a good idea," Alice said slowly, relieved at least that she could firmly put that worry to rest. "I'm not really cut out for that kind of...adventure. And besides, my life is back on the C.S Stronghold. Barnaby will probably think I'm dead by now."

Violet laughed. "And what would he say if he knew you were sitting at a table with a pirate captain, drinking cheap whiskey from a mug?"

"He'd probably say it was about time that I had some fun. But Barnaby isn't here, and I can't stay. And I hardly think that taking someone hostage is the right way to start off a healthy workplace relationship." Alice set her empty mug aside and pushed her chair back. "I should go, Captain, I've a long night ahead of me if I'm to finish those repairs tomorrow. Good night."

Alice stood up and headed for the door before realizing she didn't know which way her quarters were. Before Violet could object, she headed towards the boiler room. Alice wasn't confident she could get any work done after that whiskey, but it was better than staying with Violet and entertaining the notion of becoming a *pirate*. The thought had soured her mood.

"Alice, *wait*," Violet called, jogging down the corridor to catch up. "I didn't even show you where you can sleep tonight!"

"I'll be fine, I can sleep in the boiler room," Alice replied, still marching down the hall.

Violet, panting, finally caught up to Alice. She grabbed her arm to stop her. The mechanic's long strides made for a punishing pace, even for her. "Alice, just...wait. Wait." Violet started to catch her breath, "I'm the captain of this ship, and I order you to sleep in your quarters."

"So much for not forcing me to do anything," Alice said sarcastically. "Captain's orders, even on an old, rusted, *stolen* ship."

"I'm trying to be accommodating!" Violet said, raising her voice. "I know this isn't ideal, but I'm trying to make it as painless as possible."

"What the hell did you think was going to happen here?" Alice retorted angrily. "That you would let me sleep in a bed, have dinner with the crew, ply me with whiskey, and I'd agree to be your new mechanic? Agree to be a common thief and a fugitive?"

Violet stood straight, squaring her shoulders with her hands on her hips. Even at her full height, Alice was almost a third taller. "I told you, I—"

"I don't care, take me to my quarters. I'll finish fixing your damned ship tomorrow." Alice kicked the wall, scuffing the dull metal. "And then, you'll take me to the nearest planet where I can send a signal for pickup, and we'll never have to see each other again."

"Fine. Follow me." Violet angrily stalked down a long corridor, her sharp steps echoing down the corridor.

Alice followed silently, feeling anger and whiskey churn in her stomach. Violet stopped suddenly, and whirled around to face Alice.

"And another thing, Mechanic," Violet said icily, "don't go poking around my ship again. You'll have a crew member escort you to the boiler room tomorrow morning." She pulled a ring of keys from her waistcoat pocket. "And I'll be expecting a full report when you're done." She unlocked a door, and it swung open. "Your quarters."

Alice stood for a moment and studied Violet in the dim lighting of the ship. Her scar shone bright against her dark skin, and a stray tight curl framed her face. Alice swayed on her feet, the effect of several mugs of whiskey in her belly. Violet was a beautiful woman and a powerful captain, and the way her dark eyes sparkled with anger made Alice's head spin more than the booze.

"Well?" Violet demanded, impatient.

Alice's gaze shifted to Violet's full lips, positioned in a frown. She lunged forward clumsily and pinned Violet's shoulders to the corridor wall, kissing her hard on the mouth. Surprisingly, Violet returned the kiss, and brought her hands up to rest on Alice's hips.

Alice pulled away, releasing Violet from her grasp. "Goodnight, Captain," Alice growled, looking Violet right in the eye. She turned, entered her room, and closed the door behind her.

CHAPTER FIVE

THERE WAS A SHARP KNOCK on the steel door. "Hey, Mechanic," a stern voice said, "Time to get out of bed and fix the ship."

Alice blearily opened her eyes and groaned. Morning already? Her head was pounding and her mouth felt like sand. Memories of the previous night flashed through her mind like pieces of a puzzle. There was an argument, yes, and...a kiss?

"Oh, gods," Alice mumbled to herself. What a mess she had made. She felt her cheeks burn with embarrassment, shaking her head to try and clear her thoughts, and her vision swam.

Another knock rang in Alice's ears. "Mechanic. Now."

"Just—argh—just a minute," Alice growled as she pulled on her boots. She tightened the laces and stood up. The room spun around her and she felt sick. She squinted her eyes and pulled her goggles over her eyes to shield her from the bright light beaming from the light on the ceiling. Obviously, it had been on all night. She groggily stumbled to the door and opened it to find Kady's steely stare on the other side of it.

"Good morning, Mechanic," Kady said brusquely, surveying Alice's dishevelled appearance. "Late night, I take it?"

"Uh, yeah, something like that." Alice ducked through the door and into the corridor. "I assume you're my guard this morning?"

"You assume correctly." Kady narrowed her eyes. "I don't know *what* you said to the Captain last night, but I've never seen her so eager to get a prisoner off the ship."

Alice racked her brain – what *had* she said last night? Was that kiss real, or just an alcohol fueled dream? Still, no matter: she was here to do a job, and then get back home and put all memories of pirates, parents, and whiskey out of her mind for good.

Kady glided down the corridor, her long black tailored jacket floating behind her and her boots silent on the metal grate flooring of the ship. "I assume you'll be finished today, then? The captain is anxious to be on her way before the Coalition ship catches up to us."

"Yes, barring any complications." Alice stumbled along behind Kady, pulling herself along the walls to keep her balance. She was beginning to remember why she stayed away from whiskey – the mornings after were vicious. Her stomach grumbled loudly, and she wasn't sure if it was hunger or bile roiling in her guts. She grimaced and followed Kady down the stairs into the boiler room.

"Here's a radio, you will call if you need anything to complete the job. Don't go sniffing around on your own again. Captain's orders." Kady handed her a radio identical to the one that got smashed in the attack on the Stronghold, small and aluminum with a lit up display that read "Channel 00.2" with solar panels and a hand crank on the back for power.

"Er, thanks," Alice mumbled. She pushed up her goggles and rubbed her eyes. She would pay all the credits in the world for a pot of strong black coffee right about now. Still, the sooner she finished this job, the sooner she could get back home. Alice sat down against a wall, facing the broken boiler and all the parts laid out in order on the floor. Once she repaired an internal pilot light and finished up that safety valve, she could easily reassemble the boiler and be on her way.

She closed her eyes, just for a moment. She longed to go back to her quarters and sleep for a decade. She'd need it to get rid of this pounding headache.

"Taking a nap on the job already, are we?" a voice called from the top of the stairs.

Alice blinked to clear the fog from her vision and looked towards the voice. It was Captain Violet, with two mugs in her hand. "I, er—" she began, "I just..."

Violet sat on the steps and gestured for Alice to join her. "I come in peace. Let's talk."

Grunting, Alice hauled herself up off the floor and crossed to Violet. She sat two steps lower so they would be level with each other. "So."

"So if you're feeling anything like me this morning, you're going to want this," Violet said, offering one of the mugs to Alice.

"It's not more secret decaf coffee, is it?" Alice took the mug from Violet, smirking.

"Oh, no, definitely not," Violet said as she rubbed her temple. "I think the regular, extra caffeine, unsweetened coffee is what's necessary this morning."

"Listen, I—" Alice began.

"No, no, it's fine. Whiskey is known to make tempers flare. And besides, I was foolish for thinking you would entertain the notion of staying on as our mechanic. You barely know us, and it's not like you chose to come here." She took a sip of her coffee and looked at Alice, her eyes searching for something. It made Alice feel uncomfortable, and she shifted her weight from one foot to the other.

"I probably said some...regrettable things," Alice said, "but thank you for the coffee. It will certainly help me get a move on to get this boiler working again." Alice looked down into the mug and stared at the swirling dark liquid, wondering if Violet even remembered the kiss.

Violet cleared her throat. "In any case, Alice, there's something you should know. I've not been completely honest with you about our little invasion of your ship and liberation of Coalition supplies."

Alice looked up from her mug. "Oh?"

"That gun I threatened you with?"

Alice tilted her head. "Yes, I do have a memory of you dragging me here at gunpoint."

"It wasn't loaded."

And without another word, Violet stood up, climbed the stairs, and disappeared out of sight.

Alice couldn't quite figure Violet out. Why try to take someone prisoner with an unloaded gun? What would Violet have done if she had decided to fight back? She gratefully swallowed the last swig of her coffee and paused to savor the feeling of warmth in her hands. She set the mug on the step, hauled herself up, and got to work, with hundreds of questions swirling in her mind.

• • • •

VIOLET SIGHED AS SHE walked the corridor towards the bridge. It was obvious that Alice didn't remember the kiss, and it was just an effect of the whiskey they had shared. She stopped to rub her head in a vain attempt to ease the throbbing in her temples. What was she even doing, anyway? She was the captain of a goddamn ship, for fuck's sake! She didn't have time for trysts with mechanics or to be thinking about late night illicit kisses, she had a crew to protect and shipments to deliver. She straightened her waistcoat with a tug and scaled the steps into the command center.

"Ned, where are we at with the navigation projections?" she asked.

"Morning, Boss," Ned boomed.

Violet winced at the volume and leaned away from her large, burly navigator.

"We're on target to hit all the supply drops on time, provided the mechanic finishes that main boiler repair today." Ned swivelled his chair to face Violet. "Did she say that she'll finish today?"

"Yes, I just spoke to her. We should be golden by sundown. We can drop her off at the nearest trade outpost, and her people will pick her up from there. As for us, we'll have to be on the lookout for a new mechanic, and soon. Perhaps on Delta 4, there's a significant rebel diaspora there." Violet sat heavily in her captain's chair and turned to face the front window of the ship. She looked into the vast, dark space in front of them and couldn't help wondering if she would ever see Alice again after she fixed the boiler.

"Everything okay, Boss?" Ned asked, punching coordinates into a digital display. "You seem distracted."

"What? Oh, uh, yes, fine. I was just up too late." Violet turned in her chair to examine the ship maintenance logs, presented in green text on a black screen. She scanned the log for the main boiler, where the text read "REPAIR: IN PROGRESS." It sent a strange twinge down her spine to think of Alice down there, fixing her ship. She'd be gone soon, but Violet wanted her to stay for selfish, dangerous reasons.

· · · ·

ALICE SAT ON THE FLOOR in the middle of what looked like an organized mess, legs splayed out, bent over a small piece of equipment. A nearby cooling system thrummed softly as she worked, a familiar and comforting sound to a mechanic who had spent decades in rooms just like this one. To Alice, boiler rooms were all the same. Predictable, repairable. No surprises.

"Alright, done," she said to herself, standing up and carefully stepping around the parts strewn on the floor. She hopped over a large crate and bent down to reinstall the piece into the boiler. Another piece serviced, and a couple dozen to go. Alice was confident that she had figured out the source of the problems Violet's ship was having: the bent safety valve, and a busted pilot light that was only working half the time. When she replaced everything, the ship would be able to run at full speed for awhile, and then they'd have to find a regular mechanic.

Alice tried to imagine what a life on The Cricket would look like. A boiler room may be the same as any other, but she'd never been a fugitive before. Deserting her post on the C.S. Stronghold was an offense punishable by years in a Coalition work camp. At her age, she wasn't sure how well she would handle that kind of punishment if she were caught. Still, she couldn't help wondering what a life alongside Captain Violet would bring, even if she was brave enough to chase that adventure.

"Argh," Alice growled, frustrated with her inability to focus. It wasn't just the headache causing problems, it was the memory – or what she thought was a memory – of the kiss the night before. She picked up a screwdriver and rapped it on the bare workbench, and then flinched at the loud echo it made around the room. "Focus, Alice," she said sternly to the empty room. "Pretty soon it will be like this never even happened." She returned to the pile of tiny pieces and parts. "Alright, who's next?"

"You're next," chirped a voice from the steps. Alice turned to see the perky medic she had met briefly the night before. She stood in the doorway, wearing gray tweed shorts and a matching cropped jacket over a bright orange blouse, with matching tangerine tights that disappeared into heavy black boots. She carried a small bag, and had several pencils tucked behind her ears, along with loose locks of dark hair.

"I'm next?" Alice looked at Hyun through her goggles, with a grease smear on her left cheek.

"Yes, Captain Violet sent me to check on your burn." She gently cleared a place on the small workbench for her bag and set it down. She unclasped the bag and peered inside. "Hmm. I'm not sure I have what I need to treat your injury," she murmured. "May I see the burn?"

Alice crossed the room to the medic, tripping over a large pile of bronze tubing. She caught herself on the workbench and looked at Hyun sheepishly. "Uh, sorry. Here." Alice rolled up her sleeve and thrust her arm forward, exposing yesterday's burn.

Hyun examined the burn closely, her brow furrowed in concentration. "Hmm, yes, looks like a second degree burn. You're very lucky, you know, it could have been much worse."

Alice shrugged. "I've had worse."

"I don't doubt that," the medic said brightly, "but I'll not have someone contract an entirely avoidable infection on my ship." Hyun carefully irrigated the burn with a small bottle of fluid, and began to apply burn ointment.

"So how did a trained medic end up on a pirate ship?" Alice asked, flinching.

"It's a long story," Hyun replied as she opened a sterile bandage to wrap the burn in. "I'm sure you're far too busy repairing our boiler to listen to a boring story like that." She tucked the end of the bandage in to secure it and closed her bag. "You're all set, please let Captain Violet know if the burn seems infected and she'll send for me to tend to it."

Alice pulled her coverall sleeve down over the bandage and buttoned the cuff. "Well, thanks, Doc."

"I'm not a doctor, I'm a medic. And you're welcome," Hyun said. "Do let me know if it gives you any trouble, I'm more than happy to help." She scaled the steps with a spring in her step, and left Alice alone once again.

The mechanic listened to Hyun's steps fade down the hallway and laughed to herself. She never thought she'd meet such a cheerful pirate, and certainly not one with Hyun's impeccable fashion sense. Patting her arm, Alice realized she was grateful for the medical treatment, and she smiled when she realized that Violet had thought of her enough to send the medic to check on her burn. It wasn't even that serious – after all, Alice was a mechanic, and injuries were part of the job description.

She turned back to the hodgepodge of parts littering the floor, and stepped over the pile of bronze tubing to pick up an aluminum box. "Next up: waste burner!" She turned to the partly-assembled boiler and began to reattach the part using a small screwdriver and a pair of pliers. She hummed an old folk melody to herself as she ruminated on the history of steam power.

Slowly, piece by piece, Alice put the old boiler back together. While she worked, she couldn't help thinking about the previous night, and dissecting every detail in her mind. She thought about the feeling of the Captain's hands on her arm, the easy way she laughed, the stories they shared...and that kiss.

She knew she hadn't dreamt it, no dream had ever felt that electric.

Alice absent-mindedly shined a piece of tubing with an old rag, buffing out water spots and grease. She looked down at the tubing and sighed; she was almost done repairing the ship, and soon she would be on her way back home. Everything felt so much more complicated than it had before Captain Violet had abducted her. A part of her wished she could stay, but Alice pushed it out of her mind. She had a job to do on her own ship, especially given the level of damage the C.S. Stronghold had taken 36 hours previously.

Alice tried to push the mystery of the old map out of her mind. Were her parents rebels in the last uprising? Is that why they sent her and her brother away, and why Alice had never seen them again? Could that be why the distant relatives who raised them never showed them any affection? Alice didn't have many memories of her parents, but she could remember how gently her father would brush her hair, and how her mother would return home from her job in the lab and scoop Alice up and spin her around. Sometimes, she could almost remember their faces.

Alice's brother was younger, but they hadn't spoken in over a decade. Other than genetics, they had little in common, and their familial bond was tenuous. They fought constantly as children, and the bitterness carried into adulthood. She didn't even know where he was living now. Maybe he was a pirate, too. Alice smirked to herself; if her brother was anything, he definitely wasn't a pirate. He was even more driven by law and order than she was.

She shook her head to try and dislodge the invasive thoughts. She didn't want to think about the family she didn't have, or rebel safe houses, or a town she barely remembered. She just wanted to finish this job and return back to her normal, though dull, life.

Alice stepped forward to examine the pressure gauge, which seemed to be functioning normally. She tightened a last screw, and stepped back to admire her work. She was an accomplished mechanic who worked quickly and efficiently, but a total overhaul of a boiler, with no assistants, in less than 36 hours? That must be a record, even for her.

She stood tall with her hands on her hips, looking over the boiler to scan for anything she might have missed. If she hurried, she might be able to fix the loose coil in the ship's cooling system. Captain Violet could call her ship whatever she wanted, but a loose coil could cause serious damage if it detached. It could tear through the filtration, maybe worse.

Alice shivered at the thought of Violet's ship exploding into space dust, and turned her focus back toward her work with renewed determination.

* * * *

"BOSS, THERE'S A STRANGE reading on the radar. Something keeps fading in and out; whatever it is, it's not small." Ned turned in his char to face Violet. "Maybe you should take a look."

Violet turned and leaned forward in her chair to see the radar screen. She squinted to see the bright green shape fade in and out. "Could it be a ship? "How big does that look to you, Ned? Assuming it isn't an anomaly or defect in the radar."

Ned examined the radar as it pulsed. "Could be a ship, smaller than The Cricket, but not insignificant. It's too far outside the local planetary system to be Coalition, so at least we're okay there."

"Try to send them a radio signal. If it is a ship this far out of orbit, I want to know who it is. And I'll call in Kady to have a look at that display. If it's malfunctioning, I want it fixed as soon as possible."

Ned pushed a square orange button on the console in front of him. "Greetings, this is the navigation commander aboard The Cricket, please respond." The speakers remained silent. "Calling to the nearby ship, this is The Cricket, please identify."

Violet stood up. "Arm weapons, Ned. They could be a threat. We won't know until the damn radar is fixed." She pulled her radio from her belt. "Kady, we've got a problem on the bridge. We need to take a look."

Violet's radio crackled for a moment and then they heard Kady's voice, "Understood, Captain."

"How far away is it, Ned?" Violet squinted out the window. Whatever it was, she couldn't see it yet. She was hoping against all odds that it was nothing, just a radar malfunction.

"About 75 kilometers, Boss. Whatever it is, it's heading straight for us." Ned tapped some buttons on the console, and a screen unfolded from the ceiling showing the radar and the mystery object, with an estimated time of collision if neither ship changed course.

Kady appeared suddenly and quietly, her hooded jacket swooshing past Violet and Ned. "I'll take a look, Captain," she said, moving to the radar console and furrowing her brow as she pushed buttons that lit up green, red, and orange. "Captain, something is wrong with the radar. It isn't showing up on the screen properly, but there is another ship out here."

Violet looked at the screen, a small ship blinking in and out of existence on the failing radar. They didn't seem to show any signs of slowing down or altering course.

"30 seconds and counting, Boss," Ned said, powering up the steam cannons and solar beam weapons with a handle to his left. "I recommend we fire a few warning shots."

Violet squinted into the darkness in front of the ship, straining to see the ship that was headed straight for them. "Ned, take evasive maneuvers."

Ned tapped coordinates into the main console. The console replied with a strange garbled string of static and beeps. Ned tapped in the coordinates again, with no result. "Captain, we have no navigation or steering," he said with panic in his throat.

She leaned forward to push the inter-ship communication button again. "Cricket to unnamed ship, alter your course immediately! We are dead in the water, repeat, we cannot alter our position."

The ship on the screen disappeared and the radar console gave a long, slow gurgle of beeps.

"THIS IS THE CAPTAIN OF THE CRICKET, ALTER YOUR COURSE IMMEDIATELY."

"Boss, I really think we should fire a warning shot—"

"Do it, Ned!" she shouted. Ned engaged the steam cannons and shot a burst into space. The boiling hot water formed an arc and quickly froze into a huge icicle. The ice flew into the distance and disappeared into deep space without hitting its target. "Where the hell are they?" Violet yelled. "The bloody radar isn't showing a goddamn thing—"

Suddenly, Violet saw the ship off their port bow, about to crash straight into them. She snatched at her radio. "CALLING ALL CREW: PREPARE FOR IMPACT!"

The ship began to shake and shudder as a deafeningly loud series of crashes and explosions were heard. Violet held firm to the chair in front of her to keep her balance, studying the screens showing the ship's integrity. As the lights flickered and her ears popped with the noise of the explosions, she realized there had been no damage to the outside of her ship. "They didn't crash into us," Violet yelled to her crew, "so what the hell is that noise?"

As if on cue, the explosions ceased and the ship came to a standstill, and left them in an eerie, threatening silence. The mysterious ship had come to a stop right next to them. Violet's radio began to ring with static and white noise. As she turned it over in her hands to examine it, a man's voice came from the speaker:

"Hello, Captain. Prepare to be boarded. If you cooperate, we might let you live."

CHAPTER SIX

VIOLET TURNED AND TRIED to swallow her fear, which was quickly becoming a knot of terror in her stomach. "Kady," she said quietly, "try to round up the rest of the crew and keep them calm. Whoever this is, I'll deal with them." Without a word, Kady turned on the heel of her immaculately polished boot and silently swept down the corridor.

Violet raised her radio to her mouth. "This is Captain Violet of the unregistered vessel Cricket, please identify yourself." The radio emitted a low hum of static. "Repeat, this is Captain Violet, what can we do for you?" There was no response. Violet tried to listen for sounds of struggle from her crew or from the other ship, but only heard the hisses and pops leftover from the explosions. She pulled out her revolver and removed the holster under her arm, hiding it under the captain's seat. Pulling several bullets from the inside pocket of her leather vest, she quietly loaded the gun and flicked her wrist to snap the cylinder closed. She quickly unbuttoned the top of her white blouse, and concealed the gun within her black lace bra.

Hearing the sound of boots in the corridor, Ned picked up a large heat gun meant for repairing breeches in the ship. Heat guns were never supposed to be used as weapons, but had become favored improvised tools of assault in recent years, both with pirates and the Coalition. They were heavy and cumbersome, but for a large man like Ned, it felt more natural than to fumble with a gun holster. He moved towards the door of the bridge and settled to the left of the entrance, crouched down as much as a very tall, very broad man could be. The intruders were drawing nearer, their raucous laughter and stomping becoming louder as they approached the bridge.

Violet stood calm and firm, her feet set apart and her hands clasped behind her back. Her head held high, she set her steely stare at the entrance to the bridge. She would never allow her crew to know it, but her pulse was racing and she could feel the prickle of sweat down her spine. She hadn't been this terrified since she was a child during the last rebellion, hiding while guards ransacked her neighbors' homes. Violet concentrated on long, slow breaths as the voices grew close enough to understand.

"These fucking morons are going to regret meeting us, aren't they, Captain?" a loud, throaty woman's voice laughed.

"Aye," a man responded, stomping loudly down the corridor, "They'll rue the day they ever parked this piece of shit ship in our corner of space."

"Hey, what's that? Fuck! He's got a heat gun!" another man yelled.

Ned leapt around the corner with the heat gun as Violet lunged forward in a pointless attempt to stop him. As Ned's finger curled around the trigger, one of the invaders rushed him, grabbing Ned around the knees and bringing him down to the ground. The heat gun went off and several invaders jumped back as it scorched the metal interior of the ship, leaving black marks on the doorway and ceiling.

"I'll take him out!" the woman with the loud voice yelled as she jumped to the side of the heat gun, shooting Ned in the neck with a small gun loaded with syringes. Ned stumbled and dropped the heat gun. He wavered on his feet for a moment, and before Violet could get to him, his body went limp and he fell to the floor.

Violet shoved the woman out of the way. "What did you do to him?!" she cried, a note of panic in her voice. A striking blonde man with cropped hair and a stocky build stepped over Ned's unconscious body and grabbed Violet firmly by the shoulder.

"I'm gonna need you to calm down there, darlin'," he drawled. His icy blue eyes were rimmed with red, and he had a wide face covered in patchy stubble. "He'll probably be fine, so long as you follow my instructions." He spat on the floor. "But then, we've never used that much sedative before, so who knows. Thought it was best to be on the safe side. He looks like a big fella." The blonde man turned and kicked Ned's boot. "Nah, probably be fine."

Violet narrowed her eyes and thought about the gun hidden in her shirt. Even if she shot him right now, the rest of his crew would probably murder her, Ned, and anyone else they came across as they looted her ship of the supplies meant for starving rebel communities. "And what can I do for you?" she said coolly.

"You can call me Captain Leo," he challenged. "A man has to demand some respect, after all." He waited for her response, tugging at his belt loops with his free hand.

Violet gritted her teeth. "What can I do for you, *Captain Leo*," she hissed.

"Well for starters, you can tell me where the rest of your crew is. I know y'all aren't running this pile of shit with just the two of yous." He stared Violet down and squared his broad shoulders. She knew that he wanted to intimidate her, but she wasn't about to take that bait.

"I wouldn't know," she said innocently. "When I heard the explosions, they all scattered to their repair stations."

"Did ya like them explosions?" He grinned. "Specialized fireworks. Disables navigation and steering without blowing up any valuable cargo."

"Fascinating." Violet stared at Captain Leo. He was still holding her right shoulder with his meaty hand, and she hoped he wouldn't notice the bulge of the gun beneath her vest.

"Well, never mind that," he said cheerily. "We'll find 'em." He turned to his crew. "Fuck off and find the crew," he shouted, "and don't come back unless it's with a hostage." The small crew dispersed down the corridor, leaving Violet, Captain Leo, the loud woman, and a short, skinny young boy who couldn't have been older than 18.

"These are my seconds in command," he said, "but I don't suppose that's important to y'all. You probably just want to know what I want with your ship – don't worry, it's not worth stealing. How old is this model, 30 years old? Looks like it should have been decommissioned a decade ago."

Violet shifted her weight. "It was decommissioned a decade ago. I...liberated it from the shipyard."

Captain Leo gave a loud, boisterous laugh and took his hand away from her shoulder. "A woman after my own heart!"

"No thank you," Violet said flatly.

Captain Leo stood straight, all humor gone from his face. "Well, don't worry, darlin'," he growled, "you're a bit old for me anyway. I like my women with less sass."

Violet's gaze flicked to the woman, who frowned.

"Don't worry none," he continued, "we're just gonna be clearin' out your cargo hold and we'll be on our way."

"I'm afraid I can't allow that," Violet said evenly. "The supplies in our hold are earmarked to support the rebels in their fight against the Coalition."

"Boy, howdy," he laughed, "never thought I'd meet a pirate with political convictions. I don't give a fuck what happens to rebels, or the goddamn Coalition." He paused. "We'll be having those supplies, darlin.' Ain't nothin' you can do to stop that happening."

Violet hoped that Kady had gotten to the rest of the crew before this captain's crew found them. She hoped they'd all get out of this alive. The color had drained from Ned's face, and she felt the knot in her stomach tighten. She cleared her throat and focused her thoughts. She had to keep a cool head if she wanted to save her crew.

"I'm not sure we have much that would be of interest to you. Mostly canned food and some fresh produce." She hoped this rag-tag crew wouldn't find the death droids that were locked away. If they got hold of those, no ship in this entire sector would be safe.

"Food is good enough for me," he said slapping his flat stomach. "We're mighty hungry, and some fresh vegetables would be mighty welcome. We may be pirates, but we don't want to end up with scurvy, yes?" Captain Leo laughed at his own joke, and Violet rolled her eyes. He glanced around the room, taking stock of the console and its displays. "And besides," he chortled, "I'm sure you've got some fine goodies stashed away on this here ship. And we'll find em', yes we will."

Violet took a step back to put some space between her and Leo. "Search all you want, you're still not getting what you want."

Leo narrowed his eyes. "I'll do whatever I damn well please, bitch." He pulled a large pistol from a holster hanging from his belt and turned to point it at Ned. "I wouldn't be able to take this fella in a fair fight, but it's easy enough to shoot him dead while he's knocked out cold."

Violet's breath caught in her throat, and she couldn't even dare to move a muscle.

"Maybe I should shoot him, just to show y'all how serious I am." He cocked the pistol, and his two companions laughed.

"Yeah, shoot him," the woman giggled.

"Shut up, Josie," he growled. The woman closed her mouth and looked down. Leo looked back to Violet, keeping his gun trained on Ned. "She might be a woman, but she's a damn fine navigator," he said. "Pity she doesn't know when to keep her mouth shut."

Violet wished she knew what was going on in other parts of the ship: Where was Kady? Where was Hyun? *Where was Alice?*

· · · ·

ALICE SAT UP AND TOUCHED her head. She had been thrown off balance by the explosions and slipped on a piece of pipe that had been laid out on the floor. She grimaced and looked at her hand, which had come back with blood on her fingers. She probably hit her head when she fell down, and she had no idea how long she had been knocked out. Still, the cut didn't feel too serious, and she was able to clear the fog at the corners of her vision by shaking her head vigorously.

She saw movement out of the corner of her eye, and instinctively picked up the large wrench by her side. "Who's there?" she asked.

Kady peered into the boiler room. "Shhh!" she hissed. "The captain and Ned are in trouble. Pirates. I'm gathering the crew in the mess hall to regroup, but the intruders are looking for us."

Alice stood up, taking the large wrench with her. "I want to help. Tell me what to do."

"Nothing," Kady whispered, "I can't trust you. Just meet with the others."

Alice stuck her chin out stubbornly. "I can help. Even if I was a spy, it wouldn't make sense to side with other pirates."

Kady narrowed her eyes and studied Alice's face for a moment. "Fine. Follow me. But don't make a goddamn sound, or we're fucked." She looked down at the mechanic's boots. "And take those off. Can't have you stomping through the hallways."

Alice bent and untied her boot laces, removing them and hiding them under a pile of scrap metal in the corner that she had been sifting through.

Kady turned to climb the steps out of the boiler room, and Alice followed.

"Wait," Alice whispered, "aren't you going to take a weapon? What about the death droids?"

"The droids are locked away," Kady replied, "And if they caught me while I was fetching them, they'd know the droids are worth stealing. I can't risk that. I'll just have to improvise."

The two women crept through the corridors, twisting and turning to avoid the invading crew. Each time they would hear voices or boots on the metal grate flooring, they would hold their breath and move down an adjacent hall. They knew better than to hide in a room, where they would be cornered if discovered.

"This way," Kady mouthed, pointing down the main corridor towards the bridge.

"What if they see us?" Alice mouthed back. Kady shook her head and pointed again. Alice quietly followed her down the wide corridor, away from the mess hall and towards Violet and Ned. They inched past crew quarters, maintenance access vents, and old, unused cargo overflow rooms.

They continued silently, Alice sliding along the floor in her thick wool socks. The women approached a closet with a door left ajar. Kady and Alice exchanged a glance, and proceeded with caution. As they neared the door, an arm reached out and grabbed Alice by the wrist. Using the intruder's weight against him, Alice pulled him out of the closet and hit him with her large wrench, knocking him out cold.

Kady raised an eyebrow and nodded in approval. "Make sure he can't get out," she whispered.

As quietly as possible, Alice shoved the intruder into the closet and closed the door. She pulled a screwdriver from her belt and wedged it under the door to delay the intruder's escape.

Kady led the way, sneaking around corners as she listened for the intruders. Alice followed as quietly as she could, focusing her attention on each step so as not to stumble or fall. She wondered how Kady was so silent when she moved, when she struggled not to trip over everything in sight.

Alice wiped a bead of sweat from her brow. They were nearing the bridge now, and she could hear a muffled man's voice. She gripped the wrench tightly in her hand and hoped she would get out of this alive. She had been brought here against her will, but she felt oddly responsible for the members of the crew. And for Violet.

Kady sidled around the corner to the bridge, and gave an almost inaudible gasp. She covered her mouth for a moment and motioned for Alice to follow.

Alice turned the corner and saw Ned on the floor, motionless. Her stomach seized with worry; she hadn't known Ned long, but his friendly and welcoming demeanor had already endeared him to her. Alice slowly raised up, wrench in hand. She saw the abandoned heat gun between Ned and two members of the invading crew, a blonde woman who was looking at her feet and a young, scrawny boy. She didn't see the boy as much of a threat, but the woman could cause some problems if things went wrong.

Alice gestured towards the heat gun. Kady nodded; they both knew they'd have to act fast before anyone saw them. Alice reached forward and grabbed the woman as Kady dodged the boy and somersaulted towards the heat gun, landing on her feet with the gun in hand.

"Leo!" the woman yelled.

Alice tightened her grip on the woman. "Don't come closer," she said, "or I'll knock her out cold and come for you next. That gun in your hand doesn't scare me."

Kady powered up the heat gun, which began to pop and whirr. She grinned at the invaders. "You know, it's not your fault you've been outsmarted. We're top of the line pirates." She tilted her head, "And you're bottom of the heap."

Alice glanced at Violet, who had the top two buttons of her blouse open. Alice's stomach jumped, and she didn't know if it was seeing Violet or the near death experience that was causing the shiver down her spine.

"Are you okay?" she asked to try to cover her reaction.

Violet straightened. "Yes, I'm fine," she said calmly. "Good to see that you're both alright." She turned to face Captain Leo. "As you can see, Captain Leo, you've been outgunned. If you shoot Ned, or me, your seconds in command won't fare very well."

Captain Leo frowned. "Well, darlin', that was a mighty impressive show. I say I am impressed! A woman captain who managed to best me, well, that's a rare find indeed." He kept the gun pointed at Ned's unconscious body. "But I think y'all are forgetting, the rest of my crew is bound to find where you're hiding the rest of yours."

"Yes, that's true," Violet said, "but are you willing to risk the lives of your crew for a little bit of food and scrap metal?"

Captain Leo smirked. "Ya know, I don't really care all that much for these two anyway," he mused, "One's as useless as a box of shit and the other isn't much better. Replaceable." His finger twitched on the trigger.

Violet frowned. "You've already admitted that you're beat," she said calmly. "Leave my ship. I'll even give you some food, I don't want anyone to starve."

His eyes narrowed. "I'm not taking any fuckin' charity from a *female*. I'd sooner blow up your ship and mine."

Violet's radio zapped to life. "Captain, this is Hyun. The other crew found us, but we have, uh, disabled them."

Violet smirked and engaged her radio. "Thank you, Hyun."

Alice shifted. "Uh, Captain Violet, there's one stashed inside the empty storage closet down the hall. Might have a concussion."

Violet raised the radio once more, "Hyun, please send someone to check the closet nearest the bridge, I'm told he will need some medical attention."

"Sure thing, Captain!" Hyun chirped.

Violet's radio fell silent. "Leo, we have you backed into a corner. Give up. Leave my ship."

He narrowed his eyes. "I don't think you have the balls to kill any of us," he replied smoothly. "I think I still get to do whatever the fuck I want." He turned towards Ned. "I think I could shoot him and you wouldn't do a goddamn thing."

Violet stepped forward. "Do not. Challenge me." Her eyes flashed with fire.

Leo flashed a grin. "You don't even have a gun, darlin'." He looked at Ned's body. "Pity about this fella, but I reckon if he's not woken up yet, he ain't gonna. Betcha I could shoot him and it wouldn't make a damn bit of difference."

Quick as a flash, Violet pulled the revolver out of her bra and cocked the hammer. "Shoot him, and that's it for you and your entire crew," she said with a terrifying stillness.

Leo turned to face Violet. "Like I said, I'd rather blow up both these ships than admit defeat to a woman. I'm a pirate, not a chicken-shit military boy." He smiled and looked Violet in the eyes. "I didn't get to where I am by surrendering. I reckon we're not done here." He pulled the trigger and the gun went off. Kady screamed and Alice gasped, tightening her grip on the woman. Ned's left thigh bloomed a deep scarlet, but Ned didn't stir.

Violet stepped towards Leo and pointed her gun. "Not another move." She grabbed her radio with her free hand. "Hyun, I need you on the bridge immediately. Bring your trauma kit."

Leo laughed. "Ah, see, I knew ya wouldn't kill me. Ya ain't got the balls. Shit pirate, if you ask me." He grinned at Violet with sparkling white teeth. "You might be able to capture my dumbass crew, but I'll never leave a fight without winning."

They heard someone running down the hallway, and Hyun burst onto the bridge with another crew member. She quickly surveyed Ned's injuries. "I need pressure on that wound," she said clearly and calmly, "and I'm going to need a vial of adrenaline." Another crew member stumbled into the room with a large, heavy box of medical equipment and a canister of oxygen.

Alice held her breath and bit her lip. She looked across the room and saw a single tear roll down Kady's face.

"He needs oxygen," Hyun said to the late arriving crew member.

Leo laughed. "Ain't no point, that fella is dead." He pointed his gun at the canister of oxygen. "And soon, y'all will be too."

Violet laughed darkly. "And what do you propose to achieve by shooting the oxygen tank? I'm no fool, *Captain*. The best you'll do is exhaust our supply; those tanks have been explosion proof for half a century."

His lip twitched, and Leo gave a melodramatic sigh. "Ah, well, I was hoping to avoid any bloodshed. But—" He looked at Ned, "we seem to be past that point." He trained his pistol on Ned with one hand, while he reached into his leather duster coat with the other and pulled out a small metallic sphere.

"Recognize this? Probably not, it's brand new technology, ain't it?" He turned the small device over in his hand. "Voice activated micro droid, it can blow a hole in a ship bigger'n any traditional explosive can."

He brought the micro bot to his lips and kissed it. "What do y'all think? Am I bluffing? Or maybe I should just take what I came for and I won't blow us all into space."

Violet took a deep breath, aimed, and shot Captain Leo right between the eyes.

CHAPTER SEVEN

CAPTAIN LEO FELL TO the floor in a heap, his eyes still wide in surprise. A slow trickle of blood dripped from the small bullet hole on his forehead.

"You killed him!" Josie, the blonde woman screeched. Alice tightened her grip on the woman.

Hyun stood and gestured at the two crew members she had brought. "You two, get Ned to the med bay immediately. Do it carefully." The crew members gently picked Ned up, one by his armpits, and the other by his knees. They quickly carried him out and down the hall, and Hyun turned to Violet. "He's not dead, Captain, but he needs urgent medical attention."

Violet nodded and slowly lowered her revolver, staring at the dead Captain Leo. She stared at the gun in her hands and had a vague awareness that they might try to shoot her, too.

Kady shifted the clumsy weight of the heat gun in her arms, still pointing it at the boy, who still hadn't said a word.

For a long moment, the bridge was silent except for Josie's soft sniffles. Then she spoke, sobbing softly, "You killed him, you killed our captain!"

Violet raised her stare to meet the woman's. She cocked her revolver and brought it to eye level, pointing it at the woman. "And I'll kill you, too, if you don't get. The fuck. Off of my ship."

An eternity seemed to pass in silence before Josie slowly raised her hand to her radio. "Back to the ship, everyone. It's a bust." Alice released her, staying close enough to grab her again if she tried anything. The boy held his scrawny arms up, and Kady lowered the heat gun slightly.

Maintaining her aim, Violet used her free hand to pick up her radio. "Can someone in the mess hall please escort our guests the fuck off our ship?"

A moment, and then a reply: "Sure thing, Boss."

Josie's tears continued to fall as she sniffled. "Can we at least take his body with us?"

Violet looked at her coldly. "It's none of my business how you choose to deal with your trash."

Josie and the boy dragged the corpse of Captain Leo off the bridge and down the corridor, his boots squeaking as they dragged against the floor. It seemed to take forever. Finally, Violet lowered her revolver as she heard the last of the invaders returning to their ship. Her legs felt like wet noodles and her heart was still racing with fear for Ned, her navigator and close friend.

"Alice, Kady, you're dismissed," Violet said softly. "Alice, see to the repairs. I don't want to be stuck out here any longer than necessary." She glanced at Alice, this tall, strong woman she'd brought here against her will. Violet sighed. "Kady, please check on the console programming, make sure whatever they did can be reversed. And examine that micro bot."

"Yes, Captain," Kady replied quietly, and swooshed off the bridge in a whirl of heavy black fabric.

Alice stood in the doorway and shifted her weight. "Violet? Er, Captain? Are you alright?"

Violet looked at Alice. "Yes, Mechanic, now please start on the repairs as I asked."

The mechanic looked down at her feet, her wool socks torn up by the metal flooring. Her boots were still hidden under the pile of scrap metal in the boiler room. "Aye." She turned and left the bridge, the soft thud of her footsteps fading down the corridor.

· · · ·

ALICE RETURNED TO THE boiler room, her mind in a haze. In two days, she had been abducted, drunk, kissed a pirate – she cringed when she thought about how awkward she had been – repaired a ship, attacked by *more* pirates, and seen two men shot, one killed. The minor repairs she'd been working on the previous morning seemed like a lifetime ago.

She sighed and bent to dig out her boots. She laced up one boot, and then the other; she tightened her tool belt around her hips and cast her gaze over the chaos caused by the modified fireworks that the invaders had used. Luckily, none of the components needed to finish the repair had been damaged. She would be finished with the repair in a couple of hours at most, and the problems caused by the invaders were mostly cosmetic, aside from the reprogramming Kady would have to do.

Something on the far side of the room caught Alice's eye – a broken hinge on the maintenance access panel for the secondary boiler. She could fix that, too. Alice rubbed her eyes as if to rub out the memory of Captain Leo's corpse. "Argh, enough of this," she muttered to herself.

She pulled her goggles over her eyes, cracked her knuckles, and got to work. With any luck, she'd be done by dinnertime, and if she was very lucky, she would lose herself in the work. The next time she looked at the time, hours had passed in pleasant silence, a deliciously peaceful change from the chaos.

"Are you almost finished, Mechanic?" Kady appeared in the doorway, her pin straight black hair tied haphazardly at the nape of her neck.

Alice turned towards the door and looked at Kady through the teal tint of her goggles. "I should be finished in a few minutes. Luckily, the explosions didn't damage any of the machinery. I had to sort through some of the smaller components again, but nothing serious."

"Well, good. We're meeting in the mess hall soon to fill everyone in on what happened."

Alice turned back to the boiler she was repairing. "How's Ned doing?"

There was a moment of unsettled silence. "Hyun will be giving us an update. I don't know how extensive his injuries were, and I don't know anything more than you do."

Alice picked up a screwdriver to affix a safety plate to the pilot light. "How did you get on with that micro bot? Does it do what he said it does?"

Kady folded her arms across her chest. "We aren't friends, Mechanic, and you're not a part of this crew."

Alice said nothing, choosing instead to continue focusing on the equipment in front of her.

"It's a Coalition made explosive, but I'm sure you're aware of that."

Alice shifted her weight to peer around the side of the boiler. "I have no idea what goes on in the weapons division. I just fix things."

"Just because you helped me earlier doesn't mean I trust you. As far as I can tell, you'll tell your captain everything that happened here, expose our weaknesses. You might even be sabotaging the ship with that repair."

Alice sat back on her heels and pushed up her goggles, before saying again, "I'm a mechanic, not a spy." She turned to look at Kady. "Like I said, I just fix things. I don't have the kind of clearances to be privy to top secret artillery developments."

"Time will tell," Kady said firmly. "Are you finished now? I should escort you to the mess hall. I don't like the idea of you wandering around unsupervised."

Alice sighed. "Yes, I'm finished." She replaced the screwdriver in her tool belt. "Will Captain Violet be joining us?"

Kady narrowed her eyes. "Why do you want to know?"

Alice stood up and dusted off her knee pads. "Just...curious."

"No, she has other business to attend to. Follow me, there is food prepared in the mess hall." Kady glided down the corridors, followed by Alice's echoing footsteps.

As the two women approached the mess hall, they could hear murmuring crew members and feel the thick air of tension and uncertainty. Alice rounded the corner into the room, and saw that none of the crew members were seated; they chose instead to cluster around the tables, which held large bowls of plain, limp noodles. A hush came over the crew as Kady entered, and they looked at her expectantly.

Kady cleared her throat. "I know many of you are worried about Ned. He's a friend to almost everyone on this ship. He's a good man and an even better navigator. And you all know that his cooking is much better than mine." A few quiet titters were heard around the room. She continued, "Hyun will be arriving shortly to give us an update on how he's doing. The captain is with him in med bay, and will not be joining us for dinner this evening. As Ned was unavailable to cook us dinner, I had to make do. I know it's not what you're used to, but it's something. You all need to eat to keep your strength up and get enough sleep so that your duties don't suffer. Please, sit and eat."

A tall, muscled crew member in the back of the room said, "Thank you, Kady." The rest of the crew quietly murmured their agreement, and they began to take their seats.

As Alice wedged herself into a chair, she realized that the Cricket's crew wasn't all that large: certainly smaller than the crew that would have been used on a similarly sized Coalition vessel. It was a rag tag group, and she was curious about those she hadn't met yet. Why were they here, and why had they left home for a life of dangerous uncertainty?

Kady sat down in the seat to Alice's right and passed her the bowl of food. Alice filled her plate with the lukewarm, plain noodles and passed the bowl across the table. She sighed and paused for a moment, taking in the chatter of the crew members. She leaned over and hissed, "Don't think you'll overhear any secrets, Mechanic. I've instructed the crew to not mention any sensitive information in your presence."

Alice rolled her eyes. "Okay, then," she said. She took a bite of her noodles and realized that she might miss Ned most of all: tonight's meal was certainly less impressive than the last dinner she had on this ship. Her stomach growled with the memory of the hot, spicy food.

"Hi everyone, attention please," Hyun said loudly as she entered the mess hall. Her clothes were splattered with blood, and she looked exhausted. Stray hairs fell around her face, and the elaborate coiled braid on her head was loose and wispy. A hush fell over the room as they waited to hear her news. "I know you're all anxious to hear about Ned. He's a lucky guy: the bullet only nearly missed a main artery. He's stable now, but needs to rest. The drug he was dosed with is a strong sedative, and he'll need to sleep it off."

There was a collective sigh around the room. It was clear to Alice how important Ned was to the rest of the crew, not just as a navigator or a cook, but as a friend, too. She didn't even know the name of the cook on the C.S. Stronghold, and she suddenly felt very uncomfortable with the idea that she ate three meals a day on that ship, cooked by someone she'd never met. She shifted in her seat and shoveled another forkful of disappointing noodles into her mouth.

"The captain is with him now," Hyun continued, "so I'll take food up to her. Ned won't be able to eat until he comes around. I need to monitor Ned tonight, so if any of you need any urgent medical attention, that's where you can find me. I want to thank everyone for working together earlier to secure the mess hall, and for those of you who helped me transport Ned to the med bay." A crew member Alice hadn't noticed before handed two bowls of noodles to Hyun with forks sticking out of the top. "Thank you all again. My radio will be on silent mode so as not to disturb Ned. So, if you need me, you'll have to come and find me." She held one bowl in the crook of her arm, and held the other in her hands as she deftly stuffed noodles into her mouth.

"Thank you, Hyun," Kady said quietly. The crew nodded their heads in agreement, some with mouths full of noodles.

Hyun nodded at Kady as she turned and left the room. Alice was struck by Hyun's firm authority; she was clearly a strong leader, and confident in her position as the crew's only source of medical treatment. She'd been clear that she was a med tech, not a doctor, but Alice wondered how someone who hadn't graduated from a Coalition school could be so adept at surgical procedures like repairing gunshot wounds and not progress to medical school.

The crew returned to eating, though many were almost finished with their portion. The bowls were now empty, and the only sound in the room was that of forks on plates and the crew refilling their water glasses. One by one they got up, cleaned their dishes, and left to return to their duties. Alice had seen how those explosions earlier left her own projects in disarray; she wondered how badly theirs had been affected.

Kady stood. "Are you finished? I'll escort you to your quarters for the night. I imagine we will drop you off at the next available opportunity, and you'll be able to signal for pickup from there."

"Just about." Alice stood and grabbed Kady's plate as well as her own. She crossed to the sink, rinsed, and dried the dishes. She turned to face Kady. "Are you going to see Ned?"

"I told you, you and me, we're not friends. What do you care, anyway?"

Alice shrugged. "It's clear he has a lot of friends on this ship. He seems like a good man."

"He is a good man. Follow me." Kady turned to lead the way to Alice's quarters. "In the morning, I'll send a crew member to fetch you from your quarters when we're ready to drop you off. Make sure you're ready, once we enter colonized space we're detectable by the Coalition and we can't remain there for long, not without Ned as our navigator."

Alice followed Kady down the narrow corridor. "Understood."

She felt a bittersweet sadness about the thought of leaving the Cricket; she was eager to get home to what felt familiar, but this had been an unexpectedly positive adventure. She wanted to tell Barnaby about what had happened here, and she wondered if she should say goodbye to Violet. As they reached Alice's quarters, Kady pushed the door open. "Here you are, Mechanic," she said. "I'll be posting someone outside your door to make sure you don't decide to roam around the ship looking for secrets."

"I told you, I just fix things."

"I'm still posting someone outside your door." Kady turned to leave and picked up her radio. "Any available crew members, I need a volunteer for a night watch," she said.

"I'll be right there, Kady!" came the overenthusiastic reply.

Kady looked at Alice. "You might as well close the door, Mechanic, I'm not leaving until your night watch arrives."

Alice sighed and closed the door. The room in front of her was silent except for the low hum of the engines and the chirp of the filtration system, and she realized how bone tired she was. She peered around the unfamiliar room: after last night's whiskeys, she hadn't really looked around. The bed was larger than hers on the C.S. Stronghold, which was a welcome change with her tall, broad frame. There was a squashy, overstuffed chair in the corner with faded upholstery. There was a simple desk, a long plank of unfinished wood balanced on top of bricks at either end, with a small stool in front of it. The attached bathroom had a small bathtub much too short for her tall frame, and she frowned. A bath would have been nice. Alice looked out the window at the dark space surrounding the ship: tomorrow, they'd be near a planet where she would be dropped off. She'd be able to contact the Stronghold and request a pickup. She might not ever see the crew of the Cricket ever again.

She needed a bath, a change of clothes, and a few days – or weeks – of sleep. Alice took off her goggles and placed them on the table next to the bed. She sat on the bed and leaned back into the pillows. Before she knew it, she was deep in a dreamless sleep.

• • • •

ALICE SAT IN THE DARKNESS, cocooned in the deep hum of the ship's engines. She looked out the window and saw a desolate rock far in the distance. She had never been good with space geography, but it looked like Iota-9, which people used to call Pluto before the Coalition renamed all the celestial bodies almost 200 years ago. Alice hadn't realized they were this far out, but it made sense for a vessel trying to avoid detection. She sighed and sat up in bed. She looked at the digital interface inside her goggles on the nearby table – it was the middle of the night, and yet Alice felt wide awake.

She swung her legs off the bed and stretched her arms. The guard that Kady had posted outside her door was probably still there, and Alice felt lonely. She padded across the room and slowly opened the door a crack to see who was waiting for her to try and sneak out. She put her eye to the crack and saw a petite crew member with bright green hair tucked into a cap, slumped against the opposite wall and snoring deeply. Alice stifled a laugh and formulated a plan. Leaving the door open, she crossed the room quietly. She laced up her boots, squeezed out the barely open door, and crept past the sleeping crew member.

Alice moved softly through the corridors to the med bay, taking extra care to be as silent as possible. Her tall frame and heavy steps made it hard to be quiet, but on this occasion she managed to sneak by every room un-detected, including the mess hall where the night shift crew members were laughing and playing a game of Banríon, a card game where players collect-ed cards and built decks to challenge each other with.

"Don't you even dare," one of the players said. "You've not slept in two days, how are you still winning?!"

Alice heard laughing from the room. She stole a glance inside, being careful not to be seen. Hyun sat at the table facing her opponent, grinning.

"It's just practice," Hyun said, laying her final card on the table. She still looked tired, but more relaxed, and Alice took that as a good sign about Ned's condition.

She smiled and wondered if Violet ever played card games like that. Al-ice thought about her own Banríon deck back on the C.S. Stronghold, and made a mental note to challenge Barnaby to a game when she got back. The game was an excellent way to keep your wits sharp, and it was also a good way to distract yourself from your worries.

As Alice approached the med bay, she heard soft, even breathing from within. She entered the dark room and saw Ned sleeping soundly. His leg was tightly bandaged where he had been shot, but the color in his face had returned. It was clear that Hyun was an incredibly adept med tech; Alice had seen accredited doctors fail to save a patient under those conditions. The whole crew was lucky to have her.

She heard a rustling sound in the darkness behind her, and she turned to find Violet sleeping uncomfortably in a folding chair. Alice wondered if she should wake her or let her sleep; she found herself staring at the pirate captain, her tight curls tied back into a haphazard bun and the scar on her face shining in the dim light from the corridor.

Alice reached forward and gently touched Violet's arm. "Erm, Captain?" she whispered.

Violet's eyes flew open and she grabbed Alice's arm in a panic. "Fuck off my ship!" she yelled, before realizing it was the mechanic she'd picked up, and not another invader. She cleared her throat and glanced at Ned to make sure she hadn't woken him up. "What do you want?" she hissed.

"Uh, I just wanted to..."

"You wanted to what?" Violet replied as she released Alice's arm, her tone softening.

"To see how Ned is." Alice rubbed her arm and stepped back.

"As you can see, he'll survive. He'll probably have a limp the rest of his life from the gunshot, but he's a far sight better off than if Hyun hadn't been on board. That sedative they gave him was some pretty heavy duty stuff." Violet rubbed her eyes and stretched out her arms. "How did you get past the guard Kady stationed outside your door?"

"I, uh, don't want to get anyone in trouble," Alice said softly, crossing to the far window. She leaned forward to peer into space, and knocked over a tray of medical instruments, which clattered to the floor noisily. Alice whirled around to see if she had woken Ned, who was still sleeping peacefully. She continued, "I'm a master of silence and I sneaked past the guard?"

Violet raised an eyebrow. "Clearly," she said wryly.

Alice bent to pick up the instruments which were now strewn all over the floor. She quietly replaced them, one by one onto the table. "I don't think Kady likes me very much," she thought out loud.

"She doesn't trust you," Violet replied, standing up out of the chair. "And frankly, you not exactly easing her fears, sneaking around all hours of the night. What are you really doing here, anyway?"

"I told you, I wanted to see how Ned was doing." Alice replaced the last instrument and stood up.

"A bit odd, seeing as you'll probably never see him again after tomorrow," Violet probed. "Seeing as you decided to leave."

Alice sighed. "I told you, I can't just give up everything to be a mechanic on a pirate ship. I have a life and a plan that doesn't include being arrested—" she gestured at Ned, "or shot at."

Violet reflexively felt for her gun, which was still safely holstered under her arm. "And what does that plan include, then? A white picket fence, a vegetable patch, a quiet retirement?"

Alice shuffled her feet. "Something like that."

The captain scoffed. "Sounds like a good way to die of boredom. Don't you want something for your life other than basic rations? Where do you think you'll find this idyllic existence? The cities are fucked and the farm land is all owned by the Coalition. But maybe you've been too isolated on that goddamn ship to know that."

Alice bristled. "And what, fending off pirates and Coalition bounty hunters is your idea of the perfect existence?"

"The only reason they were able to catch us is because we weren't at full power. If you had finished those repairs sooner, those pirates would never have even gotten close enough to disable our radar and navigation."

Alice narrowed her eyes. "You're goddamn lucky it got fixed at all. This ship should have been decommissioned twenty years ago. You're flying on borrowed time, Captain. Without a full-time mechanic, another problem is inevitable – and most younger mechanics won't know what to do with this old analog system." She crossed her arms. "But I suppose you know that, which is why you abducted me, plied me with whiskey, and tried to convince me to stay."

Violet stared at the mechanic, her eyes full of fire. "You kissed *me*, Mechanic."

Alice felt blood rising in her cheeks and took a step backwards at the sudden realization that Violet remembered that. "I—but you—I was drunk!" she stuttered.

"Do you always kiss strange women when you drink?" Violet challenged, raising an eyebrow. "I'm not here to offer you a fairy tale. I offered you a job on my ship. I have a responsibility to this crew and to the people I promised to help. I'll find another mechanic; they won't be as good as you, but they will be enough."

Alice could feel her stomach tied into knots. "Violet, I—" she started, her voice raising.

Ned stirred in his sleep and the two women's eyes met.

"Don't wake him," Violet scolded quietly. Alice crossed the room and stood in front of the door.

"Violet, I—" she tried again.

"It doesn't matter. You're dismissed, Mechanic." Violet looked over her shoulder at Ned, who was returning to a deep sleep.

"Should I, uh..." Alice began. "Should I say goodbye to you tomorrow before I go?"

Violet looked up at her.

"No."

· · · ·

ALICE SAT AT THE EDGE of her bed, eyes bleary amd dry. A soft knock at the door roused her back to reality, and she blinked to clear her clouded vision.

"Uh, hello? Mechanic? We're about to dock."

She felt exhausted, as if she hadn't slept at all. Alice sat up and groggily laced up her boots. She didn't want to think about her last conversation with Violet, so she pushed it out of her mind, thinking instead of what maintenance the C.S. Stronghold would be needing. She began to make a mental checklist in priority order of everything she would need to accomplish. Alice opened the door and saw the crew member with bright green hair who had fallen asleep on her watch.

"Uh, morning," Alice said. "How long until we dock?"

The crew member handed Alice a peach, likely stolen from the Stronghold, and a carton of milk. "About 30 minutes. Kady wanted to speak with you on the bridge before you go."

Alice nodded and followed the petite woman through the corridors to the bridge, eating the peach as she shuffled along. She pocketed the peach pit when they reached the doorway.

"Mechanic," Kady said over her shoulder, not even bothering to look at Alice. "I trust you finished the repairs?"

"Yes, plus a maintenance overhaul of the secondary boiler systems. You're in good shape for now, but you will need a full time mechanic sooner or later. Unless you intend to keep kidnapping mechanics every time something goes wrong."

Kady shifted in her seat. "I don't much care for spies on the ship, so it's likely we will find a permanent mechanic, yes."

"You'll need to upgrade some of the thermal couplers within the next month or two." Alice added.

"Noted." Kady examined a display in front of her and squinted at the unfamiliar readings. "We'll be docking at the trading beacon soon, Mechanic. I trust you have all your belongings?"

"I wasn't exactly invited to pack for this little excursion," Alice replied. "I'm ready to go. Please give Ned my best and wish him a quick recovery." She paused. "And tell the captain..."

Kady looked at Alice over her shoulder. "Tell the captain what?"

"Never mind, it's not important. I hope you have an uneventful journey from here."

"So what will you be telling your Coalition captain about your time with us, spy?"

"There's nothing to tell. I was abducted, I fixed a boiler, I was dropped off. And I'm not a spy. I fix things."

"Mm. I'm sure." Kady stood and faced Alice. "You're dismissed, Mechanic. Thank you for your services. You'll be escorted to the cargo bay, and you may disembark as soon as we touch ground. We won't be sticking around, I'm sure you understand why."

Alice nodded. "Understood."

The green-haired crew member gestured for Alice to follow her, and the two passed through the ship without conversation. They passed through the crew's airlock into the main cargo bay, and Alice stood near the door, which would open as soon as they landed.

"Uh, bye," the crew member said awkwardly as she clambered back through the airlock. She pressed her palms against the glass and shouted, "Just don't touch anything!"

Alice heard the landing gear engage, and she braced herself against a support beam. The ship was descending quickly now, and it wouldn't be long before she was off this ship and sending a distress call to be picked up. No doubt they had been looking for her, but she had no idea if they thought she was alive or dead. She hoped that Barnaby would be happy to see her, at least.

The ship landed hard, and the hydraulic cargo bay door began to hiss as it started to open. Alice bent to slide under the door when she heard a voice.

"Mechanic! Uh, Alice? Wait!"

Alice turned and straightened.

Violet was at the top of the ladder waving something.

"Just wait a second!" She shouted as she began to descend the ladder. About halfway down, she moved her feet to the outside of the ladder and slid the rest of the way down, landing gracefully on the balls of her feet.

Violet crossed quickly to Alice. "I just wanted to give you this." She handed Alice an envelope, her hand brushing against the mechanic's and lingering a moment longer than necessary. "Now, go! We can't stay!" Violet turned and jogged towards the ladder as Alice ducked under the door into the bright sunshine. As soon as her feet touched the airship dock, the Cricket was already beginning to pull away.

Alice opened the envelope. It contained the yellowed map with her parents' house circled. She flipped over the map and found some kind of code that looked like it had been written a long time ago, possibly when the map was originally in use. Unfortunately for Alice, she wasn't skilled in the art of code breaking.

A note fluttered to the ground, and Alice bent to pick it up.

"I hope this helps you unravel some of those mysteries in your past.

I'm sorry.
-V"

CHAPTER EIGHT

"I MISSED YOU, ALICE." Violet sat straddled over Alice, who was leaning back on the bed. "I chose you over piracy, Alice." She leaned forward and buried her face in Alice's loose silvery waves. She entwined her hands in Alice's hair, pulling it around to the left and kissing her neck. Alice found her hands on Violet's hips and pulled her closer.

"Captain, I..."

Violet continued to kiss her neck down towards her shoulders. "Shh." She kissed Alice deeply as she pulled the strap of her tank top down over her shoulder. "Don't say anything."

Alice breathed deep and closed her eyes. She hadn't been with anyone for a long time. Violet kissed Alice's shoulders and slid her hands down her back. She leaned forward to push Alice back onto the pillows and ran her hands up and down the mechanic's burn scarred arms. She pushed down Alice's other tank top strap and kissed her left shoulder.

"Alice?" a man's voice asked. "Alice, are you in there?"

Alice's eyes flew open. Disoriented and annoyed, she struggled to hold on to the last fleeting moments of the dream. "Uh, yes? What?" she replied as she jumped out of bed and put on her standard issue coveralls and buttoned them up. She wondered where the hell she had left her other boot.

"Alice, calm down, it's just me. Did you oversleep again? Open the door!"

Alice opened the door, her hair still in yesterday's braids and with one boot on, her coveralls half buttoned. Her goggles sat crooked on top of her messy, bedraggled hair. Barnaby raised an eyebrow.

"Still catching up on sleep then I see?" He pushed the door open and moved past Alice to sit on her rumpled bed. "It's been two weeks, are you not yet recovered from your little adventure?"

Alice searched under a pile of dirty laundry for her boot. "I told you, I'm on double shifts this week to catch up on repairs. Plus Captain Allen has me training a new mechanic." She opened the closet door and lifted up a spare set of coveralls – her boot wasn't in there, either.

"A new mechanic? What for? I thought they already had shifts covered." Barnaby leaned back on the bed. "Besides, you've never been bothered by double shifts before. It's not like you have any kind of social life outside our morning wake up calls."

Alice continued searching for her boot in a basket full of holey wool socks that needed repair. "Captain Allen realized lately that I'm unlikely to be immortal, it seems," she said, dumping out the basket. "He wants to be prepared in the event I am 'unable to adequately perform duties.' I guess he realized that being stranded without a lead mechanic isn't the best idea for a merchant vessel, even a Coalition one."

Barnaby leaned over and uncovered a boot that had been hidden under a sheet. "Looking for this, then?"

Alice rolled her eyes and took the shoe. "Anyway I've just had a lot on my mind." She laced up the boot and haphazardly dumped the socks back into the basket.

"Ah yes, like your pirate queen?" Barnaby asked, wiggling his eyebrows.

Alice shot him a look. "No, other things." She sat on the bed next to Barnaby. "And I told you, I was drunk."

Barnaby leaned against her. "It's the most action you've seen since...Victoria? What's that, seven years now?"

"Something like that. Now go away Barns, I need to get breakfast before I head to the boiler room."

"Lucky for you, I like to travel with meals on hand," Barnaby said, producing a squashed bran muffin from his pocket. "Now you have no excuse not to tell me what's going on."

Alice snatched the muffin from his hand and took a big bite. "Told ya Barns," she said with a mouth full of muffin, "it's nothing. Just gotta get my focus back." She swallowed and took another bite.

"Bullshit, Al," he said with a note of seriousness. "I can tell something is up. Why won't you tell me?"

"It's complicated," she replied when she had finished the muffin. "I'll tell you when I'm ready. Maybe." She thought about the old map and frowned.

"Okay, just tell me this," he pressed, "is it the captain of that pirate ship?"

Alice rolled her eyes. "No, Barnaby, it's not the captain. I'm not some lovelorn teenager, I can handle a drunken kiss. I just need to think about how long I want to be on this ship, figure out if retirement is even going to be possible at this point."

"You save every credit you earn, why are you even worried?"

"We don't all have cash handed to us under the table for favors and trade deals, Barns. Some of us have to actually plan for our future."

"Darling, you know you'll just end up living in a wing of whatever lavish property I buy. You'll barely even know I'm there."

Alice wrinkled her nose. "No thanks, I prefer my living arrangements without having to hear your midnight visitors."

"Suit yourself then," he said. "But you know the offer's always open to you." He stood up and walked to the door. "Just promise me you'll let me know what's going on with you when you're ready."

"I promise. Now get out, I need to finish getting ready before I go to work." Barnaby smiled and closed the door behind him.

Alice stood and walked to her desk, where the envelope Violet had given her was hidden in a false compartment under the top drawer. Alice couldn't risk whatever this map was being found during a random inspection of crew quarters. She hadn't been inspected in years, she was too respected by the captain and the crew, but she couldn't be too careful. She hadn't told them anything about Violet or her crew when they picked her up at the trading beacon near Iota-9, and she knew that made Captain Allen suspicious despite their decades of working together.

Alice told the investigator that they had kept her far from the bridge of the ship, and that she had no idea where they had taken her in the system. She lied confidently, saying that she was kept in isolation when not working on their boilers. She said she didn't know their names, their plans, or where they were headed next. Though she had worked for the Coalition her entire adult life, she couldn't bring herself to sell out the crew of the Cricket. She smiled to herself and wondered if Kady would still think she was a spy, just before her heart pounded with the thought she was selling out Captain Allen and the Coalition. What a mess she'd found herself in.

Alice lifted the bottom of the desk drawer and retrieved the envelope from the secret compartment. She took out the map and squinted at the code on the back. What could it mean? She'd been spending late nights examining the code for any kind of hint, going so far as to compare it to books of old codes she had found in the restricted Coalition library archives, but she wasn't a code breaker by trade. She sighed. The secrets of her past were locked tight, and frustratingly so.

Violet's note peeked out from the envelope, and Alice took it out and laid it flat on her desk, smoothing out the creases. She lightly ran her fingertips over the florid script and marvelled at how anyone could write so beautifully when in such a rush. She wondered what Violet was doing now, if they had made it to the drop zones yet. She wondered if Violet ever thought of her, or of the drunken kiss in the dark corridor. Her mind wandered back to the dream she had woken up from just a few minutes previous, and Alice scrunched her eyes closed to try and remember every detail, most of which had already dissipated into fragments in her mind. She wondered what the dream meant: was it just a subconscious stream of thought, or a sign of something more?

Alice shook her head to try and clear her thoughts. She was unlikely to ever see Violet again, and she needed to focus on the repairs that were behind schedule, and training this new recruit. Her apprentice had little potential and Alice was struggling to keep her cool with her. The recruit was fresh out of Coalition training and no older than 18, with plenty of enthusiasm but no love for the trade. Alice wouldn't have been surprised if the girl requested a transfer.

Alice placed the note and the map back inside the hidden compartment and closed the drawer. She took a deep breath, opened the door to her quarters, and stepped into the harsh florescent light of the offensively lit corridor.

* * * *

VIOLET SAT AT HER DESK, where she had been all night. She hadn't slept more than a couple of hours a night since the confrontation with the invading pirates. When she did sleep, she dreamt of Captain Leo's wide, dead eyes as he laid dead on the floor of her ship. In the dreams, she watched his limp corpse fall to the ground and heard the screams of his second in command. It replayed every night, and she always awoke in a cold sweat, her heart pounding in her chest. She pulled a small bronze pocket-watch out of her vest pocket and checked the time. It was finally morning. These nights were long, and she couldn't risk her crew knowing that she was struggling to come to terms with what had transpired. She was the captain, and that meant she had to be strong, especially with Ned still on the mend.

Violet stood and stretched her arms over her head. "I should probably change my shirt," she muttered out loud to the empty room. She rummaged through a heavy oak trunk at the foot of the bed and pulled out a crisp white blouse. It was the last one, and she knew she would have to clean her clothes eventually. She dressed, buttoned the shirt, fastened the toggles on her vest, and headed into the hall.

The captain walked the halls, breathing deep the scent of the ship. It smelled like hot metal and toast; the night shift was about to swap with the day shift, and crew members were quickly scarfing what breakfast they could before their duties began. She walked purposefully through the corridors, an outward picture of strength and composure. Turning down a dark hallway, she knocked on the only door there.

"Kady, are you in there?"

"Come in, Captain," came the reply.

Violet opened the heavy steel door into a makeshift lab, where Kady was working behind a long table littered with equipment for testing and programming droids. The detonation bot sat in the middle of the table, where Kady was examining it closely through yellowed lab goggles.

Violet closed the door behind her. "Any progress on that yet? Does it do what he said it does?"

"I'm still evaluating it, Captain. I know it's taking me far longer with this than with other technologies we've encountered, but this is top of the line Coalition grade explosives. This kind of stuff was always kept behind top security clearance when I was there, so who knows how he got his hands on it." She straightened and dusted her hands off on her worn, threadbare lab coat. "I can tell you that it does have strong explosive properties, but I won't be able to replicate that kind of technology for several months at least."

"I don't want you to replicate it," Violet replied. "I want you to learn how to disarm them. I'd rather not have a repeat performance of the invasion a couple weeks ago if at all possible. Who knows how many of these things are out there?"

"My early analysis would be that they might be able to be disarmed with a strong electromagnetic pulse, but I'll have to test that outside the ship, maybe at the next drop zone."

"Right, like the pulse that 'temporarily disarmed' our droids on the Coalition ship when we....when we got Alice?"

Kady pulled the goggles down around her neck, where they hung limply. "Yes, like that. I'd like to develop a way to disable them permanently; if these are common Coalition weapons now, we need a way to combat them. We aren't all a crack shot like you, Captain."

Violet flinched at the mention of her shooting skills. "Yes. Well, keep at it Kady. Is there anything else you need? I can try to get hold of any necessary materials. This is my top priority for you right now."

"A decent mechanic would be nice. I'm an excellent scientist and a competent programmer, but some of these components might fare better under the supervision of someone who deals with the physical elements."

"You're more than competent at programming, Kady, you're the best I've ever seen. Did you ask Alice for help with it before she left?"

Kady wrinkled her nose and shook her head. "No."

"She might have been a help in the small amount of time she was still on the ship after it happened. I'm sure she would have helped if you had asked."

"She claimed she had no knowledge of devices like this."

"Well it stands to reason that's true, especially if you're right about it being top level security clearance."

"Regardless, Captain, she returned to the C.S. Stronghold. I didn't want to provide her with any more information than necessary, given I'm sure she sang like a canary to officials after she was picked up."

Violet frowned. "If that were true, Kady, we'd already have been arrested by Coalition forces. She didn't know where we were headed but if she told them about our confrontation with Captain Leo's brigands they would have known our approximate location. Those pirates don't stray far from their caches."

"Maybe she's helping them lure us into a trap, then."

"I don't think Alice would do that."

"Permission to speak freely?"

Violet narrowed her eyes. "Granted."

"You barely know her, Captain. She could have been memorizing everything about the Cricket in order to report back to her captain on the Coalition ship. We did abduct her, after all." Kady turned to an old, outdated coding device and lazily tapped in a command.

"Do you disagree with my methods?"

"I don't think it was a good idea to aim for the top Coalition mechanic, that's all. But I'm not in command here, you are." The detonation bot beeped quietly and gave off a hazy green glow. Kady made a note on a small pad of paper, and tapped in another command.

"That's correct, I am." Violet let a moment pass in an uncomfortable silence. "I think you're forgetting, Kady, that she wasn't the only Coalition employee to ever set on this ship."

Kady huffed and stepped back from the table. "Yes, but I stayed. I didn't return to the Coalition. I also wasn't abducted, I joined you of my own accord."

"You're also a good deal younger, Kady. Change like that gets harder the older you get. Alice has had a lifetime of service with the Coalition, it's all she knows." Violet pressed a hand to her temple; she could feel another headache on the way, brought on by a lack of sleep. "Anyway, this isn't about Alice."

"If we can find a decent mechanic, I might be able to solve this problem sooner than without one. But if not, I will make do."

"Noted."

"Is that all, Captain?"

Violet could feel the exhaustion tugging at the corners of her mind, and she knew she would drink through a week's ration of strong coffee today. "Yes, that's all. Good work, I'll leave you to it."

Violet returned to the dark hallway, and made a mental note to have someone repair the flickering light overhead.

• • • •

ALICE'S LIMBS WERE heavy and sore from a week of double shifts in the boiler room, and she felt every step as she climbed the stairs back to her quarters. Repairs were progressing; she had just completed work on the main boiler and the C.S. Stronghold was now back to full strength. They had been dragging along on secondary systems since before Violet and her crew had attacked.

She thought again of Violet, of cheap whiskey, and of the letter that was still hidden in her desk. She paused on the stairs and squeezed her eyes shut, but she wasn't sure if she was trying to remember the dream or forget it. She shook her head to clear her thoughts and continued up the steps towards her quarters.

Alice reached the top of the stairs and turned left. Hers was the only room down this isolated hallway, a rare perk of working with Captain Allen for decades. As she approached, she could see that the door was ajar. Alice began to walk faster as she neared the door, and her heart began to race. Who else had keys to her room? She made sure she locked it every day when she left; there were too many young recruits on this vessel who like to stir up mischief after their shifts were over. Alice pushed the door open, and her breath caught in her throat. Her entire room had been searched, and whoever had searched it didn't take any cautions to cover their tracks. Her mattress was overturned and leaning against the wall, and the trunk at the foot of her bed had been emptied, the contents strewn all over the floor. In a panic she climbed over an overturned storage unit to reach her desk – was the letter still safe? She threw open the desk drawer and pried open the hidden compartment.

The letter was safe, and then immediately tucked it into the inside pocket of her coveralls. She was glad for those woodworking courses she had taken all those years ago, because the seams of her secret cache were perfect and undetectable. Was this a routine search by an overzealous security officer, or something else? She hadn't given them any reason to suspect that she had more information about Violet and her ship...at least, she didn't think she had. There was a note on the top of the desk with a hastily scrawled note:

"Inspected by Security Officer Smith"

Alice felt anger rising in her chest, adrenalin-laced blood coursing through her veins. She hadn't done anything wrong, she didn't choose to be abducted. She never asked for any of this, and now her loyalty to the Coalition was being questioned anyway. Stepping around her belongings, she set to march straight to Captain Allen's office. She moved through the ship quickly, the heel of her boot echoing percussively down corridors. She reached the captain's office, and saw that his light was on. She rapped sharply on the door.

"Captain Allen? I have a matter that I need to discuss with you urgently." She could see him through the glass on the door, his tiny spectacles perched on his nose as he examined maps and charts laid out on his desk.

He looked up and gestured at the door. "Ah, Lead Mechanic Alice Green. Come in. What can I do for you?"

She opened the door and quickly closed it behind her. "Captain, I just discovered, after working a double shift to complete repairs faster, that my room was searched by a Security Officer Smith." She crossed her arms in front of her and continued, "Searched is a loose term for it, actually, he tossed everything in there. It will take hours to clean up the mess."

Captain Allen took off his spectacles and placed them on the desk in front of him. "Alice, you know that these random searches are mandatory for all Coalition crew members and regiments."

"I haven't been searched like that in over twenty years, Captain," she retorted. "Is this a new recruit, overstepping established protocol, or have I done something to make you question my decades of loyal service on your ship?"

"Alice," he said as he looked up at her, "please sit down." He gestured at a folding chair leaning against the left wall.

She unfolded the chair and sat down heavily, looking at the captain expectantly. "Well?" she asked.

"Alice, your service record has been exemplary. You're possibly the best mechanic in the entire Coalition fleet. In fact, I've had to fend off transfer requests from the military vessels for years, who wanted you as their mechanic."

"And?"

"And I'm grateful that you're my mechanic."

"Yes, so grateful that you've asked me to train my own replacement," she said wryly. She probably shouldn't be speaking to Captain Allen this way, but she was angry and this was the last straw.

"Alice, you know why you're training a new mechanic. When you left, we had to wait for a Coalition crew to drop off a replacement to get us running again. And that mechanic...well, he left a lot to be desired."

"When I *left*?" she asked incredulously. "I think you mean when I was abducted."

Captain Allen laced his fingers together and leaned back in his cushioned leather chair. "Well, yes. We're glad to have you back, of course."

"Yeah, well, tell that security officer that there's nothing to find in my room. I don't appreciate being treated like a new recruit, Captain."

"Are you *sure* there's nothing to find?" he asked with a crooked smile. Alice's blood ran cold, and she was sure the envelope in her pocket was going to start beating out loud like a telltale heart.

"Uh," she began, and then cleared her throat. "Yes, I'm sure."

"Alice, I won't lie to you. Some of the higher ups aren't quite convinced that you told us everything you know about that situation. Now, I stood up for you, told them you're a loyal Coalitionist, and that on this ship, your word is gold."

Alice willed herself to breathe normally. "But?"

"But I've been authorized to offer you a promotion...*if* you can give us information that leads to the capture of the pirate crew and their stolen ship."

"My quarters get tossed and now you're offering me a promotion?" she asked.

The captain laughed. "I know, sometimes this is just how things happen. The promotion would come with a substantial raise and a backdated retirement account. You'd have enough credits in six months to retire comfortably."

Alice took a deep breath. "And all I have to do is give you information that I already said I don't have?"

"Level with me," he said, leaning forward in his chair and laying his forearms flat on the desk. "I think you may have forgotten something useful in the excitement of it all. Maybe if you take a day to rest, you'll remember a location, or some information about those goddamn droids they were using."

Alice stood and replaced the metal folding chair against the wall. "Thank you, Captain," she said slowly. "I'll get a good night's rest and see if anything comes to mind." She crossed to the door and opened it.

"Come now, don't ruin what could be a great opportunity just for some pirates. They don't deserve your loyalty. Don't risk your future on common thieves."

Alice nodded slowly and closed the door behind her, exhaling softly. Whatever she was going to do, she needed to talk to Barnaby.

She crossed the ship in a blur, moving on autopilot towards her friend's lavish private quarters. A million thoughts flew through her mind, thoughts of Violet, and promotions, and a quiet retirement on a farm in a peaceful region. She reached Barnaby's door and knocked.

"Barnaby? I need to talk to you."

There was no answer from within. Alice frowned and knocked again. "Barns? I know you're in there, we don't dock for another 36 hours."

She furrowed her brow. "Goddamnit Barnaby, this is important!" She tried the door handle, and to her surprise it swung easily into Barnaby's room. She stuck her head inside and reached for the light switch.

"Barnaby, for fuck's sa—" she stopped short when the light illuminated the room. It was empty, the trunk missing from the foot of his bed. The red satin sheets had been stripped from the bed, which was now just a bare white mattress. She opened the cupboard, and none of Barnaby's expensive suits remained; she was greeted with the sight of empty hangers.

She walked to the bathroom and turned a light on, and in confirmation of her fear, she realized his shaving kit and personal effects were missing, leaving a bare counter.

Barnaby was gone.

CHAPTER NINE

"WHAT THE HELL?" SHE muttered under her breath. Barnaby was her closest friend, and they told each other everything. She had even told him about the kiss with Violet, and even now she felt her cheeks warm with a blush. Where had he gone, and why hadn't he told her about it? What could he have been hiding?

Alice whirled out of his empty room, leaving the door wide open. There was nothing left in there to protect, anyway. She marched back to the captain's office, where he was still sitting in his comfortable leather chair, examining aerial maps. Without knocking this time, Alice walked right in and stood near the door.

"Captain!" she said a little too loudly.

Looking up from his work, he raised an eyebrow. "Yes, Alice? Did you remember something already?" he asked hopefully.

"What? Uh, no," she said quickly. "I was just wondering where Barnaby was."

"Aren't you two thick as thieves? I thought he would have told you. He's on a weekend trade mission finalizing a deal for some raw materials. Should be back in a few days at the most."

Alice thought about Barnaby's empty room. All of his many fancy suits were gone, along with his bed linens, every pair of shoes he owned, all of his personal effects. It was obvious that the captain wasn't aware of Barnaby's intent to stay wherever he had gone, and she wasn't about to fill him in before she knew what was going on. She cleared her throat. "Oh. Thanks."

"Is that all, Alice?"

"Er – yes, that's all," she replied. "Sorry, I should have just checked the mission rota."

"It's alright. Don't forget what I said, now – you stand to gain a great deal if you happen to remember some information about those pirates that help the Coalition capture them, or disable those droids."

"Yes, Captain, I'll try to remember something. Retirement would be nice."

"Alright then, Alice. I've got some work to finish. You're dismissed."

He picked his glasses up off the desk in front of him and smoothed out the large map that covered the whole desk.

It was a map of the nearby systems, Alice noticed, seeing the planets, Coalition bases and satellites. The suspected rebel bases were marked with red Xs, dotted around the map. Alice's eyes were drawn to a little flag on an area near Iota-9. Could it be that they had already discovered where Violet's ship was hidden even without her help?

Tearing her eyes away from the map, she stammered, "Er, uh, yes Captain. Thank you."

She backed out of the room and closed the door behind her as her mind raced. Could she even entertain the notion of giving her up for a promotion and early retirement? And where the hell was Barnaby? *Barnaby.* She thought about how she had left the door to Barnaby's room standing wide open. If she didn't want anyone else to rat him out, they couldn't see an empty room. She walked as quick as she could back to the room, trying not to run or look as worried as she was. She rounded a corner and almost ran straight into the new recruit she had been training.

"Hello, Alice!" she said brightly. "I was wondering, what if we bypassed the secondary boiler to—"

"We can chat later, Trudy," Alice said quickly. "I have to...uh, I have to get something from my room."

"Oh, I can tag along, we can chat on the way!" Trudy replied.

Alice thought about Barnaby's room, standing wide open to passers-by to see that he had left. Her new recruit was annoyingly plucky and determined. Alice had to get rid of her, and fast.

"Actually, Trudy, I need you to run diagnostics on the air filtration system. I think I noticed a loose fan belt earlier. Radio me when you're finished."

Trudy looked relieved to have a task to do. "Aye, Alice!" As she turned down the opposite corridor, Alice remembered something – she never got around to repairing Violet's air filtration system. She hoped someone would remember to check on it.

Alice was relieved to see Barnaby's door still wide open in the empty hallway. She jogged the last few steps and closed the door behind her softly. She heard the latch engage, and she locked the door as well. She didn't need anyone discovering her poking around in the empty room, she was in enough trouble as it was already. Maybe she had missed something that would tell her what the hell had happened, and why he had abandoned his very well paid post as a merchant trader for the Coalition.

The room was as empty as it had been minutes prior: no bed linens, no shoes, no suits. No personal effects on the table next to the bed, and no trade contracts strewn over the desk. Alice crossed the room to the desk and ran her hands over the leather writing surface. It was scratched from heavy use and the many hours he sat here, writing up trade deals that favored him as much as they did the Coalition.

She opened the desk drawer, and suddenly remembered that she had fitted his desk with the same false bottom that hers had. Alice impatiently pried up the wood, positive Barnaby would have left her a note explaining his absence. She saw a yellowed piece of paper and she eagerly snatched it up. She unfolded it and read,

• • • •

FRANÇOISE,
I'll be waiting for your next letter. We have details to discuss.
-N

Her mind raced. Who the hell was N? And furthermore, who the hell was *Françoise*, and why had Barnaby hidden a note addressed to him? An under-the-table trade partner, maybe an old lover? Why had he hidden it in the secret false drawer if it was just a lover's note? What the hell was going on? Pocketing the note, Alice replaced the false bottom and closed the drawer. She gave the room one last confused look, turned off the light, and closed the door behind her, hoping that nobody would investigate his absence for a few days. She hoped he was safe, wherever he was, but she couldn't help feeling hurt that he hadn't told her. It worried her, and made her think that whatever his reason was, it was worse than anything that had happened to either of them before.

• • • •

ALICE TRUDGED BACK to her own room and locked the door behind her. She had almost forgotten what a mess the security officer had left it in, and she huffed angrily at seeing it again. Decades of loyal service to the Coalition, just to be treated like a new recruit and treated to a surprise inspection. She easily hefted the mattress back into place and picked up the rumpled Coalition blanket off the floor. After making the bed, she surveyed the mess. Everything had been tipped out of drawers and toppled out of her trunk, strewn across the floor. She grimaced when she saw her book of maintenance repairs, thrown into a corner with a bent cover. Inspections were one thing, but wilful destruction was another. She began to clean up, her mind racing with everything that had happened in the past hour. Her room had been searched, because Coalition higher ups didn't believe that she didn't remember any relevant information. They were right, of course, but Alice still felt angry that they sent someone to tear apart her room.

Then she thought about the Captain's offer: give up Violet and her crew, tell them how the Coalition targeted droids worked, and receive a promotion, a pay raise, and early retirement. She could buy a little farm in the country and forget that any of this had ever happened. She could adopt a dog, raise some sheep, learn to knit. She would never have to fix another boiler again, or work a double shift, or worry about what would happen to her job when this new recruit learned enough to replace her. Alice angrily stuffed two spare coveralls into her trunk. She didn't do politics, she was just a mechanic, exactly as she'd always said to Kady. She didn't want to make this decision; no matter what she did it wasn't going to be easy. Betray the Cricket and its crew members, damning them to harsh punishment, but being hailed a hero for the Coalition while she enjoyed an early retirement? Or keep Violet's secrets and face whatever consequences they would levy on her for not providing information? It wasn't fair, and she felt a hot wave of injustice wash over her skin.

She tossed a spare boot into the wardrobe and kicked the door closed. It was a little cleaner, at least. Peeling off her damp, dusty coveralls, she dumped them in a basket near the bed. She stood in her black tank top and matching boxers and took a quiet, deep breath. Alice crawled into bed, her thoughts swirling around her head. Where was Barnaby, and who was N? Who was Françoise?

What was she going to do?

How long would she even have to make that decision?

How why she even managed to end up in this mess in the first place?

Alice's radio buzzed and crackled.

"Alice?"

She tossed her goggles onto her bedside table, where they landed noisily next to the lamp. She grabbed her radio and answered, "Uh, yeah?"

"It's me, Trudy! You said to tell you when I finished the diagnostics on the filtration system?"

Alice rubbed her eyes. She had forgotten about the task she gave the new recruit, but she also hadn't anticipated her working through dinner to finish it. "Uh, yeah. And?"

"Well I couldn't find a loose belt, but I did find some lime scale build up around some of the coolant connections."

"Er—okay, good job. Is that all?"

"Well, um, seeing as we're about to dock early, I was hoping for some shore leave. Captain Allen said I report to you directly, and—"

Alice gripped the radio in a panic. If they were docking early, there was a reason for it. Had they discovered Barnaby's empty room? Were they preparing to put more pressure on her to provide information about Violet and the Cricket?

"Dammit," she whispered to herself. Time was running out, and she didn't even know what was going on yet. Then, louder, she added, "Take whatever shore leave you want, Trudy. Just be back before the ship leaves port." There was no response from the radio, and Alice knew that the young trainee mechanic was likely excitedly packing a bag for shore leave, where she would meet up with friends, drink illegal swill, and dance. Alice knew that she only had a short amount of time to find answers, and that time was already ticking away.

Without turning on the light, she dressed quickly. She didn't bother to brush her hair, leaving it in the day's messy, tangled silver braids. She tugged on her boots and tucked the laces inside, not even stopping to tie them properly. Leaving the dark room, she patted her inside pocket to make sure the notes were still there: her note from Alice, and Barnaby's note from the mysterious N.

She locked the door behind her and crept through the hallways. Most crew members would still be asleep and unaware they had docked early. The night crew was a skeleton one, and they would be preoccupied with contacting their superiors to request shore leave, just as Trudy had. Alice quietly walked the halls, not even sure what she was looking for. She reached Barnaby's room, and the door was still locked tight. It was unlikely they knew he was missing yet. Her mind raced. Her boots thudded quietly along the halls as she headed to the captain's office. She didn't know what she would find there, but she couldn't think of anywhere else she would find any answers. She passed a night crew officer and called to him, "Hey! Know why we docked early? It's messing with my maintenance schedule because my trainee wanted shore leave."

He turned and waved. "Nah, heard there's some important government representative who wanted to meet the captain. That's all I heard, though!"

"Thanks," Alice replied with a wave. She wondered who it could be, and why. Representatives didn't have much to do with merchant vessels, even if they were Coalition owned and the largest in the fleet. Trading goods like raw materials and components wasn't exactly front page news. Quietly, she continued along the halls towards the office.

As she approached, she heard muffled voices through the door. She crouched around the corner and strained to listen.

"...pirates. These...dealt with. Coalition policy...harsher punishments."

Alice leaned closer and peeked around the corner. The man in the captain's office was tall and bald, his dark features handsome and striking. She recognized him from the newspapers: he was the head of rebel prosecution. He was known for his harsh opinions of rebels and pirates alike, whipping up anger and distrust among Coalition loyalists and average citizens alike. There had even been a few stories of unofficial Coalition militias meting out vigilante justice in rural areas. Alice wondered what he was doing aboard the Stronghold. Whatever the reason, it couldn't be good.

The door opened, and the man continued, "This is the new position, Captain. The Coalition can't take these attacks lightly. I know you're not a military ship, but you're one of the fastest in the fleet and you're going to help us track them down, with or without the help of your mechanic. Make sure she understands, our offer won't be on the table much longer. We need information on the ship or those droids."

"Aye," Captain Allen responded.

The man turned and said over his shoulder, "Fucking pirates, eh?"

The captain laughed. "Fucking pirates," he replied, "should string up the lot of them."

Alice leaned back on her heels and her breath caught in her throat. She knew that pirates didn't have a good reputation among Coalition captains, but the thought of anything happening to Violet or her crew members made her stomach turn. The work camps for rebels and pirates were already known for being merciless and sometimes cruel; how much worse could it get?

The man closed the door behind him and walked down the steps towards the main entrance of the ship. Alice knew that asking a trade vessel to track pirates was unprecedented, and she worried about what that meant for Violet. Surely they wouldn't have returned to that place near Iota-9, right? She just wanted to buy some more time to figure out what she was going to do.

Alice felt sure that early retirement was off the table for her now.

· · · ·

"CAN'T BELIEVE WE GOT screwed out of extra shore leave," a passing new recruit said as Alice ate her dinner of basic rations. "I was hoping for a couple of days at least."

Alice took a bite of stale bread and swallowed hard. The crew hadn't been happy about being called back from shore leave so soon, but when an important Coalition prosecutor shows up to talk to the captain, there wasn't much room for debate.

The new schedule and rota had been posted in mid afternoon, and Alice had been first to read it. The C.S. Stronghold was changing course to head towards Iota-9, and the schedule indicated that they would be picking up some rare components. No mention of tracking any pirates, and no mention of Barnaby. They didn't know that he was gone yet, and probably wouldn't until he missed the liaison in two days. It was obvious that Barnaby had planned his escape well – but what the hell was he escaping from? She dragged the bread through a puddle of watery red sauce on her plate, leftover from the bland, starchy noodles she had just eaten. They were tasteless, but adequate. Alice couldn't help but feel like everyone was watching her, even though in reality none of the other crew members knew what was going on. To them, this was a fairly routine schedule adjustment. They didn't know about missing trade dealers or hidden pirates. Most of them probably didn't even know her name; besides Barnaby, she didn't have many friends here.

Most of the crew was Coalition military, and new recruits at that. Merchant vessels had long been training grounds for trainees to learn the ropes and get used to protocol and procedures before being reassigned to a military ship. The crew was a near-constant rotation of trainees, except for a few core staff like herself, Barnaby, and Captain Allen, of course. Alice was happy with her own company, and she would occasionally meet old friends on shore leave. This was the first time she had felt this isolated and alone. They had left port about an hour ago, much to the dismay of her new trainee. Trudy had returned to the ship with bright makeup and curled hot pink hair, obviously meant for a night on the town. Alice felt bad for her, and gave her the night off. Trudy had seemed grateful for that, at least, especially after working through the night on that air filtration system that didn't actually need any repairs. Alice still felt guilty about that.

They were moving at full speed towards Iota-9, and her heart was pounding faster with every moment that passed. At this rate, they would reach the planetoid by morning. She hoped that Violet and her crew was nowhere to be found. She hoped that Barnaby was okay. She hoped she would be able to avoid the captain, and his inevitable probing questions, followed by tempting promises of promotions and pay raises. She had plenty of hope, but an equal measure of worry.For the first time ever, she wished she really *was* a spy and knew how to get information.

Alice stood and cleared her plate, placing it on a conveyor belt that automatically washed the crew's dishes. She looked around at the room, full of glum, disappointed crew members. There was no drinking allowed on Coalition vessels, so any drunken debauchery had to take place on shore leave only, in illegal but well-known back rooms, hidden by fake fronted grocery stores and sometimes, the town library. Being caught with alcohol was a major offense, so Alice had never bothered with trying to stash any. She knew some of them would probably be dipping into secret reserves tonight, regardless of consequences. She also knew she wouldn't be sleeping tonight: there was too much at stake. She didn't know what she was going to do, or even how she would make that decision, but she did know that time was running out. She headed to the boiler room, where her head was always clear. Alongside the low hum of the equipment, she was able to figure out impossible repairs and invent new methods. It's where she felt most at peace: people were unpredictable, but boilers were all the same at their core. Heat. Water. Steam. Energy.

She descended the steps into the boiler room and surveyed the organized mess around her. Piles of boxes, filled with components and wiring, still lined the walls. She had forbidden the new recruit from moving anything; this was still her boiler room as long as she was on this ship. The cargo crew hadn't removed the boxes of broken droids yet, and they were piled in the corner. A few boxes were missing, the ones that Violet's crew had stolen.

She sat on the stool in front of the workbench and took a deep breath, thinking of Violet, of Barnaby, of her future on this ship or off of it. She wished she could warn Violet somehow, but it was impossible without control of the long range communications. As a mechanic, she didn't have access to the bridge on Coalition vessels and wouldn't have known how to use them if she did, so that idea was out.

Alice spotted one of the broken droids, which had rolled underneath her bench. Smiling, she picked it up and started pulling it apart: small projects like these were perfect for thinking things over. "Alright, you," she said to the droid, "Tell me your secrets." She unscrewed the back panel and removed most of the wiring. She furrowed her brow when she spotted something behind the wiring, a small, shiny, round sphere. She pried it out and gasped: it was the same as the detonation bot that Captain Leo had threatened Violet's crew with. These droids weren't broken: they just hadn't been activated yet. Alice put the detonation sphere down carefully. She wondered if Violet had known what she was stealing. And how had Captain Leo gotten his hands on one that was activated and outside its host droid?

What was a merchant vessel doing with all these? They traded weapons, of course, but they were rarely on board more than a few days. Weapons were in high demand these days, and military vessels were always in need of new and improved explosives.

She looked at the boxes of droids in the corner and realized that there must be at least 200 droids in them. If they all had these detonation spheres, that's a lot of damage waiting to be dealt. Alice pieced the droid back together and placed it in one of the crates. She wondered if Captain Allen knew what they were. Though they had worked together for decades, she didn't really know him on a personal level. His remarks about pirates this morning had surprised her and made her feel distrustful and alone. She missed Barnaby more than ever, and for a moment she almost allowed herself to miss Violet, too. She felt helpless and frustrated. She wasn't going to betray them, but she didn't know how she could help Violet or her crew either. She didn't even know where they were. If she wasn't going to betray them, then what?

Alice picked up a box of lightbulbs and hurled it against the wall in frustration, where it made a series of satisfying smashing noises. She paused and took a deep breath, and when she shifted her feet, shards of broken lightbulbs crunched under her boots. Alice squared her shoulders and nodded her head; her decision was made. She unclipped her radio from her belt.

"Captain? I think I remember something that would help."

CHAPTER TEN

"BOSS?"

Violet opened an eye and looked around her room. "Yeah?" She sat up and rubbed her eyes, wondering why Ned was knocking on her door in the middle of the night instead of calling her on the radio. Whatever it was, it wasn't good.

"Boss, our communication system is down. None of the radios are functioning, and the radar is going haywire. Might be a hardware problem, or it could be that we're not getting enough power to the system."

"Fuck. Okay." She pushed off the pile of plush, soft blankets and swung her legs over the side of the bed. It was cold, but the shock to her system was almost as good as a cup of coffee. "I'll meet you on the bridge in five minutes."

"Roger that, Boss."

She heard Ned's uneven gait fade down the hallway. He had recovered from his injuries, but he had to walk with a cane now, and probably would forever. She shivered and stood to get dressed: white blouse, tan leather vest, riding pants, and her thick leather lace up boots. She looked in the mirror across the room and saw a woman who looked exhausted and unkempt. Violet huffed angrily at her reflection and tied her tight black curls back. That was better, at least a little bit.

She locked her room and dragged herself up to the bridge. "Alright Ned, show me what's going on," she said as she entered the room.

"I woke up Kady too," he said, turning in his chair, "Maybe she will see something I haven't yet."

Violet sat in her captain's chair in front of the main console. The map that displayed radar was flashing intermittently, and she noticed that Ned had already abandoned his radio on the other side of the room. She wondered how long he had tried to repair the problem on his own before waking her and Kady.

"I don't think it's a power problem, Alice repaired and serviced the main and secondary boilers before she left. Could be the wiring, a ship this old is prone to equipment breaking down over time."

"I had a look and I didn't see any stripped wiring or exposed connections, but I wasn't able to get underneath the console to look at the main feed." Ned gestured at his leg. "If I got down there, I don't think I'd be able to get back up here."

"Alright, Ned. I'll have a look." Violet knelt down and opened a hatch near her chair. There was a ladder that led down into a dark shaft, which was for servicing problems just like this. She looked into the dark space and strained her eyes. There were cobwebs strung across the ladder, and Violet swallowed hard. She could handle pirates, the Coalition, and almost everything in this system, except the spiders. She really, *really* hated spiders.

Violet climbed down the ladder into the shaft, which activated motion sensor lights along the walls. She examined the wiring as she climbed; it was old and dusty, but nothing looked out of place. A large spider crawled over a bundle of wires, and she recoiled, clinging to the ladder.

"I don't see anything down here either," she called to Ned. Frowning as she tried to keep an eye on the spider, she climbed the ladder back onto the bridge and replaced the hatch. Violet stood up just as Kady glided into the room, looking like she hadn't missed even one moment of sleep.

"Captain?"

"I was checking the wiring beneath the main console, looking for loose connections or exposed wire. I didn't see anything." Violet aggressively dusted herself off, paranoid that the spider had escaped the service tunnel by hitching a ride on her clothes.

"Could be an internal dialog problem, did someone already check on the power supply?" Kady sat next to Ned and began making notes on a stray piece of paper.

"I haven't checked yet, but I don't think it's a power supply problem. Alice repaired and serviced things before she left."

"Unless she sabotaged it," Kady challenged.

Violet shot her a look, and Kady met her glare and shrugged. "You never know, Captain," Kady continued, "she could have loosened some connections or added sediment to the boilers. Those methods would work on an old ship like this one, and she would know how to do it."

"Alright. Ned, are you okay with those steps into the boiler room?" Violet asked, her brow furrowed. Maybe Alice had sabotaged the boilers; she had been abducted, after all. Maybe the kiss was just a ploy to keep her distracted and unaware that her ship was being damaged.

"Aye boss," he replied as he used his cane to stand up from his chair. "Hyun says I'm okay to do stairs, just no climbing or feats of strength. Not yet, anyway," he continued with a wink. He left the room, leaving Kady and Violet alone on the bridge.

"Captain, I didn't mean—"

"It's fine, Kady. You're right to want to check."

"It might not be the power supply."

"Yes, let's hope it isn't. There aren't many prized mechanics flying around this part of space." Violet sat in her chair and looked at the flashing displays again. "I don't like this, Kady. It leaves us vulnerable," she said, quickly turning the conversation away from Alice and back to the problem at hand.

"I'm going through the coding, maybe I'll find what's affecting it."

"This reminds me too much of when we got attacked by Captain Leo," Violet said nervously. "I really don't want to repeat that." She felt her breathing become shallow, and forced herself to take a long, deep breath.

"We're lucky we have Hyun with us. Who knows what would have happened to Ned otherwise," Kady said as she squinted at a screen full of bright green scrolling code.

"He would have died, Kady." Violet let a moment of uncomfortable silence hang over the room. "Have you checked those new security protocols we installed?"

"Yes, there's now a thermal proximity monitor spliced into the system. No one will be able to sneak up on us. It has a separate power supply, too. It's unaffected by the current issue."

"Good." Violet squinted at the blinking radar display. They were unlikely to encounter anyone out here, this far away from a Coalition base or a trading beacon. Still, the memory of Captain Leo's dead body being dragged off the bridge was burned into her memory, and she couldn't shake the feeling that something was seriously wrong.

"I'm not finding anything wrong with the coding," Kady mumbled to herself. "It's like our communication system is wrapped in an aluminum blanket, nothing can get in or out. Same with the radar. Almost like a re-verse...cloaking device?"

Violet nodded and gestured for Kady to continue.

"Instead of shielding your ship, you would disable the other ship's radar and communications. In effect, you would be invisible to the other ship un-til you either passed them by or got close enough to fire on them."

"Do you think that's what is happening now?" Violet asked, panic ris-ing in her voice.

"Well, I'm not positive, no. Even if that is what's happening, it could just be a passing pirate vessel that doesn't want anyone knowing it was here."

"Best to be prepared, maybe we should—"

The thermal proximity monitor began to flash red and emitted a long, shrill beep.

Violet reached for her radio before she remembered that it had been disabled. "Fuck!" she yelled, running into the corridor. "GET TO YOUR STATIONS," she bellowed, "PREPARE FOR AN ATTACK. TELL EVERY CREW MEMBER YOU SEE. COMMS ARE DOWN!"

She sprinted back to the bridge and squinted out the front window. "Who the fuck's out there?" she asked out loud. She thought of Ned, down in the boiler room checking on the power supply, and vulnerable with his injury. She realized that her pistol was back in her quarters, and she couldn't leave Kady alone to run and get it. Whoever had disabled their communi-cations and radar, she hoped that they would just pass by. Her heart raced and blood pounded in her ears as panic rose in her chest. She felt like she couldn't breathe, and the room grew fuzzy around the edges.

"Captain?" Kady asked forcefully. "What is the plan?"

Violet blinked and tried to shake the blurry edges from the corners of her vision. "Do we know where they are yet?"

"Not yet. They are within 50 kilometers, they have to be to trigger the proximity alarm."

"Can we engage the weapons stations?"

Kady moved to Ned's chair and furrowed her brow as she pressed a series of buttons. "Weapons are functional and staffed by the appropriate crew members."

Violet struggled to gain control over her breathing; it felt like her lungs were unable to process enough air, and her shoulders sent tension down her arms and into her fingertips.

"Captain?" Kady looked across the room at the captain.

"Get down to the armory and tell them to hold fire. I can't call them when the radios are down. Return fire if they fire on us, but under no circumstances are we to shoot first." Kady swept out of the room, leaving the captain alone on the bridge. Violet turned to look at the radar display again, willing it to function again. If she just knew where to look for the other ship, they could try maneuvering out of its way.

Violet stood and stared into the black space on the other side of the window. It was so dark out here that sometimes it felt almost hopeless, like the last shreds of sun had been swallowed by the empty space between planets. She tried to focus on the invisible horizon, to see a ship swimming through the darkness; anything to calm her shredded nerves.

From the corner of her eye, Violet spotted some movement amongst the black. Without taking her eyes of the ship, she said softly, "There's a ship approaching on the starboard side. They're running without lights so as not to be detected. Kady will keep things calm in the armory." Violet inhaled and held the air in her lungs for a few moments, and then slowly breathed the air out through her nose.

"They're headed for us," she said to the empty bridge, sitting in her chair and taking the throttle in her hands. In that moment, Violet felt like she was floating above herself. Her actions were pure instinct, the result of training at the academy before she defected to be her own captain on her own stolen ship. She gripped the throttle and set the ship on a course to turn towards the nearest trading beacon. If the other ship wasn't looking for trouble, they would just pass by. She turned the ship, keeping the other one in her sights as they glided through the dark. The other ship turned to follow them, and turned their lights up to full power. They knew they'd been spotted, and there was no point in hiding now.

"Don't shoot yet, just stay calm. We don't want any trouble, we're of no threat to you," she said to the empty room.

Violet stared into the darkness, trying to make out the name of the other ship. It was newer than hers, but not Coalition issue. She couldn't quite read the name, but could see that it had been painted with precision. Violet reached for her radio once again before remembering the block on their communication systems, and she unclipped it from her belt and placed it on top of the console. She'd need that radio as soon as systems came back online.

The ship was close now, no more than a few kilometers away, and heading straight for them. Violet gasped softly when the ship's name came into focus. It was the Captain Leo. She shook her head. Of course a man like that would name his ship after himself. She thought again of his body being dragged off of her ship, and understood why they had come back to stalk them once again. This new technology was certainly impressive, and Violet wondered how they had acquired it so soon after their last encounter.

The captain continued to weave her ship through the darkness; there was no sense in allowing herself and her crew to be a stationary target. The Captain Leo continued to follow them through the darkness, and Violet knew that they were ready for a fight.

With a flash of light, Violet could see that they were preparing to fire their weapons. "Hope you're all holding onto something sturdy," she said out loud.

"Aye Boss," Ned replied from the doorway.

"Ned!"

"It's not a problem with the power supply."

She laughed in spite of herself and replied, "Yes, Ned, I figured that out."

She braced for impact and an exploding shell slammed into the hull. She leapt out of her chair to read the diagnostic display on the other side of the bridge. The air filtration system had been hit, nothing immediately serious. The radar display blinked off for a moment, and then returned, fully functional.

"Ned, we've got radar, do we have radios?"

She threw herself back into her chair and pulled the throttle all the way back.

"Going to full speed, we'll burn through our power reserves but we might be able to just about escape!"

The ship slowed to a crawl and began to shudder and shake.

"Ned, I thought you said there was nothing wrong with the boilers!"

"There wasn't when I was down there!"

"Get someone back down there to fix whatever the hell is wrong with my ship, we can't keep taking damage like this!"

Ned hobbled to his chair and bellowed into his radio, "SOMEONE GO FIX THE MAIN BOILER, CAPTAIN'S ORDERS!"

Violet knew that getting a boiler fixed in the middle of a firefight was unlikely; she had to keep pivoting the ship if they were going to survive this. Starboard, port, port, starboard. She could see that the rest of her crew was returning fire, and saw a piece of the Captain Leo detach and disappear into space.

Another explosion shook the ship, and she saw the loading bay door shoot past the front of the ship. It was a good thing there was an airlock on this ship, or that area would be totally inaccessible until they landed somewhere.

"Ned! Did those extra supplies we picked up last week get strapped down?" She was envisioning the hard won supplies floating in space, no good to anyone.

"Aye Boss, I did it myself."

Violet focused on pivoting the ship to avoid as much enemy fire as she could. It was clear that Captain Leo's crew was out for revenge, not for pillaging or theft. She remembered the detonation droid and worried what would happen if they were able to shoot those across to their ship.

The radio on the console crackled and hissed. "Captain – we've got another incoming ship on the port side!"

"For fuck's sake, who is it now?" Violet stole a glance at the radar, and she saw it, a ship coming in fast, and it was large.

"Ned, I can't take my hands off the throttle, this thing can't autopilot itself through a firefight. Tell Kady and the rest of the crew to keep focusing fire on the ship that's shooting at us until we know what's going on."

"Aye Boss." Ned relayed her instructions to the rest of the crew over the radio, and he stood up from his chair and looked to the port side out of the front glass. "Boss, that looks like a Coalition ship. Too far away to see anything else."

"Goddamnit. GODDAMNIT." There was no way she could escape this without full power, and certainly not with pieces of her ship hanging on by mere bolts. She thought of all the people that would be let down if they were captured, which seemed inevitable. The hungry rebel bases and surrounding areas would starve under Coalition tactics. Her entire crew would be tried for piracy, and some of them for treason, too. Abandoning the Coalition wasn't an option these days, and it was punishable by a life sentence in the work camps. No trial, no jury, just a Coalition judge to sentence you.

Violet's mind raced as she tried to think of any possibility of escape.

The radio came to life again with Kady's voice. "Captain, the Coalition ship...it's the C.S. Stronghold."

Violet's blood ran cold. Alice had sold them out, she was sure of it now. How else would they have found them? This was it, then, they'd all be imprisoned, people would starve, and it would all be because she was stupid enough to trust a mechanic she'd abducted.

"Ned, I..." she said in a small voice.

"It's not over yet, boss." He squared his shoulders and tied his long ginger hair into a loose bun. "We'll fight to the last if we have to."

Hands firmly gripping the throttle, she continued to maneuver the ship back and forth. If they took any damage to their main systems, they wouldn't be ending this encounter alive.

"Captain, the Stronghold has slowed, and they are sending a trade shuttle."

Violet furrowed her brow. Why would they send a trade shuttle when they could just wait for military backup? Or, at this rate, wait for the Captain Leo to blow them apart? She spotted the trade shuttle, a small two person craft, off the port bow. The steam from the boilers left a trail of tiny ice crystals as it approached the Cricket. She couldn't even keep the shuttle out, not when the loading bay door had been blown off several moments previously. She took one hand off the throttle to take the radio on the console. "Attention, all crew members: do not engage with the Coalition craft that will likely land in our loading bay in a few moments. Focus your fire on the engaged ship."

"Boss, are you sure that's a good idea? We're being boarded by Coalition, shot at by a rival ship, and we have no power."

"We're running out of options, Ned. I can only hope that whatever Coalition lackey they're sending won't be too comfortable with the current situation of being shot at with exploding shells by another ship."

The Cricket shuddered softly as the Coalition shuttle landed in their cargo bay. Whatever was going to happen, it was going to happen fast. She watched through the glass as another piece of the Captain Leo disappeared into the darkness. As battles went, they were evenly matched, and if the Stronghold hadn't showed up, the Cricket might have had a chance at survival. Another explosion rocked the ship, and the lights flickered and dimmed. Their generators had taken damage, and it was only a matter of time before radar, navigation, and air filtration failed. Violet knew they were fighting on borrowed time.

The moments seemed to stretch on forever, and it was difficult to tell how much time had passed. The ships continued to blast bits of each other into space, the Coalition shuttle was on board and its occupants somewhere on the ship, and systems were minutes away from failing. Violet gripped the throttle and gently swayed the Cricket, trying to avoid as much incoming fire as possible. She began to imagine a Coalition security officer coming onto the bridge and arresting her and Ned. She couldn't leave her seat, and Ned's leg was still healing; they wouldn't have a chance at fighting them off, not with the Stronghold a short distance away. In all likelihood, they had already informed the nearest military vessels of their location.

"Ned?"

"Yeah Boss?"

"I just wanted to say—"

At that moment, the lights returned to full power and the console lit up with all its functions and displays. She could hear the engines ramping into gear, and she felt power return to the throttle. She grabbed the radio and shouted into it, "Did someone repair the main boiler?"

After a moment of silence, Kady replied, "None of us have left the armory, Captain!"

Violet looked at the fully functional console and grinned. "Ned, chart us a course home and let's get the fuck out of here. We'll deal with our Coalition visitors once we're out of range of the Captain Leo."

"Course charted, Boss. You're clear to engage main boilers."

Violet pulled the throttle back and the Cricket lurched forward and began to pick up speed. It still wasn't full power or strength, but it would get them out of this mess, and that was all she needed. The ship soared through the black space, leaving the Stronghold and the Captain Leo behind. Hopefully, if they were lucky, neither ship would be able to follow them fast enough. With a sigh of relief, Violet watched the ships fade into the distance and disappear off the radar display. She could hear cheering from the armory; her crew had done good and they knew it. She knew there would be repairs, and they needed to find a mechanic as soon as possible, but for now, they were safe, provided Kady zapped the Coalition chips on whoever flew that shuttle aboard.

"Ned, take the controls and set to auto pilot. I'm going to go down to the boiler room and see what the hell is going on. Let me borrow your gun." Ned presented a large revolver with a long barrel and a brushed steel finish.

"It's loaded, Boss."

Violet grabbed her radio and took the gun from Ned, holstering it under her arm. "Kady, take some crew members and do a sweep for our Coalition visitors, they'll need their chips deactivated *right now* or our head start isn't going to count for much."

"Copy that, Captain," came the reply from the radio.

Violet walked the corridors of her ship, confident that Kady and others would apprehend the Coalition crew that had boarded them. There would only be two invaders maximum, because those shuttles only fit two people. The onboard safety controls prevented extra passengers, and there was almost no way to override it. She kept a hand on the revolver she had borrowed from Ned, just in case the invaders felt confident enough to start shooting. When she reached the boiler room, she heard someone walking around at the base of the stairs. She unholstered the gun and quietly descended the stairs, ready for anything.

A tall figure was standing in front of the main boiler, which now had a hasty patch applied to the lower left corner to cover a gaping hole. Violet squinted at the invader, who was wearing Coalition regulation coveralls and an air filtration helmet that obscured the face.

"Stop, or I'll shoot!" Violet shouted, pulling back the hammer of the revolver.

The invader removed the helmet, and long silver hair tumbled out.

Alice grinned. "Hello, *Captain.*"

CHAPTER ELEVEN

VIOLET STOOD STARING at the mechanic, her mouth opening and closing wordlessly. Alice set the helmet on the ground and took a step towards the captain.

"Violet? Er, Captain?"

"How – what – uh," Violet stuttered. She'd been convinced that Alice had sold them out to the Coalition, and now she was standing in her boiler room. Violet's gaze flicked between the patched boiler and Alice, trying to decipher what had just happened. Alice had a streak of dark brown grease across her left cheek, and her right eye was bruised a deep purple.

"Could you lower the gun, please?" Alice asked quietly.

"Oh," Violet answered, lowering the revolver she had borrowed from Ned and holstering it under her arm.

Footsteps pounded down the corridor leading to the boiler room, and they both looked towards the door, Violet looking back over her shoulder. A group of crew members descended the steps and came into view, led by Kady, who had a small revolver in one hand, and the Coalition chip disabling device in the other. She spotted Alice, and anger flashed on her face.

"*You*! You sold us out to the Coalition!" she shouted. The rest of her group filtered down the stairs after her, all pointing weapons.

"She just patched the pressure leak in the boiler," Violet interjected, turning to face Kady. "And I would thank you very much to not point weapons at me."

The group lowered their weapons, but Kady held hers steadily. "Don't worry, Captain, I have impeccable aim."

"I'm aware. Lower. Your weapon." Violet squared her shoulders and stared Kady in the eye. "Captain's orders."

Kady huffed angrily and holstered the small gun on her hip. "Captain, it's obvious that she gave them information on us. Whatever she says now, it doesn't matter."

"She hasn't said anything yet, but first, you need to disable that chip in her arm or they'll be on our asses before we can even regroup." Violet turned to Alice and looked up at her. "What the hell are you doing here?"

"What, no 'thanks for saving our asses?' From where I'm standing, that pressure leak was about to cause you a whole lot of trouble." Kady held out the device and aggressively pushed it into Alice's arm. Alice flinched away from the small zap of electricity that prickled beneath her skin. She shifted on her feet, and Violet could see Alice's knee begin to swell under the torn, dirty coveralls.

"How did the Coalition find us, then, if not for you telling them our recent coordinates? You want us to believe that they just happened to come across us, this far from a Coalition base or a trading beacon?" Kady asked, incredulous. "And what did you tell them about your chip? Did you tell them we deprogrammed it? Do they know we have that technology?"

Violet turned and put a hand on Kady's shoulder. "Thank you for your passion, Kady, but I think I should do the questioning, don't you?"

Kady lowered her gaze and stepped back. "Sorry, Captain."

Violet faced Alice and raised an eyebrow. "Alright, Mechanic. How about you start by answering Kady's questions, and then we'll continue?"

"I didn't compromise your position, they already knew you were near Iota-9. I don't know who gave them that information, but it's likely they already had it by the time I returned to the Stronghold after I, uh, we...parted ways."

"Then how did they find our exact position?"

"You were having a firefight in dark space. You think anyone passing by within two thousand kilometers didn't see that display of bravado? They knew your approximate location, and that little space fight did the rest."

"It was Captain Leo's ship," Violet replied, and surprised flashed across Alice's face.

"How did you know the boiler would need repair? Because you sabotaged it before you left?" Kady interjected hotly, and Violet shot her a look.

"I didn't. At first, I thought you just hadn't noticed the Stronghold yet and were preoccupied with the other ship. It wasn't until I got here that I realized your power was failing, and I ran all the way from the loading dock."

"How did you bypass the loading bay door air lock? It should be impassable without the code," Violet questioned.

Alice looked at her feet. "I may have smashed the lock. You, uh, might want to get that repaired." She looked at Violet with a smirk. "I'll repair it myself."

Kady rolled her eyes at the crew member next to her, who shrugged silently.

"Why did the Stronghold stop advancing on us? Were they waiting for reinforcements from a military vessel?"

Alice tilted her head with a twinkle in her icy blue eyes. "I may have, uh, *disabled* their main and secondary boilers. They have no thruster power or propulsion."

Violet furrowed her brow. "Disabled?"

"I smashed in the safety valves with a very big wrench." She shrugged and grinned impishly. "It will take them a few hours to repair them at the very least. It should be enough time for us to get to a safe location."

"Us," Violet repeated, and she felt a wave of relief crash over her. Relief, and a quiet anticipation, laced with a triumphant boost from their narrow escape. "And what about your chip?" she asked, gesturing at Alice's arm. "They had reinstated it, but do they know how it was initially disabled?"

Alice shook her head. "When I got back, I had to go to the medical bay for an examination, standard protocol. The med tech scanned my arm and obviously it didn't pick up. They figured it became accidentally demagnetized from the electro magnetic pulse when you boarded. Obviously new chips aren't affected by that but mine is an earlier generation model. They don't know about the deprogramming gun."

Without turning, Violet said, "Kady, the rest of you, you're dismissed. Begin assessing what needs repairs and delegating to the correct crews. Anything more substantial that needs specialist attention, make a list for Alice and she will see to it that crew members get proper training to address the matter."

"But Captain, she—" Kady protested.

"Kady, I have a very large gun, and Alice has a pair of pliers and some boiler tape. I think I'll survive. Get up to the bridge and assist Ned. Make sure our radar and comms are working, and then chart a course home."

Kady whirled around and stalked up the steps, leading the rest of the crew back into the main part of the ship and leaving Violet and Alice alone in the boiler room.

When the crew's footsteps and chattering had faded, Violet spoke. "Alice, you must realize this all sounds very far fetched. How can I convince my crew that you didn't sell us out? What am I supposed to tell them, to ease their fears? To ease my own reservations about your very timely reappearance?"

"You can tell them I gave up a luxurious retirement with a generous pension to come back."

"Is that true?"

Alice leaned back against the damaged air filtration system to relieve the pain in her knee. "The Coalition made me a very attractive offer if I gave up information on your last known location or those droids you used to ransack the Stronghold and steal their best mechanic." She grimaced and shifted her weight. "As you can see, I'm here on the Cricket, and not preparing to live out the rest of my days on a small farm, far away from all this mess."

"If they thought you had information, why offer you anything? Why not just threaten your job instead?"

Alice brushed a stray hair from her face and replied, "They needed me to train my replacement first. The newest recruits from the Coalition engineering academy aren't trained in older systems because they're mostly obsolete now. Still, that knowledge is very useful in troubleshooting even the newest rigs."

Violet rubbed her temple. "I believe you, Alice, this just all feels...very coincidental."

"Maybe not as coincidental as it seems," Alice replied. "I had to act fast, but somehow, it worked."

"What worked? *Did* you give them our location?"

"I told you, they were already headed towards a location near Iota-9. I figured I'd have until morning to enact my plan, but your firefight meant I had to move faster and get out of there sooner, or you'd all have been arrested as soon as military support arrived."

"That leaves a lot to the imagination, Alice. I'm struggling to see how this all came about without you giving them any information. You said they already knew to head in this direction, but how? Even if they had old information, they had no reason to believe we had returned to the same location."

Alice shrugged. "I overheard a Coalition representative give the captain orders to return here and look for you. I think he just got lucky that you were engaged in a very loud, bright confrontation right as we were passing."

"And what, they just let you take a shuttle over here? Or is that black eye you've got supposed to be evidence to the contrary?" She gestured to Alice's swollen eye, which was getting larger and more purple by the minute.

Alice bristled. "*Supposed to be evidence*? I lied to a captain I worked with for decades. I gave up a cushy retirement and comfort to come back here. I smashed their boilers so they wouldn't be able to follow us. I stole a shuttle and took some punches on my way out. I thought you'd be happy to see me...I guess not." Alice grunted softly and grabbed at her shoulder.

Violet's gaze softened and she took a step towards Alice, reaching out for her shoulder. "Are you alright?"

Alice flinched away from Violet. "I'm fine. Dislocated my shoulder on my way off the Stronghold when I engaged the emergency door in the loading bay."

"I'll get Hyun," Violet said softly and reached for her radio.

"I said, *I'm fine.*" She rubbed her shoulder gingerly and scowled. "Hyun can see to my shoulder later. We need to talk about this boiler. First of all, one of the explosions damaged your air filtration system, and that loose belt I warned you about shot into the boiler and punctured it, which is why you lost pressure and power. It's patched for now, but you won't be able to get anywhere near full speed, and you'll need to land somewhere so I can source the parts to repair it properly. It's going to take at least a week. And then, I'll—"

"Alice," Violet interrupted, "I am glad you're back."

Alice's cheeks flooded with color and she looked down at her boots. "I, uh...good." A moment passed and then she continued with a grin, "Is the mechanic position still open?"

"I think we can work something out," Violet laughed. "I can't offer fancy retirement packages, though, and you're likely to spend thirty percent of your time in mortal peril. What say you to that?"

"Aye, Captain."

Their eyes met for a quiet moment, and Violet could feel her pulse quicken. She tore her gaze away and looked towards the stairs.

"If you won't let me call Hyun, you can at least show me the Coalition shuttle you stole. Come on, let's go have a look. Grab your mask, you'll need it in the loading bay."

Alice crossed the boiler room and met Violet at the stairs, where they headed towards the loading bay and the stolen shuttle.

"So tell me, Mechanic," Violet began, "won't they be able to track the shuttle?"

"Nah," Alice replied nonchalantly, "took a wrench to the navigation panel."

"Is that your solution for everything?"

"Not everything, just when a little elbow grease is necessary." Alice rubbed her shoulder and winced. "It can be repaired, if you're interested in having a shuttle and not just parting it out for profit, but Kady will need to reprogram some things before that can happen."

They turned down a bright corridor lined with storage shelving, stocked full with bags of rice, flour, and sugar.

"I'll talk to her. Might be useful to have a shuttle, especially once we get through this round of supply drops."

"Mm," Alice replied. "You might want to consider a paint job, too. They'll be looking for that shuttle, and even though the tracking chip has been disabled, it would look out of place in the kinds of places I would guess you're – er – we're heading to."

"Won't it still be recognizable as a Coalition shuttle?"

"They outsourced shuttle production to a private company two years ago. They have different technology than civilian shuttles, but other than the paint they look the same."

Violet wrinkled her nose and looked over at Alice. "What kind of civilian has the credits for a private shuttle, much less a large private vessel?"

"The kind that work for the Coalition," Alice replied. "Government contracts are lucrative." Alice paused and rubbed her knee.

"I see you're coming around to our kind of ideology, then? Is that why you came back?"

"I don't really know why I came back. It just seemed like the right thing to do. And besides, a relaxing retirement seemed boring after the adventure I had here on the Cricket." She straightened up and followed after Violet with a slight limp as she tried to keep weight off her knee.

The captain walked confidently through the ship. She knew every bend and corner, because she had studied the schematics for weeks before they liberated it from the scrap yard. "And what about your friend, what was his name? Barnaby?"

Alice massaged her shoulder as she walked, and was quiet for a moment. "Barnaby left. Took everything from his room and went on a trade mission. I don't even think the captain knew yet that he had left. He didn't leave me anything, I just found a note in his room from an old lover. It's nothing to go on."

"I'm sorry, Alice, that must be difficult." Violet looked back at Alice. "I'm sure he's okay."

"He's an incredibly smart, clever man, I'm not worried about his well-being," Alice said with a tinge of bitterness. "I just thought we were close enough that he would tell me where he was going."

"We'll keep an ear to the ground for information, if you like. We pirates have a network of little birds that sing for us."

"If he doesn't want to be found, he won't be. Barnaby has a lot of money and even more shady connections. He could be living on Delta-4 under a new identity by now for all I know."

• • • •

THEY REACHED THE LOADING bay airlock, and Violet looked through the window and laughed when she saw that the combination lock to gain access to the ship had been smashed in, just as Alice had said. Violet grabbed an air mask off of a peg near the door, and they both strapped masks over their faces. Violet shoved open the door, and they entered the airlock.

The airlock was rudimentary, a functional but old design. There was the door leading into the ship, which had been protected with a combination lock before Alice smashed it in. The other door led to the loading bay, which was now unprotected from the harshness of space with the cargo door gone, torn off in the firefight.

"It's a damn good thing Ned and the others tied these crates down, or they'd all be floating through dark space by now," the captain said, patting the side of a worn wooden palette. "Best be sure we use some more tie straps from now on, especially if people are going to bust through the loading bay door," she said with a wry smile, and turned to admire the shuttle. "Well, she's a beauty, that's for sure. What should we call her?"

"I've never named a ship before," Alice replied, and wondered what kind of responsibilities came with that.

"Well, we can think about it," Violet said thoughtfully. "Maybe I'll ask the rest of the crew for suggestions."

Alice nodded and opened the pilot's hatch on the small shuttle. There wasn't much room on these small vehicles, only two seats and a meager amount of space for luggage or cargo. These were meant for making trade deals and negotiation in a neutral area; after the deals were made, cargo was transferred between ships on the ground. Actual trades rarely took place in space. These shuttles were also frequently used for diplomatic meetings, and for the private owners of these crafts, secretive affairs with lovers.

"Have a look, Captain," she said proudly. "Almost fully functional, aside from navigation. Might need some small repairs."

Violet leaned inside and peered at the navigation panel, black and lifeless with part of the screen caved in by Alice's wrench. She smirked and looked back over her shoulder. "Well it's a good thing we have a mechanic now, to fix it. It could really help us in the future. Well done."

Alice reached inside to grab a large canvas sack she had brought with her, full with things she usually took on shore leave: spare coveralls and underthings, her deck of Banríon cards, and whatever else had settled at the bottom of the bag. It was the only thing she'd had time to take when she left, and was now all she owned. When she tried to lift the bag from the passenger seat, her shoulder exploded with pain. She gritted her teeth through the pain, but couldn't help but let out a small whimper.

Violet's face clouded with concern. "Alice, I'm calling Hyun in. You need your injuries seen to, and then you need rest. You can meet up with the rest of the crew at dinner tonight. We're going to be talking about drop strategies and the next vessels to hit for supplies."

Alice raised her eyebrows in surprise. "Which vessels to hit?"

"Yes, if you didn't get the memo, we are pirates, Alice," Violet replied, "and now you are, too."

Thoughts swam in Alice's head; the pain from her shoulder and knee clouded the edges of her mind now that the adrenaline of her escape had worn off. Her bruised eye socket had begun to swell, and she struggled to keep that eye open at all.

Violet called Hyun on the radio and requested her assistance, and then she turned back to her new mechanic.

"Alice, let's go back inside the ship. Come on now, I'll get your bag and drop it in your room. You remember where that is, right?"

Alice nodded. "Yes."

"Alright then," Violet said as she slung the large canvas bag over her shoulder. The bag was almost as tall as she was, and half as heavy. "Let's get you to the med bay. Hyun wants to take a look at that shoulder, and I think you should ice that eye."

"Not a good look on me, huh?" Alice asked jokingly.

Violet looked over her shoulder and winked through her face mask. "I wouldn't say that."

Alice felt her face flush and coughed nervously. "I guess I should head to the med bay, then?"

"I'll walk you there," Violet said as she entered the airlock with Alice.

"I'm okay, I'm sure you're busy with preparing repair schedules. I can start assigning easier tasks at dinner tonight if you're ready."

Violet cocked her head as though considering Alice's offer, and then pushing the second door into the ship, she removed her air mask and said, "Okay, then. See you there. Get that shoulder looked at, and get some rest. The rest of us will hold down the fort until tonight."

Violet went in the direction of Alice's quarters, the same ones she had slept in before. Alice removed her own air mask and turned left down the corridor and towards the med bay, and hopefully, some pain relief. She walked slowly, favoring her right leg. Her knee throbbed, and she knew she would be feeling that for some time to come. Whoever had engineered human knees certainly needed a lesson, that was for sure.

Hyun was waiting for her outside the med bay with a big smile on her face. "Alice! Welcome back!" she yelled down the hall, her arms wide and ready to embrace her with a warm welcome.

Alice couldn't help but feel a surge of warmth in her stomach and a smile spread across her face in spite of the pain. "Hyun! Good to see you!"

"Wow, you really got us out of a bind there," Hyun said. "It's a good thing you came along, or who knows what would've happened."

"I'm not sure everyone would agree with you," Alice laughed, remembering Kady's hostility.

Hyun gave a dismissive gesture. "Don't worry about them. They'll come around. I'm glad you're back, it's nice to know there's a mechanic around to get us out of messes we find ourselves in. Hop up on this table here."

Alice grimaced as she pulled herself up onto the table. She hadn't realized before how tall Hyun was: not as tall as herself, or as Ned, but significantly taller than Violet and Kady. "You going to fix me up, doc?"

Hyun looked over a pair of large orange framed glasses that perched on her nose. "I'm a med tech, not a doctor." She smiled and continued, "I never actually graduated. Would have been first in my class, though."

"Why didn't you – AH – graduate?" Alice asked as Hyun easily popped her shoulder back into place.

"It's a long story, really. A tale to tell over a game of Banríon, maybe. Do you play?"

"I do, actually. Brought my cards mostly on accident, but I do have them." Alice tried to wiggle her fingers, and was dismayed when sharp stabs of pain shot through her shoulder.

Hyun pulled a fabric sling from a drawer and started to wrap it around Alice. "You'll need to wear this sling for awhile, until your shoulder is stronger. Make sure you rest it, I know how you engineers are, always poking at something."

Alice grimaced as Hyun fastened the sling. "Thank you."

Hyun turned and handed her a cold cloth packed with ice. "Here, put this on your eye, it's swelling." She turned back to the cabinets and pulled out a bottle. She shook out two capsules and handed them to Alice with a cup of water. "And take these, they should help with the pain so you can get some sleep. You'll be okay, and I'll see you at dinner."

Alice returned to her quarters and found her canvas bag propped up in the corner where Violet had left it. She surveyed her new home, and sat on the bed. She laid back on the pillow, and propped up another pillow against her shoulder so she wouldn't roll over on it in her sleep. She felt the capsules Hyun had given her start to take effect, and she drifted into a quiet, exhausted sleep.

• • • •

CHAPTER TWELVE

VIOLET PASSED ALICE's door for the third time that morning, and stopped to listen through the door, yes, for the third time. The mechanic hadn't woken up last night, and Hyun had suggested they all let her sleep until morning. This time, Violet couldn't hear anything through the door, no quiet snores or rustling of bed sheets. She thought of Alice's swollen face and was suddenly gripped with worry, and couldn't resist the impulse to slowly push the door open to check on the mechanic. Alice lay on her back, her bruised face nestled on the extra pillows that Violet had sent down for her. It was clear that Alice's eye would be swollen shut for at least a few days, and her shoulder, still in the sling that Hyun had provided, would likely take weeks to heal.

Violet eased the door shut behind her and took a step closer to the bed, stepping around the discarded torn coveralls that lay in a heap on the floor. She leaned over Alice, who wore nothing except a faded tank top and a pair of boxer shorts, and watched closely as her chest rose and fell with the rhythm of deep sleep. At least Violet knew that Alice was still okay, still sleeping off the excitement of the previous day, and not in any medical danger. She grimaced when she examined Alice's eye, puffy and purple. Violet gently brushed a stray hair from Alice's cheek, then straightened. Even beat to hell, Alice was still the most attractive woman Violet had seen in quite awhile, and her pulse fluttered when she thought what might happen if Alice awoke right at that moment. The captain put the thought from her mind and quietly exited the room, latching the door behind her. She rested a hand on the closed door for just a moment, gathering the focus she needed to meet Ned and Kady on the bridge.

"Are we nearing the port?" Violet asked Ned.

"Aye Boss, a few hours, maybe more depending on the thrusters."

"Thank you Ned, I'll take the bridge for awhile if you want to get something to eat or stretch your legs."

Ned stood from his chair, using his cane for balance. "Aye Boss, I'd kill someone for a sandwich."

"No need for homicide, Ned," she laughed. "I'll radio you when I need you."

He nodded in acknowledgement and hobbled out of the room confidently, his large stature as imposing as ever, even with the cane.

Violet turned towards her second in command. "Kady."

"Yes, Captain?" she answered tersely, not looking away from the screen in front of her.

"I think we need to have a discussion about what happened yesterday."

"I apologize for my insolence," she said flatly, "I recognize that you have final say on this ship. It won't happen again."

"Kady, we talked about this before. Alice isn't a spy. Without her, we wouldn't be here, we'd all be on our way to a work camp."

"Without her, we'd have been *just fine*. Are you telling me you believe her ridiculous story that the Coalition already knew where to look for us?"

Violet sat in her captain's chair at the helm and looked out into space. "Does it really matter? She committed treason to get back here. She's just as vulnerable as the rest of us now."

"Unless it's a ruse to get us to trust her, so that she can give up the locations of the bases we're helping, and give them the droid technology."

"Kady, we didn't exactly have a choice yesterday. Even if she was a spy, which I don't believe she is, what was our other option? Wait for the military ships to arrive? The Stronghold may have been temporarily disabled, but their backup would have arrived in less than an hour."

"I just think it's naive to let her have full access to the ship."

Violet turned to look at Kady, whose eyes were still on the screen. "So you think I'm naive?"

Kady looked up, startled. "Captain, no, I—"

"It's fine," Violet interrupted. "I understand your concerns, and I have noted them. I think that we can trust Alice. If I'm wrong, I will turn the ship over to you and retire somewhere quiet."

"You'd hate retirement," Kady replied, the tension lifting. "You would be retired for five minutes before you liberated another ship and took to the skies again."

"You're probably right," Violet said, laughing. "But please know that I value your insight, Kady. I might not always agree with you, but I want you to feel heard on this ship. We're not the Coalition, and I'm not a traditional captain."

"Thank you, Captain," Kady said, her tone lighter than before. She cracked a small smile.

Violet felt keen to change the subject away from Kady's actions the day before, satisfied that at least some progress had been made."Did you and the others finish the repair schedule?" she asked, looking over a clipboard on Ned's desk.

"Yes, except for the more complex procedures that will need a mechanic's eye. I suppose Alice will be taking care of that, whenever she decides to leave her quarters." Kady's tone was still heavy with disdain, and Violet was annoyed at the resigned frustration in Kady's voice.

"She should be awake soon, Hyun gave her some pain relief and a mild sedative yesterday. It would seem even that's enough to knock our mechanic out."

"Our mechanic," Kady repeated, sighing in resignation. "Well, I assume she'll be able to take point on the bigger repairs and source the tools and materials when we touch down."

"Yes, that's the plan. I spoke with her about it yesterday." A moment passed in silence, and then Violet continued, "Did you talk to the crew about shore leave when we reach the port?"

"I did, and they seem excited about having a night off. They've all been informed to be back by the following midday to commence repairs."

"And how about you, Kady? Have any plans?"

"I have a meeting with a former Coalition scientist to discuss the emerging detonation bot technology."

"Oh, a *meeting*, is it?" Violet asked with a wink.

"Yes, a meeting. I thought it was productive to discuss our findings and see if there is more to these than meets the eye."

"Not worried this scientist is a spy, then?" Violet gently teased.

"She blew up the lab she was working in before she defected, so no, I am not worried that she's a spy."

Violet raised her eyebrows in surprised. "Well alright, then." She couldn't remember a single instance of Kady dating, and she had never mentioned any past relationships. "No chance for romance, then?"

Kady examined the screen in front of her with a furrowed brow. "I don't have much interest in romance, Captain. I prefer my own company, or the company of my friends, the crew on board here." She turned and looked at Violet. "People don't seem to understand that I'm not lonely or pining for any lost lovers, I'm happy as I am."

The captain paused and nodded thoughtfully. Even through her honesty, Kady seemed uncomfortable even talking about the idea of being with someone. Violet nodded again, now resolute. "Then you'll hear no more talk of romance from me," she assured her second in command. "Your life is your own."

Kady nodded. "Thank you. Captain, shall I fetch Ned for you? I have to prepare my notes for this meeting, if you don't need me urgently on the bridge."

"I'm okay here on my own, let him enjoy some time before we enter orbit."

Kady glided out of the room, leaving Violet alone with her thoughts about repairs, supplies, and the mechanic who found her way back onto her ship.

• • • •

ALICE AWOKE IN HER pitch black room, and blearily looked towards the goggles on the table near her bed. The time display suggested that it was nearly noon, but she couldn't have slept that long, could she? Almost an entire day? She could smell the faint aroma of cedar wood and pine, and wondered where it had come from. Oddly, it reminded her of Violet.

She sat up and touched her bruised eye socket and winced. It was even more swollen, and she couldn't even open her eye to test her vision. She dragged her heavy limbs out of bed, the previous day's events swimming in her mind. Her stomach clenched into a knot as she felt the full weight of what she had done: she'd be branded a traitor now, guilty of treason. The punishment for such crimes was to hang on the gallows. There was no going back now, not after this. She pushed the thought of gallows and work camps out of her mind. Dwelling on her choices wouldn't change them, and she wasn't even sure she would change what she had done, given the chance.

She chose a fresh pair of coveralls from her canvas sack and kicked the dirty ones on the floor of her room into the corner. She'd have to ask about laundry facilities on the Cricket; back on the Stronghold, all the crew laundry was done by the cleaning crew. She hadn't washed her own clothes since she was in engineering school, a long time ago.

Rubbing her sore shoulder, she realized that it was now covered in a rainbow of bruises leading across her collarbone and up over her shoulder onto her back. It was swollen enough that even the sling Hyun had given her felt tight, and it was clear there was no way she'd be able to get into her coveralls.

"Well, fuck," she said to herself. She didn't have anything else to wear, so she pulled the coveralls to her waist and clumsily tied the sleeves into a knot. She'd just have to walk around in her black tank top and coveralls, and that was that. She laced up her boots and left the room, but didn't bother to lock the door. There was nothing worth stealing in there, anyway. Not unless someone wanted her dirty laundry or a deck of Banríon cards. Some were considered valuable, but she suspected that the crew on this ship earned far more from pillaging Coalition ships than they would pawning some cards.

Alice rubbed her good eye blearily and glanced down the corridor. It was empty; at this time of the day most of the crew would either be working or breaking for some lunch. Her own stomach rumbled in protest, and she felt woozy from hunger.

She ducked through the low doorway of the mess hall, and everyone fell silent. She had never felt so out of place than right in the moment, and for a split second, she wanted to run back to her quarters. Alice looked around the room for a familiar face, but didn't recognize any of these crew members other than a vague recollection.

"Alice! Hey, Alice!" The mechanic turned and saw Hyun, smiling and gesturing towards her. Ned sat across from her, his injured leg propped up on a spare chair. "Over here, you can sit with us!"

Relieved, Alice walked past the rest of the crew and sat at their table. The others slowly began to talk and chat once again, and she was grateful for their friendliness.

"Has anyone fed you yet? You look a little dazed," Hyun said with mild concern.

"No, I only just woke up. What the hell was in those capsules you gave me?"

"It was only a mild sedative," she replied, laughing. "It's rare for anyone to sleep that long, but I thought it was for the best. Just sit tight, I'll get you some food. Ned kept some of the best sandwiches in the locked cooler, and you look like you need one." Hyun leapt up from the table and bounced into the kitchen area.

"So, Alice," Ned said, bemused. "Couldn't stay away from us, eh?" His long red hair was tied back into a loose bun, and his thick beard was neatly trimmed.

"Uh, something like that," Alice mumbled.

"I heard Kady wasn't impressed that you were back," he said with a sideways glance.

"You could say that," Alice replied. "She thinks I'm a spy. I'm sure she's not the only one here who thinks that."

"Well, are you?"

Alice looked at Ned and tilted her head. "Do spies usually commit treason against their employers?"

"No, I guess not," Ned laughed. "In any case, I never got to thank you for helping save my life. So...thanks." He took a huge bite of his sandwich, which left a pile of crumbs on the plate.

"I didn't really do anything. Hyun is the one you should thank, not me."

"Oh don't worry, he did," Hyun said as she slid a plate in front of Alice and sat back in her seat.

The sandwich looked delicious: poached eggs delicately placed on slices of ripe avocados, perched on perfectly baked bread, fresh from that morning. Alice tore into the sandwich, and in that moment she knew she could definitely get used to the quality of food here. Captain Violet and the Coalition's questionable ethics aside, the food alone was worth committing treason for.

"The way I figure, he owes me his good leg as thanks for making sure he didn't lose the other one." Hyun smiled broadly and continued, "Eat up, Alice, you need the energy to heal. How is your shoulder? That bruising looks fierce."

Alice quickly chewed through a bite of sandwich. "Hurts like a bitch," she said as she swallowed. "But thank you for fixing me up yesterday."

Hyun sat back in her chair and crossed her legs. "It's my job, after all," she said warmly. "If the swelling doesn't go down in a few days, make sure you come and find me."

"I will," Alice said between bites. She hadn't realized how ravenous she was until she started eating. The food was delicious, and before she knew it, the sandwich was gone, and only a sparse pile of crumbs remained.

"Better?" Hyun asked.

"Mm. Yes," Alice replied with a satisfied smile.

Make sure you hydrate, too," Hyun advised. "The sedatives really took it out of you. Maybe don't take any more of those," she laughed.

"Not if you want anything repaired on time," Alice mused. "From what I can tell, it's going to take a lot of crew hours to get everything back into working condition. I haven't even done a full examination yet."

"The boss will give you a team to take on lower level repairs," Ned said. "There isn't anyone on board who knows engineering, most of them are converted Coalition traders and military members. There's only about twenty of us on board, but we manage. I'm sure someone will volunteer to help with the more complicated stuff."

"I'll need it, especially with this shoulder. Plus I still have a wicked headache from this bruised eye socket."

"It looks like it hurts," Ned said.

"Yeah, well, you should see the other guy," Alice said with a laugh.

"If you need more ice or anti-inflammatory capsules, you know where to find me," Hyun interjected, "I've got to get back to the med bay to finish inventory after the firefight. We lost some bottles and equipment that got smashed."

"I want a rematch of Banríon later," Ned said as Hyun stood up. "I'll win this time."

"Aw, Ned, maybe. But I doubt it." Hyun laughed as she cleared the dishes from the table and made her way out.

"So, Alice. How do you feel about being a pirate now?" Ned prodded, licking crumbs from his fingers.

She sighed and gave him a comical look. "Can I get back to you on that?"

Ned chuckled. "Of course. Have you been to see the boss yet?"

"No, I just woke up and came straight here. I can't think on an empty stomach." She looked towards the galley, wishing another sandwich would appear. She felt like she was still starving, which was strange for her. On the C.S. Stronghold, basic rations were usually enough to keep her fed.

"Can anyone?"

Alice shrugged. "I suppose some people aren't as bothered by it, but I'm pretty useless until I eat breakfast. Or in this case, lunch."

"We'll be docking in a few hours, you'll probably want to have a list of supplies ready before everyone heads off on shore leave. Once they leave, there's no getting anyone back before Boss says so."

"It's the same on any ship I guess," Alice said. "Everyone needs some time to get away from their duties. You're right though, I should do my examination before then so the captain can have things picked up. I assume that we'll be docking at a trading beacon?"

Ned laughed. "A pirate trading beacon, so maybe."

Alice raised her eyebrows in surprise. "Is that like a black market?"

"Of sorts. Where we're headed, it's pirates only. We all contribute funds to keep the base shielded from Coalition scans. As far as they can tell, it's just a small derelict space station, not a thriving community of cutthroats and thieves."

"So you'll be sourcing supplies from other pirates? What if we run into Captain Leo's crew?"

"I wouldn't worry about that. There's one rule there: no infighting, or you'll be banned. Pirates who get banned don't tend to stick around for long before the Coalition catches up to them."

"And where exactly is it we're going?" Alice asked.

"It's a small moon off of Eta-7. We call the port Bradach. If you didn't know what you were looking for, you'd think it was just a small science installation with a skeleton crew. Nothing worth sniffing around. They scramble transmissions and use fake data to make it seem like there's only a few people there, when really, it's a whole city."

"One day into being a pirate, and I'm already learning the ways of the black market," she chuckled and shook her head, "talk about an initiation."

"Oh," he added as he unclipped a radio from his belt, "Boss wanted you to have a radio. I guess you're official now," he said with a smile. "Welcome to the crew."

• • • •

ALICE WAS NEARLY COMPLETE with her inspection of the damaged equipment when the Cricket docked. The repairs would be extensive, that was certain; the main systems needed significant work, and there was other things that needed to be fixed, like the outside loading bay door. She wondered how Violet was going to raise the credits to pay for the supplies, but then, Alice wasn't familiar with the black market.

She was crouched behind the main boiler, hunting for an exit puncture. She couldn't find one, which suggested that the piece of shrapnel from the air filtration system was still kicking around inside the boiler. She'd have to completely drain and disassemble the boiler, find the shrapnel, and reassemble it. With her bruised and swollen shoulder, she would definitely need some help. It was a good thing there were extra pairs of hands to help out, or it would take months to get everything repaired. Even with the entire crew working on rotating shifts, it would still take almost a week to complete all the work.

Alice found the social dynamic of the Cricket intriguing. The captain added herself to the work rotation schedule, something that never would have happened on a Coalition vessel. Rank dictated strict roles there, and the captains of Coalition vessels almost never assisted with repairs unless it was absolutely critical and lives were at risk. On a merchant ship, that had never happened in the decades of Alice's service for the Coalition.

She backed out of the small corner using her good arm, and sat back on her heels. She pulled a pad of paper from her pocket and added a note to the bottom, under a heading entitled "Primary repairs:"

Drain, clean, and reassemble primary boiler. Re-patch. Team size: 2-3.

Alice put the notebook away, and tucked a pencil into her messy braid. A stray piece of hair stuck to her cheek, and she brushed it away awkwardly. She knew that braiding her hair was going to be an impossible task until her shoulder had healed, and she was dreading trying to shower. Her new radio crackled to life.

"Alice?" came Violet's voice.

"Yes, uh...Captain?" Alice replied. It still felt odd to call anyone except Captain Allen that.

"The team heads are meeting to discuss the revised repair schedule before everyone leaves for shore leave tonight. Could you come up to the mess hall with your inspection notes and equipment list?"

"I'll be right there." Alice heaved herself off the floor, a difficult feat with one arm in a sling and a swollen knee. She dropped her tool belt on the workbench and climbed the steps out of the boiler room. On her way to the mess hall, she briefly wondered to herself if she was entitled to shore leave yet. She then wondered if she would ever be able to rewire her thoughts to be more pirate and less Coalition.

When she reached the mess hall, familiar faces were seated around a table. Kady, Ned, Hyun, and Violet we waiting for her repair recommendations. There was one free seat next to Violet, and she eagerly sat down. The relief of pressure on her knee felt exquisite.

"Do you have your list?" Violet prompted.

"Oh, of course," Alice responded as she placed a creased piece of paper on the table. "My suggestion is to start with the major repairs first, using larger teams, and branch off into small groups to work on more rudimentary fixes. I've also included a materials list of the supplies needed, which I've already cross-checked against spare parts you have in the boiler room."

Violet cocked an eyebrow and looked at Alice. "Impressive."

Kady rolled her eyes and interjected, "It's hardly unreasonable to expect that a lifetime Coalition engineer be efficient. They take entire classes on that."

Without turning her head, Violet responded, "Kady, I'm going to assign you to Alice's repair detail. I think you two should get to know each other as the head of programming and the head mechanic."

Kady huffed quietly, but didn't say another word.

"There's a significant amount of materials needed, including a brand new loading bay door. I'm not sure what kind of currency..." Alice trailed off.

"We use credits, just like everyone else. Ours are just more...creatively acquired," Violet said with a smirk "Sometimes we barter directly with merchants; we have relationships with some that give us what we need in exchange for supplying them with rare finds that we liberate from merchant vessels."

"Credits..." Alice said quietly.

"Yes, Credits," Violet said.

"No, sorry, it's just...I just realized...never mind."

"Realized what?"

"The Coalition will have frozen my account by now. My entire life savings is in there. It's for the best, I suppose, they're able to track everything these days."

"It's been transferred to a secure, untraceable account," Kady said with acid. "I took care of it while you were sleeping off those sedatives."

"Oh...Oh, wow. Thank you," Alice said quietly.

"No need. They were *captain's orders*."

"You won't be able to access that account for a few weeks while our contacts sort out new identification for you, but we'll make sure you're taken care of until then," Violet added. "Now, to the next order of business. Ned, are you okay to meet your merchant contact tomorrow to source these high level materials?"

"Aye Boss, got it all set up. Found him some rare stuff he's been asking for, so we're golden."

"Good. And Hyun, you know what we need to restock the med bay?"

"Yes, we only need antibiotics and a couple of other things. We're lucky that the med bay didn't take more damage."

"And you're okay to source that yourself?"

"Yes, but we'll have to wait until the next supply drop, I have a contact who works in a hospital there who gets me untraceable supplies. There's nothing here on Bradach that we need."

"Okay, excellent. And Kady? Do you need anything from the rest of the team?"

"I don't need anything," she replied with a surly tone. "Not unless you can get me more of those detonation droids to examine, but that's impossible."

"Oh," Alice said excitedly, and her eyes lit up. "I forgot to say! I brought a box of them with me. They must still be in the shuttle."

"You. Forgot. That you had a box full of explosives?" Kady asked incredulously.

"Ah, well, it was kind of a last minute decision when I left. I thought they were just deactivated droids at first, but I disassembled one and found the detonation bot inside the core. I was worried what they might be planning, so I...stole them."

Kady sat back in her seat, silent.

Violet nodded in approval. "Theft is a good first step to piracy," she said, bemused. "I guess you have plenty to keep you busy now, Kady," she added.

"It would seem so," Kady replied through gritted teeth.

"Aw come on, Kady," Ned interjected, "give Alice a break. Spies don't usually provide their enemies with cutting edge weapon technology, do they?" he said as he playfully elbowed her.

Kady folded her arms and said nothing. A moment of awkward silence passed before Violet continued.

"I'll have the crew divided into teams for the repairs by the time everyone gets back from shore leave. I'll take a look at Alice's suggestions and work up a repair rota for everyone. Please assure the rest of the crew that they'll get extra shore leave if repairs are completed ahead of schedule."

"Aye, Boss," Ned affirmed.

"Alright, you're all dismissed. Have fun, make sure everyone knows to be back by midday tomorrow."

Ned and Hyun chatted about their evening plans as they left the mess hall, with Kady following silently behind, leaving Alice and Violet alone in the room.

"How about you, Alice?" Violet asked. "Any shore leave plans for tonight?"

"Ah, I'll probably stick around the ship if that's alright." Alice gestured to her shoulder and eye. "I feel like I'm not exactly in top form for a wild night in a pirate black market town."

Violet smirked. "I don't know, I bet that black eye would be popular in the taverns here. You could hustle yourself an arm wrestle, or have a night of passion with a strange pirate, perhaps?"

Alice blushed. "I, uh...I...I don't really get out much, I guess." She couldn't help but think that the only pirate she wanted to spend the night with was sitting next to her, but she knew she would never say that out loud. She coughed loudly to clear her thoughts, and refused to make eye contact with the captain.

Violet laughed. "Okay, well, no pressure. There's bound to be a few of us who stick around on the ship, so feel free to head here for dinner later. Or you can get something in town, if you like."

"I'll think about it," Alice said as she stood up. "After all, how many times do you get a first night in a pirate town?"

CHAPTER THIRTEEN

"YOUR PLAY," VIOLET said with a smirk.

"I think you've got me backed into the corner here, Boss," Ned chuckled as he laid a card on the table.

"You're sunk, that's for sure," Kady added as she looked on from the corner of the room, where she leaned against the wall with tall, knee high black leather boots that featured wide silver buckles along the sides.

"Did either of you see Alice this evening? I was wondering if she had decided to sample Bradach culture and visit a tavern or two," Violet asked nonchalantly. "I suggested it to her earlier today, but she didn't give any indication of her plans."

"I haven't seen her since this afternoon," Ned replied.

"Well, if she did take shore leave, I hope she doesn't get herself into trouble. Or maybe a little bit of trouble would be good for a new recruit, who knows?" She felt a tinge of disappointment that Alice had decided to spend the night on the town, after all.

"Someone who can smuggle an entire crate of high level explosives in a small trade shuttle without a second thought can probably take care of herself," Kady mumbled.

"So you're past thinking that she's an evil Coalition spy?" Violet asked.

"I'll admit, it's *unlikely* she's a spy. I had a look at those droids she brought with her, and they all seem to have that detonation bot at their cores. Doesn't seem like the kind of thing the Coalition would want ending up on the black market. But I still don't trust her."

Ned looked at his cards thoughtfully and rearranged them in his hand. "Have you figured out how to disable them yet?"

"No, but I have a meeting tonight with a scientist that could help me get a breakthrough. I'll take notes and report back tomorrow."

"You don't have to spend your shore leave working, you know," Violet said as she played another card with a grin. "Your turn, Ned."

"I enjoy my work, and besides, this is the only time the scientist had free to meet me here. She's been very busy working with rebel groups on growing sustainable food for the surrounding towns indoors, without the aid of natural sunlight."

"Impressive. Do you think that's something we could implement here on the Cricket?"

"Perhaps, I'll know more tomorrow." She arched her back in a wide stretch, and the long heavy cloak she wore for outings fluttered.

"I give up, Boss, there's no way I can win this match now," Ned said, laying his cards face down on the table. "Bested once again! I should stick to the drunks in the taverns, those are the only poor souls I can beat with this lousy deck."

"I told you Ned, you need to pare down the number of direct attack cards in your deck. They make for some flashy plays, but you're left with no defense," Violet laughed.

* * * *

THE SOUND OF LAUGHTER drifted down the corridor as Alice approached the kitchens. She was starving, her stomach rumbling angrily, and with no idea where else she could find food, she gave up on waiting for the mess hall to clear out and leave her to eat in peace. "Oh, I thought you'd all be out on the town," Alice said as she entered the room. "I just came down looking for some dinner."

"Help yourself to what's on the counter," Ned said as he gestured towards the kitchen. "I left out some things for those who chose to stay aboard. We're the only ones here, so feel free to load up if you're hungry."

"Oh, Alice, I thought you'd left," Violet called to her as she rustled in the kitchen. "No one had seen you for awhile so..."

"I was working on some schematics for a couple of upgrades for you to consider. With a few minor additions, we can increase maximum speed by about ten percent." There was a crash, followed by the sound of things falling to the ground. An orange rolled out of the kitchen and came to a stop by Kady's feet.

"Are you alright in there?" Violet asked with a laugh.

"As it turns out, preparing food one-armed isn't as easy as you'd think." Alice poked her head out of the kitchen. "I knocked over a plate of tasty looking citrus fruit."

Kady bent and picked up the orange, and began to peel it as she leaned against the wall.

Alice gathered up her plate of food and sat at the table next to the card game. "Playing Banríon, are you?"

"Do you play?" Ned asked.

"I do. I was the best on my ship," Alice replied smugly.

"Oh ho ho," Ned said with a false mocking tone, "aren't *you* impressive?"

"Either that, or I played a lot of drunk crew members who couldn't read their cards straight." She laughed, and it made her bruised eye socket throb with a dull pain. She gently prodded it, and it felt just as swollen as it had when she woke up.

"Did I hear someone say they're playing Banríon?" Hyun asked loudly as she strode into the room.

Ned and Violet quickly stacked their cards and put them away into cases. "Just finishing, actually," he replied.

"Ah, shame," Hyun continued, "we could have had a tournament! As it happens, I'm off to a professional game this evening, I just came by for a snack before I left."

"Well I hear Alice has been throwing fruit around in the kitchen if you're interested," Violet said as she packed her cards away into a small, tan leather case.

Hyun laughed. "Sounds good to me." She grabbed an apple from the counter and took a bite. "You know what I say, never play hungry!"

"I should head out, this meeting is across town and it will take me awhile to find the location. This scientist is very secretive, but I don't blame her." Kady headed towards the door. "I'll see you all tomorrow, then, good night," she called over her shoulder, and whisked down the corridor, her cloak trailing her artfully.

"Wish me luck," Hyun said as she followed Kady out the door. "I hear there's a new player, and I've not played him before."

"Good luck!" Ned shouted, slightly too loud. Alice winced at the boom of his voice, rattling in her ears.

"Hyun plays Banríon professionally?" Alice said, with a hint of awe in her voice.

"That's how she keeps her family fed," Violet replied. "They lived in a rebel area, and the Coalition cut off supply drops to try and drive out the rebels. She was able to get them relocated to a safer settlement, but she still uses her winnings to buy them food on the black market." Violet snapped her card case shut and leaned back in her chair. "She's kind of a big deal on the circuit."

"Wow."

"Don't ever play her," the captain said with a laugh, "she's too good at the game. She's thrashed us all, even when we made her play with a beginner's deck."

"Definitely don't let her hustle you into betting on the game, either," Ned added. "I lost my favorite pocket watch that way."

"That was your own fault for being cocky with that new card you'd bought."

"What card was it?" Alice asked.

"It was the Lava Flow card, it took me months to track down," he replied proudly. "I couldn't believe it when it turned up in a card resale shop in Bradach."

Alice wrinkled her nose. "That's a card that's only good for quick damage. It does nothing for your defense."

"That's what I told him!" Violet cackled.

Ned rolled his eyes. "Yeah, well, you'll both be sorry when my Lava Flow card decimates your decks."

"Let's see your deck then, Alice," Violet encouraged. "Did you bring it with you?"

"By sheer luck and coincidence, it was in the one bag I grabbed on my way off the Stronghold." She produced a thick deck of cards held together with a rubber tie from her pocket, and placed it on the table. "But if I show you my cards, you have to show me yours." Alice immediately blushed at her own comment. "I, uh, I just mean if you see mine, I'll lose the element of surprise!"

Violet playfully snatched up the deck and untied them. "Oooh, a mystic deck, how mysterious," she said. "Not many people play mystic any more."

"Old habits die hard, I guess."

Violet sifted through the cards. "You have some really rare cards in here," she said, clearly impressed.

"I've been playing since engineering school, that's a lot of years to collect cards. There's only a few I'm still looking for, but they were first editions and nearly impossible to find unless you're willing to shell out some serious credits for them." Alice reached across the table for Violet's card case. "Well let's see what *you've* got then."

Violet reached out reflexively, and their hands met on the case. Alice looked at Violet and tilted her head, and Violet just stared for a moment. "Oh, uh, sorry," she mumbled as she pulled her hand back.

Ned looked at Violet, and then at Alice. He cleared his throat. "Well, chums, I've got big plans tonight, big plans indeed. I should be going, yes I should," he said awkwardly, and cleared his throat again.

"Ned, are you okay?" Violet asked.

"Yes, yep, I'm fine, just have plans to get to." He stood up and grabbed his card case from the table. "See you both tomorrow afternoon!" He quickly hobbled out the door, and they heard his uneven steps fade down the corridor.

"That was...strange," Alice said after a moment.

Violet cleared her throat. "Uh, yes, it was. I haven't seen him move that fast since before he got shot. Maybe it's a sign he's healing quicker than Hyun had anticipated."

Alice opened Violet's card case and began to examine the cards. "You play a cleric deck, that's interesting."

"If you get the right card drops, you can just build up extra lives, and your opponent will never be able to catch up. I've never beaten Hyun, though, none of us have."

Violet looked at Alice's plate of untouched food. "You know, I haven't eaten yet either, and that plate of leftovers looks a little uninspired. Do you want me to make us something?"

"Oh, no, I don't want to be a bother," Alice said as she clumsily shuffled Violet's deck with her uninjured hand. "I'm fine with the leftovers."

"It's no bother, I'm hungry. Easier to cook for two than for one."

"I thought you didn't like to cook." Alice straightened the cards and stacked them in the corner of the table.

Violet shrugged. "I don't mind it, when the company is right."

"Alright then, if you're sure you don't mind."

"Great!" Violet jumped up from her chair, leaving Alice's cards on the table in a neat pile but taking the plate of cold leftovers. "Is there anything you don't like?" she continued over her shoulder as she went into the galley.

"Uh, not really," Alice replied. She decided to follow Violet into the kitchen galley, instead of sitting alone at the table. "So, uh...how come you're not going out tonight?"

Violet looked up from the counter, where she was slicing a fat loaf of crusty wheat bread. "I and the other senior crew members: Ned, Kady, and Hyun, that is – we take turns with one of us staying on board in case something happens. We keep an eye on the logs, make sure nothing on the ship gets stolen. It's my turn to stick around this time."

"So do you usually go out?" Alice asked, annoyed at herself for being so curious about the captain's social habits.

"Well, yes, sometimes. Didn't you get shore leave when you worked for the Coalition?"

"The Stronghold was a ship where recruits were trained. Apart from a couple other senior staff members, the crew was always rotating in and out. Most of them young, straight out of school, and keen to get a little rowdy. Shore leave was a good opportunity to enjoy the peace and quiet."

"Alice, I want to ask you something," Violet said as she filled a pot of water. "Why did you really leave the Stronghold? As captain of this ship, it's my responsibility to understand our opponent's weaknesses, where they have vulnerabilities. I never thought I'd see you again."

Alice shifted nervously and looked down at her boots. "I don't know, it just kind of...happened. Barnaby was gone, they were pressuring me for information."

"Oh come on, I bet it was a feat of impressive ingenuity to escape," Violet said with a sparkle in her eye. "Like how did you get that?" she asked, gesturing at Alice's black eye.

"To keep things abbreviated, my original intention was to feed them some false information and hope they never found you in the first place. I went to the captain to tell him you had held me somewhere near Delta-4. I planned to plead ignorance when they got there and you were nowhere to be found."

"But they did find us."

"Yes, I was too late. By the time I came up with a plan and called up to the captain, your ship had already been reported on the Coalition long radio band. A passing private vessel saw your firefight and called it in."

"So what then?" Violet began to chop some alarmingly large cloves of garlic, and the kitchen was filled with the aroma.

"I thought if I disabled their boilers, and made it look like an accident, you would have a chance at escaping."

"Smashing in the safety valves looks like an accident?"

"No," Alice replied with a laugh. "No, that wouldn't look like an accident. The recruit I was training caught me in the act of disabling them. Clocked me in the face with...I don't even know, something heavy. After that, I didn't really have time for subtlety."

Violet spread the crushed garlic and tomatoes onto the bread and pushed it into a large, brick lined oven. "And then you stole a shuttle."

"And then I stole a shuttle."

"But wait, how did you know that you'd be able to land the shuttle here? The loading bay door wasn't blown off until halfway through that fight."

Alice grinned. "Pure luck. I figured I would just try to get to the nearest trading beacon, ditch the shuttle and hitch a ride to somewhere else. I hoped I'd be able to get in contact with you and..."

Violet raised an eyebrow. "And?"

"And, I don't know, ask you to pick me up, or something," Alice said sheepishly. She knew that she had to convince Violet that she came back to the Cricket because she wanted to join her crew, not just because things had gotten dicey aboard the Stronghold.

"So you wanted to come back?" Violet asked, staring at the boiling water full of pasta, watching it bubble and roil in the pot.

"I had to finish what I started, didn't I?"

Violet gestured at Alice's arm, where the Coalition chip was lodged just below the skin. "And what were you going to do about that?"

"Yeah, I..." Alice ran her fingers over the chip reflexively as it rested under her burn scarred skin. "I know where it is, I'd just have to..." she swallowed hard. "...remove it."

"That's surprisingly badass," Violet said in an approving tone. "I don't know many who have attempted slicing a Coalition chip out on their own." Violet rubbed her own arm and grimaced, running her fingers of the crisp cotton of her shirt where it gathered at her elbow.

"Yeah well, let's just say I'm very glad it didn't come to that."

Violet looked at Alice out of the corner of her eye, and Alice felt her stomach do a somersault. "Um, that looks like it might be done," she mumbled, gesturing at the pasta in the pot.

"Oh yeah," Violet said absent-mindedly, "yeah, let's eat." She gingerly pulled the crisp, toasted bread from the oven and divided the pasta evenly between two plates, smothering it with a thick red sauce from a jar.

"It smells delicious." Alice reached out to pick up a plate, and Violet playfully slapped her hand away.

"Not yet, you beast," she said laughing, "I haven't seasoned it to perfection yet."

"My apologies, chef," Alice replied with a smile and a bow.

Violet revealed a small glass container in her hand, which she deftly shook over both plates. "Ah, yes, my secret ingredient!"

Alice looked at the bottle suspiciously. "Okay, but what is it, really?" When Violet gave a coy smile, Alice rolled her eyes and laughed. "Come on, who am I going to tell? Is this what you've really been hiding from the Coalition?"

The captain snorted a laugh. "Dried chillies from a friend who grows them. I get him untraceable, rare replacement parts for old ships—"

"— and he gives you chillies. Seems a bit, I don't know, unequal." Alice took her plate and sat down at their table, deeply inhaling the scent of the spicy dish.

"You might think that, until I tell you that these are the rarest in the Near Systems. I don't break these out for just anyone, you know," Violet said with a wink.

Alice took a bite and her eyes rolled back into her head with delight. "Holy shit, Violet, this is actually delicious."

"Aren't you glad I didn't let you eat sad leftovers?" Violet asked with a smirk.

"Mmm."

"You know," Violet said between bites of pasta, "you risked a lot coming back here."

"I'm trying really hard not to think about it." Alice slurped up another fork full of pasta and chewed thoughtfully. "It's certainly a change of pace for me."

"Well, just know, I appreciate the help."

Alice nodded, her mouth full of charred bread. Somehow, every meal she ate on the Cricket seemed better than the last. She wasn't sure if that was just the truth, or just her own perception after decades of basic rations aboard Coalition vessels.

"And at least I don't have to go looking for a new mechanic now," Violet continued, "I wasn't really looking forward to reading through all those 'pirate mechanic' applications, you know?"

"And what precluded me from having to submit an application? Have you checked my references?" Alice asked, laughing. "You never know, I might have stolen an extra loaf of bread from my last job. Or, you know, a shuttle."

"Your reputation proceeded you." Violet used a slice of the crispy bread to mop up the sauce left on her plate. "You are the best, and everyone knows it."

Alice blushed and shoveled the last of the pasta into her mouth to save her from having to respond. She never had learned how to take a compliment.

"Do you want to play around?"

Alice choked on her pasta and her cheeks burned. "I'm sorry?"

Violet stared at her quizzically. "Do you want to play a round?" she asked again, nodding towards the piles of cards at the edge of the table. "I promise I'll go easy on you."

"Excuse you," Alice said, swallowing as she regained her composure. "I don't need your pity plays, I can handle myself just fine."

"Alright then, how about we make it interesting, seeing as you're so confident?"

"What, like a bet?"

"I have something you might want," Violet said suggestively.

Alice blushed bright red and stammered, "I – uh – what...what's that?" She turned her face towards the door so Violet wouldn't notice.

Violet sat back in her seat with a swagger, her hands clasped behind her head and her boots crossed at the ankles. "You mentioned that you've been looking for first edition mystic cards," she said as she began to slowly shuffle her deck. "I'm going to guess that the holy grail for you is the Fog of War card."

Alice whipped her head back around. "You do *not* have that card, you're teasing me."

"Oh, I've got your attention, have I?" Violet asked playfully.

"No one who plays Banríon would risk that card in a bet. It's one of the rarest, and you could sell it for....for, I don't know, a lot."

Violet shrugged. "I don't play mystic decks, and it's just been sitting in a drawer for a couple of years now. And I'm a pirate, Alice, what makes you think I'm hurting for credits? I don't need to sell interesting finds, I keep them for leverage."

"Leverage?"

"Leverage, or a fun night in placing bets with new crew members," Violet added. "I have an idea." She cleared the plates and disappeared into the galley.

"What are you doing?" Alice called.

"Just reliving some memories," Violet answered as she returned to the room with an enormous bottle of whiskey and two matching mugs. She wiggled her eyebrows and raised the bottle above her head.

"Oh gods, not that again," Alice said with a laugh. "I barely survived the last encounter with your whiskey."

"I find that most people play better after a wee dram," Violet said as she poured whiskey into the mugs. "If not better, then at least with less of a predictable nature.There's nothing more dull than a game where the players only enact defensive cards. Let's get things going in here! She took a long drink from her mug. "Your turn, Alice," she said, nodding towards the second mug.

Alice gave a fake exasperated sigh. "Oh, *alright then*," she said with a wink as she took a drink. "So if I win, you'll just hand over this incredibly rare card worth loads of credits?"

"Sure."

"And what if you win?"

"I get to ask you for a favor."

"What kind of favor?" Alice asked,wary of the vague request. She didn't like how elusive Violet was being, but it couldn't be anything worse than committing treason and stealing a shuttle, could it?

"Nothing illegal," Violet answered.

"What about dangerous?"

Violet thought for a moment. "It's very unlikely to be dangerous. Though I suppose some may disagree."

"So what, like upgrading the water pressure in your room? Finding some kind of rare artifact? What?"

"That's the deal, Alice. You win, you get the rare card; I win, I ask for an as-yet undisclosed favor."

Alice sat back in her chair and took another sip of whiskey. She wasn't in the business of being in debt to someone, even in a light hearted way...but she really, *really* wanted that card. Annoyed at her sling, she unfastened it with one hand and let it fall onto the table, sighing at the feeling of additional freedom.

"Don't tell Hyun that I took that off," Alice said with a grimace.

Violet crossed her heart with an x motion and promised, "I wouldn't dream of it."

Alice leaned forward and cracked her knuckles. "Alright then," she said with a glint in her eye, "Your play first."

The captain shuffled her deck with one hand while she stared Alice down. "Prepare to be annihilated."

"We'll see about that." Alice refilled their mugs with whiskey and sat back in her seat, feet planted wide and her arms crossed in mock defiance.

"Mmm," Violet murmured as she looked at the cards in her hand. "Alright, try this on for size: I play Haunted Cleric. He's unkillable and generates health when not attacking or recovering."

"Impressive card," Alice said, "that one's pretty rare. Who did you steal that one from?"

"I won it in a game, *actually*."

"Too bad I have a Force Recovery card," she said, laying the card on the table. "So much for your health generation, eh?"

Violet narrowed her eyes. "Alright, Mechanic, I see what I'm working with now. You're a woman who knows her deck." She drew a card from her deck and laid it on the table. "Standard Monk card, nothing to worry about."

"I'll play a Vengeful Fae. Double damage when I control two other fae types." She raised her eyebrow and looked at Violet with a challenging eye.

"Damn, Alice, you're pretty fierce right out of the gate. What, no foreplay?" Violet laughed.

Alice blushed crimson and cleared her throat awkwardly. "Well, uh, I mean, I—"

"How does your Vengeful Fae feel if I equip my Monk with an Aerial Artillery card?"

"That doesn't seem very monk-like," Alice grumbled.

"Au contraire, my mechanic, some of the bloodiest wars in history were fought over religion."

"Yes, but how many monks were manning huge anti-aircraft cannons?"

Violet shrugged. "Probably a few. Your play."

"I play Siren's Song. None of your actionable cards can attack for the next two turns." Alice said with a self-satisfied smirk. "How does your Monk feel about that? Oh, and that triggers the Vengeful Fae's secondary ability, which is playing a second card whenever I play a card that affects the opposing player's attack sequence." Alice leaned forward and raised an eyebrow. "So I'll be playing the Fae Queen card."

Violet gasped softly. "I didn't see that in your deck!"

"Couldn't give away all my secrets, now could I?"

"That's cheating!"

Alice laughed. "It's not cheating to conceal a card from a potential opponent who's hungrily pawing through your deck!"

"Hungrily pawing," Violet repeated with a low growl. "Alright, well there's no way I can come back from that play, the Fae Queen is a game ender in almost every circumstance, unless you have something built into your deck to combat her."

Alice leaned back and shrugged nonchalantly. "Précisément."

"And where did you acquire that little beauty from?"

"Barnaby got it for me as a gift a few years ago, said he traded for it on a mission. I used to play a druid deck, but when I got this card, I built a whole new deck around it."

"So you have a druid deck kicking around somewhere, too?" Violet straightened her cards. "I love a good druid deck. Versatile. Flexible."

"No, I traded most of them away to build this one."

"Well, damn," Violet said with a laugh, "I was hoping for another game, and one where I won't have to face your Fae Queen."

"I just got lucky with the card drops," Alice said, laughing. "But I did win."

"Best two out of three?" Violet asked hopefully. Alice shook her head. "Oh come on, Alice, you have to let me get warmed up first! Best two out of three!" Violet begged.

Alice sighed and nodded. "Oh, alright then."

Violet leaned forward and filled their mugs again. "Drink more. It's the only chance I have at winning." She took a swig from her mug, and waited until Alice matched her.

"I'll play first," Alice mumbled, as she shuffled her deck awkwardly.

"Do you want some help with that?" Violet reached across the table and took Alice's cards, and their hands brushed for a moment.

Alice eyed her suspiciously. "Don't stack my deck."

"I would never," Violet said with mock sincerity. "On my honor as a pirate, I promise I shan't stack your deck, even though I guarantee I would win if you don't pull that card." Violet delicately shuffled the cards, being careful not to bend or damage them, the way only a seasoned player would. She pushed the deck across the table to Alice. "Alright then, your play."

"Hmm," Alice said, considering her cards. "Alright, here we go: how about my Enchanted Shprite, er – Sprite," she said as she laid the card on the table. She blinked a few times to clear the haze from her vision, induced by the third mug of whiskey. "Normal damage, acts as a defender when it's my opponent's turn."

"Playing it safe this round, are we?" Violet shifted through the cards in her hand. "I thought you were a maverick, Mechanic."

"Yes, well, when I don't have the perfect starting hand, I tend to play a bit more, hmm, conservative."

"What shall I play?" Violet considered.

"Come on, we don't have all night," Alice urged.

"Don't we?" Violet asked with a grin. "Did you have some plans you're keeping secret?" She waited a moment and examined Alice's face, her icy blue eyes sparkling. She hadn't intended on spending the evening with her newest recruit, and yet, something about it just felt right. "Alright, how about...how about my Sister of Condolences?"

"Shit." Alice rolled her eyes. "How did you manage to pull that straight off the bat?"

"I'm lucky, you know." Violet laid the card on the table. "Double damage when she's the only card on the table, and she has an entry bonus of removing an opposing team's card." She gestured towards Alice's Enchanted Sprite card. "Go on then, Sprite, off you go."

Alice reluctantly slid her card off the table, and placed it back into her main deck. "Goddamnit."

"So that's double damage to you then, Mechanic," Violet cackled gleefully.

"Argh," Alice growled. "Alright, double damage to me." She adjusted a many faced die on her side of the table and examined the cards in her hand. "Alright, well, if that's how we're playing, then I'll play the Witch in the Woods card. She has research, defense, and attack abilities, but is vulnerable to fire."

"Okay," Violet began slowly. "Then how about a Righteous Knight? She has high defense and rallying capabilities."

"Fine, fine." Alice pored over the cards in play. "Perhaps..." she trailed off. Then, she felt Violet's boot lightly graze against the side of her leg, and her stomach did a somersault. She dropped the cards in her hand onto the table, and one fell face up.

"Aha!" Violet cried. "You've chosen the Tidalwave card?" She broke into fits of giggles. "Why would you play that? It only affects cards that *you* have in play!"

"That's not fair!" Alice said, her voice rising with indignation. "You—you—"

Violet met her gaze. "I what?"

"Never mind!" Alice huffed. "Okay, so that's my cards out of play, *well done*."

"What did *I* do?" Violet asked innocently.

Alice narrowed her eyes. "Nothing, *I guess*." She couldn't help but wonder if that had been accidental or intentional. Violet was a pirate, after all.

Violet laid a card on the table. "I'll play my simple Monk again. No real threat for now." She gave Alice a wide, confident grin.

Alice drew a card and smirked mischievously. "Ah, Captain," she said, "I don't know how to tell you this." She slowly and deliberately laid a card on the table, and Violet's grin turned into an open mouthed gasp.

"I can't believe you pulled that card."

"What can I say? Whiskey gives me luck," Alice laughed as she took a deep swig from her mug. "Read it and weep, Captain. The Pragmatic Magick card. Renders all cleric powers unviable, and it's also a permanent card on the playing field." She sat back in her seat, satisfied, and stifled a small hiccup.

"Did you know that I play a cleric deck?" Violet asked. "Why else would you have that card in your deck?"

Alice smirked. "You pilot types are all the same, you fancy yourselves heroes and play cleric decks. I just came prepared, and I got lucky."

Violet threw her cards down on the table in mock disgust. "I guess that's two out of three." She looked up at Alice through her eyelashes. "I suppose I owe you that card now."

"I guess you do." Alice sat back in her seat and crossed her arms confidently. "I still don't know why you bet that card."

"Sometimes, it's worth the wager." Violet hauled herself out of her seat. "Come on then, the card is in my quarters."

Alice followed the captain out of the mess hall and through the corridors, heading towards her quarters. "So, what was the favor going to be?" she asked.

"It's not important." Violet said coyly, as she rounded a corner down a dark corridor, lined with overturned old wooden apple crates.

"Come on, just tell me. I just want to know what I would have been getting myself into."

Violet turned abruptly and faced Alice. "Are you sure you want to know?" She swayed slightly on the spot, plied with the outlawed alcohol she had shared with Alice.

"Uh...yes?" Alice replied with a furrowed brow.

Violet took a wide step onto a crate, so that she was eye level with Alice. She raised an eyebrow and leaned in close. "You're not going to kiss me again, are you, Mechanic?"

Alice jerked back. "What? I—uh—er—" she stuttered, as her cheeks blushed a bright red in the dim light of the corridor.

"What, you didn't enjoy it?" Violet asked softly. "I did." She stretched her arms out and clasped her hands behind Alice's neck and gently pulled her closer. She paused a moment and fixed her eyes on Alice's. "I am glad you came back, whatever the cost."

"I—uh—" Alice started.

Violet leaned in and kissed Alice slowly on the mouth. "You're a fabulous mechanic."

Alice stood speechless, staring at Violet.

"And you're not a bad kisser either." She leaned in again and kissed Alice deeper and harder, parting her lips and exploring her mechanic's mouth with her tongue. She gave a soft, involuntary moan as Alice kissed her back.

"Captain, I—" Alice began as she pulled away.

"What's wrong?" Violet whispered.

"I just, I, um—should we?"

Violet ran her hands down Alice's back. "Should we what?"

Alice laughed softly. "You don't actually have that card, do you?"

"Of course I *have the card*," Violet replied indignantly. "Is that what you really want?" She hopped off the crate and looked up at Alice.

"I just want you to show it to me, er, in your room." Alice nodded towards the end of the corridor. "I'm not very good at this." She looked at her feet, embarrassed and awkward.

Violet gently grasped Alice's trembling hand and led her down the hall towards her quarters. "Follow me."

They reached Violet's quarters, and she unlocked the door, pushing it open with her free hand. "I'll show you that card," she whispered.

Alice followed the captain into her chambers and pinned her against the door, pushing it closed. "I had a dream about you, you know," she murmured as she leaned in for a kiss. Violet smelled of cedar wood and pine, an earthy, sensual scent that Alice found oddly familiar. She found herself burying her face in Violet's neck and breathing deep the woodsy, comforting scent.

"Mm," Violet moaned softly. "What was the dream?"

Alice stroked Violet's face, tracing the scar on her cheek. "I could show you," she whispered, leaning in for another kiss. Their mouths met, hot, wet, and hungry. Alice kissed the captain hard with one hand smoothing the fabric over her hips, and the other stroking her neck.

"Show me," Violet breathed.

Alice pulled her to the bed and laid back. She grasped Violet's hip with one hand and pulled her on top and stared. "I, uh," she muttered awkwardly.

"Stop talking," Violet ordered as she straddled Alice. She leaned forward and kissed Alice again. "I love a woman in uniform," she whispered mischievously, as she ran her hands over the mechanic's tank top. "I like this, by the way," she said softly, gesturing towards the sleeves of Alice's boiler suit tied around her waist. "You should wear it like this all the time."

"Why do I feel like I'd never get any work done?"

"You're probably right," Violet said as she untied the sleeves and unzipped the rest of her boiler suit, slipping her hands inside.

Alice reached up with her good arm and flipped open the toggles on Violet's leather vest. She pulled it off the captain and tossed it on the floor; she started to unbutton her crisp white shirt, which revealed a lacy black bra underneath. "I didn't peg you for a femme," Alice murmured, gesturing to Violet's underthings.

"I wear them for myself, not anyone else," the captain answered as she slipped off her blouse. She reached down and lightly pressed on Alice's bruised shoulder. "Does that hurt?" she asked.

"A little."

Violet pulled back. "I'm sorry," she said as she lightly traced the bruise around the edges with her fingertips.

"It's okay. It's healing. I'll be good as new before you know it." Alice toyed with the waistband on Violet's pants, tugging at a belt loop playfully. "Could have been worse."

"You could have died," Violet said, unbuttoning her trousers. "I'm glad you didn't."

Alice felt her body come alive with excitement, and resented her injured shoulder. "Don't say that, you'll make me paranoid," she answered.

Violet reached under Alice's tank top and sighed, "Oh, Alice. You're a beautiful woman." She pushed up the tank top and traced Alice's nipples. "There's just something about you..." she trailed off.

"Something about me that what?" Alice prompted as she tugged at Violet's bra with her good arm.

"You're just— I like you more than I've liked a woman for a long time." Violet swung a leg over Alice and hopped off the bed. The captain pulled off her trousers and tossed them onto the chair in the corner. She slowly removed her bra, keeping eye contact with Alice the entire time. Her small, dark breasts sat high on her chest, and Alice gasped softly at the sight of her nearly naked body. "So...what now?" she whispered.

"Take those off too," Alice said, nodding at Violet's underwear. "The dream re-enactment should be as accurate as possible." She felt heat in every part of her body, and her heart pounded in her chest.

Violet stepped out of her underwear and said coyly, "Now you, too."

"I wasn't naked in my dream," Alice answered defiantly.

"You were in mine," Violet responded flirtatiously. "Shouldn't I get to live out my fantasies, too?"

"I'm the one who won the game," Alice said.

"I don't care," Violet said. "Take it off."

Alice obediently wriggled her hips out of her coveralls and kicked them onto the floor next to the bed, leaving herself in her black tank top and matching boxer shorts.

Violet raised an eyebrow. "Those, too," she said, gesturing to Alice's underthings.

"I can't get the top off without some help." Alice whispered, nodding towards her bruised shoulder. She pulled her boxers off and left them next to her on the bed.

"I don't want to hurt your shoulder." Violet leaned forward and pulled a small knife from her bedside drawer. "May I?" she asked, gesturing towards Alice's tank top.

Alice closed her eyes and nodded. "Okay," she said quietly.

Violet pulled the shirt taut and nicked it with the knife, pulling at it until it tore and revealed Alice's large, round breasts. She inhaled sharply and leant down to kiss Alice's nipples softly. "Oh, Alice," she murmured as she straddled her once again. "You don't know how much I wanted you to come back." She kissed the mechanic deeply and pushed her groin against Alice's hips. "I yearned for you."

Alice's body felt like it was on fire; she hadn't felt like this in years, maybe ever. She reached forward and ran her fingers over Violet's body, coming to a rest at her hips. "You know," she said, "in my dream..."

"Mm?" Violet prompted.

"You shushed me."

"Shhh," Violet whispered, running her hands over Alice's body. "What else?"

"I woke up before it finished."

Violet traced her fingers over Alice's soft belly and wide hips. "I think I can make sure you finish this time." She ran her hands up Alice's thighs as she kissed her breasts and traced the faded stretch marks along the edges.

Alice breathed deeply in anticipation. "Oh, Captain," she said quietly.

"Call me Violet."

"Oh, Violet," Alice corrected herself, "don't make me wait."

Violet teased Alice, lightly grazing the folds of her labia. "I won't make you wait much longer," she whispered, slipping a finger inside.

Alice gasped. "Oh," she whispered.

Violet explored Alice, kissing her deeply. "Are you glad you came back?"

"So glad, "Alice sighed.

"Do you want me?" Violet asked, pressing further.

"Yes," Alice rasped, leaning into Violet. She hadn't felt like this in an eon, in decades, maybe.

Violet pressed further, and harder. "Alice, please," she uttered softly, "don't make me wait any longer. I want to feel you."

"I'm not, uh, I haven't done this in a long time," Alice murmured nervously. "I don't think I'll be any good at it any more. I'm out of practice, and— "

"Shh," the captain shushed her again, and slid deeper into Alice with a slow, purposeful rhythm. "It's alright. Just be with me, in the moment."

Alice searched blindly with her hand, pressing against Violet. "Tell me what you want," she whispered shyly.

"Touch me," Violet begged. She looked at Alice with her deep brown eyes, the yearning written all over her face. The captain leaned forward and kissed her again, their lips brushing gently against each other.

Alice pushed inside, and Violet gasped. Alice felt warmth pulsating from her core, an unstoppable cadence that was pushing towards an inevitable crescendo. Breathless, she uttered, "Violet, I'm— "

"Yes, Alice," Violet replied, pressing further and harder. Alice gasped and cried out. Violet raised an eyebrow. "That didn't take long."

"I told you, it's been awhile," Alice replied breathlessly. "Let's go again." She stretched up and kissed Violet on the breast. She felt like she had been reawakened, like she'd been in a dormant, icy room for years. Violet's every breath spurred Alice onward, and she let herself rediscover the joy of being this close to a woman. She wrapped her bruised arm around Violet's waist and pulled her closer, ignoring the sharp pain throbbing in her shoulder.

They moved in tandem, gasping and kissing, until both were left breathless, satisfied, and laughing. They laid side by side on Violet's bed, amongst her soft, plush purple blankets, and tried to catch their breath.

"So, " Alice breathed laboriously, "what was the favor?"

Violet laughed weakly. "I was going to ask for a kiss."

CHAPTER FOURTEEN

ALICE AWOKE TO BRIGHT sunlight streaming through a window high on the wall. She smiled to herself, recalling the previous night's events, and reached out for Violet but instead found an empty bed. She sat up and propped herself against the headboard. Alice surveyed the room and saw the Fog of War card propped up against a lamp on the table next to the bed. She leaned over to examine the card and a note that laid beside it.

The spoils of our battle, as promised.

-V

"Where the hell did she go?" Alice muttered to herself. She searched for her boxers, which were half hidden under the bed. She pulled them on and looked at her torn tank top in dismay.

"Fuck," she said quietly. She had no idea what time it was: there was no analog time display in Violet's room, and she had left her goggles in her room the previous day. She couldn't just sprint through the ship topless when crew members might already be back on board. There was only one option: wear her boiler suit, and that meant stuffing her injured shoulder into the sleeve. Alice tugged the legs of her suit on, and did a couple of hops to get them to settle into place around her hips.

Alice stretched her bruised shoulder back to fit her arm into the sleeve, and was blasted with a stab of excruciating pain. She let out a yelp and pulled the suit over her shoulder as tears sprang to her eyes. She was definitely regretting allowing Violet to slice up her tank top. The mechanic stole a glance at herself in the ensuite bathroom and recoiled. "Gods, what a mess."

Her braids were falling apart, with long strands of silver hair pulled free and floating rebelliously around her pale face. Her blackened eye was now turning shades of green and yellow, and made her look a little bit undead. Her shoulder throbbed and pulsed with the constriction of the sleeve, and Alice grimaced. If she could just get back to her own room without seeing anyone, she could put on a fresh tank top, and maybe ice her shoulder before breakfast...or lunch. She still wasn't sure what time it was.

Alice opened the door a crack and peeked outside into the corridor. She didn't see anyone, and couldn't hear any footsteps, so she closed the door quietly behind her.

"What. Are you. *Doing.*"

Startled, Alice whirled around and found herself face to face with Kady. "Oh, Kady, I didn't see you there. Or hear you. Ahem."

"I knew you were a spy. Sneaking around in the captain's quarters, *again*? Seems like a bit too much of a coincidence, don't you think?"

"Well last time I was looking for a key, and I didn't know it was her room, and-"

"I don't care about your excuses. I caught you sneaking out of her room! What were you looking for in there?"

"I wasn't— I'm not—" Alice stuttered, searching for the right words. She couldn't very well tell Kady the real reason why she was leaving the captain's room alone, could she?

"I'm taking you to the captain," Kady said icily. "I know you are injured, so I won't try to restrain you. Just don't try anything."

"Thank you for that, I guess."

"Let's go, Mechanic," Kady said, prodding Alice in the back. "To the bridge."

They walked in silence, Alice's boots thudding heavily along the corridors.

"Alice!" Violet shouted when she saw the mechanic turning the corner into the bridge. "Did you see the n—" she stopped short when she noticed Kady behind her, eyes full of fire.

"Captain, I found her sneaking out of your room. *Again.*"

Violet's gaze flicked to Alice, who gave an almost imperceptible apologetic shrug. "Kady," she started, before realizing she didn't know where to go from there. She cleared her throat and squared her shoulders. "Kady, you're dismissed. I'll deal with this."

"But *Captain*, she—"

"We will discuss this later, Kady."

Kady spun on her heel and stalked off the bridge, muttering angrily. When the sound of Kady's fury faded down the corridor, Violet turned to Alice.

"You couldn't have been a little bit more careful?" she hissed.

"Are you kidding me?" Alice replied loudly. "You know she's like a ghost, creeping around the ship silently and trying to catch me in the act of something suspicious. How does she even manage to move around that quietly?"

"Keep your voice down," Violet said quietly. She waited a moment and then continued, "Kady was a skilled gymnast when she was young, before she worked for the Coalition as a scientist. Those skills of grace have carried through to adulthood, and are very useful when raiding a ship. As you well know."

"She worked for the Coalition, and *I'm* the spy?" Alice whispered incredulously.

"It's a long story, and one you should hear from her."

Alice tried to cross her arms, and pain shot through her shoulder. She gave an involuntary whimper and furrowed her brow.

Violet stepped towards Alice and tenderly touched her shoulder. "Are you alright? Should I call Hyun?"

"No, I'll be fine. I was trying to get back to my room to grab a fresh shirt."

"What happened to the shirt you were wearing last night?" Violet asked. Alice raised an eyebrow at her, and Violet laughed quietly. "Oh, right. Sorry."

The captain saw Ned approaching the bridge, and said loudly, "And that's final, Mechanic. Here's your list of primary repairs that need delegation from other crew members, see that they get completed."

Alice squinted in confusion, not having seen Ned. "Wha—?"

"Mornin', Boss," Ned said with a jolly tone as he entered the bridge and sat in his seat. He wiggled his eyebrows at Alice and added, "Mornin', Alice."

"That will be all, Mechanic," Violet said sternly. "You are dismissed."

Alice rolled her eyes at Violet and mouthed, "Are you kidding?"

Ned looked from Alice to Violet and laughed. "Alright then," he chuckled.

"What?" Violet asked.

"Nothing, Boss. Just getting ready for the day."

"Actually, Ned, I've just given Alice a list of repairs that need delegating, but she needs to examine some systems first. The air filtration access panel for the starboard side of the ship is in your quarters, is it not?"

"It is, you're right about that."

"Will you please let Alice in so that she can have a look? You can supervise her presence if you like."

Ned laughed again. "Sure thing, Boss." He leaned on his cane and stood up from his chair. "Hey, Alice," he said over his shoulder, "follow me, I'll show you."

Alice followed Ned's heavy, uneven footsteps through the ship. "It shouldn't take long, to uh, look at the access panel," she offered.

"Just take your time," Ned replied as they reached his quarters. He unlocked the door and continued, "Just don't look around too much, my room is a mess." He winked and pushed the door open.

Alice stepped through the door and laughed; Ned's room was completely spotless. "This is messy?"

"If you prepare people for the worst, they'll be thrilled when they discover something better."

"I'll remember that." Alice looked around the room for the access panel. "Uh, where...?

Ned gestured towards the far wall. "Behind that painting."

The painting was of Ned, and exquisitely done. In the painting, he was naked from the waist up, perched on a rock in front of a beach. He also had a large, fishy tail. Alice considered the painting for a moment. "It's very well done. Unique."

"It is, isn't it? It's my favorite thing that I've ever stolen from an ex-lover." He looked appreciatively at the painting. "He was terrible in bed, though."

Alice looked back at Ned. "You stole a painting of yourself? As a merman?"

"I used to pose for an artist. This one was my favorite, so I stole it on my way out. I figure it was my payment, so to speak."

"Uh, can you...?" Alice asked, gesturing to the painting and then to her shoulder. "I'm afraid I'd drop it if I tried to move it one-handed."

"Oh, of course," Ned replied, edging around Alice and leaning his cane against the wall as he removed the painting and carefully propped it against the bed. "There you are," he said, pointing at the access panel.

"Er, thanks," Alice said as she examined the panel. She was wishing she had picked up her goggles before having a look, the diagnostic tools alone would have helped. She pulled a lever that released the panel, and looked inside.

"So Alice," Ned began, "did you have an interesting evening last night?"

Alice turned her head and smacked her forehead on the door of the panel. "Shit."

"You alright?"

"Yeah, it's just, er, never mind. Yes, er, no? My evening was uneventful, I guess." Just the thought of the previous night sent memories flooding into Alice's mind, and she could almost feel the heat even now.

"Ah well, I'm sure the boss will be pleased when we get next shore leave, it will be my turn to stick around on the ship then."

Alice fiddled with a knob inside the panel. "Does she like to go out?"

"She's a red blooded human, like any of us," Ned said as he reclined on his bed, "she likes to have a good time, and why shouldn't she?"

"And she has a good time with, uh, other pirates, I suppose," Alice continued, feeling deflated.

"Why, are you interested?" Ned asked with a saucy edge to his tone.

"What? *No.*" Alice aggressively yanked on another lever with her good arm.

"You wouldn't be the first woman to fall prey to her charms, you know," he added. "She's a beautiful woman." He waited a moment. "Don't you think?"

"Yes —er, no — uh— " Alice stammered.

Ned guffawed. "I'm just playing with you, Alice." He sat up. "It was an unfair question."

"Well, what about you, then?" Alice challenged, desperate to change the subject. "What did you get up to last night?"

"I watched Hyun trounce a load of cocky gits in that tournament. Honestly, I don't know why those guys keep challenging her and betting huge sums of credits. She wins every time. Maybe it's pride, I don't know."

"And then what?" Alice pressed.

"And then I spent the night with a man I fancied, is that what you're fishing for?" he laughed. "I'm not as guarded as the boss, and I spend my free time having fun, not studying like Kady does. She's too smart for her own good, I think."

"Violet said she used to work for the Coalition." Alice replaced the access panel and turned to Ned. "Why does she hate me so much, then?"

"Kady has her own reasons, and they aren't mine to tell," Ned replied. "I don't think she hates you, she just doesn't trust you. And you don't help yourself, you know, sneaking around the captain's quarters. What was that all about, anyway?"

Alice turned back to the panel so Ned wouldn't see her cheeks glowing red. "She uh, asked me to get something from her room."

"Hmm. Alright then."

"Okay, that panel is functional and doesn't need much work, so that can be assigned to any member of crew. That repair won't take much more than a coil replacement, which anyone can do."

"Alice."

She turned to Ned. "Yeah?"

He studied her face. "Nothing, never mind."

"Um, okay." She screwed the panel back into place.

"Alice, I have to meet a trader this evening to discuss the acquisition of some of the materials we need for the repairs. Maybe you should come with, make sure the quality is up to par."

"I'll have to ask the captain."

"She might be the captain, but we're still pirates," he offered. "You can do whatever you want. Meet me at the Purple Pig later if you want to come. I'll even buy you an ale," he winked.

"It's a date," Alice said, smiling. "I'm not the kind of woman to refuse the offer of a free ale."

"And Alice?" Ned added. "Just give Kady some time to get to know you. She's a good, loyal friend to the people she trusts."

"Well I'm not sure that she'll ever trust me," Alice replied, "but I'll keep that in mind."

With a nod to Ned, she closed his door behind her and massaged her throbbing shoulder. She needed to get her arm out of this suit, and she needed ice. Her stomach growled loudly, and she was also reminded that she needed breakfast, too. She turned towards down a corridor leading towards her quarters and found Hyun knocking on her door, holding the sling she had left in the mess hall the night before.

"Hyun," Alice called down the hall, "I'm not in my room, I'm here." She picked up her pace to meet the medic at her door.

"Missing something?" Hyun asked, holding up the sling. "I found this in the mess hall this morning. If you don't wear your sling, your shoulder won't heal properly!" She frowned at Alice. "I know you mechanic types resent not having full use of your limbs, but if you don't follow my instructions, you will regret it."

"I know, I know, I'm sorry," Alice pleaded as went to take the sling from Hyun. "I just had a few whiskeys and—"

Hyun pulled the sling out of reach. "No, you'll need me to make sure your shoulder hasn't swelled too much. And what are you doing with it in that suit?" she asked incredulously. "Come then, I'll help you get your arm out without too much fuss—" Hyun said as she reached for the zip on Alice's suit.

Alice blocked Hyun and stepped back. "I'm not wearing a shirt under this," she whispered.

Hyun rolled her eyes. "What! Alice. Alright, into your room then. Don't worry, I won't look. I'm a medical professional, besides."

The two women entered Alice's room, and Hyun closed the door behind them. Alice unzipped the top half of her suit, and allowed Hyun to help ease her injured shoulder out of the sleeve.

"What were you doing that you forgot to put a shirt on under your coveralls this morning, then?" Hyun asked.

"Er – nothing," Alice evaded. "I just forgot."

"You forgot." Hyun waited until Alice had pulled on a new tank top, and began to fasten the sling around her neck. "I imagine that would have been quite painful, getting that on this morning."

"It, uh, was," Alice admitted with a wince.

"You know Alice, you can talk to me. I may not be an actual doctor, but I take privacy seriously. What were you doing last night? If I know what you were up to, I might be able to make some suggestions that will help your shoulder heal faster."

Alice felt panic rising in her chest. "I— "

"Did you sleep with someone last night?" Hyun asked gently.

Alice stared silently, and gave an almost imperceptible nod.

"Okay. Listen, if you don't want to keep your sling on when you're spending the night with someone, that's fine. I even understand leaving the sling here on the ship when you left to meet them last night. Just remember to put it back on after."

"Mm," Alice mumbled in agreement, relieved that Hyun thought she had met someone off the ship, and not spent the night with her captain. She had a moment of relief before realizing that if Hyun ran into Kady, they would both probably figure it out. She had to rely on Hyun's discretion, and trust her not to mention this conversation to anyone.

"Hold still, I'm checking for swelling," Hyun said as she gently prodded Alice's shoulder. "You really should be more careful, your joint is susceptible to further damage until it heals." Satisfied, Hyun reattached the sling with a clasp behind Alice's head. "Your eye is looking better too, no sign of residual trauma." She raised an eyebrow and looked her right in the eye. "Alice, if you ever need protection, I have options in the med bay."

The mechanic let out a laugh that was more like a bark and said, "That's never really been an issue for me, if you know what I mean. I uh, don't get around much."

"Come on Alice, you're old enough to know better," Hyun scolded her gently. "Unless you've both been tested, you should always be using protection." She paused and waited for Alice to answer.

"I'll, uh, keep that in mind," Alice mumbled, her cheeks burning with embarrassment.

"Just remember, I have options available. We can have fun but stay safe!" Hyun chirped.

"I heard you did well at your tournament," Alice said brightly, trying to shift the conversation. "Ned told me."

"Yes, I did very well. I took the entire winnings, fifteen thousand cred-its."

Alice gave a low whistle of awe. "Hyun that's loads."

"It's not unusual for a tournament of that size, and the buy in is substan-tial."

"If you make such good money being a professional card player, why do you work as a med tech on the ship?"

"Because if I didn't, you fools wouldn't have anyone to take care of you when you get sick or injured," Hyun said brightly. "I have to chase all of you around as it is just to make sure you aren't making your injuries worse!"

"I suppose that's true," Alice laughed. "Well in any case, I'm glad you're here."

"Good. Now don't let me find your sling not on your person again, si?" Hyun scolded. "At least two more weeks of full-time wear, and then we can re-evaulate."

"Aye," Alice said with a grin. "I know now not to cross you, or you'll be at my door at all hours!"

"You may be new to the ship, Alice, but I still care about your well be-ing. I'll see you later." Hyun gave Alice a nod and a grin, and closed the door. As her steps faded down the hall, Alice heard her mutter, "Why can't they all be good patients, like Ned?"

• • • •

ALICE WAS FINISHING a long day of altering the repair schedule and recommending projects that could be delegated. She had 10 pages of notes regarding the ship's repairs and routine maintenance that had gone unat-tended for months, and she hoped that the crew was up to the challenge. She hadn't managed a team before; it was always her sole responsibility to keep things up and running when she worked for the Coalition.

She checked the time display on her goggles and realized she would have to meet Ned at the Purple Pig soon. She didn't even bother to run a brush through her hair or change her suit; it's not like she had anything else to wear anyway. Even on the Stronghold, her time off was so rare that owning civilian clothing was almost pointless. She knew she looked like a mess, but they were just meeting a trader, so what was the harm?

Alice headed into the center of Bradach, towards the Purple Pig tavern. She wasn't expecting much, after all, dock side taverns weren't usually known for their shining hospitality, and in a pirate town, it was probably worse. She reached the tavern, an old brick building with a wooden swinging sign hung above the entrance. It was painted white with a fat purple pig that had light blue fairy wings. The building looked like it had been here awhile, and Alice found herself wondering just how long the pirate port of Bradach had been around.

She pushed open the heavy, solid oak door and was greeted with the noise you'd hear in any good tavern: happy chatter from the patrons, jaunty live music, and the satisfying sound of clinking glasses. The sights, however, were not typical of any tavern Alice had ever been in.

The pine wood floors were sparkling clean, and the walls covered in plush deep purple velvet. Antique lanterns hung from the ceiling and gave off soft light that bounced and played in the rafters. There were over sized sofas in the corners, piled high with large square cushions. Some sat on the cushions on the ground beside low tables, playing various card games. The tall stools at the counter were brushed copper metal with padding that matched the walls. The bar was stocked with every kind of illegal alcohol you could think of, as well as some so rare Alice had never seen any in person.

"Alice!"

She squinted her eyes and looked around. Finally, she saw Ned in the corner, waiting at a table with two pints of a deep amber ale. She wove her way through the tavern, carefully edging past other patrons, and sat in the seat next to him.

"Alice, you made it! What do you think of our humble little tavern?" he asked loudly, to be heard over the din of patrons and music.

"I wouldn't call this humble," she chuckled, "but it's really nice. I almost regret not coming out last night and letting my hair down!" She took a look at Ned, who was dressed in a dapper fashion, with a tailored leather vest which fastened with wide brass toggles and deep green velvet trousers that disappeared into tall, heavy brown boots with buckles that matched his vest. "Oh, I, uh, feel a little under dressed."

"I wouldn't worry about it," Ned reassured her, "I only dressed up to impress." He winked at Alice and surveyed the tavern. "Our trader isn't here yet, but he's always punctual, so should be around any moment."

Out of the corner of her eye, Alice spied Violet at the bar, leaning against a stool and talking to a very attractive woman with a crop of tight curls flopping over one eye, with the sides shaved into an intricate pattern, and the most impressive cybernetic prosthesis Alice had ever seen, proudly displayed beneath dungarees that had been hastily chopped into shorts. She felt a surge of jealousy course through her veins. "I thought no one was allowed off the ship when it wasn't shore leave?" she asked Ned, not taking her eyes off of Violet and the mysterious woman.

"Nah, that's Coalition talk, that is," he said, realizing who she was looking at. "There are some rules as to when we can disappear for awhile, like when we have scheduled drops, or when we're on a Coalition controlled planet. But here on Bradach, as long as the work gets done on schedule, we can do what we like. Violet's the boss, she makes the final decisions, but most of us still have a say on how things get done." He put a hand on her arm and continued, "Alice, darlin', you need to learn how to be a pirate." He stood up. "I'm going to get us another pint while we're waiting."

Alice's first pint of ale sat untouched as she stared at Violet. The captain was laughing and gesturing, and the mysterious woman leaned forward and tucked a hair behind Violet's ear. Alice felt her blood grow hot at the same time that she realized: she wasn't the only woman Violet yearned for.

"I didn't realize you'd be here," she heard a familiar voice say. "Wow, you really look like hell. What happened to your face?"

She turned her head and gasped; she couldn't believe her eyes. "Barnaby?!"

"Keep your voice down, Alice, they don't know me as that name here," he said as quietly as he could and still be heard above the din.

"You what? How—you're the trader that Ned is meeting with?"

"Ssh, yes, I—"

"Where the fuck have you been?" she demanded.

"Honestly, love, please keep your voice down, I—"

"Oh, right, I forgot you two knew each other." Ned sat down with two pints of ale and pushed one towards Barnaby. "Barnaby, is it? I guess I can stop calling you Françoise, then?"

Alice snorted. "Françoise?!"

"Alice, honestly, I'm trying to stay under cover!" He looked around nervously at the other pirates in the tavern.

"Don't bother, Barnaby, half the tavern heard her." Ned gestured around at the tables of patrons engrossed in conversation. "As you can see, none of them give a shit what your name is."

Alice narrowed her eyes and looked at Barnaby, and then at Ned. "Wait," she said, putting the pieces together, "you," she pointed at Barnaby, "left a note from him," she nodded at Ned,"in the secret panel of your desk when you left."

"Ah right, well thanks for getting that away from prying eyes, then." Barnaby took a swig of his ale. "Been on the run, you know."

"Yeah, well, I figured something was up when I discovered that you had emptied your room before a routine trade mission. How long before they figured out that you were gone for good?"

"Well thanks to you, I suppose, I had a few days extra head start before they knew I had missed the pick up. I heard that someone had smashed in the boilers before taking off in a stolen shuttle." He raised an eyebrow at Alice. "I know I said that you needed more excitement in your life, but I never imagined you'd go so far as to become a pirate."

"You didn't seem surprised to see me," Alice said. "How did you know I had joined the crew of the Cricket?"

He shrugged nonchalantly. "I have contacts."

"You talked to Ned, you mean."

Ned held his hands up. "In my defense, I didn't know you were friends. I casually mentioned that we had a new mechanic on board who was former Coalition."

"And upon hearing that there was a new Coalition mechanic you didn't think to inquire if it was me? You didn't even want to know where I was?" she asked Barnaby angrily.

"I don't usually have heart to hearts about my personal life when I make trade deals, Alice," Barnaby retorted.

"Alright, alright," Ned intervened. "It certainly seems like you two have a lot to catch up on, so it's good that Barnaby will be joining us on the Cricket after repairs are completed. He's our inside man on Coalition information, and the next vessel we're planning to hit is one of the raw supplies transport ships. Barnaby's going to tell us where it is, and when." Ned grinned. "It's like a happy reunion!"

Alice stared at Barnaby. "You know where all the transport and trade ships will be, and when," she said coldly. "You sold them information on the whereabouts of ships so they could be pillaged."

Ned laughed. "Don't make it sound so serious, Alice, it was just supplies." He took a swig of his ale. "It's not a big deal."

Alice narrowed her eyes. "I was *kidnapped!* You sold me out, didn't you, Barnaby? For a few credits, you risked my life?"

"I had met Ned before, I knew they wouldn't hurt you!" he said, trying to defend himself.

"Did you know that we were attacked by another pirate ship while I was there? That Ned was hurt, that I could have been?" She felt anger rising in her chest, accompanied by betrayal. How could her best friend sell her out like that?

Barnaby sat silent and shame faced.

"What kind of friend does that?" she demanded.

"Alice, it's not like I had a choice, they froze my accounts—"

"Who fucking cares? That's your own fault!" she said, her voice rising in volume. "I can't believe you, Barnaby, honestly this is the lowest—"

"Well it all worked out, didn't it?" Barnaby yelled back. "You left the Coalition anyway to join your little pirate queen crush on her piece of shit ship—"

Ned cleared his throat loudly. "I know you're both new here, but there's only one rule on Bradach, and that's no fighting...and that includes tavern brawls." He gathered up the empty glasses. "Let's all just take a deep breath and calm down, because this is my favorite tavern, and I don't want to get kicked out of it. Another round?" He didn't wait for an answer before he stood and left to get more pints of ale.

Snapped out of the moment, Alice immediately looked around, and was relieved to see that Violet had disappeared. She definitely didn't want her to hear what Barnaby had said, especially since she was busy flirting with some new woman.

"If you're looking for that captain of yours, she left ten minutes ago," Barnaby said gently. He reached out to pat her on the arm.

Alice recoiled. "No, I just—"

"She left alone, Alice." Barnaby sat back in his chair, dapper as ever. "I saw the other woman, too, when I came in."

"Why can't you just stay out of my life?" Alice shot back. "I'm never going to forgive you for this, you know. Never."

"Alice, come on," Barnaby said, reaching across the table again. "I was going to split the money with you anyway."

"Bullshit," she said, staring him down. "But you absolutely will be splitting it with me now, and don't think I'm not going to ask Ned what he paid you."

"But Alice—" he started.

"Oh, no, absolutely not. You don't get to sell me out to pirates and get away with it. I know you don't care about me, but you do care about money, so that's what I'll be taking, thank you."

"I do care about you!" he protested. "I made him promise they wouldn't hurt you, and that you'd be returned to the Stronghold safe and sound."

"And what if Ned had been a liar, Barns?"

"But he wasn't."

"But what if he was? What if they had decided to keep me in some terrible cell in the brig, and not let me go back? What if I had been hurt during the attack from the other ship? Gods, Barnaby, do you ever think about anyone other than yourself?" she asked, exasperated.

"Come on, Alice," he tried.

"Honestly Barnaby, this is such a betrayal. I thought you were my friend." She shook her head with disappointment.

"I am your friend."

"No, not now. Maybe not ever." Alice picked up her full pint of ale and drained it in one long drink as she stood up from the table. "Wire my half into my account by tomorrow afternoon, Ned has the details."

"Your account wasn't frozen?"

"I guess you aligned yourself with the wrong people," Alice said over her shoulder. "My credits were all transferred to a secure account the moment I set foot on the Cricket. That's what people do for you, when you don't fucking sell them out at the first opportunity." She paused. "And don't fuck Ned around on the materials. I'll know if it's sub-par." She stormed out of the tavern, feeling angry and betrayed.

She walked back to the Cricket along the cobblestone roads, feeling very alone.

CHAPTER FIFTEEN

ALICE HAD BEEN SURPRISED by how fast the crew had completed repairs. On her own, on the Stronghold, it would have taken her weeks, maybe even months. But everyone banded together into teams and tackled projects simultaneously, and now they were almost ready to leave Bradach and deliver some supplies to people who desperately needed them.

She also gained a trainee: the petite crew member with the green hair who had fallen asleep guarding her door the night before she went back to the Stronghold. Not even a month had passed since then, but it felt like a lifetime. The trainee's name was Ivy, and she had a good aptitude for engineering. She never attended the Coalition schools, but she had good instincts, so she was a natural fit. Alice was glad for the help, and knew that Ivy's training wasn't a threat to her role here on the ship – besides, it would take years to train her properly, even with her quick wits.

"Ivy, toss me that box of screws, would you?" Alice held her good arm out in anticipation. She had gotten pretty good at managing with one arm over the past week.

"Sure thing, Boss!" Ivy replied enthusiastically as she lobbed the box over to Alice, who caught it easily.

"I told you, call me Alice."

Ivy nodded. "Okay, Alice." The trainee was wearing faded denim overalls over a black shirt with rolled up sleeves. Her green hair peeked out from under a gray flat cap, and her short black boots were scuffed with use.

"So, is the name and the hair color a coincidence, or intentional?" Alice asked playfully.

"Ivy is a chosen name, but I didn't choose it because of my hair or vice versa. I just like the name, and I like having green hair."

"That's fair enough," Alice replied with a smile. "I'm glad to have you on my team, Ivy."

Ivy blushed and smiled. "Thanks, Boss – er, Alice."

"What's the status of those air filtration repairs?" Alice asked, looking at a sheet of paper littered with notes and ticked boxes.

"Oh, I meant to say, I completed those repairs this morning."

"Oh, great!" Alice said enthusiastically, ticking off another box on her paper. "That just leaves some minor work in the galley, but there's another team working on that this afternoon." Alice pushed her goggles up onto her head and grinned at Ivy. "Looks like you and I have some free time," she said with a wink.

"Oh, uh, actually, " Ivy began, "can I...?"

"Honestly, Ivy, you can do whatever you want. I'm not actually your boss. You want to head into town, grab a pint at the Purple Pig?"

"I actually, uh, have plans," Ivy mumbled as she blushed a deep red. "There's this girl, and I really like her, and—"

"Oh gods, just go!" Alice laughed. "Have fun, be safe, you know the drill. I'll see you later, thanks for your help."

Ivy nodded at Alice and grinned, before she turned and leapt up the steps and pounded down the corridor and out of sight.

Alice was left alone in the boiler room, and she took a deep breath and sighed. Now that the repairs were almost finished, they would soon be on their way, and wouldn't return to Bradach until they had dropped supplies at three different far-flung locations. It might be weeks, or even months, before she would be able to enjoy a pint of ale in the Purple Pig again. Bradach had a certain charm to it, and if you didn't know it was a settlement of pirates and castaways, you'd never know it from the opulence in the tavern, or the kindness of the local merchants. It felt like even strangers went out of their way for each other here, something that was incredibly rare in Coalition settlements these days.

"Bridge to boiler, are you still on board?"

Alice unclipped her radio and replied, "Aye, Captain, still on board. Did you need something?" There was a moment of silence from the radio, and Alice could feel herself getting tense. She had been avoiding Violet since the morning after their night together. She couldn't talk to her, not after she found out that Barnaby had sold her out to Violet and her crew in the first place. Violet must have known, and kept it a secret. She probably also knew where Barnaby had gone, and lied about it the entire time.

"I just saw Ivy sprint off the ship, everything okay down there?"

Alice chuckled. "Yes, we're all done here, and I think she had some plans she was anxious to get to. Just waiting on the team to finish those minor repairs in the mess hall, and we're golden."

"Meet me at the Purple Pig in fifteen minutes, I need your help."

"Help?" Alice asked, but there was no answer. "So much for having freedom to do whatever I want," she said out loud to herself. She didn't bother to change her clothes or brush her hair; whatever the problem was, it sounded urgent. She hurried up the steps, down the corridor, and off the ship into town.

* * * *

WHEN ALICE REACHED the Purple Pig, she pushed the door open and squinted as her eyes adjusted to the darkness. She looked around, and saw Violet about to sit down at a table in a dark corner, across from a dimly lit figure with a wide brimmed hat on. Without a word, she wound her way through the tavern and sat beside Violet, giving her a questioning look.

"You remember Josie," Violet said through gritted teeth with a forced smile, "She invaded our ship, and now she's their new captain."

Alice turned and looked at Josie, the brassy-haired woman who had been the now dead Captain Leo's second in command and navigator. "Hello, Josie." The mechanic sat up in her chair and squared her shoulders in an attempt to make herself look more intimidating. It wasn't necessary: her size made her an imposing figure to most who didn't know her.

"Josie wanted to have a chat about how we're going to supply compensation to them for killing their captain. I suggested Bradach as a neutral meeting ground, and they just arrived this afternoon. Isn't that fabulous timing?" she asked flatly.

"Compensation," Alice repeated, "for killing their captain, who almost killed Ned and threatened all our lives. Of course."

"We lost Captain Leo, and I think someone should have to pay for that, don't you?" Josie challenged. "We had to drag him off the ship ourselves, even."

"And what *compensation* are you asking for?" Violet asked angrily.

"We want half your food stores, and half a ton of scrap metal, so we can sell it for profit."

"*Half a ton*?" Violet asked incredulously, standing up out of her seat. "What kind of—"

Alice put a hand on Violet's shoulder and gently nudged her back into her seat. "Well, from where I'm sitting, Captain Violet, she might have a point."

"She *what*?" Violet narrowed her eyes at Alice. "They traumatized half our crew, they shot Ned!"

"Josie, listen," Alice interrupted, kicking Violet's shin under the table. "We just don't have the kind of stock you're looking for."

"Oh, uh, yes," Violet added quickly, following Alice's lead. "We don't have half a ton of scrap metal to give you. As you might know, we sustained considerable damage after the firefight with you. It has cost us over a week of repairs, as well as a substantial portion of our liquid assets."

"I've seen what goes on and off that ship," Josie protested. "I know you have it, and you're going to give it to me and my crew."

"Or what?" Violet asked innocently.

"Or we'll blow you out of the sky again," Josie replied. "It took a week of repairs to fix what we did last time, what makes you think we won't do it again?"

"Josie, I can understand—" Violet began.

"Understand what? That my captain and mentor got blown away by a rival pirate, and his body dragged off of a ship like some roadkill?"

"I can understand," Violet tried again, "that you're upset, and that he meant a lot to you. Why that is, I will never grasp, because he was a mean, vicious—"

Alice kicked her under the table again and shot her a look.

Violet cleared her throat. "What I'm trying to say, is that I can understand why you wanted to meet here and ask for these provisions. However, we cannot fulfill your request now, and nor do we intend to. I respect you as a captain, but that's just not how things work."

"Then we'll follow you off Bradach, and as soon as we're outside the range of the cease-fire, we'll take our half ton of scrap metal from the wreckage of your ship." Josie sat back in her seat, looking very satisfied with her negotiating tactics.

"You got the jump on us, twice, because of your very clever anti-detection systems. Unfortunately for you, my programmer has been working on a solution night and day, and we now have sensors to counteract them. We're bigger and have more firepower, you'd never win in a fair fight."

Josie's self-satisfied smirk turned to a scowl and she stood up from her chair. "I don't know who you think you are, Violet—"

"Captain. *Captain* Violet," she replied with acid in her tone. Violet reached into the deep right pocket of her jodhpurs and produced one of the bots. "Do you see this?" She set it down on the table and pushed a button on the top, and it came to life with little whirs and beeps. "It targets whoever we tell it to, and it delivers a fatal burst of electricity. Enough to stop a heart."

Josie flinched at the bot's beeps and sat back in her seat.

"We've stolen everything we've ever wanted from ships with these," Violet continued, tapping the bot, "and they're also very adept at defense. You attack us again, and we know you're coming? You'll be boarding a ship amidst a swarm of these."

"I'll just shoot you out of the fucking sky then, and pick up the pieces amidst your corpses," Josie shot back.

Violet shrugged. "You could, maybe, *if* you surprised us, which is *very* unlikely now, and if we didn't just install a much more powerful set of artillery. Or you could just stay the fuck out of our way." Violet leaned across the table and raised an eyebrow. "*Or*, you could help us."

"Help you? I just threatened to kill you," Josie laughed sarcastically.

"All in the day of a life as a pirate," Violet added. "If you helped us, then we'd split all the profits fifty-fifty."

"And what would we have to do, then?"

"Do a few supply drops occasionally, nothing drastic."

"Supply drops where?" Josie asked suspiciously.

Violet sat back in her chair. "Rebel townships, mostly. Well away from front line initiatives. It's to keep people there from starving. We raid Coalition vessels, keep some for ourselves, distribute the rest."

"And I suppose you'd provide us with some of those death droids? The ones that target Coalition chips?"

"Absolutely not. It's our technology, and we won't be sharing it with you. I'm sure you have your own ways of raiding ships," Violet said, and mumbled, "like brute force."

Josie laughed dryly. "Get fucked, Violet." She stood up from her chair. "Stay the hell out of our way. If we come across you in our sector again, I can't be responsible for any damage your ship takes."

Violet rolled her eyes. "Okay then, Josie. The offer stands if you ever change your mind."

"Fat chance of that," Josie spat over her shoulder as she left the tavern.

"I suppose that went well," Alice ventured.

"As well as I had expected it to," Violet replied, putting her boots up on Josie's now empty seat. "It would have been interesting if she agreed to work with us, but I suspected she would do what she did. In any case, I don't think they'll be coming after us, not until they up their game a bit." Violet slapped a gold coin on the table. "Fancy a drink?"

Alice gawped at the coin. "I've never seen a coin like that in real life."

"It's Bradach, people will deal and trade in whatever has worth. I won this in a game of darts last night, and now I want to spend it on dinner. With you." Violet put a hand on Alice's knee. "Have you been avoiding me, Mechanic?"

Alice pushed Violet's hand away and stared at the bar on the other end of the tavern. "Violet, I have to know," she began, "I have to know if you knew that it was Barnaby that told you where I'd be and how to abduct me."

"I should have known this was the reason you were being distant." Violet took her boots off the chair and twisted in her seat to face Alice and took her hands. "I promise you, I didn't know. Ned gets contacts, he gets information, and I don't ask questions. I didn't make the connection until Ned told me what happened last week."

"I don't know, Violet, it seems hard to believe."

"I'm a pirate, and a cheat, and a liar, but I don't cheat or lie to my crew. That includes you." Violet gave an earnest smile, and dragged the coin across the old wood of the table.

"So I'm just another member of the crew now, is that it?" Alice asked with a smirk.

"A crew member with certain perks, how about that?" She reached out and placed her hand on Alice's knee again, and this time the mechanic didn't push her away.

"I'll take it." Alice accepted Violet's offer, but couldn't help wondering if she was the only woman Violet had set her sights on. She remembered the mysterious woman in the torn dungarees and frowned.

"So, dinner?" Violet asked as she picked up the coin on the table and wound it through her fingers. "My treat? I heard that Kady's cooking on the ship tonight, so I recommend accepting my generous offer."

"You know, I think you're all a little too hard on Kady about her cooking. It may not be the kind of gourmet stuff Ned cooks, or have special rare chillies from your secret stash, but she does her best. She's a scientist, not a chef."

Violet raised her eyebrows in surprise. "I didn't think I would hear you defending Kady, given your previous interactions."

Alice shrugged. "She seems like a good person, but she doesn't trust me. She just wants to protect her family."

"Alright, alright," Violet said, laughing. "I hear you, I'll be nice." She leaned forward and whispered in Alice's ear. "Please have dinner with me?"

"Okay," Alice replied mischievously. "But you have to pick up the tab for the ale, too."

Violet grinned. "It's a deal!" She jumped up out of her seat with the coin. "I'll order for us."

"How do you know what I want?"

"I don't, I just know what I want you to try before we leave tomorrow."

Alice raised an eyebrow. "If I don't like it, I'm going to eat yours instead."

"Don't even think about it," Violet said as she strode over to the bar to order their food.

Alice watched her as she leaned on the bar with one arm, chatting to the barkeep casually. She was struck again by how frustratingly attractive Violet was, in a nonchalant, understated way. Her practical riding pants allowed a full range of movement while hugging every curve. Her blouse was unbuttoned just enough to look casual, with the sleeves rolled up to show off her toned, smooth arms. Even the scar on her face, shining bright against her dark skin in the dim light, was sexy. Alice tried not to think about that night, just over a week ago now, when she saw Violet's lacy black bra. She swallowed hard and tried to clear her head.

"Alice! Are you even listening to me?" Violet was beckoning her over to the bar, grinning. "Come on, food's up, and I can't carry it all by myself."

"Huh? Oh!" Alice jumped out of her seat and tripped over a table leg. She caught herself on a chair with her good arm and pushed herself back up. "Sorry I'll uh, be right there."

"Remind me to never send you on a stealth mission," Violet laughed as she handed a plate and a pint of ale to Alice. "Here, now, try not to send that flying all over the tavern on your way back to the table, huh?"

"No one ever accused me of being graceful," Alice grumbled, annoyed that she embarrassed herself in front of Violet again. She hadn't even had a drop of ale yet, and already she was acting like a fool.

The pair sat at the table, and Violet nodded towards Alice's plate. "Go on then, eat up," she said. "I think you'll like it."

Alice eyed her plate with suspicion. "What is it?"

"It's this great vintage recipe, using pasta and cheese."

"It's just pasta and cheese?" Alice poked at the food on her plate suspiciously.

"It's good, I promise." Violet, who had ordered the same thing, shoveled a huge forkful into her mouth and moaned. "Mmmm, it's *so good*."

Alice felt her stomach do a somersault, and followed Violet's lead before she had too much time to think about it. "Mm, Violet," she said with a mouth full of pasta, "this is actually really delicious. How is it just pasta and cheese?"

"Well, I'm sure there's other ingredients in there somewhere," Violet replied after taking a swig of ale, "but I'm not the chef so I don't care. I just know this is what I order whenever I have dinner here."

"Whatever it is, it's amazing," Alice said with awe as she stuffed more into her mouth.

When they had finished, the barkeep came over and took their plates away. "Good food, friends?" she asked. She was short, with a shock of messy blue hair and a worn, faded black apron. She grinned at the pair and swept their dishes from the old weathered oak table.

"Ugh, *yes*," Alice replied. "I want to eat that every day until I die."

"We may be pirates, Alice, but I have no intention of getting scurvy," Violet chortled. The barkeep laughed and whisked their empty plates back into the kitchen, stopping at the bar to fill a tankard with ale and chat with the patron perched on the stool.

"I don't even care, it would be worth it," Alice said with a satisfied sigh. "Thank you, Violet." She took a long swig of her ale, draining the glass. "Do you want another ale?"

"I already asked the barkeep to bring us another round," Violet replied. "Let's just, I don't know, just talk, until we have to get back on the ship. After we leave tomorrow, it's going to get pretty busy for a few weeks."

"What do you want to talk about?" Alice watched the foam drip down inside her empty cup slowly, sliding along the frosted glass before coming to a rest in the bottom.

"Anything."

Alice paused for a moment. "Anything?"

"Whatever it is, Alice, just say it," Violet encouraged. She obviously wanted to straighten things out between them.

"Okay, who was that woman you were with in here last week?"

Violet tilted her head. "You saw me with her, while you were waiting for Barnaby, didn't you?"

Alice nodded. "Yes. Tall, graceful, incredibly attractive..."

"You're not...*jealous*, are you?" Violet teased.

"I might be. Who was she?"

Violet ran a finger around the rim of her empty glass. "An old friend."

"That's all I get? 'An old friend?' That's not very reassuring," Alice said grumpily. The more evasive Violet acted about this woman, the more she suspected she had been right about her being another one of Violet's lovers. Just how many 'old friends' did Violet have?

"An old friend, yes."

"The kind of old friend that you— you know what, never mind." Alice tried to smooth a stray hair back into place. She huffed into her empty glass and craned her head around, willing the barkeep to show up with their pints and break the tension of this awkward conversation. She wished now she'd never brought it up in the first place.

"I assume you also saw that I left alone, no?"

"Barnaby saw, I didn't. Though he and I aren't exactly on speaking terms at the moment."

"Ned mentioned that you told Barnaby to wire half his fee into your account. Did he?" Violet seemed eager to change the subject away from the mysterious woman.

Alice examined the bottom of her glass and tried to push the idea of Violet and the woman from her mind. "Yes, he did. But it doesn't change the fact that he sold me out."

"Well it worked out, didn't it?" Violet mused. "You joined us in the end, anyway."

"That's not the point!" Alice huffed. "He didn't know that you would stick to your word, you're a *pirate*."

"And so are you, now."

Alice paused for a moment to consider what Violet said. "I guess so, but still. He was supposed to be my friend." She paused as the barkeep set down two new pints of ale, and removed the empty glasses. She noticed she had a book tucked into the pocket of her apron, the pages dog-eared and worn. "He didn't know that the crew would be so nice, or that you would be so alluring and attractive." She took a deep drink of her ale.

Violet raised an eyebrow. "And I didn't realize the mechanic we were abducting was quite so..."

"Quite so what?" Alice prompted.

"Well, you know." The captain took a long drink of her ale, and Alice could tell she was trying to buy time.

"Quite so what?" Alice repeated.

Violet set her glass down and leaned across the table. "Well, let's just say, I'll be a little disappointed when that sling comes off and you aren't walking around in a black tank top any more," she said huskily.

The mechanic leaned forward and rested her chin in her hand on the table. "I think we could probably work something out."

Violet reached across the table and traced a scar on Alice's arm. "Are you ready?"

"For tomorrow? I guess, I don't really know what the plan is." Alice felt shivers travel up her arm where Violet's hand was resting.

"Are you ready to go, I mean."

"Oh – uh, yes." Alice drained her glass and stood up. "I'm ready."

They left the Purple Pig and ambled slowly back towards the ship, as the sun dipped over the mountains on the horizon. The sky blazed fuchsia and gold, and the air was heavy with humidity, produced as a bi-product of the enormous steam-powered machines that kept the atmosphere breathable. There were no birds here, and not on many of the outer planets or their moons. The ecosystems weren't stable enough for their delicate physiology, not yet.

Lost in the beauty of the moment, Alice reached across and touched Violet's arm as they walked, just for a moment.

"You know," Violet said, "it's the mirrors that mimic day and night here. In actuality, this settlement gets 42 years of summer. In a few years' time, the poles will be reversed, and it will be 42 years of winter, and the sun won't rise, and they use artificial light instead, generated by thousands of light-bulbs strung across the city."

"I never thought I would see sun that never sets." She paused. "Well, it does, just not very often. Every 84 years."

"I think I'd like to see the sun set here," the captain pondered. "Even if I never see it rise again, it would be worth it."

"Maybe we could see it together," Alice replied hopefully. "Assuming you haven't found yourself a replacement mechanic by then," she continued with a smirk.

Violet poked her playfully. "Somehow I doubt I'd be able to replace the best mechanic in the Coalition on a whim," she said as she looked into the distance. "Come on, I want to show you something."

Alice followed her down an alley that was hidden from the main road, and bathed in the golden light of a perpetually sunny afternoon. "Where are we going?" she asked.

"Just keep following me," Violet said over her shoulder as she turned down another hidden alley, where the walls were completely covered in bright red ivy. "I promise it's worth the walk," she called to Alice as she climbed over a stack of abandoned produce crates, probably abandoned by a trader months ago.

Alice gasped when they arrived at their destination: a small, impeccably kept garden, surrounded by brick buildings that reached high into the sky. It was lined with white terraced fencing, covered with juicy purple grapes hanging from the vines. In the center of the garden was a small fountain of deep red terracotta pots, allowing water to calmly cascade from one to the other, back into the base of the pond with satisfying, continuous splashes.

At the far end of the garden, there were tall, thick bushes covering a wide secondary entrance that was lined with cypress trees, two rows deep. You could see the tops of the trees emerge past the brick buildings and wind their way down towards the dock.

"Why is this here?" Alice asked with awe.

"Just a little hidden treasure, for those who know where to find it." Violet picked a grape from the white fence and popped it into her mouth, smiling at the mechanic. She then led her to a large cherry tree in the nearest corner of the garden, lush with pink blooms that scattered petals onto the grass below it. They sat next to each other on a large tree stump under the branches, and Violet snaked her arm around Alice's waist.

"Alice," she said quietly.

"Mm?" Alice replied, turning her head to face Violet.

Violet reached up behind Alice's head and intertwined her fingers into Alice's braids. She gently pulled her forward, and kissed her softly.

Alice placed her hand on the small of Violet's back and pulled her in closer. "Kiss me again," she whispered.

The captain obliged, and Alice felt like she was losing herself to a fantasy, to wishes for more kisses, more intimate dinners, and more whispered words across all the vast space in the Near Systems.

"Oh, Alice," Violet sighed. "What are you doing to me?"

"Whatever it is, I don't want to stop," Alice murmured, lost in the moment. She kissed the captain again, longer and deeper than before. She thought about other women she had kissed in her life, but none of them measured up to Violet. She found herself wondering how she measured up to the other women Violet had ever kissed, and she pulled away.

"What's wrong?" Violet asked.

"Nothing, I—" Alice saw something out of the corner of her eye, at the far entrance of the garden. Bushes rustled softly, and she squinted at the distant foliage. "Uh, Violet, I think someone else is here."

Violet scooted away from Alice and smoothed her curls back behind her ears. "Well, it's not that unlikely that someone else would be here," she said, clearing her throat.

"Who do you think it is?" Alice asked, wiggling her eyebrows.

"I don't know everyone who comes to Bradach, Alice, I'm just—" Violet jerked her head back in surprise. "*Ned?*"

Alice burst out laughing. "You're teasing me, Violet, no way is that..." she paused and stood up, shading her eyes from the light with her hand. "Violet, you're not going to believe this."

"Believe what?" Violet asked as she stood on top of the tree trunk and tried to see.

"It's Ned and Barnaby."

They watched as the pair emerged from the bushes laughing, and were about to approach when they saw Ned wrap Barnaby in an embrace and kiss him.

"Whoa," Alice breathed.

"You got that right," Violet whispered. "Let's get out of here before they see us too and it gets awkward."

Alice nodded, and the two crept towards the entrance.

"Alice?" came a voice from across the garden. "Alice, is that you? It's me, it's Barnaby! Please talk to me!" He rushed across the garden with Ned close behind, limping with his cane.

"Oh, gods," Alice muttered as she reluctantly turned around. "Uh, hi, Barns. Enjoying the, uh, weather?"

"Alice, I just wanted to talk to you. I didn't think I'd see you here."

"Just getting some fresh air before we leave tomorrow."

"Captain?" Ned asked with a laugh. Violet had been trying to hide behind Alice and look nonchalant. "What are you – oh."

"Nothing happened!" Violet said nervously. "We were just walking back after having dinner!"

Ned shrugged. "I won't say anything if you don't. None of my business anyway."

Violet looked relieved and quickly added, "Yes, thank you, I mean good, uh, because nothing happened anyway."

"We'll talk later, Barnaby," Alice interjected.

"Alice, should we...?" Violet hinted, nodding towards the entrance.

"Alice, Wait!" Barnaby shouted anxiously. "I just wanted to talk, and —"

Ned cleared his throat loudly. "Boss, I had something I wanted to speak to you about. On the bridge. On the ship."

Violet furrowed her brow at him. "Surely that can wait, I don't want to —"

"It's urgent," he said, staring at Violet like he was trying to communicate telepathically.

Violet sighed and looked at Alice, who was boring holes into Barnaby with her angry stare. "Alice, maybe we can— "

"It's fine," Alice said through gritted teeth. "We'll meet you back on the ship."

Violet and Ned backed out of the garden and hurried down the nearby alley, their boots echoing faintly on the cobblestones.

"So," Barnaby began. "Are you and her an item?"

"I don't want to talk about it." Alice kicked at a small stone and watched it bounce across the lush, thick grass.

"No, I mean, it's good, good for you, and—"

"I definitely don't want to talk about it with you," Alice spat. "I'm still angry at you, Barnaby. You fucking sold me out. What kind of person does that?"

"I told you, I was desperate, and —"

"That's no excuse!" she shouted, her anger boiling over. "Even at my lowest, it never would have occurred to me to sell you for a few credits just to save my own ass. You were my *friend*."

He shuffled his feet on the soft, mossy grass. "I learned my lesson." He stared at his polished shoes, which had become encrusted with mud.

"I doubt that." Alice sighed angrily."And what the hell are you doing with Ned, anyway? He's a nice person, and a good friend, *unlike you*. Don't be messing around with him, he deserves better."

"Alice, come on, just talk to me. I sent the money, just like you said," he pleaded.

"I know," Alice huffed. "Barnaby, I just don't think I want to talk to you right now. And I definitely can't be friends with you again, not after what you've done." She could feel a headache coming on, and rubbed her temple.

"You're all I've got left," Barnaby said quietly.

"Apparently not. Maybe you should have thought about that before selling me off," Alice snarked, looking in the direction that Violet and Ned had left in. "You always knew how to manipulate people."

"Alice, I'm sorry. Truly, genuinely, supremely sorry. If anything had happened to you, I don't know what I would have done with myself."

"Found yourself a new lackey?"

"Fuck's sake woman, I'm trying to apologize, and you know how rare that is for me." He took a hesitant step towards her, his hands held up in defeat.

Alice sighed. "Barnaby..."

"Come on, I said I'm sorry. And I am! I am very sorry. I'll do whatever you want, to make it up to you."

"Stay away from Ned," she said with a steely glare. "If you're going to be on the Cricket with us, it's not appropriate."

"Anything, except that. He's different, Alice."

"Yeah, he's actually a decent human being," she retorted. After a moment, she continued, "Is it really different with him? Be honest, because he's nothing like your usual conquests."

"It really, really is." Barnaby furrowed his brow and added, "Just don't tell him I said that."

Alice narrowed her eyes at Barnaby, trying to decide if she should ever forgive him. She sighed and rolled her eyes, saying, "Come on, *Françoise*. We have a pirate ship to catch."

CHAPTER SIXTEEN

VIOLET WOKE WITH A start, drenched in a cold sweat. She had been dreaming about Captain Leo again; dark, visceral nightmares that terrified her even while awake. She sat up in bed and hugged her knees as she cried softly, trying to muffle any sound of her distressed sobs. She had a tough couple of weeks after the incident with Captain Leo and his crew, with nightmares at night and anxiety during the day.

Still, she thought she had left that all behind – after all, he was dead, and his crew wouldn't be bothering them anytime soon, if ever. She was certain she'd scared the new Captain Josie off for good. And still, the nightmares persisted.

She wiped away the tears with a trembling hand. "I just need some more sleep," she whispered to herself reassuringly. It was the middle of the night, so she didn't want to wake up Hyun, but she needed something to help her sleep. Violet groggily stood up and dressed herself in the previous day's clothes, pulling on her boots and tucking the laces into the top, instead of lacing them up properly.

The captain made her way through the ship, and the lack of sleep coupled with the persistent nightmares made every shadow seem like a threat. She shook her head to try and clear her thoughts as she opened the door to the dark, empty med bay. Violet rifled through the cabinets, looking for something that would help her sleep and get back to work in the morning. She had pilfered some sedatives from the med bay in the weeks following the incident, usually at night under cover of darkness. While it was true that she didn't want to wake Hyun, it was also true that she didn't want her crew to see any weakness in her.

"Captain?"

Violet spun around, a bottle of pills in her hand. "Oh, Hyun, I...what are you doing awake?"

Hyun shrugged off a bright pink, sequined tuxedo jacket and tossed it on the back of a chair. "I just finished my last tournament game."

"Did you win?"

"Of course."

"I don't know why they even let you compete any more," Violet laughed nervously, desperate to distract Hyun from the subject of sedatives being pilfered in the middle of the night.

"They sure as hell *wish* I wasn't allowed to compete," Hyun snorted. She sat down and crossed her legs over the arms of the chair casually. "Did you need something, Captain?"

"Oh, I just needed something to help me sleep."

"The sedatives you've been nicking under cover of darkness, when you think I won't notice, are in that cupboard over there," she said, nodding at a set of cabinets on the far wall. "I moved them when I realized someone was stealing them."

"Stealing!" Violet said incredulously. "I just needed something to get some rest!" She opened the cabinet and took the bottle of sedatives out, slamming the cupboard door shut. How dare Hyun accuse her of stealing from her own goddamn med bay?

"You know, Captain, sometimes when someone with no history of insomnia is suddenly struggling to sleep, there's something else going on. Are you okay?" Hyun asked gently. She began to unpin her complicated, coiled braid of dark hair, and toss each pin onto the counter, where they landed in a neat pile.

Violet put the bottle on the counter beneath the cabinet. "Of course, of course."

"What happened last month would rattle anyone, it's understandable that you're experiencing some trauma." Hyun shook her long dark hair loose and tousled it before letting it settle over her shoulder.

"I'm not rattled," Violet said defensively. She turned to look at her medical technician, someone she trusted her own life and the lives of her crew with. Hyun was absolutely indispensable on her crew, but sometimes her intuition was almost annoying.

Hyun rested her elbows on the arms of the chair and clasped her hands. "I'm not a doctor, but I still practice patient confidentiality. Whatever you tell me stays with me. I'm like a steel vault, buried under six feet of concrete." She nudged the door closed with her foot, and kicked off a pair of bright pink patent leather combat boots.

"Hyun," Violet began.

"It's alright," the medic encouraged. "Just sit down in that chair there, and tell me what's been going on."

Violet sat down gingerly and relaxed into the chair. "I don't know, it's just these nightmares. Always Captain Leo or his crew, just seeing his dead eyes over and over again."

"And during the day?"

"I almost lost it during the last battle," Violet said as she started to cry. "My hands were shaking, I couldn't breathe."

"Sounds like some pretty intense anxiety." Hyun sat relaxed in the over-stuffed chair, her legs flung over the sides. She blinked her soft, brown eyes at Violet and stayed silent, to encourage the captain to continue.

"It's not anxiety, it's—"

"Anxiety," Hyun interrupted, "and it's trauma induced." She leaned forward in her chair and looked at Violet across the room. "Captain, it's not unusual for people to experience events that affect them on an intense, visceral level. We all cope in different ways, but I really think you need to talk about it more."

Violet shook her head in defiance. She knew she couldn't speak, or her voice would break from crying.

"Or you could write about it maybe?"

The captain shook her head again, exerting all her effort to not fall apart in front of Hyun.

Hyun sighed. "I can give you some sedatives tonight, but stop nicking them from my med storage. It's difficult to keep track of what I have when things go missing." She didn't get up from her chair or open the door yet, she just sat and waited for Violet to choose.

"I've never killed anyone before," Violet sobbed as she buried her face in her hands. "Kady says we had no choice, that he would have killed us all and it wasn't a bluff, but...but maybe if I had tried something else, come up with a better plan, then maybe—"

"If that's what Kady says, then I would believe her," Hyun said gently. "You did what you had to for this crew, and to save Ned. Another few moments and I'm not sure I would have been able to bring him back from that induced coma."

"I know, I know, but I just keep thinking, what if? What if we had out-smarted them, what if I had scared them off, what if something *had* happened to Ned, more than just a cane and a limp?"

"Ned is alive because of you," Hyun reassured her, "and in case you haven't noticed, I think he likes the cane. He thinks it makes him look tough."

Violet laughed through her sobs. "Of course he would, vain fool."

"And our systems have been upgraded, with the help of Alice and Kady. No one will be able to sneak up on us again."

"I know it's irrational, I just can't shake the feeling that it will be worse next time."

"That's the anxiety talking," Hyun said. "I can give you some exercises to help ground you when the anxiety gets too loud. It's hard work, but worth it."

"Can't you just give me the sedatives instead?"

"Sedatives aren't a fix for trauma. They work short term, to help you get rest, but in the long term they aren't doing you any favors, Captain. It's tough but sometimes we have to face our demons if we want them to go away."

"What are your demons?" Violet asked.

Hyun paused for a moment and smoothed out her black dress as she uncrossed her legs. "I have a terrible fear of flying."

Violet stifled a laugh. "That can't be true, you're part of a crew on a ship!"

"My best friend died in a collision when I was young. I was terrified for weeks, I would wake up in the middle of the night screaming, having dreamt that I was on a ship alone, and it was plummeting into Earth."

"Oh gods, Hyun, I'm sorry."

"It was a long time ago." Hyun looked out towards the window and sighed. "And yet, sometimes it feels like it was just yesterday. I miss her."

"Wait, but those battles must have petrified you! How did you manage?"

"If I didn't have people to take care of, I probably would have been hiding inside that cupboard," she said, gesturing to the cabinets that lined the wall. "It's one of the reasons medical science captured my interest, if I have someone else to look out for, I can't focus on my own anxiety in situations like that."

"Wow, I...I didn't know."

"You aren't weak for experiencing trauma, or anxiety, or anything else. Your strength lies in how much you care for this crew, and in how you pick up and keep moving. Your strength shows with every decision you make, and that's why this crew follows you. It's why we love you."

Tears fell silently down Violet's face as she took in everything that Hyun said. "Thank you," she said, pushing herself out of the chair and standing in the middle of the room.

"Now, let's talk about how we can work through this," Hyun encouraged.

Violet threw her arms around Hyun and hugged her, tears flowing freely down her face.

· · · ·

"ALRIGHT, EVERYBODY, let's talk plans," Kady said loudly to get the crew's attention. "The captain has tasked me with telling you all what's what, and I have to say I was more than happy to accept the job." Quiet titters of laugher sprouted around the room, and Kady grinned. "As you all know, the repairs have all been completed, and it's a job well done by everyone," she announced, clapping. "And as you all also know, it's time to get on with our jobs, and that means we're planning a raid on a merchant vessel. Thanks to Barnaby here," she continued with a grimace, "we know where it's going to be, and when. He's been our inside contact for some time now, and even though he's been ousted from the Coalition, he still has information." She coughed and muttered, "Or so he says."

"We should reach the ambush point a few hours after we depart Bradach, and if everything goes to plan, which it will, we'll reach the first drop zone in a couple of days. As usual, you're all free to spend your spoils and your time as you like, as soon as the supplies have been delivered."

"What about the ship's radar systems? Will other ships be able to sneak up on us again?" Ivy asked from the back of the room, where she was leaning against the back of a chair.

"Our systems have all been upgraded, thanks to... Alice...and myself. We now have secondary measures in place to prevent any cloaking devices or programs from disabling our radar."

"Oh, neat," Ivy said, scribbling notes in a tattered old notebook.

"We'll have three drops from this raid's resources, one on Delta-4, and two on a moon off of Epsilon-5, but on opposite ends. We'll be delivering food and medical supplies that we will be liberating from the Coalition merchant vessel later today. The raid will be executed as normal."

"For those of us who are, um, *new* here, what exactly constitutes normal?" Alice asked.

"Surely you saw what that looked like from the other side, no?" Kady replied sarcastically. Violet poked her head into the mess hall and raised an eyebrow at Kady, who scowled before continuing, "Ah, that is to say, we will ambush the ship, disable their systems, board the ship to collect whatever we need, using the murder bots to keep them in check. Then we'll pack up and be on our way."

Alice nodded, her brow furrowed.

"Is there a problem, Mechanic?" Kady asked suspiciously.

"No," Alice replied, "I was just wondering if it might be more effective to disable their navigation, too. It would take them some time to boot it back up, and give us a greater chance of escape without any tail."

Kady raised an eyebrow and nodded. "Yes, that would work," she said with grudging respect.

"When we board, I'll need to access their main console. If I could just get some cover while I work, it should only take about..." Alice calculated in her head, looking at the ceiling, "about ninety seconds. A couple minutes max if they have anti-tampering measures installed onto the wiring."

"How the hell do you expect to get around anti-tampering measures that quickly?" Violet asked from the back of the room. "Some of the most accomplished engineers and coders can't do it in an hour, much less a few seconds."

Alice turned her head to face Violet, and grinned. "I invented the anti-tampering measures for Coalition vessels. If you know just the right spot to pry open, there's a weakness in the cable that allows for manipulation."

"Well you heard her," Kady said, gesturing at a tall, broad shouldered young man in the corner of the room. "Jasper, you'll stick with Alice and cover her while she disables the navigation."

"Are you going to tell them about our latest achievement? Or rather, your latest achievement?" Ned asked loudly.

Kady cleared her throat and raised her arms, gesturing for quiet. "I've been working on deconstructing the algorithms responsible for Captain Leo's radar invisibility, and I think I've figured out how to make it work for us. It would make us virtually undetectable until we were ready to board the vessel."

"Have you tested this new technology?" Violet asked. "It seems risky to depend solely on untested programming."

"No, but we'll have an opportunity to test it this afternoon, when we raid the trade vessel," Kady replied defensively. "And we won't be using that as our sole means of defense; we'll use all the usual measures as well."

"Then how will you know if it worked?" Violet challenged. "I'm not comfortable risking the crew of this ship, no matter how advantageous the technology we may acquire."

"If Alice can disable the navigation in the main console, it would be easy enough for her to grab their historical radar data as well," Kady shot back, and then looked at Alice for confirmation.

Alice nodded. "I can do that."

Violet looked back and forth between Kady and Alice. "I trust you, Kady," she said firmly. "I may not be convinced – yet – but I know that you won't take any unnecessary risks where this is concerned. In fact, I'm quite interested to see the outcome. Being invisible to our enemies, well, that would be a game changer for us."

The rest of the crew murmured their approval. When it became clear that neither Kady nor the captain had anything else to say, they began to break off into small groups and disperse, clearing the hall as they chattered animatedly down the halls.

"Oi, Alice," Ned said as he leaned back in his chair. "You ready for this? First big raid, eh?"

Alice feigned insult with an exaggerated gasp. "You mean we're going to *raid* a *ship*? I didn't know that's what pirates did, I thought we would just hang around and drink ale!"

Ned slapped his knee and roared with laughter. "Alright, alright, I just wanted to check in. You feeling okay about it all?"

"As long as no one busts me while I break into that comms panel, I'll be just fine. If Kady can verify that this new technology works, it could be really amazing, don't you think?"

"Aye, it would be a help." He studied Alice's face for a moment. "So what was going on in that garden yesterday afternoon?"

"I could ask you the same thing," she retorted. "And I wasn't the one tripping out of the bushes, so I'm not sure you're in any place to be asking questions there, my friend."

He raised an eyebrow and sat back in his seat. "Alright, okay. I just like to know what's going on around the ship."

"You're nosey and a shameless gossip, Ned," Alice said as she rolled her eyes. "You keep my secret—er, not that I really have one, and I'll keep yours. No doubt Kady would be *thrilled* about the idea of you cavorting with a Coalition spy."

"Don't you have some boilers to fix or something?" he asked playfully. "Get out of here, before I tell the captain you're slacking on the job."

Alice jumped up from her seat and spun around. "Oh no, anything but that!" she shouted sarcastically, and laughed. "I suppose there's no harm in one more check before we arrive. I can teach Ivy some of the inspection protocols anyway."

Ned nodded, his friendly, bright blue eyes crinkled with a smile. "See you at the ambush site, soldier."

She gave a mock salute, spun on the heel of her boot, and mock marched out of the mess hall and into the corridor. Once she was out of sight, her gait returned to normal, and she headed for the boiler. Ivy had been such a keen and attentive student that she expected to find her there, studying the manuals and practicing the disassembly and reassembly of the small engine Alice had given her.

Alice hadn't been here very long yet, but it already felt like home, more than the C.S. Stronghold ever had. She was respected here, the head mechanic with a promising apprentice and control over all the repairs and service schedules. She already had more friends here than she had when working for the Coalition: Ned and Hyun both went out of their way to include her and make her feel welcome, and Violet – well, she was still trying to figure out what that was all about.

She also knew that she wasn't ready to forgive Barnaby, not yet, not after what he had done. He had betrayed her trust, and potentially put her life in danger. Then again, his rash, selfish decisions are also what had led her here, so could she really stay angry at him forever?

Upon reaching the steps down to the boiler room, she called down, "Ivy, are you down there? I wanted to talk about some inspection protoco—" Alice reached the last step and discovered Violet leaning against a workbench, with no Ivy in sight.

"Oh, uh Violet, er, Captain," she mumbled. "What can I do for you?"

"I just wanted to stop by your office and see how you're feeling about the raid."

"Why is everyone asking me that today?" Alice asked, with a touch more defensiveness than she had intended.

"Because you're green, and green pirates get their crew mates killed if they aren't ready," Violet said with a stoic tone. "I think you're going to be just fine, but I need to hear it from you for me to really believe it."

"I'm fine," Alice said flatly.

Violet scanned Alice's face for any trace of doubt. "I was just going to have you stay on the ship this time, you know. Take care of the boilers and the engines, wait for us to get back and debrief you."

"What, because I'm too 'green' to take care of myself?" Alice scoffed, adjusting her sling. "I did manage to disable an entire Coalition vessel, steal a shuttlecraft, and land it on a requisitioned ship just a couple of weeks ago, in case you've forgotten."

"Alice, I just—"

"And, *and*, I supervised the repairs of this entire ship. From the boilers all the way down to the goddamned lightbulbs. But I guess I'm too *green* to be trusted on a mission with my crewmates, right?" Alice kicked a screw that was near her boot and it flew into the wall with a small metallic clink.

"Alice!"

"What!"

"Just *calm down*, I just wanted to make sure you're okay with it. This should be an easy job, but anything can go wrong, and you have to be prepared for that. I can't have you losing your cool during a raid and endangering someone else's life. I know you're smart, and strong, and capable. I just need to know that you can also keep it together; you were in the Coalition for decades, I can't imagine turning pirate is an easy transition."

Alice looked sideways at Violet and stepped towards the workbench. She rested her arm next to Violet and moved in close. "You might be surprised, Captain."

Violet ducked under Alice's arm and stepped away. "Not here."

"Why? You're the captain, you can do what you like."

"I have to maintain the respect of my crew, Alice."

"Oh, and I guess being seen with an ex-Coalition mechanic would make you look bad, would it?" Alice said with a barbed tone. "How very presumptuous of me." She turned and hauled herself up with one arm to sit on top of the workbench. "You didn't seem to have any problems with it the first night we had dinner after I came back."

Violet blushed. "No one was here, they all had shore leave!" she said defensively. "And keep your voice down. I think Ned already knows, after seeing us yesterday."

"Gods forbid," Alice said with an eye roll, "I'd hate for him to think that we were *together*."

"Alice, we're...we're not *together*. Not like that."

The mechanic turned her head away. "Okay."

"I just mean, it's complicated, and—"

"I have a lot to get finished, Captain," Alice interrupted. She wasn't in the mood for playing games with Violet about what they were or weren't to each other.

Without a word of protest, Violet silently backed out of the room. As her footsteps faded, Alice wiped an angry tear from her cheek.

• • • •

"HEY ALICE, YOU ALMOST done?" Alice's bodyguard yelled from the doorway. He was a tall, broad man with wide shoulders and a chiseled chest: just the kind of person you'd want watching your back. He wore jodhpurs like Violet's, only they were black and tucked into matching huge black boots that were covered in straps and buckles. He wore suspenders over a faded, pale blue shirt that was unbuttoned to his sternum, and carried one of the large heat guns that were used for industrial welding on ships.

"Just...one more...second..." she replied as she dug into a cable with a large pair of pliers.

"We've got Coalition crew headed this way, won't be long before they hear us," Jasper said uneasily.

She yanked on the cable and pried out a tiny black box that was attached to the console by several wires. "I just have to download the data," she said calmly as she plugged a small chip that Kady had given her into the box. It made an angry beep and flashed red. "Got it, let's go!" she shouted as she hauled herself to her feet with her good arm. She stashed the pliers in her tool belt and took out her enormous wrench as her weapon of choice in case they got cornered. She hoped she didn't have to use it.

"Let's head back to the ship then, the cargo crew is almost finished. Kady has the main crew hostage with the droids, but there's a few rogues hiding, and I don't want to have to bust any heads today."

Alice looked at her wrench apprehensively. "Me, neither," she replied.

They moved swiftly and quietly through the ship, tip toeing around corners to avoid any Coalition crew members who had avoided Kady's bots. They turned down the final corridor, and could see Violet beckoning them onto the ship, parked in the loading bay of this enormous trade vessel.

"Home free," Jasper said with a handsome grin and his deep, butterscotch smooth voice.

Suddenly, a Coalition military officer leapt in front of them from around a corner, blocking their exit. "You're not going anywhere, pirate scum," he spat. "You and the rest of your crew are about to be arrested and taken to work camps."

Jasper held up his heat gun and shrugged at the officer. "I think, actually, you're going to let us get back on our ship, and then we can all get on with our day."

"What makes you think you can steal from the Coalition and get away with it? I'll have you arrested!" He straightened his shoulders. "I'll kill you myself!"

"That's a bit harsh, doncha think?" Jasper asked with a gleam in his eye. "Listen, officer, we've never once been caught, and we aren't starting today."

Alice lifted her wrench above her head with one arm, in a way she hoped looked menacing. "Yeah," she added.

Violet was waving them back to the ship, but she couldn't see the Coalition officer in front of them. Alice watched as the last of the cargo crew hauled huge crates up the ramp and onto the Cricket. If they didn't leave soon, any SOS call that the Coalition ship had sent before Alice disabled their navigation would be received and acted upon by any other nearby vessels.

"Come on, man, just step out of the way and pretend we incapacitated you. We won't tell your superiors, and no one else on this ship is going to admit to what happened here, either. Tell your accountant to make an error in the ledger, or lie about produce spoilage due to a broken cooling coil. You don't want to admit you were had by *pirates*, now do you?" Jasper said convincingly.

"After all, that would be an automatic demotion, wouldn't it?" Alice added, her arm starting to tire from holding the huge wrench aloft. "Why let your entire Coalition military career go to waste, just for a few measly crates of food and scrap metal?"

The officer hesitated and looked at Jasper, and then at Alice. "Did anyone else confront your crew?"

Jasper grinned. "No, sir."

"I just don't know how you caught us by surprise, as if out of nowhere," the officer muttered. He cleared his throat and continued, "Would you at least do me the favor of pretending you incapacitated me?" He looked at Alice's wrench suspiciously. "And please don't hit me in the face."

Alice smiled. "Of course I'm not going to hit you in the face," she chirped. "Jasper, tie him up and lock him in the custodial cupboard across the hall."

Jasper deftly hog tied the man with complicated knots and stowed him in the cupboard, locking it from the outside with a lock pick he pulled from his pocket and wedging a nearby crate in front of it.

"Well done, partner," Alice laughed as she holstered her wrench and slapped Jasper on the back. "Now let's get the hell out of here."

They sprinted to the ship and up the ramp, and the Cricket sped away at full speed, the cargo hold bursting at the seams with produce, canned goods, ammunition, weapons, and scrap metal.

Alice stood in the loading bay amongst overflowing crates and bent to catch her breath. "That...was...great," she declared with labored breaths. "I wonder if that officer realizes how much we took." She took a long, deep breath and stood up straight.

"Well if he doesn't now, he will in the morning when someone pulls him out of that closet," Kady said as she strode into view. "Nice work on disabling their navigation, Alice. Did you get their data?"

Alice tossed the small chip to Kady nonchalantly. "Of course."

Kady caught the chip effortlessly and nodded, "Thank you. I'll know by dinnertime later if that cloaking shield worked."

As she turned to leave, Alice interjected, "Kady, that officer mumbled something about how they had no idea we were coming. Obviously you'll want to check the data, but I think you did it."

Kady gave her an awkward half smile, half sneer as if she didn't know what to do with her face, before swiftly turning and leaving the room.

"Jasper, nice job with those knots," Alice nodded approvingly.

"I grew up in Scouts," he said proudly. "Learned every knot there is."

"I didn't realize the Scouts were still around."

"Of *course* the Scouts are still around," Jasper replied in disbelief. "*Who wouldn't want to be in the Scouts?*" he muttered as he walked away, waving at Alice over his shoulder and setting his heat gun on a crate near the loading bay air lock.

Alice sat on a sealed crate heavily and sighed contentedly, unhooking her tool belt with her good arm and setting it on the ground beside her boots. Maybe she had a knack for this piracy thing after all.

"You handled that well," came Violet's voice from behind a crate.

Alice jumped. "I didn't realize you were still in here," she mumbled grumpily, recalling their earlier conversation. How dare Violet think she wasn't capable, after all she'd done to come back here? And she hadn't liked how dismissive Violet had been about their...well, whatever it was.

"That raid will last us the next few supply drops, as well as being significantly profitable," Violet offered. "Not only did we grab fresh produce, but we also nabbed a great deal of other supplies, too." She took a step towards Alice. "I heard Ned is planning some amazing culinary delight with some of the spoils."

"Don't come too close, Captain," Alice said, her tone dripping with acid. "You wouldn't want the rest of the crew to think that you're associating with the lowly mechanic."

"Alice, come on, let me explain!"

"You don't have to explain. I understand everything perfectly clear: I'm a mechanic on this ship. A well paid one, to be sure, but that's all I am to you. Just the mechanic." She leaned forward and hopped off the crate. "I didn't come back just for you, you know," she said as she stomped towards the airlock door, "I came back because I liked everyone else on the ship, too. I don't expect anything from you."

"Alice, wait!" Violet called to her.

But it was too late. Alice was gone through the airlock, leaving Violet alone in the loading bay.

• • • •

"HOW IS YOUR SHOULDER feeling?" Hyun asked as she unfastened Alice's sling.

"Okay, I guess? It doesn't feel as tender or swollen any more."

Hyun gently prodded Alice's shoulder. The bruising was completely healed now, and her skin had returned to it's usual pale shade. "You're right, the swelling is gone." She took Alice's wrist and slowly stretched her arm out until it was fully extended. "How is that?"

"Fine, fine. It doesn't hurt or anything."

"Good. And this?" Hyun rotated Alice's arm, holding her elbow.

"No pain. Feels a little bit strange, though."

"That's to be expected, your muscles will have slightly atrophied. I'll help you with some physical therapy over the coming weeks to get you back to one hundred percent with that arm. For now, you're good to turn in your sling."

"Oh, gladly," Alice laughed. "It's hard repairing things with only one arm." She flexed her bicep weakly and wiggled her wrist and fingers. Ah, freedom! "Any big tournaments coming up?" Alice was fascinated by Hyun's career as a professional card player, and was keen to know more.

Hyun sat on a wooden stool and put her pink combat boots up on a box of files. "There's one at our next drop zone in a couple of days. The winner's sum isn't very much, but I'll still go to protect my reputation. Plus my family lives nearby, and my mother likes to watch me play."

"That's really sweet," Alice said as she shrugged on her boiler suit and zipped it up over her black tank top. "Are you close with your family?"

"My father died when I was young. Starvation. But my mother and I are very close, yes."

"Oh, gods, I'm sorry, Hyun." Alice looked at the floor, unable to meet Hyun's gaze.

Hyun shrugged. "I was very young, I don't remember him much. I only remember how sad my mother was, for a long time."

"I don't remember my parents, either. I was sent to live with some distant family on a farm, far away from the fighting in the first rebellion. I don't know anything about them at all, really." Alice thought of the yellowed map that Violet had given her, now stashed safely away inside a drawer in her quarters. "Any siblings?" she asked after a moment.

"Nope, it was always just me. My mother was young when she married my father." Hyun leaned over and opened a drawer, pulling out a small burlap sack. "Want some candy?" she asked, gesturing with the bag towards Alice. "It's like a honeycomb, I don't know really. I won it from Ned in a bet, so it must be good."

Alice hopped off the table and plunged her hand into the bag. "I'll never turn down something sweet," she said as she stuffed a piece into her mouth. "Oh my gods this is delicious," she added, chewing slowly.

"You should arrange a bet with Ned too," Hyun giggled. "He always loses. I highly recommend it." She set the bag on the counter and pointed at Alice's shoulder. "Come see me if you have any pain or swelling. It's looking good, but you'll need to do some gentle motions to get back to full strength."

"I will."

"And don't slouch," Hyun scolded gently, "it lengthens healing time."

Alice pulled her shoulders back and stood straight. "I will probably forget that."

Hyun winked. "Don't worry, I'll remind you. Now get going, I hear we're not too far from the drop site."

"I'll see you around, I guess?" Alice asked hopefully. She still hadn't fixed things with Violet, not really, and sometimes she felt a little lonely with everyone being so busy with their jobs on the Cricket. She had been avoiding Barnaby, and while Ivy was great company, she was still just a kid, no older than eighteen.

"If you're not doing anything later, I'm making Ned go to my favorite food stand with me. They have the best bibimbap you'll ever taste."

"I'd love to!" Alice replied cheerfully. "I'll see you later, then."

Hyun waved her off, before turning her attention back to her honeycomb candy that she won from Ned and stuffing another piece in her mouth.

CHAPTER SEVENTEEN

"OKAY, PEOPLE," VIOLET announced, "we'll be landing in a few minutes; Kady is piloting the landing today. We have a lot of crates to transport, with most of them going to the city outskirts. Our contacts will be meeting us at the dock with transport. The rest of the crates need to be taken to the traders in the city center to sell." Violet nodded at Ned. "You'll have your usual team to take crates to sell, and I'm also sending Barnaby with you this time to help broker a more favorable deal."

"Hyun, you're with Kady and her team today, since these are your old stomping grounds. Alice?" Violet looked around and spotted the mechanic near the airlock.

"Yes."

"Alice, I want you to go with them too, to replace me. I have an important meeting, so I won't be joining the rest of the team."

"Sure thing," Alice replied coldly. A meeting with who, she wondered? Probably that attractive woman from the tavern. Or another woman, maybe. She huffed quietly to herself.

The ship began to shudder and gently shake as they crossed through Delta-4's manufactured atmosphere. It wasn't quite identical to Gamma-3's, but it was close, and it was inhabited by hundreds of small colonies and two large cities on opposite sides of the planet.

Violet's radio buzzed softly. "Preparing to land, Captain," came Kady's voice.

The ship set down smoothly on the surface, and the crew sprang into action like a well-oiled machine. Ned's team set to work compiling the crates that needed to be sold at the market, while Hyun jogged down the ramp to talk to someone at the port who was waiting with a small team of people, each waiting to load crates onto a nearby train. Alice watched as Hyun chatted animatedly and hugged one of the men enthusiastically.

"Alice, are you ready?"

Startled, Alice turned to find Kady standing behind her, wearing a pair of heavy duty work gloves.

"Are you ready, or what?"

"Um, yes, sorry." Alice bent to pick up a large metal crate, and heard a loud screech from the dock.

"ALICE!" Hyun yelled. "DO NOT pick up that crate, you need to rest your shoulder!"

Alice paused, stunned, still holding the crate in mid air. Hyun glared at her, and Alice slowly lowered the crate to the ground and stepped away from it, holding her hands in the air.

"I guess you'll be helping the loading team then," Kady said with a smirk. "Do you think you can manage telling them what can be loaded on top of what?"

"I, think I can manage that, yeah."

Kady nodded in the direction of the dock. "Well get going, then."

The teams worked fast, peppered with lively, familiar conversation. Alice directed the stacking of the crates inside a cargo container on the huge steam train, standing with a manifest list and ticking off things as they were loaded. There was fresh produce, non-perishable food items, ammunition, and cloth.

When the last crate was loaded onto the train, Alice gingerly hopped off out of the cargo container and squinted as she looked for Kady and Hyun.

"Alice, over here!"

She turned and saw Hyun in the next container, beckoning for her to join them. She jogged lazily to meet them, and hoisted herself onto the train. "So, is that it then?" she asked.

"No, we'll go with them to their community and talk to the leaders there, see what they need for the next time we make a drop."

Alice looked around at the train, filled with crates that acted as seats for the team members. "How is it that they have access to a train to use for transport? Aren't they worried that the Coalition will do a spot check?"

"You grease the right palms here, and anything goes," Hyun replied matter of factly. "We're far enough from a Coalition base that checks are rare anyway, and seeing as the locals drive the train, we're solid."

"You can get away with almost anything," Kady added. "It's not a long journey to the colony. Take a seat, Mechanic."

Alice sat down heavily on a large crate and leaned back against the wall of the train. The train puffed and wheezed as it lurched forward, and the rocky, red landscape of Delta-4 was like a photograph through the frame of the doorway. They passed craggy mountains and dusty craters as the train chugged forward towards their destination, and Alice's mind wandered as Kady and Hyun chatted amicably about their plans for shore leave.

The mechanic's mind turned to the yellowed, old map again. She was frustrated that she might never learn the truth about her parents. There wasn't anyone left alive who would know, and even if they were still living, they probably wouldn't tell her anyway. She thought of her childhood home, marked as a rebel base, and wondered if her parents would have been proud of the decisions she'd made recently, leaving the Coalition and joining a pirate band who delivered goods to rebels. She shook her head to clear her thoughts. It didn't matter what they would have thought, and she felt too old to be seeking approval from long-dead relatives, in any case.

• • • •

THE TRAIN SLOWED AND the brakes hissed as they pulled into the Red Top rebel community. The team members gripped their makeshift seats for balance as the train screeched to a halt, and Alice looked out the open door at the small community outside. There were small, wood sided cabins dotted across the horizon, with larger buildings nearer the train. Children played in the street, shrieking happily as their parents looked on.

"It's lovely here," Alice said quietly. "I didn't think it would be like this. "

"You thought they'd be starving and squalid, you mean?" Kady asked. "They would be, if we left it up to the Coalition. There was a rebel base here a few years back and the Coalition found out about it. They threatened the whole community, locked people up in prison, forcibly adopted their children out to wealthy childless Coalition patrons."

"Gods," Alice whispered softly.

"And when no one would give up the rebels, they stopped all trade in and out of here. Traders in the city were threatened with steep fines and five years of work camp duty if they were caught trading or helping this community in any way." Kady stood up and silently leapt down, off the train. "By the time we found out about it, people here were starving. Children were dying and people were terrified."

"So all this is just because of the supply drops you do?" Alice asked with awe in her voice.

"Us, and a few other pirate vessels. We have a sort of unspoken agreement," Hyun interjected as she hefted a crate off the train. "But yes, without our help, it's likely this community would have died out. Some would have tried to relocate, change their names, build a new identity. But that all takes huge amounts of credits which most of them didn't have, and wouldn't ever be able to earn or save."

"Well it's really astounding what you've accomplished," Alice said as she gingerly hopped off the train. "Honestly, you'd have no idea what the Coalition does if you don't see it first hand in places like this. I had no clue."

"Some of us paid attention to the world around us," Kady said with a bitter tone. "Of course the Coalition isn't going to tell you what they're doing that's terrible and wrong. You have to open your eyes and look for yourself."

After a moment of awkward silence, Alice looked around. "Is there anything I can do to help?"

"Their people will unload the train," Hyun answered, "so we're not needed for that. You're welcome to join us as we talk to the community leaders, though."

Alice nodded and followed Hyun and Kady through the small town, and she couldn't help but notice the rubble of old buildings that had existed before the Coalition pulled them down. They reached one of the small cabins, which had once been painted green. The paint was flaking at the sides and faded from the elements. Hyun pushed open the door and with a huge smile called, "Zane! It's so good to see you!"

Alice followed them into the cabin, which was brightly lit from the open windows on every wall. Zane was a lean, tall man with the dark skin and bright, friendly eyes. He had thick brown dreadlocks that were tied back, and reached halfway down his back. He sat behind a desk that was piled high with papers, some yellowed with age and curled at the edges.

"Hyun!" he shouted happily as he stood up from his desk and crossed the room to give her a hug. "I've missed you, where have you been?" He squeezed her gently and then released her, keeping a friendly hand on her shoulder.

"Oh you know, pillaging ships, winning tournaments, the usual," she said with a grin.

"And Kady, how are you?" he asked with a kind smile.

"I'm well, thank you," Kady responded warmly. "How have things been here? How are your supplies looking?"

"Ah, straight to business as usual, I see," Zane said with a wink. He sat behind his desk and dropped a pile of paperwork onto the floor to clear some space. "I'll be honest with you, it's been difficult lately," he said.

"Why, what's wrong?" Hyun asked.

"Well, there was an outbreak of measles, we're vulnerable ever since the Coalition started refusing us the vaccines we need a few years back. We lost a few people, the ones with weakened immune systems, and those that struggle to be further away from the sun than on Gamma-3."

"I'm really sorry to hear that," Kady said as she stood in the middle of the room.

"We got things under control, but our medical supplies have been decimated. If anything else happens in the near future, we'll have no way to properly treat people."

"Why didn't you send us a message?" Hyun asked gently. "I could have made sure we brought some supplies with us, to tide you over."

"Well, that's the other problem," he said, his voice full of exhaustion. "The Coalition has been monitoring communications from this sector. I think they might suspect that we're getting supplies from somewhere. There haven't been any in person checks, but they are keeping an eye on us from afar."

"We'll see what we can do about disabling that, at least temporarily," Kady said with a worried tone. "You need to be able to contact us about things like this."

"In the meantime, send someone back with us to the ship, I have some medical supplies I can spare," Hyun added. "We can send back antibiotics, supplements, anything else you need."

Zane nodded. "Thank you. Without you and the others, we'd have nowhere to turn."

"It's no problem," Hyun replied earnestly. "We're happy to help."

"And who is this?" Zane asked, nodding towards Alice. "I don't remember seeing you before."

"Oh, I, uh," Alice began.

"She's *ex-Coalition*," Kady sneered. "She was their best mechanic for decades, so they say."

Alice furrowed her brow at Kady. "Yes, I was a Coalition mechanic for most of my life, working on various merchant trading vessels. A couple of weeks ago, I smashed the boilers, stole a shuttle, and escaped." She saw the look of surprise on Zane's face and added, "It's kind of a long story."

"Well, it certainly sounds like an eventful few weeks for you, Alice," he laughed. "You're very welcome here, and I thank you for your help."

"Anything I can do, please ask," Alice said.

Zane nodded. "I will." He looked back to Hyun and Kady, his hands folded on the desk. "I can send someone back with you to collect medical supplies," he said, "but other than that our needs haven't changed. Our community may be small, but it is growing as other rebels find their way here and take refuge." He offered some papers across the desk. "Here's our food requirements; even though we've grown as a community, we don't need any more than usual. We welcomed a new member recently who has the ability to cultivate plants in the soil here. It's been a real boon."

Kady reached forward and took the paper, examining it. "This is all doable," she said pensively. "So if nothing else changes, we'll return to Red Top in a few months with the next supply drop."

"That would be fantastic, thank you," Zane replied. "I don't know where we would be without your help. If you had told me five years ago that the livelihood of my community would be dependent on the generosity of pirates, I would have called you a fantasist."

"Well, we live in different times, now," Kady added pensively. "Things aren't the way they used to be. Times are hard, and we all have to stick together. You never know if we'll end up needing help from your community someday."

"That's for certain," Zane agreed as he stood up from his desk. "If that's all, then you can head back to the city and enjoy the rest of your time on Delta-4. I imagine the receiving team will have emptied the train by now."

Hyun nodded. "I hope that the next time, we can stay a little longer. It would be nice to spend some more time here and have a real catch up with you and the others."

"I understand. After all, you have others to help as well," Zane replied. "I will look forward to seeing you soon." He stood in front of his desk and gave Hyun a long hug, and then waved at Kady. "Have a safe journey back to the city. Alice, it was nice to meet you."

Alice nodded. "And you."

• • • •

THE TRIO LEFT THE CABIN and trudged back to the train, which they found empty. Hyun waved at the train conductor at the front of the train and boomed, "WE'RE READY TO HEAD BACK, NOW!"

Alice laughed. "Hyun, I'm always surprised by how loud you can be."

"I took some voice lessons as a child," she shrugged as they all climbed aboard.

The train hissed into life and began to chug and rattle as it started the journey back to the city. They sat in silence, each lost in their own thoughts, planning their time off in the city. Alice thought about the good meal to come, and how she wanted to explore the city the next day, wandering aimlessly through the busy streets. The landscape zoomed by through the open door, the wind whistling through the empty train. Kady's long, loose hair flew around her face, while Hyun's dark coiled braid sat motionless atop her head. Soon, the sights of the city came into view, with tall skyscraper buildings and wide, squat blocks of houses. It didn't matter what planet you were on, or which city you were in, they all looked the same. The train came to a halt in the center of the city, exactly where they wanted to be. Ned waved eagerly from the station, across the tracks.

Alice, Hyun, and Kady disembarked, hopping off the train and over the pathway to the other side of the tracks.

"Done at the market already?" Kady asked quizzically.

"You know, for a Coalition trader, Barnaby makes a hell of a deal," Ned grinned. "Record profits, I'd say."

Hyun raised her eyebrows. "And how much are we talking?" she asked.

"Five thousand credits," Ned announced proudly, "apiece."

Alice nearly fell over with shock. "Five thousand credits? That more than I made in three months on the Stronghold!"

Ned doubled over laughing. "Welcome to being a pirate, Alice," he said as he caught his breath. "Now shall we get some food?"

"I have something to attend to," Kady said mysteriously, "a meeting that I cannot miss."

"A meeting, eh? Well, I guess it's just the three of us for bibimbap, then, eh?" he asked, looking hopefully at Hyun and Alice.

Hyun nodded. "Follow me, it's not far!"

Kady waved goodbye and headed back towards the dock, and the trio followed Hyun as she wound through the city, down tight alleyways and around hidden corners. Before long, they reached a courtyard filled with different food stalls, and the air was thick with the aroma of spices and roasted food.

"Oh, how I love it here," Ned said happily. "So much choice! "

"The Korean stand is at the far end," Hyun said, pointing at a large stand on the other end of the courtyard. "Better get in quick, before they run out."

They hustled toward the stand, and stood in line as they waited patiently for their turn. The pair that were dishing out food gave broad smiles to every customer as they handed over deep bowls filled with delicious food.

Hyun ordered for all of them, as she spoke Korean to the pair managing the stand. It was clear that they recognized her, and as an added bonus, they included an extra heap of rice into each of their bowls. She grinned and handed Alice and Ned their bowls, and then took her own. Together, they scouted out a place under a tree where they could sit and eat.

Alice devoured her food, while savoring every bite. The bowl was filled to bursting with brown rice, roasted vegetables, fresh, firm tofu, and an egg on top of it all.

"Hyun, this food, " she said as she shoveled another mouthful, "this is amazing." Alice broke the yolk of the egg with her spoon smeared it over some rice.

"I told you, didn't I?" Hyun replied as she stuffed more rice and tofu into her mouth. "It's the best there is, no matter what planet you're on."

They finished in silence, the only sounds were those from other customers of the market and their own hungry slurps. As they all sat under the tree, full of delicious food, Hyun surveyed Alice out of the corner of her eye.

"Alice, let's go shopping!" she cried enthusiastically. "You need something to wear other than those old Coalition coveralls all the time."

Alice wrinkled her nose. "I don't enjoy shopping. Most things aren't exactly tailored for women of my size. Tall women with wide hips and fat stomachs rarely get a choice of what to wear. And I'm happy in my coveralls!"

"Nonsense! I know a place just around the corner," she said gleefully as she pulled Alice out of her seat. "Come on, Alice, haven't you ever wanted to express your individuality?" She thrust the stacked, empty bowls at Ned and gestured for him to return them.

Alice looked at Hyun in her electric blue shirt and bright pink combat boots. "Uh, not really?" she replied.

"You're going to love it," Hyun insisted as she pulled Alice across the courtyard, with Ned following behind. "And if you don't, then I'll never bother you again."

A few short moments after they entered the shop, Alice's arms were full with various articles of clothing. Trousers, vests, shirts, and belts, it seemed as though Hyun had thought of everything. "Hyun, there's too much choice!" Alice laughed. "I've never seen so many different things that would fit me."

"Go try things on, and come out when you've decided on the things you like," Hyun said excitedly, bouncing on the balls of her feet.

Alice dumped the armful of garments onto the bench inside the curtained dressing area. She tried on one thing, then another, and another. She would look into the mirror with each thing and wrinkle her nose, longing for her familiar and comfortable coveralls, ragged and worn as they were. She tried on a pair of trousers that she liked, and added a shirt, a jacket, and a wide belt. She pulled on her boots and laced them tightly, and then took a deep breath and pulled back the curtain.

"EEEE!" Hyun squealed. "You look amazing. Do you love it?" she asked.

Alice turned and looked in a mirror on the wall. "Oh, uh, yes, actually." She had chosen a pair of deep, aubergine purple trousers that hugged her wide hips and soft belly, tucked into her familiar, scuffed boots. Her blouse was a simple crisp white, with gleaming, iridescent buttons and a keyhole neckline. She had also chosen a tailored black jacket, with large brass buttons on both sides, joined with a matching brass chain across her waist.

"Holy gods, Alice," Ned said quietly, "you look fantastic."

Alice looked in the mirror and smiled at her reflection. "I do, don't I?"

Hyun grabbed her hand and pulled her towards the door. "Don't worry, I already gave the shopkeep your credits I.D.!" she shouted. "Let's go have some fun!"

As she was pulled towards the door, Alice picked up her crumpled boiler suit and tucked it under her arm as they left the shop. "Thank you!" she shouted to the shopkeeper as the door closed behind her.

CHAPTER EIGHTEEN

VIOLET WAS WANDERING through the central market of the city, bathed in the cool glow of the sunset when her stomach rumbled loudly. Her meeting had lasted far longer than she had anticipated, and now what she really needed was some food. She scanned the stalls as she walked: leather vests and bags, made from synthetic, lab grown fibres, a stand covered in aromatic empanadas, a ship's captain recruiting a new crew, a table with a huge cauldron of thick, sticky noodles. Violet couldn't help but drift towards the cauldron, hypnotized by the sweet and sour aroma.

She paid for an extra large portion of noodles and dove in as she sat on the curb in a quiet side street. The noodles were covered in a thick savory sauce, paired with green leafy vegetables, crisp pea pods, and perfectly fried tofu. She brought her chopsticks to her mouth and stuffed her cheeks with the delicious food, and ate with unbridled enthusiasm. As she ate, she watched the people of the city go about their lives: lovers arguing in low tones as they walked the streets, children playing in alleyways, an old man biting into an empanada and grinning the kind of smile that only food can bring.

An attractive, tall woman was leaned against a wooden post with her back to Violet, who found herself staring a little too long. The woman was wearing impeccably tailored clothing, with the longest silver mane of pin straight hair Violet had ever seen.

That wasn't Alice, was it? It couldn't be, Alice only had her coveralls, and besides, she was out with Hyun and Ned tonight. There was another woman with her of similar stature, with a wide smile and bronzed sepia skin. Violet watched the women with curiosity as she ate; she smiled despite her mouth being full of noodles as they gently flirted with each other, with a subtle touch of the hand and lots of laughter.

The woman with the long silver hair turned around, and Violet nearly choked on her noodles. The sexy, self assured woman spending her evening flirting with a stranger *was* Alice.

"Violet?" she asked incredulously from across the street. "Are you *following* me?" Alice's face was full of shock, and anger, and a little bit of smugness.

"Alice! Alice? No, I—" Violet tried to say, her mouth full of tofu.

"So you're saying this is some kind of strange coincidence?" the mechanic asked, raising her eyebrow. "That seems improbable."

Violet swallowed her noodles. "No, I didn't know it was you—"

"*You didn't know it was me?* How many other tall, older women with silver hair do you know?"

"Just— hang on!" Violet shouted as she crossed the street. "I just didn't recognize you is all," she said defensively, even though it was an obvious and clumsy lie. Violet paused to regain her composure, took a breath, and turned to the other woman. "Hello, many apologies for my rudeness, I'm Captain Violet of the Cricket, nice to meet you." She held out her hand to the woman, who shook it firmly.

"Hiya. I'm Jhanvi," she said with a thick southern drawl. "So *this* is the Captain, is it?" she asked Alice with a sideways glance and an impish grin. "I can see the problem."

"Uh, what? No? This is, uh—" Alice stammered, blushing a crimson red. "She's, uh..."

Violet raised an eyebrow. "I didn't realize I had such a widespread reputation," she said to Alice. "I'm sorry again for my rudeness, please enjoy your evening...together. Jhanvi, very nice to meet you."

The captain turned on her heel and moved swiftly down the street. She folded the box of noodles closed, her appetite ruined by thoughts of Alice and Jhanvi spending the evening together. "Get it together, Violet," she muttered to herself as she marched back towards the ship, her polished boots thudding heavily on the paved pedestrian roads.

• • • •

VIOLET SAT IN HER SEAT on the bridge, picking at the leftovers of her noodles unenthusiastically. She had been determined to finish her food, to not think about Alice, or Alice and Jhanvi, or how she had barely recognized Alice from behind because she looked so amazing in her new clothes.

It was late, and Violet was the only one left on the ship. She had volunteered to take Ned's place keeping an eye on things; her interest in spending the night in the city had been dulled by the evening's events.

She looked out the large window at the port in front of the ship, filled with ships of every shape and size; lifting off and landing in tandem against the taffeta blue fabric of the sky. She set her box of noodles on the main console, chopsticks sticking out at the top. She leaned back and closed her eyes, thinking of simpler times, before the budding new revolution, before Captain Leo, and before she had ever met Alice, the sturdy, attractive mechanic who was driving her thoughts in circles.

Against the silence of the ship, Violet heard the airlock door open, and then close. Someone had returned to the ship, but who? Ned, or Kady? One of the other crew members? She stood up from her seat and peered down the corridor. She saw a flash of black jacket headed towards the boiler room, and ran back to her radio.

"Bridge to boiler," Violet said sternly into her radio, "are you there? Report."

A moment passed, as Violet stared at her radio waiting for a reply.

"Boiler here, what's the problem, Captain?" Alice's annoyed voice echoed around the room.

"I seem to be having a problem with the central console and I think it may be hardware related."

Another moment passed, and Violet bit her lip in anticipation of Alice's reply. Violet didn't blame her for being frustrated, and she wanted to make things right. She liked having Alice around and enjoyed her company, and hated the idea of her spending the night with someone else, a strange and unfamiliar feeling for someone as romantically detached as Violet.

"I'll be right there."

Violet quickly hid her box of noodles behind Ned's usual seat, on a small shelf behind the navigation console. She smoothed her curls back into their bun and tucked a stray hair into a pin. She heard Alice's heavy footsteps approaching, and tried to look nonchalant, leaned against the main console.

"What seems to be the issue here, Captain?" Alice asked flatly.

"I think there's something wrong with the main console, maybe the wiring?" Violet said innocently. "I don't think it's down in the access shaft, though."

Alice studied the display and tilted her head to the side. "Is it the map display acting up?"

"Er, yes?"

"Hmm, yes, it could very well be a wiring problem..." Alice trailed off.

"Here, sit in my seat, you might be able to see the problem more clearly."

Alice sat in the captain's seat and leaned forward to examine the console, her brow furrowed in concentration.

Violet stood behind her and leaned in close. "Do you see the problem?" she whispered slowly in Alice's ear.

"No," Alice replied sternly. "I don't see any problems with the main console. If that's all, Captain, I'll make a note to have Kady check the programming when she returns on board tomorrow."

Violet placed her hands on Alice's wide shoulders and massaged gently. "Are you sure you don't see any issue? Maybe you should take a closer look."

Alice leaned back in the captain's seat. "Captain, " Alice began, "I'm not sure this is a good idea."

"What, afraid that Jhanvi might find out?" Violet whispered as she kissed Alice's neck. "She's very pretty, I can see why you'd be interested in her."

"No," Alice mumbled, "we're just friends."

"Didn't look like friends earlier tonight," Violet said, kissing Alice's ear. "Looked like much more than that, if you ask me." She continued to massage Alice's shoulders as she kissed her neck softly.

Alice sighed involuntarily. "No, just friends. She's helping me with a project."

Violet lightly bit Alice's neck. "Are you sure about that?"

Alice jerked away. "Ouch! And yes, I'm sure. Besides, what does it matter to you anyway? We're not *together*, remember? Those were your words!" She was brought back to reality with the pinch of Violet's bite, and she remembered why she had been avoiding the captain in the first place.

"Oh, Alice," Violet whispered, "don't you see what you're doing to me?"

"Captain, er, Violet, " Alice protested, "this isn't fair."

"All's fair in love and war, is it not?" Violet mumbled, and then dragged her tongue across Alice's neck, up to her earlobe.

Alice turned her head and kissed Violet full on the mouth, raising an arm up behind the captain's head to pull her in closer. "If you don't stop, then someone might see," she warned.

"Everyone is out in the city, except for us."

"What if someone comes back early?"

Violet walked around the chair and sat in Alice's lap. "They won't." She kissed Alice slowly, and deeply, her hands running over Alice's breasts under her new blouse. "You look amazing in this, by the way."

"Hyun picked it out," Alice laughed quietly, reaching out for Violet. "I like it, too."

"Don't get me wrong, your boiler suit is alluring in its own way, but the way this hugs your curves," she ran her hands down over Alice's hips and squeezed, "is very easy on the eyes."

"I'm glad you like it," Alice whispered as Violet ran her hands over her. "I was hoping you would."

Violet kissed Alice's neck as she slowly unbuttoned her blouse, one shiny button at a time, exposing her black tank top underneath. She pushed the blouse back, and pushed up the tank top to expose Alice's full, soft breasts. She moaned softly as she kissed Alice's nipples and ran her hands over her breasts, down to her waist, and played with the waistband of her trousers.

"Violet, " Alice mumbled.

"Sssh," Violet replied as she kissed the mechanic. "Don't you want this to happen?"

"That's not fair, " Alice continued, as she unlatched her belt and unbuttoned her trousers. "Of course I do."

Violet pulled at Alice's trousers, and she lifted her hips so that they fell to the floor. The captain kissed her thighs gently, tugging at her boxers.

"Violet," Alice tried again.

"Call me Captain," Violet said mischievously as she dragged Alice's boxers to the floor.

"Captain," Alice whispered, "you know what I want." She locked eyes with the captain and stared intently, almost daring her to continue.

Violet knelt down in front of Alice and wrapped her hands around the mechanic's thighs as she kissed her gently, each kiss higher than the last. She reached a thicket of silver hair and buried her mouth as Alice gasped.

"Captain," Alice breathed.

The captain explored Alice with her tongue, tracing the outline of her labia and teasing her entrance. She ran her tongue across either side, stopping in the center and wrapping her hands around Alice's waist.

Alice rested her hands behind the captain's head and pulled her in closer as she moaned. "Captain, don't stop," she begged.

Violet buried her face further, feeling voracious and wild. She grasped Alice's hips and pulled her in closer. She loved the feel of the mechanic's soft belly, and ran her hands over Alice's soft hips and thighs. She buried her face where Alice's thighs met and sucked, teased, and circled. Violet knew she was good at this, and Alice's surprised sighs and quiet moans proved her right.

The mechanic writhed against Violet's mouth, and cried out, her thighs shaking. She was left gasping as Violet sat back on her haunches with a sly grin.

"Enjoyed that, did you?" she asked, pleased with herself. She cocked an eyebrow and waited for Alice's response.

After a moment, Alice finally caught her breath. She stood up to regain her composure and pulled up her boxers and trousers, and re-buckled her belt. "Well, Captain," she said flirtatiously, "that was of utmost quality." She turned towards the door without another word.

"Wait, where are you going?" Violet asked desperately.

"Good night, Captain," Alice called over her shoulder.

Violet sprang up and followed the mechanic, catching her gently by the wrist. "Alice, where are you going?" she asked deviously. "Don't you want to know what *I* want?"

Alice raised an eyebrow and gently traced the scar on Violet's face. "Alright, what do you want?" she whispered.

"Follow me," Violet replied, placing her hands on Alice's waist, "and I'll show you." She walked backwards, keeping her hands on the mechanic's body, pulling her gently down the corridor towards her quarters. She paused where the corridor came to a fork and stood on her toes to kiss

Alice deeply, reaching up to weave her fingers through her long, loose silvery locks. She almost hadn't expected to get her way with Alice, not this time. She felt her old, familiar swagger rise up with her success.

"Oh, fuck it," Alice whispered into Violet's neck. She reached for Violet and embraced her, lifting her off the ground. Violet wrapped her legs around the mechanic's waist and held tight to her, as if Alice was a lifeboat in the middle of the ocean. Her kisses felt like fire, like warmth spreading across every inch of her skin and sinking down deep into her bones. Alice held her in her arms and walked to Violet's quarters, kissing her all the while. She fumbled for the doorknob while Violet kissed her neck; after she opened the door and took them both through, Violet kicked the door closed. Neither of them emerged from the room for the rest of the night.

CHAPTER NINETEEN

ALICE WOKE ALONE IN Violet's bed again. Dim sunlight cast long shadows in the room, and she knew it wasn't long after dawn. She sat up against the headboard and saw that the captain had left her a note:

I'll leave breakfast for you in the mess hall, something special I picked up in town yesterday.

Don't let Kady see you this time.

-V

It was almost exactly the same as last time, which was exactly the opposite of what Alice had wanted.

Rolling her eyes, Alice swung her muscular legs over the side of the bed and stretched her arms. As she had predicted, her shoulder was pulsing with a dull throb, no doubt a result of the previous evening's activities. She gently massaged her shoulder and rotated it slowly. The mechanic got dressed, but in no hurry. She looked in the mirror and grinned; she certainly did look good in these new clothes. Her hair was tangled and messy, the result of sleeping with it loose. She combed her fingers through the worst of the knots and braided her hair into two long braids, the way she usually wore it, and fastened them with pins she found on the counter.

Her stomach rumbled loudly. "Time to go," she said out loud to herself. She grabbed her new black velvet jacket from the back of the chair in the corner and shrugged it on. With one last glance in the mirror, she cracked open the door and peeked out. She looked both ways and listened intently but the ship was silent and motionless. The rest of the crew hadn't returned yet, and not even Kady would be able to sneak up on her today.

Alice squeezed out the door and gently closed it behind her. The lock made a soft, satisfying click when it latched. She wandered towards the mess hall slowly, yawning and rubbing the sleep from her eyes as she walked. As she neared the mess hall, she could smell something hot and sweet, and it reminded her of being a small child, before she was sent away from her parents. She peered around the room and spotted a small plate on the counter. There was a large sweet bun sitting atop the plate, oozing with a sugary glaze and sprinkled with cinnamon. Alice eagerly took a bite and sighed happily. The sweet treat was still warm, no doubt heated up by Violet and left for her. She savored every bite, chewing slowly with her eyes closed, trying to grasp the fleeting childhood memory.

As she swallowed the last bite, she couldn't help but lick the crumbs from the plate. She'd have to ask Violet where she got that from, because she wanted to eat it every morning until she died. She turned and quietly made herself a mug of coffee, a rarity for her but it felt right this morning. With a satisfied sigh, she slumped back into a chair to drink her coffee with introspection and deep thoughts. There was something oddly enticing about contemplating the mysteries of life while nursing a mug of hot liquid, and Alice indulged her urge to take a moment to enjoy the peace of the empty ship.

She sat in the empty hall, hands huddled around the comforting warmth of the mug as steam lazily rose and disappeared into the air. Slow, quiet sips, underpinned by the distant sounds of chatter and footsteps as crew members started to return to the ship. Alice reached the bottom of her mug, and made herself another cup, not wanting to squander this rare moment of peace. She thought of plans to upgrade some of the ship's systems, of Ivy's progress in her training, of her argument with Barnaby, of Jhanvi, of Violet, and of the mystery clouding her past.

Finally, she drained the last sips of lukewarm coffee from her mug and stood, stretching her arms up over her head. She rinsed the mug and placed it back in the cupboard quietly as two crew members whose names she couldn't remember noisily flopped down at a table to eat their breakfast and prepare for the day. The morning had grown late, and Alice knew they would be preparing to leave soon, to head towards the next drop zone. She waved and smiled at the newcomers and left the hall.

Feeling inspired by her morning respite, Alice took a brisk pace through the ship towards the bridge. She wanted to present some ideas for improvements that would increase the efficiency of the Cricket and hopefully give them a speed boost as well. She approached the bridge and heard Violet and Ned talking softly, their voices tense with worry.

"I don't know, Boss. The transmission only came through a few moments ago."

Violet paced, obviously teeming with nervous energy. "How long would we have to make a decision one way or another?" she asked, an edge to her voice.

"Not long," Ned replied. "The Coalition could be here any moment."

"Fuck!" Violet yelled as she kicked the console access panel. "Goddamn it."

"Anything I can help with?" Alice offered, leaning casually against one side of the doorway.

"No, Alice. Just make sure we can be ready to go at a moment's notice." Violet sighed angrily and unclipped her radio from her wide brown belt. "Kady, I need you up on the bridge, immediately."

"Aye, Captain," the radio crackled.

"What the hell happened?" Violet demanded, looking at Ned. "We were just there yesterday!"

"I'm not sure, Boss, but Kady mentioned they suspected the Coalition was monitoring their communications, possibly looking for rebel activity, or to put a stop to any supply drops." Ned nervously ran a hand through his long, loose hair as he examined the navigation display in front of him. "If they know it was us who supplied the community..."

"Yes, Ned, we all know. Treason, times two." Violet looked out the window at the port, bathed in cool blue light. "If we were going to help, how fast could we get away? Is it even worth trying?"

"Not any longer than usual. If Alice and Ivy can keep the boilers warm, then I can chart a course for the next supply drop, but we'll have to take the long way around to keep the heat off our tail."

Violet drummed her fingers against the rough canvas headrest of her chair. "What kind of help are they asking for?"

"The transmission said that they'd been spotted by Coalition sensors, and were anticipating an attack. If that's the case, they'll all be rounded up and dumped into camps." Ned shook his head and added, "Even the children."

"But that's against the inter-planetary rights conventions!" Alice interrupted. "They can't do that, it's barbaric!"

"The Coalition does whatever they please," Kady said as she swooshed past Alice. "Children or not, they're all traitors in their eyes."

"Kady, good. I'm sure you've heard, but the rebel community has been detected by the Coalition." Violet resumed her pacing across the bridge, her hands clasped behind her back. "The question is whether we try to assist them and risk being captured, or ignore their transmission, and—"

"And leave them to be arrested," Kady finished. "I found and disabled the Coalition monitoring chip yesterday afternoon after Zane told me his suspicions, lodged in their communications tower. I guess it was too late for that. They already knew."

"Do you think the Coalition knows it was us that organized the supply drops?" Violet asked.

Kady shrugged. "There's no way to know that, unfortunately. We can't monitor their communications."

"What about the death droids?" Alice suggested. "It would give them a source of defense against the Coalition, and I bet they could replicate the design if Kady showed them how to rewrite the programming."

"I'm not comfortable with that kind of technology being handed out to everyone who asks for our help," Violet said sternly. "If it was misused, or discovered by the Coalition, there's no telling what could happen. At least if the droids stay with us, then we know how they are being used."

"Alice might have a point, Captain," Kady ventured, "we could always pick them up at the next drop. We wouldn't even have to be there in person to help them, just drop off a box of the droids."

"And what if they can't figure out how to activate them? Or what if they activate them before it's necessary? Then it's blood on our hands." Violet thought of Captain Leo's dead eyes once again and shuddered. "I don't want to be responsible for starting a violent altercation."

"So you're happy to let children to be taken to work camps? Because that's what's going to happen if we don't do anything," Kady replied angrily, her eyes flashing with fire.

"Of course I don't want children to be taken to camps!" Violet shot back. "But I don't want to see my crew being executed, either! We're pirates, not goddamn freedom fighters."

"Aren't we?" Alice asked quietly. "I came back because I saw injustice, and I wanted to fight against it. Why bother to help at all if you won't lay it all on the line?"

Violet turned her intense gaze to Ned. "And what about you, then? Are you happy to risk treason charges and execution?"

Ned took a deep breath. "Boss, if we don't do the right thing, who will?"

For a moment, the bridge was silent as they all considered their options. Without the loud hum of the engines, the only sounds were those of the port. People shouting to each other, cargo being loaded and unloaded, ships landing and taking off. It felt like the outside world was continuing to turn, while time was frozen onboard the Cricket.

After a long silence, Violet looked up from her boots. "Alright, then." She stood tall and squared her shoulders. "Kady, take Jasper with you. Take two boxes of droids, show them how they work. Tell them not to activate them unless *absolutely necessary*. Then come right back."

Without another word, Kady swept out of the room, quick as a flash of light.

"Ned, get everyone back on board, if they aren't already. Anyone not on board when Kady and Jasper return will have to stay here and wait until the next drop to get picked up." Violet turned to Alice, still leaning against the door frame. "Alice, get Ivy and head to the boilers, keep them hot so we can leave as soon as they're back."

"Aye, Captain," the mechanic replied. "For what it's worth, I think this is the right decision."

"Two weeks out of the Coalition, and you're more of a rebel than most lifelong pirates," Violet chuckled as Alice turned to leave. "It's good to have you as part of the team."

Alice smiled. "I'll keep those boilers piping hot for you, Captain." She paused for a moment, then continued, "Thank you for leading us to do the right thing." Her footsteps thudded heavily down the hall, and Violet heard her call Ivy on the radio.

• • • •

VIOLET TURNED TO NED. "So, old friend, what do you think? Will we escape with our lives, or be executed for treason?" she asked with a tinge of dark humor.

"Kady and Jasper are a good team," Ned replied evenly, "and they'll get the job done. We can trust them." Ned studied the navigational display for a moment, and then turned to mark a red X on a map that was tacked on the wall beside him. "It will take us a little longer to get to the next drop zone," he calculated, "if we want to stay well far from any Coalition probes."

"Yes, I think that's wise." Violet studied the main console monitor, searching for any Coalition ships on the radar. They were safe, but not for long.

"It will add an extra day or so, maybe more if we have to swing wide around any merchant vessels."

Violet nodded slowly. "Yes." She began to pace again, walking back and forth between the doorway and the front window. "Ned, reply to the transmission and let them know we're on our way, tell them to be ready with a team. Don't give any details other than that, just in case the Coalition is still managing to monitor communications."

"Aye, Boss."

"How long will it take Kady and Jasper to get there and back, do you think?" she asked, her voice thick with worry. "I don't want to have to leave without them, especially if the Coalition is sending military vessels. Kady is still in their system from her time with them, and they'll know who she is. She'll be tried for treason." Violet anxiously smoothed her curls back behind her ears, her hands shaking. "Maybe I should have sent someone else."

"Boss, you know she's the right person for the job. She's quick, she's quiet, and she knows those bots inside and out. And Jasper will keep an eye out. They'll be fine." Ned swiveled around in his high backed chair and leaned forward, towards a small microphone that was attached to a large radio device. It was brown and square, with a series of knobs and buttons, and emitted a low hum when Ned turned it on. "Attention, we have received the transmission, have a team ready at the meeting point to receive assistance, over."

Violet continued to march back and forth across the bridge as they waited for a reply. Several minutes went by in silence, and the captain felt her heart racing faster with every passing moment. "Ned, what if they've already been found out? What if we just sent Kady and Jasper into a trap?"

She tried to swallow the lump in her throat, but it remained, threatening to let tears spring to her eyes. "Answer, goddamnit!" she yelled at the radio.

The radio remained silent, and the air on the bridge became harder to breathe. Violet paced, and Ned watched the radio intently, gripping the edge of the desk with white knuckles.

"If they borrowed steambikes from the port, they'd be arriving soon," Ned muttered anxiously. "Still no response."

The captain's heart was pounding in her throat with every passing second. Nightmare scenarios raced through her mind as she imagined her crew being arrested and executed. She imagined Kady and Alice, former Coalition members, receiving the worst treatment, probably starvation, followed by torture for their betrayal.

She stifled a sob as a tear rolled down her cheek and dripped down her chin onto the floor. "Ned, why aren't they answering?" she asked quietly.

"I don't know, Boss," he whispered. "I don't know."

Violet stared at the radio, willing it to crackle to life, praying that Kady and Jasper were okay. Against the silence inside the ship, the port was lively and cheerful, a juxtaposition that Violet found jarring. She heard the low hiss of the boilers being heated, and tried to grasp that tiny morsel of comfort in knowing that Alice and Ivy were doing their best to make sure they'd all be celebrating a daring escape later, instead of spending the night in a cold, dank cell aboard a Coalition military vessel.

Ned cleared his throat. "Boss, what are we going to do if they don't come back?" he asked.

"Fuck! I don't know!" she yelled, dragging her hands over her hair and pulling at her bun. "Maybe I should go after them."

"We need you here, Boss," Ned said quietly.

"Well I need to know what's going on over there," she said angrily, her fear turning to red hot fury in her mouth. "Fuck protocol, I need to save my crew." She unholstered her revolver and pulled bullets from the inside pocket of her vest, carefully loading the gun and snapping the chamber closed with a deft flick of her wrist.

"Boss, I—"

"Ned, you can fly the ship if I'm not here. If we don't come back, leave. That's an order."

"Fuck orders, I'm not leaving without you or the others," Ned replied, his voice rising with frustration. "Orders be damned, I will not abandon any member of my family." He stared at the captain intently, his eyes flashing with determination. "I may not be able to run after them," he said, gesturing to his cane, "but I can goddamn well make sure no one gets left behind."

"If anyone gets arrested because you were too stubborn to follow orders—!"

"No one is getting arrested. Now go if you're going!" he yelled.

Violet nodded curtly, holstered her revolver, and sprinted through the ship, heading for the loading bay. Her boots pounded against the floor as she ran, adrenaline coursing through her veins like venom. As she reached the airlock, she punched in the security code and waited for the airlock to process. "Hurry up, damn it!" she yelled as it hissed with pressure.

The airlock opened into the loading bay, and she ran to the emergency open lever. She yanked on the lever, and the hydraulic door began to pop and creak as it slowly opened. Violet ducked under the door, and saw two steambikes racing towards the ship, emblazoned with the Coalition crest.

CHAPTER TWENTY

VIOLET'S BREATH CAUGHT in her throat as she tried to climb back under the door. A latch snagged her belt loop, and she yanked to try and free herself. "Ned! Go!" she shouted into her radio, knowing full well that she wouldn't survive outside the airlock once they were outside the terraformed atmosphere. "Go! Coalition!" She felt the ship begin to shudder and shake as it came to life, and she pulled furiously on her belt loop, desperate to free herself and close the loading bay door.

With a mighty yank, the belt loop snapped and she fell to the floor in a heap. She dragged herself to the lever, and as she started to pull it, she heard a voice over the din of the ship.

"Captain! Wait! It's us!"

Violet squinted at the approaching steambikes, and as they neared, she recognized Kady's long black jacket and Jasper's tall, broad silhouette, tailed by faceless Coalition soldiers in black visor helmets. She gasped with surprise and tried to reverse the closing door, but it was too late; the ship's safety protocols wouldn't allow the door to be opened while the engines were engaged. With horror, she watched the door slowly lower as the bikes reached the ship.

She shoved a tall crate under the door, using all her strength and body weight, and reached for her revolver. The door crashed into the crate, crushing the top half as it struggled to close. It was enough: Kady and Jasper slid under the door on their bikes as the ship lifted off the ground and out of reach of the Coalition soldiers. The crates shifted and slid as the trio scrambled for the airlock, dodging loose cargo as the Cricket ascended into the upper atmosphere. The air became thin and hard to breathe as they prepared to leave the planet.

As the Cricket left Delta-4, the air left the loading bay, sucked out into the vast darkness through the partially open loading bay door. Violet, Kady, and Jasper fell into the airlock and gasped for breath as they waited for the airlock to fill with oxygen. As air began to flow, their breathing regulated. They sat in a heap inside the airlock, and Violet threw her arms around

Kady and Jasper, tears flowing freely. "What..." she wheezed, "what the hell are we going to do with Coalition steambikes?"

Kady laughed weakly. "Just seemed like a good idea, to wait until the last possible moment like that." She wrapped an arm around the captain and squeezed, returning the embrace. "We're okay, Captain. We're alright."

"Boss! Boss? What's going on down there?" Ned's panicked voice came through Violet's radio. "Are you okay?"

Violet unclipped the radio. "Aye, Ned, I'm okay. It wasn't Coalition. It was Kady and Jasper."

"Thank the gods," Ned replied, his voice breaking with emotion. "Now get up here, all of you!"

The airlock opened into the ship, and they tumbled out into the corridor. Kady leapt to her feet and extended a hand to Violet with a grin. "Mission accomplished, Captain."

Violet accepted the hand up, and hauled herself to her feet. "Accomplished, indeed. Now let's go see Ned on the bridge."

Jasper nodded to the captain. "If it's alright with you, I'd like to sit down a moment." He was a large, imposing man, but his hands were shaking with stress. He leaned against the door frame of the airlock and heaved a heavy sigh.

"Take all the time you need," Violet replied gently, squeezing his arm. "It will be a little while before we need you again."

They walked the halls of the ship, panting with exertion. Kady moved silently as always, but Violet's steps thudded heavily and echoed down the corridors. The ship began to pick up speed, and the hum of the engines was a comfort to both, like the feeling of being cocooned in a womb. The captain reached out and placed a hand on Kady's shoulder, a wordless expression of pride and gratitude. Kady smiled back at her and placed her hand over the captain's as they approached the bridge of the ship.

Ned was waiting in the bridge doorway with open arms, tears streaming down his face, blotchy with emotion. "Captain! Kady..." he sobbed. "I thought..." he trailed off as he wrapped them both in a tight embrace.

"It's alright, Ned," Kady said softly. "Everyone is safe."

He sniffled and held them tighter. "Never do that again," he mumbled, his face buried on Violet's shoulder. "I don't think my heart could take the stress."

Violet laughed gently and patted Ned's long, loose ginger locks. "Alright, Ned, I promise. Now let's get the hell out of this sector, shall we?"

Ned released the women and stood straight as he wiped the tears from his red, puffy eyes. "Yes Boss." He cleared his throat dramatically and furrowed his brow. "We'll be exiting the sector in about an hour. Hopefully no one tailed us."

"I think we got a clean getaway," Kady offered. "I don't think anyone chased us back to the port."

"How about you tell the whole crew about it over dinner tonight?" Violet asked. "Ned, do you mind cooking?"

His face lit up with a wide grin. "Boss, nothing would make me happier. I've had a special dish planned since we nabbed those supplies, and I think tonight is the right occasion. A celebration!"

Violet nodded. "Aye, it's settled then. Set the course and get to the kitchen, I'll keep an eye on things up here." She looked to Kady, who looked bedraggled and unkempt from her daring escape, her long dark hair escaping from its strict bun, and a long tear in her coat. "Kady, I think you should go relax before dinner. Check on Jasper if you don't mind, I think the poor guy is a bit traumatized."

"I will. He's the best bodyguard we've ever had, but I think today's near miss may have upset him. I'll ask Hyun to have a look at him too, if he's not feeling better by dinner. I'm sure he'll be fine, just needs some peace and quiet, and maybe a long soak in the bath."

"Make sure he knows that his presence at dinner isn't necessary, if he needs the sleep or the silence of his quarters," Violet said. "And tell him I said thank you for another mission well done. And that goes for you, too, Kady."

Kady nodded and swept out of the room, straightening her damaged jacket as she went. Ned followed, an arm around her shoulders.

• • • •

THE CREW APPLAUDED as Kady and Jasper entered the mess hall, with loud cheering and whistling in celebration of their successful mission. Hyun gave them a standing ovation with tears in her eyes and a smile on her face. All the tables in the mess hall had been pushed together to form a long table that spanned the length of the room, and they were covered with trays heaping with hot, steaming food. Ned pushed a cart into the room from the galley, and it carried a huge, multi-tier cake topped with fresh berries and toasted meringue. He cleared his throat to get the crew's attention.

"The piece de resistance!" he cried proudly, gesturing towards the cake with both arms. "It took me all afternoon, but look at it! It's fucking gorgeous!"

The crew applauded and cheered again, both for Kady and Jasper's return, and for Ned's cake. Tonight was a celebration, that was for sure, and one like Alice had never seen before.

Violet entered the hall with a large dusty green glass bottle in each hand. "I've been saving these for a special occasion," she declared loudly, "and tonight is it." She handed one of the bottles to Ned and nodded, and they each popped the corks of the bottles. "A toast," she began, "a toast for the safe return of two of our own. Kady, Jasper, you did us proud today." She and Ned poured the champagne into the crew's mugs as they walked around the huge table, and finished by pouring themselves a mug, too. "I've never been so proud to have you all as a crew. You all risked life and limb to help others today." She raised her mug in the air. "If you ever scare me like that again, I'll kill you myself."

The crew tittered at that.

"To Kady and Jasper!" Violet yelled, and the crew cheered and drank from their mugs. "And to Ned, who made an absolutely stunning cake," she said, toasting again. "I'll be eating the entire thing by myself, if you're all not careful. Now, let's dig in! Don't let this generous spread get cold."

All at once, the crew began to dig into the huge trays of food. Alice eyed a large bowl, heaped with steaming, creamy mashed potatoes topped with cracked black pepper and chives. She scooped a mound onto her plate and passed it to Hyun, who was sitting on her left. To her right, Kady perched on the edge of her chair, chatting amiably with Ned across the table as she piled her plate high with rosemary roasted aubergine kebabs and crispy filo pastry, filled with Greek cheeses and fresh spinach.

Alice reached for the plate of stuffed squash, filled with spiced brown rice, and delicately slid three slices of squash onto her plate. Her stomach rumbled loudly, and she realized she hadn't eaten anything since the sweet bun that Violet had left her early that morning. When she looked down at her plate, she realized someone had placed a bowl of piping hot chipotle sweet potato soup at her place. She greedily tore a hunk of bread from the fresh loaf on the table, still steaming from the oven, and slathered it with butter before dipping it into the soup. As the bread melted in her mouth, she knew with certainty that Ned's soups were her absolute favorite, and a warm reminder of her first night on the ship.

The crew chattered sporadically as they ate, stuffing sumptuous food in their mouths and praising Ned's culinary prowess with every other bite. Alice stole a glance at Violet, who was already working on her second piece of cake. It seemed as though the captain may very well eat the whole thing, if the rest of the crew didn't claim their pieces soon. She closed her eyes to savor the rich flavors of the meal, and she felt a sharp stab in her elbow.

"Ouch!" she said sharply, and opened her eyes. Barnaby was now seated to her left, having changed places with Hyun, and he was holding a fork and grinning. Alice rolled her eyes. "What do you want?"

"To talk," he replied cheerfully. "Come on, Al, stop punishing me. I said I was sorry, and I miss you."

Alice glared at Barnaby as she shoved a forkful of potatoes into her mouth. She didn't appreciate that he was ruining her culinary experience, and she just wanted to stuff her belly with food in peace. She looked sideways at a bowl of pasta, drenched in a creamy sauce with fresh peas and spinach.

"Please, Alice." Barnaby reached across the table and piled a large portion of the pasta onto her plate. "Isn't there anything I can do to make it up to you? I just want to talk."

She swallowed, and took a long drink from her mug, still full of champagne. "Barnaby, I just need some time, that's all." The bubbles fizzed in her mouth and tickled her nose, and she took another swig. "I just can't believe you would sell me out, pass me off to strangers and hope for the best. I know I said it before, but it just baffles me that you would do something like that."

Barnaby looked at Alice, and then at Violet on the other end of the table, who was pouring out more champagne into the mugs at each seat. "And like *I* said before, it's not like it didn't all work out," he rebutted. "What's going on with that anyway?" he asked, gesturing at Violet with his fork.

"None of your business," Alice said, chewing on a mouthful of the creamy pasta. "It's nothing."

"That bad, eh? Well chin up, you never know what may happen." Barnaby skewered a fried mushroom on Alice's plate with his fork and brought it to his mouth. Before he could take a bite, she snatched the fork and stuffed the entire mushroom in her mouth.

"Don't steal my food," she said after she swallowed. "There's an entire table of food, get your own."

"But yours looks so much tastier," he teased. "Can't I have one?" He stole his fork back and aimed for Alice's plate again.

"Buzz off," Alice laughed, shooing him away from her plate. "How are you liking it here anyway?" she asked. She might as well at least try to let him repair their relationship, and she wasn't in the mood for an argument tonight anyway.

He heaved a sigh and puffed out his cheeks. "Well, it's certainly not as comfortable as my quarters on the Stronghold, but I can't complain in my position. Beggars can't be choosers, as they say."

Alice leaned in. "Not spending your nights in Ned's room, then?" she inquired in a hushed tone. "I would have thought that was a sealed deal by now."

"I'm working on it. It's complicated."

"So?" she challenged, waving her fork at him. "What's the problem? He's nice, he's cute, what's the hold up? He's sure as hell better than the last few you've ended up with. Didn't the last one steal a sizable chunk of credits from you?"

"Don't remind me," he groaned. "Anyway, I like Ned, I just don't want to rush into anything. I'm not sure he does, either." He grabbed a half full bottle of wine from across the table and topped up his mug. "It just seems like so much is changing so fast, and I don't know how to keep up."

"You're not getting any younger, old man," Alice said, rolling her eyes. "I guarantee you're not going to find a man better for you than Ned. At least I know he won't put up with your bullshit." She chewed the last of her bread thoughtfully. "I still can't believe that you left the Coalition just before I did. Weird coincidence."

Barnaby grimaced. "Maybe not that much of a coincidence," he admitted. "I was hoping you'd leave too, once you realized I'd gone. When you told me what happened on the Stronghold after they took you, I thought maybe you would want to come back here. But then weeks went by and you were back to pulling double shifts like normal, and I knew I couldn't wait any longer to leave. That trade mission was my last chance to get out before they'd figure out what I'd been doing. I found a communications tracker on my radio, so I knew they'd be on to me sooner or later."

Alice raised her eyebrows in surprise. "Why didn't you just tell me?"

He shrugged. "You weren't ready to leave yet."

"I was so worried, Barns. And then to find out you'd left after selling me out? It was a lot to process. We've always told each other everything, and then suddenly there were all these secrets everywhere. I felt so alone." She traced her finger around the rim of her mug, dragging a bead of condensation and watching its trail.

"I am genuinely sorry, Al." He took her hand and smiled cautiously. "I promise I won't sell you to pirates again?"

She spat out a laugh. "You had better not, you fool. With a friend like you, who the hell needs enemies?" She pulled her hand away from him and ruffled his hair.

Barnaby's eyes lit up. "So we're friends again?"

Alice sighed. "Fine. But I swear, one more thing and that's it. I will live on this ship for the rest of my life without talking to you if you pull any more stunts like that."

"Alright, alright," he replied, defeated. "I'm going to grab some of that cake before it's all gone. Want some?"

"Nah," Alice said, patting her belly. "No room."

"Your loss," Barnaby said with a wink as he slid out of his chair and strode over to the cake.

Alice stretched her legs out under the table and observed the room, lively with chatter and laughter from the crew's celebrations. Jasper and Hyun were poring over cards laid out on the table, their half empty dishes shoved to the side. Ned and Kady hovered near the cart with the cake, and Ned gave Kady another hug as his eyes glistened with tears. Alice even felt herself welling up as she watched them, touched by their incredible friendship.

Her mind wandered back to the afternoon, when Violet had nearly vaulted off the ship in search of her crew, and wondered if she herself would ever have done that for her. In truth, Alice was more than happy to volunteer to stay on the ship and tend to the boilers. She had never been a woman of great courage, at least not until recently. She may have stolen a shuttle, destroyed Coalition boilers, and helped the crew steal cargo and information from another vessel, but the courage didn't feel natural yet. It felt forced and clumsy.

She watched as Barnaby flirted clumsily with Ned, trying desperately to get his way. Barnaby laughed at something Ned said, and reached out to touch his arm. Ned raised an eyebrow at him and smirked mischievously. Kady rolled her eyes at both of them, and turned her attention back to handing out slices of cake to the crew. Alice glanced around the room, looking for Violet. The captain was nowhere to be found, and she had an odd impulse to search the ship for her. They hadn't spoken since that morning, and she had a craving that couldn't be sated with food.

The mechanic pushed herself away from the table and cleared her dishes, stacking them atop the others in the galley. She was glad it wasn't her night for dish washing, although she suspected others would pitch in to help whatever poor soul was on the galley roster for that day. She waved absent-mindedly to the rest of the crew and said her good night as she sidled to the door.

Outside of the mess hall, the ship was quiet and peaceful. As the voices faded, the only sound was the thud of her old boots on the metal floor. She strained to listen for sounds from the bridge, or the boiler room, or Violet's quarters. Alas, decades spent in boiler rooms had deteriorated her hearing, and outside of speaking directly to someone, it was difficult for her to hear anything other than the low hum of the ship's engines and her own footsteps. She breathed deep the scent of the ship: roasted vegetables from the mess hall, the dust on unused crates in corridors, the thick, acrid smell of lubricant for the engines. She wandered through the corridors without a sense of purpose; she walked because it felt like the right thing to do after a huge meal like the one she had just finished. She rounded one corner, and then the next, weaving her way through the ship and back.

"Alice!"

She nearly jumped out of her skin with surprise; her thoughts had been so invasive and loud that she had lost awareness of her own surroundings.

"Violet? Er, Captain?" she said.

"Didn't you hear me calling you? I've been trying to catch up with you since the last corridor," Violet laughed, closing the distance between them with a lazy jog.

Alice tapped her ear. "Sorry, I didn't. Occupational hazard, I guess."

"Did you enjoy the celebration?"

"It was amazing. Nice speech." Alice reached out and laid a hand on Violet's shoulder affectionately, tracing the edging of her leather waistcoat.

Violet nodded. "It was, wasn't it?"

"I really don't want to think about what would have happened if they'd been captured, or if those really were Coalition on all those steambikes."

"Let's not think about it, then." Violet shrugged and gave a strange smile that Alice wondered was hiding something.

"Violet, I was so worried for you," Alice murmured huskily as she gently tugged on a stray curl, which hung over Violet's scar.

"Alice. Don't." She pushed Alice's hand away gently and took a step back.

"Don't what?"

"I've only gotten this far in life by not dwelling on near-misses. We're all safe, we helped the community there, and we celebrated with food and champagne. Tomorrow is another day, and there's another one after that. We have more drops to do, and maintenance to complete, and supplies to redistribute."

"Okay, okay," Alice said quietly as she stepped forward and laid a hand on Violet's shoulder again. "I'm just glad *you're* safe." She squeezed gently and smiled.

Violet sighed deeply and closed her eyes, reaching up to run her fingers over Alice's hand. "And I'm still glad you came back to us. I couldn't train Ivy myself, she already knows more than I do."

"Give her a few years, and I guarantee she'll be innovating new techniques and methods that neither of us have ever heard of." Alice curved her hand around the back of Violet's neck and pulled her in close. "How is it that you manage to attract all these talented people, Captain?" she asked.

"Just my natural charm and charisma," Violet said with a smirk. "But I have to say, landing a renowned Coalition mechanic was one of my more impressive feats." The captain's shoulders relaxed into Alice's hands.

"What about Kady, the renowned Coalition scientist?"

"Shut up, Alice," Violet said with a laugh. "Take the compliment."

Alice leaned down and kissed Violet gently, barely grazing her soft, full lips. With one hand still behind the captain's head to pull her close, she raised her other hand up to rest it on Violet's hip. "Compliment received," she murmured.

Violet leaned into the kiss and Alice felt the edges of the moment blur. It felt right to be with the captain, and despite trying to resist each other, it was clear that it was difficult for both of them. Alice felt a flutter of excitement at the thought.

Violet pulled away from the kiss and hissed, "Alice! Did you hear that?"

"No?" Alice replied.

"Someone's coming. Come on, follow me." Violet pushed open a door and nudged Alice through it, closing the door behind them.

"A broom closet? Really?" Alice whispered, rolling her eyes at Violet's paranoia. She was the captain, and a pirate, so why the hell was she so worried about one of the crew seeing them together?

"Shh, they're getting closer."

Alice tried to listen for voices or footsteps, but couldn't hear anything over the noise of a nearby air filtration unit. She pressed her ear to the door and closed her eyes in concentration. Finally, she heard muffled voices laughing as they stopped in the corridor outside.

"Shit, they stopped out there," Alice said in a barely audible breath.

The closet was dark, the only light coming from under the door. She felt around for a light switch, but didn't find one. As the laughter outside continued, her eyes began to adjust to the darkness, Violet's face forming from nothingness. She felt Violet's hand snake around her waist and pull her closer, and she bent her head and kissed the captain, quiet and light.

Violet pulled Alice into the kiss, gently biting her lower lip and kissing her deep and slow. She wrapped her other arm around the mechanic's waist and held her tight as she nuzzled and kissed her neck.

Lost in the moment, Alice leaned into the kiss. She reached out for Violet, and connected with a mop handle instead, knocking it over with a huge crash. They sprang apart and waited for their inevitable discovery from the crew in the corridor. They waited, but no one came in.

"I think they're gone," Violet whispered.

Alice leaned in for another kiss but Violet put her hand up to stop her. "We're playing with fire, Alice," she said firmly. "Someone could have seen us, together in this closet. And what would they have thought then?"

Alice shrugged in the darkness. "They would have thought that two adults were having some fun," she retorted.

"I don't want to be kissing you in a broom closet."

"Then kiss me outside of one," the mechanic challenged, her hand on the doorknob as she leaned in for another kiss. She playfully jiggled the knob and laughed.

"Alice!" Violet said in a worried hush. "Alice, if anyone sees!"

"Okay, okay, never mind." Alice straightened her shoulders, her mouth set in a frown.

"Alice, come on—"

"It's fine, Captain. I understand," she interrupted. She didn't understand, but the last thing she was going to do was beg. She smoothed her braids and opened the door, flooding the closet with light from the corridor. "Good night."

"Alice!" Violet called after her.

"Goddamnit," Alice mumbled to herself, the sound of her boots echoing down the empty corridor, "Fuck."

CHAPTER TWENTY-ONE

VIOLET AWOKE WITH A start to the sound of her radio crackling and hissing on the table next to her bed. The room was completely black, except for the dim blinking light from the radio, which wasn't even strong enough to cast a shadow. She bolted upright and snatched the radio from the table, knowing that there must be something very wrong for a crew member to call her when she was off-duty.

"Yes? Captain here, report," she said quickly into the radio.

"Er, Boss, I think you should see this. Can you meet me on the bridge?" Ned replied, worry vibrating around every syllable.

"I'll be right there," Violet said, already dressing in yesterday's clothes. Whatever it was, it had Ned worried enough to wake her, and there was no time to hunt for a clean shirt. She didn't even bother to lace her boots, she just tucked the laces and threw open the door, awkwardly jogging towards the bridge as she buttoned her shirt and pushed up the cuffs to rest in the middle of her forearms. When she arrived at the bridge, Ned and Kady were already staring at the main screen. Violet looked up, and there they all were: a transmission from the Coalition, with all their photos, stamped with WANTED in red, and signed 'by order of Corporal Allemande.'

"What the hell happened?" Violet demanded.

"It would seem the Coalition figured out that it was us who helped the rebel community back on Delta-4," Kady said carefully. "Most of the crew are wanted for piracy and abetting rebels. Alice and I, we're wanted for treason."

Violet sat down heavily in her captain's chair, beneath the alarming display. "And Barnaby? He's not wanted for treason?"

"I don't think the Coalition knows he's with us on the ship. I checked the database, he's wanted for fraud and financial crimes, which we already knew."

"Ned, how wide do you think this transmission went? How many ships and trading beacons will have seen this?" Violet asked, studying the display. She was struck by the photos they had used; most of them were old and out of date. Kady's photo was from her time in the Coalition, and she looked even younger than she did now, no more than a teenager. She didn't know where Ned's photo was from, and wondered if an old lover had supplied it. He was young and lithe, with short cropped ginger hair and a clean shaven face. If you didn't know him, you might not even recognize him from the photo. Her own photo was from decades ago, from when she studied in the Coalition flight school. It was before she even got the long silvery scar on her face, and it was an odd shock to stare at her much younger self. Alice's photo was by far the most recent; it looked like a photo from her Coalition I.D. badge. Photos of each crew member scrolled across the screen, their names and ages included. The only photo missing from the lineup was Ivy's.

"Probably everywhere in the near systems, if I had to make a guess. If you look at the small print, they've included a very helpful list of infractions."

Violet squinted at the display. "It looks as though they're blaming us for every pirate raid in the nearby systems over the past five years. Some of these are on the same date, at opposite ends of the galaxy, how the hell would we have accomplished both?"

"They mean to make an example of us," Kady said, a hint of worry in her tone. "If they can catch the pirates that did all these things, the Coalition looks strong, and piracy will die down for awhile after they execute us."

"Kady!" Violet interjected, whipping her head around to meet the scientist's unfocused gaze. "Stop, that's not helping."

"If we get caught, Alice and I will be executed first. The rest might get lucky, might live out your lives in a work camp. But not traitors. Not former employees, guilty of *treason*." Kady's lower lip wobbled as she tried to hold in her tears.

Violet massaged her left temple and closed her eyes, facing the front window of the ship. "We're not going to get caught. We'll figure something out." She leaned back into her chair and tried to think, tried to push away the clouds of sleep for a clear thought. She needed coffee. "Ned," she said quietly, "I need some coffee, lots of it, and extra strong. And wake Alice and Hyun, they should know what's going on as senior members of the crew." She paused a moment. "And wake Barnaby, maybe he can give us some insight here."

"Aye, Boss," he replied softly, and the two women heard his uneven footsteps fade down the corridor.

"It's only a matter of time, now," Kady said, and tears welled up in her eyes. "We can't evade them forever. They have our *pictures*. They have all our pictures."

Violet stood and wrapped Kady in a wordless embrace, allowing her a moment to cry and mourn for the moments before she knew she was wanted for treason. The captain hugged her tightly, gently smoothing her long, dark hair. Kady let a strangled sob slip, and buried her face in the captain's shoulder like a small child, wrapping her arms around the captain's neck.

Alice arrived in the doorway of the bridge, looking surprisingly awake and alert, given the time. "Oh, shit," she said when she saw Kady's tear stained face. "What happened?"

"Alice, good," Violet said, keeping one arm around Kady. "We have important matters to discuss." She looked the mechanic up and down, a grease rag tucked into her belt and a smudge on her cheek. "Alice, were you still *working*?"

The mechanic shrugged. "Couldn't sleep, so figured I would examine some of the systems for possible upgrades." She looked worriedly at Kady. "What's going on?" she repeated.

Violet gestured at the main display with her free hand, which was still rotating through the photos of each crew member, WANTED stamped in red at the bottom.

"Oh, shit," Alice said again softly, watching the photos fade from one to the next, as her own face stared back at her. "Well, that's me done for treason, isn't it?"

"It would seem as though they are trying to pin all the major piracy over the last five years on this ship's crew alone," Violet replied. "It's unfair, but that's standard for Coalition policy."

Alice stifled a nervous laugh. "I haven't even been here two months, how can I be made responsible for five years of piracy?"

"According to this transmission, you were feeding us information for years, including dates and locations of cargo drops."

"That wasn't me, it was Barna—wait, why isn't Barnaby on here?"

"The Coalition doesn't know he's on the ship with us. He's only wanted for fraud and financial crimes, which are a lower priority than piracy and abetting rebels," Violet explained.

"Well at least one of us isn't wanted for treason, eh?" Barnaby said blearily as he appeared in the doorway. "Funny how they pinned all that on you, Al."

"'Funny' isn't the word I would choose to use, Barns. I could be executed." Alice tugged at her braids nervously. "I kind of expected this after I left the C.S. Stronghold, but it hits harder seeing it in black and white on a public transmission."

"We both could be executed," Kady said, swallowing another sob. "They'll kill us both."

"What should we do, Boss?" Ned asked, having caught up to Barnaby.

Violet took a deep breath and patted Kady's shoulder. "We're going to figure this out, that's what we're going to do. No sense in rolling over and giving up, now is there?" She stretched her neck in a circle and squared her shoulders. She rubbed the sleep from her eyes, and took the large mug of coffee that Ned was holding out to her. It was strong, just how she wanted it. She took a long drink and focused on the hot, almost burning warmth as it slid easily down her throat. Her senior crew members looked at her expectantly, waiting for her solution that would fix everything.

"Ned, call a meeting first thing, as soon as the shifts change. Everyone needs to know what's going on. You and Barnaby are to stay here with me on the bridge and talk about potential solutions to this situation." She squeezed Kady's shoulder gently. "Kady, you and Alice need to work on that stealth shield. Did you have a look at that data we stole from the last vessel?"

"Yes," she sniffled, "from the data, it appears that it worked."

"Good. Take Alice to the lab and work together on shoring it up. I don't want to rely on untested technology, but if we have to, then we will."

"*Untested technology*?" Barnaby said incredulously. "Why not just hand Kady and Alice over right now, then? You're going to risk their lives on some fanciful stealth shields?"

Violet narrowed her eyes at him. "You are a guest here on my ship, sir. Remember that before you challenge me on my bridge, or we'll drop you at the next trading beacon and let you fend for yourself."

"Boss, he's just concerned, he—" Ned interjected.

"We're all concerned, Ned," Violet said forcefully. "It's a concerning situation, and we're going to do the best we can to work through it. I don't need some two bit fraudster telling me how to run my ship. Kady is one of the best scientists in the near systems, and Alice was a celebrated Coalition mechanic. I have faith that they will succeed." She glared at Barnaby. "Sit."

He sat obediently, perching on Ned's chair.

"Ned, you'd better brew up more coffee. We're all going to need it today."

• • • •

KADY BENT OVER THE desk, her earlier panic and tears replaced by a laser focus and unshakable determination. Alice watched with admiration as Kady scribbled out code on a piece of scrap paper with a tiny nib of a pencil. The scientist's brow was furrowed in concentration as she worked, checking her scrambled notes every few moments.

Alice leaned against a table as she waited for her to finish, sipping a mug of lukewarm coffee. Her thoughts turned to the situation at hand, and the knot in her stomach tightened once again. The image of her face on the screen kept replaying in her mind, over and over again. She remembered when she'd had that photo taken. It was only about six months ago, when it had come time to renew her official Coalition I.D. card. Barnaby had spent the entire morning that day teasing her about it, and had tried to get her to change her hair for the photo. "This is how I look every day, why would I change it?" she had asked. Now she wished that she had, even though it was unlikely to make her look different enough to avoid detection.

"What about this?" Kady asked, yanking Alice from her deep thoughts. She pushed a piece of paper across the desk, covered in tiny scribbles of code, even filling the margins of the page.

Alice tugged her goggles down over her eyes to examine the paper. "Well I admit I don't know as much as you about coding, but the science seems solid. I never thought of inverting a radar wave to appear invisible on sensors. How did you come up with that?"

"After examining Captain Leo's data, and our logs from that incident, I noticed that they were using an external wave to disable our radar. Which, yes, works, but we were also aware early on that something was wrong with our systems. We were on guard. With this, hopefully they won't even know we're there. We'll be invisible."

"Impressive," Alice mumbled, poring over the data scattered all over the desk.

"It will only work if you can realign and invert a signal. I can code, and I can do the science, but I don't know where to begin with hardware."

Alice wiggled her eyebrows and twirled a small screwdriver. "Now that I can help you with," she said confidently. "I'll need a radio, preferably an old analog one. And some other bits, let's see here. " she began to make a list of random pieces, scribbling in mechanic's short hand. She grabbed her radio from her belt. "Ivy? Ivy? I know it's early, but I need your help."

"Mmmf, yes?" came the muffled reply.

"Can you come to Kady's lab? I have some equipment I need. I've made a list."

"Right away, Alice," Ivy mumbled.

"I think this could really work, Kady," Alice said hopefully. "As long as we get it right." She offered a smile, but it faded on her lips before Kady looked up at her. She was just as worried and panicked as Kady was, and it showed.

A quiet, solemn moment passed. "I guess we're in the same boat now, aren't we, Spy?" Kady asked solemnly.

"Yes, I guess we are. So we'd better make sure this thing works, or we're both in trouble."

"What will you do if we get caught?" Kady looked down at her notes again, but Alice saw the scientist tearing up again. Beneath her tough, intelligent exterior, she was just as human. Just as vulnerable to emotion and fear.

"I don't plan on getting caught," Alice replied sternly, trying to bolster Kady's confidence. "Getting tortured and executed isn't exactly in my life plan."

"What about stealing a shuttle and joining a pirate crew, was that in your plan?" Kady smirked now, and Alice knew her act of confidence was starting to work.

Alice laughed. "No, I suppose it wasn't. Still, we can do this. We can." She waited a moment for Kady's response, but the scientist was buried in her notes again, intent on finding a solution. Alice glanced down at the code Kady had written, and examined it. It was simple enough, just binary, but it might just hold the key to their survival, at least until they figured something else out. What would be next? Hacking the Coalition data archives to erase all mention of themselves? Even so, the Coalition would still be looking for them. Change their appearances, change their names? Would the Coalition ever stop looking for them?

She sighed and poured herself another cup of coffee from the flask Ned had sent them away with, drinking deeply from the matching blue enamel mug. She nibbled on the corner of a flaky pastry he had given them, but neither mechanic nor scientist had any appetite after the early morning discovery of their faces plastered on a Coalition transmission.

"Alice?"

There was a soft knock on the door of the lab, and Ivy poked her head inside. "Alice, I brought some things I thought you might need to get started."

Inside the crate in her arms was a random assembly of parts and tools, gears, sprockets, and springs. There was also another very large container of coffee, and a basket of fruit. Alice eagerly took the crate from Ivy, handing over the list of materials she had made with the other hand. She stood with the crate balanced on her hip.

"You're a gem, Ivy. Thank you, I know it's early."

"Is everything okay?" she asked with a worried tone. "It's not like you to call me when I'm not on shift."

"There will be a meeting in the mess hall soon with the rest of the crew, the captain will explain everything. Thank you again for the parts, and the coffee. If you could get the rest of the items on my list after the meeting, I'd really appreciate it." She tried for a smile again, because she didn't want Ivy to worry.

"Sure, anything," Ivy replied with a tentative smile. "I'll see you in a little bit, then."

Alice nodded. "In a bit. Don't be late for the meeting."

Ivy nodded and left. Alice poured another mug of coffee and passed it wordlessly to Kady, who immediately began to drink it. Some things were better left unsaid, and the need for caffeine at a time like this was one of them. Alice gestured at the basket of fruit, but Kady shook her head and looked down at her notes, frowning.

The mechanic began to unpack the crate, and was surprised at how intuitive Ivy had been in assembling an assortment of things. She could already begin working on the project with some of the supplies; she pulled a notebook from the bottom of the crate and began roughly sketching a draft of what the completed device would look like. The pair worked in silence, refilling coffee for each other as needed. It was an unexpectedly comfortable working arrangement, and Alice felt grateful for the quiet company.

"You know how I ended up here, don't you," Kady said as she broke the silence.

Alice looked up from the crate. "No, Violet and the others wouldn't elaborate. I know you used to be a scientist for the Coalition, but that's all."

"I'm sure you think I'm a ridiculous hypocrite."

"The thought did cross my mind," Alice replied with a wry smile. "But I guess I can see why you'd be distrustful of Coalition mechanic."

Kady sighed and rubbed her eyes. "I worked in their artificial intelligence division up until a couple of years ago. I started working in their labs when I was 15, too young to know any better."

"Fifteen is young for a lab position."

"Too young," Kady agreed. "I thought we were working towards a better future with safer ships that could use autopilot features beyond the near systems. I helped develop algorithms that would be able to predict ship collisions and avoid contact with debris both in dark space and within terraformed atmospheres."

Alice nodded. "I know that autopilot technology has come a long way since I was first in engineering school. I don't know much beyond that, though."

"I was in the lab late one night, the last one there. I was getting ready to lock up when I noticed a stack of files my supervisor had left on the table. It was against procedure to not lock files away, so as I was about to return them to their drawer, I spotted part of a page that was peeking out from a folder. I couldn't help myself, I just looked."

"And what was it?"

"Plans to use the coding I'd been developing to create autopiloted crafts to drop bombs on rebel sites. To use the algorithms to plot beyond the nearby systems and strip mine whatever planets and moons they came to for resources."

Alice shook her head in confusion. "But strip mining is prohibited. They can't do that, it could disrupt all kinds of unknown ecosystems. And if they had autopiloted crafts, we'd probably be caught or dead by now."

Kady smirked. "Yeah, probably. Except by the time I finished reading all the files I was so angry that I destroyed all my own work. I set fire to all the data and escaped, met Violet in Bradach shortly after when I was earning money by deactivating Coalition chips for deserters."

"Well I must say, I'm impressed," Alice said. "And I understand your caution. I may not have set fire to a lab, but I'm here to stay."

Kady poured herself and Alice another mug of coffee. "I know. Now what do you say we get back to work?"

• • • •

DAYS PASSED QUIETLY on the Cricket, the crew tending to their duties as usual. The ship felt hollow without the usual laughter and chatter, and it began to take a toll on each crew member. Some became insular and depressed, while others developed bitterness and anger. All of them were scared.

Kady and Alice worked together quietly, passing notes and mugs of coffee across the table and discussing options for their stealth shield device. Violet and Ned discussed how to handle the situation going forward, with the help of Barnaby's insider knowledge of Coalition bureaucracy. Hyun's med bay was kept busy with the steady stream of crew members desperate for something to help them sleep; it seemed as though insomnia was a plague, and none of them were immune. Jasper rarely came out of his room, except to complete his shifts on duty. Kady and Alice worked together quietly, passing notes and mugs of coffee across the table and discussing options for their stealth shield device.

The tension was like a planet's atmosphere in the early phases of terraforming: humid, heavy, and hard to breathe.

Violet walked the corridors of the ship, determined to make her presence felt. She couldn't fix their problems single-handedly, and nor could she offer guarantees and assurances that they'd all make it out of this alive, but she could hold her head high and give them hope that they would find a way out of this mess. For now, they were hidden in dark space, far from any trading beacons, planets, or moons. There weren't even any other vessels out this far, and those that passed nearby were those of other pirates. The darkness here was oppressive and complete, with no light from stars or moons. The space around them was silent, except for the gentle hum of their own boilers, powering their air filtration and power.

They couldn't stay here forever, though, and so she hoped that her senior crew members had made some progress with their plans. She hadn't seen Alice in days, not since they first discovered the transmission. Even amidst the chaos of the situation, a part of her felt eager to see the mechanic's face again.

She knocked on the door to the lab and gently opened the door. Alice and Kady were working side by side, the desk strewn with papers, and a small analog radio in the middle, with something like an antique antennae attached to the top of it. There were mugs of cold coffee on almost every surface, and the scrambled eggs and muffins Ned had brought them that morning had been left untouched.

"Good morning," she ventured quietly as she swung open the door.

Alice looked up, and Violet nearly gasped. The mechanic's face looked almost gaunt, and the deep purple crescents under her eyes showed that she hadn't been sleeping. Her coveralls were wrinkled, the elbows smudged with the gray shine of graphite from pencils.

"Alice," Violet said quietly.

"Captain." Alice nodded.

Violet cleared her throat. "Are you both alright? Can I get you anything?"

"We're fine, Captain," Kady said without looking up from her notes. "It would seem we make a good team, at least so far."

"Have you made any progress?" Violet couldn't help but stare at Alice's exhausted, malnourished face. It was clear the mechanic needed a hot meal and a good night's sleep, but Alice wasn't eating, and sleep was a luxury they couldn't afford until they had a way out of this mess.

"We should have a prototype by this evening, assuming Kady's code interfaces correctly with the device. Early tests have been promising." Alice blinked slowly, almost as if she was trying to sleep standing up.

"Maybe you should both take a break," Violet ventured. "It doesn't look like you've even eaten your breakfast."

"I don't really have an appetite when my life and the lives of my crew mates are on the line," Kady muttered. "And it would seem Alice feels the same."

Alice nodded in agreement. "Aye."

"But if anyone needs a break, it's her," Kady continued, gesturing towards Alice. "She hasn't slept in days."

"I'm fine. I'll sleep when the prototype is completed," she defended herself as she wobbled on the spot, her legs weak from exhaustion.

Violet looked at Alice worriedly, her brow furrowed in concern. "Alice..."

"Don't worry, Captain, Ivy is handling the main systems," Alice assured her. "She's more than competent."

"That's not what I'm worried about."

Alice looked up and narrowed her eyes. "Then what's the problem?" She tossed a screwdriver onto the workbench noisily and stared at Violet, hands on her hips.

"I just worry. Are you sure you don't need a break?" Violet asked gently.

"I *said*, I'll sleep when the prototype is complete."

Kady looked up in surprise at Alice's tone, glancing from the mechanic to the captain. "Er, Captain, I think we're alright here. We just want to get this finished so we can test it. Alice is tired, as am I, but we're so close to having a prototype. I promise we'll sleep when we're finished."

Violet scrutinized Alice's face, looking for a reason to order her back to quarters for her own good.

Alice caught her eye and squinted. "I'm *fine*, Captain."

Violet sighed, defeated. "Kady, let me know if you need anything. Alice...try to get some rest." As she retreated from the lab, she heard the familiar sound of coffee being poured into a cheap enamel mug. She was worried about Alice, worried about all of them. She had been forcing herself to eat, more for fuel than enjoyment, choking down dry sandwiches and watered down juice. She couldn't blame Alice for not eating, not sleeping, not when she was facing execution if they were all caught. They'd all be facing life sentences in work camps, but Kady and Alice would have no hope of a reprieve. As the years passed, the Coalition laws against treason only grew more inhumane, allowing torture and painful execution methods. Violet swallowed the lump in her throat and blinked back tears for the third time that day.

• • • •

THE CAPTAIN MADE THE rounds on her ship, gently reassuring her crew that they were working on a plan to get them all out of this mess. The crew members respected Kady and Alice, and it seemed like just knowing they were planning something eased the tension. She felt exhausted, her well of emotional energy depleted from the past few days. She stopped in the mess hall for yet another cup of coffee, which didn't even taste pleasurable at this point, just hot and bitter. She prepared it in a daze, her movements automatic and joyless. Time moved around her, and she felt detached. She drank her coffee silently, staring at the wall of the galley and tried not to vividly imagine their capture and subsequent punishments. She bit her lip hard, trying to force herself back into the moment.

"Boss?" Ned asked gently. "Are you alright? Your lip is bleeding."

"What? Oh." she replied, wiping her mouth with the back of her hand. A bright red streak flashed across her dark skin.

"Do you want something to eat? I was about to make some lunch." He gestured towards the galley hopefully and mimed making a sandwich.

"I'm not hungry."

"How about I make two portions anyway, and you can decide after I'm done if you want it or not," he offered. "If not, I'm sure someone else will eat it."

Violet nodded.

"I've got some fresh sourdough from this morning. I bake when I'm stressed. We have some leftovers I can repurpose into sandwiches?"

Violet nodded again, sucking on her bottom lip to stop the bleeding.

Ned began to potter about in the galley, slicing loaves of bread, pulling out leftover roasted vegetables, and preparing a herb sauce for the sandwiches. He worked in silence, but kept an eye on Violet, who didn't look well.

"Any update from Barnaby with thoughts on how to get out of this mess?" she asked flatly. She had hoped the fraudster's experience in scheming would have given them more intel on how to fix their problem. So far, Barnaby hadn't been much help, and she was starting to resent his presence on board.

Ned eyed her from the corner of his vision. "He's still adamant that we need a scapegoat if we want to get out of this for good." He whisked together herbs and oil to make the sandwich spread, and dolloped it generously onto the sliced bread.

Violet frowned into her mug and took a sip of the lukewarm, bitter beverage. "Scapegoats don't just grow on trees, Ned. And how would we even convince the Coalition to go for that?"

"Discussions are ongoing," he said, nervously piling the bread high with roasted aubergines and peppers. "We'll come up with something."

"If we don't, then lives are on the line. Have you made that clear?" she asked bitterly. "We allowed him onto the ship because we were under the illusion that his information would be paramount."

"He cares about Alice, too." Ned paused and searched Violet's face. "I know he hasn't made a good first impression, but he wants to help."

"Are you saying that just because you're sleeping with him?" Violet asked pointedly.

Ned put the metal spoon down noisily and glared at Violet. "We're not, actually, not that it's any of your business."

"I'm the captain, anything that affects my crew is my business," she shot back.

"I don't think I agree." He picked up the spoon and angrily flung a pile of matured cheese onto the bread. "It's not like this is an easy situation for any of us."

Violet sighed and put a hand on Ned's arm. "I know. I'm sorry."

"Boss, there might not be any good solutions to this. We might lose people before this is over."

"We're not going to lose a goddamn soul," Violet replied firmly. "I don't care if I have to break down the doors to the Coalition head offices myself. We still have supplies to deliver, and people to help, and I will be damned if they force us into a corner."

Ned looked at her with disbelief. "You still want to do the supply drop?"

"We can't let people starve just because the Coalition has put a little heat on us, Ned." She swiped at a droplet of the oily liquid and licked her finger. Delicious, of course.

Ned wordlessly sliced the sandwiches diagonally and set them on plates, his face set in a scowl. He wiped his hands on his apron and hung it on a nearby hook, and pushed one of the plates towards Violet.

"Kady and Alice said they might have a working prototype," she offered hopefully as she picked up the plate and examined her lunch.

"I think I agree with Barnaby on this," he replied, "I don't want to be relying on untested technology. It's too risky." He took a bite of his sandwich, and a piece of aubergine flopped soggily onto the plate.

"Do you doubt their abilities?"

Ned chewed his food, and then frowned. "Of course not, they're the best there is. But no one has ever perfected a cloaking shield before, and we'd be risking our necks putting it to the test."

"What other choice do we have?" Violet challenged, arranging her sandwich and taking a bite. "We won't find a scapegoat that the Coalition wants more than us all the way out here, and even if we did, there's no guarantee they wouldn't just pick us up too."

"We could wait."

"If we wait, all that cargo will go to waste. Then they've backed us into a corner, and then what?"

"And we wait until we can do more tests, or come up with a better solution," Ned replied angrily. "I don't want to see anyone in danger."

"We're past that, Ned," Violet said softly. "We're all in danger now. If we wait, if we stay here, they'll find us eventually. They did before, they will again. Just takes one nearby vessel spotting us to sell us out, and then what? We'd be sitting ducks."

"Fuck this," Ned said, throwing his plate down. "This is bullshit, Boss." One of the sandwich halves slid to one side, exposing the filling.

"Yes, but it's also the job. You knew we wouldn't be able to fly under the radar forever."

Ned sighed and picked up the intact half of his sandwich. "Let's hope this device they're working on doesn't fuck us all over," he said sourly. "I'd rather not spend the rest of my days chained up in a work camp."

"Well that feeling is mutual, I assure you."

Alice's voice echoed up the corridor, "It works! It works!" she shouted. Alice staggered into the room and collapsed into the nearest chair, holding the device aloft. "It...works."

Kady followed behind and gently took the device from Alice and placed it safely on the table in front of her.

"It works? Really?" Violet asked hopefully. "How many simulations did you run? What kind of tests?"

"It passed every simulation we ran, and it also worked in the fifteen tests we ran," Kady said proudly. "I think it might be ready for a real test."

"What kind of real test?" Ned asked skeptically. "It sounds dangerous, especially under the current circumstances."

"There are some friendly pirate vessels a short distance away that we could approach, ask if they saw us," Kady replied. "But we're confident it will work."

Alice slumped down in her chair, already succumbing to exhaustion. Kady prodded her, and she sat straight in her chair. "Yes, confident," she added.

"What are we waiting for?" Violet asked. "Let's give her a test run, then!"

The group raced to the bridge, with Alice trudging behind, her every step sounding heavy and laborious. Violet set the device on the main console and turned to Kady. "Do we have to hook it into something?" she asked.

"Yes," Kady replied, moving towards the console, "I'll wire it into the main navigation and radar panel. It should work, I've engaged it."

"Ned, where's the nearest friendly ship?" Violet asked.

He examined the screen at his desk, and then the map on the wall. "About 400 kilometers."

"Lay in a course, let's see if they see us coming."

"Aye," he replied.

The engines roared into life, the boilers already hot from keeping the systems running while they hid in dark space. The Cricket lurched forward and began to pick up speed as they headed towards a friendly pirate vessel, known to them from many years of collaborations on assisting the rebel communities of the nearby systems.

"How long?" Violet asked.

"No more than a few moments, stand by," Ned replied.

Violet watched Alice lean against the doorway and struggle against sleep, her eyelids heavy with the weight of exhaustion.

They waited, and before long the vessel came into view.

"Approach, but slowly," Violet instructed.

"Aye."

The Cricket inched closer to the vessel, and Violet held her radio in her hand, waiting for a call from the ship. No call came. With every passing moment, her hope grew in her chest. Finally, they were side by side with the vessel, and the name, The Marshy Hag, was close enough to read.

"Kady, disengage the device," Violet said, and she held her breath in anticipation.

Without a word, Kady flipped a switch on the device. After a moment, Violet's radio crackled to life.

"Ope! Violet? Captain Violet? Golly, where did you come from? We had nothing on our sensors, and there you were!"

Violet turned and grinned at her crew. "It would appear that the device is functional. Congratulations, Alice, Kady." She brought the radio to her mouth and responded, "Hail there, Marshy Hag, just checking in. How are you all doing?"

"Just fine, just fine Violet – we saw you lot on a transmission the other day, did ya know?"

"Yes, we're aware, same old tricks from them eh?"

"Ah yeah, you'll outsmart em, y'always do. We'd love to stay and chat but we're late for a supply drop, we'll have to catch up later, how about Bradach in three weeks?"

"See you then," Violet replied, not wanting to get into the gritty details of their current situation. The ship sped out of sight and the senior crew members all breathed a sigh of relief, and Ned sat back in his seat with a grin. Kady smiled confidently, and as they turned, they saw Alice slumped against the door, fast asleep.

"She missed it," Kady said, disappointed.

"It's alright, she'll be pleased nonetheless. I'll be sure she makes it to her quarters."

Violet left her other senior crew members to celebrate on the bridge and guided a half asleep Alice to her quarters. She pushed open the door and led Alice to the bed, where she promptly fell back against the pillows. The captain removed Alice's boots gently and dropped them to the floor. She turned to leave, but noticed again the sorry state of the mechanic's coveralls, caked in grease and oil from several days wearing the same thing. Violet unclipped the toggles and pulled them down over Alice's shoulders, and rounded the bed to pull them over her hips. She dropped them on the floor in a heap and thought better of it, folding them under her arm to take and wash for her. She pulled a blanket up over her and whispered, "Thank you, Alice, we couldn't have done it without you."

She kissed her on the cheek and as she turned to leave, Alice mumbled, "I love you, too."

CHAPTER TWENTY-TWO

"ALRIGHT, PEOPLE, DON't get cocky. Just because the cloaking device is functional doesn't mean that no one will recognize you in the city. Keep your heads down, don't attract any undue attention. Get the supplies to the drop zone, have dinner at a tavern, do as you will, just be smart." Violet stood on a table in the mess hall, addressing her crew. After the test was successful, news spread through the ship like wildfire, and she was now looking into cautiously hopeful faces.

"Hyun, I'm very sorry that you'll have to miss your tournament. Hopefully things will calm down soon, we're working on a more permanent solution."

"I understand, Captain," Hyun said brightly, "it's for the best. And besides, there are other ways to play in the tournaments without my face being seen – like with an earpiece in a willing actor."

"Is that even tournament legal?" Violet asked, laughing.

Hyun shrugged. "Does it matter?" She grinned and buttoned a tailored emerald green jacket, much more demure than her usual style, and yet she still looked impeccable.

The crew tittered and whispered, and it was the happiest Violet had seen Jasper since he and Kady narrowly escaped on those Coalition steambikes. Most of the crew had prepared for the drop by wearing hooded jackets that shielded their eyes, or colorful printed scarves wrapped around their faces as was the custom in this city, which was a very welcome coincidence.

"You all know the drill: be back on board by noon tomorrow so we can head to the last scheduled drop. After that, we'll turn our attention towards getting our faces off of Coalition screens." Violet shooed them out of the mess hall with a grand gesture. "Go on, be safe. Have fun!"

They filtered out of the room, breaking off into small groups as they prepared to meet their drop zone assistants with the heavy, laden crates of food, medicine, and supplies. Violet nimbly hopped off the table and sat in the nearest chair. She propped her boots up on the table and leaned back into her seat with a satisfied sigh.

"Boss?" Ned was approaching from the galley with a bottle of vintage red wine they had stolen from a merchant vessel a few months back. The dark green glass was dusty, and he carried two mugs with him. "Boss, isn't it my turn to stay on board? Don't you want to get out and stretch your legs?"

Violet opened an eye. "I don't mind, Ned." She noticed the mugs and bottle, and raised an eyebrow. "Though it seems you might have plans."

He cleared his throat awkwardly. "I, er...no. Just a quiet night in for me."

"With two mugs and a bottle of wine?" she teased.

"I was going to ask if you wanted some," he said, preparing to uncork the bottle.

She waved him away. "No, no. Go have your fun. I'll keep watch."

"I insist, Boss," he urged, "please go relax in the city. I'll stay on board." He paused and narrowed his eyes. "Unless *you* have plans on board. I didn't see our fair mechanic in that crew meeting."

"Oh please, Ned, don't be ridiculous," she replied nervously. "I could never become romantically entangled with a member of my crew. It would be unprofessional."

"Did you get the notice that we're actually *pirates*?" Ned laughed. "I'm not sure professionalism matters all that much to the likes of us."

"Well, it would be messy, then." Violet's mind wandered back to the previous evening, when Alice had unconsciously declared her love, and felt her cheeks burn with the memory. "Anyway I was just feeling tired, but maybe you're right, maybe I should spend some time in the city. It's not as if many would recognize me from that old photo anyway."

Ned leaned on his cane. "It's a rebel sympathizer area, Boss. Unlikely anyone would turn you in anyway. They know which side their bread is buttered."

"Yes, well, okay. You've convinced me. I'll see you in the morning." Violet nodded to Ned and his wine with a wink, and turned left down the corridor towards the loading bay door and the exit of the ship. She had no intention of leaving the ship, in fact. At least not yet. But she couldn't risk Ned suspecting her growing entanglement with Alice even more than he already did. She looped around the back of the ship, far from the mess hall, the bridge, and Ned's quarters. She took the long way towards the boiler room, where she hoped she would find Alice and discuss the sleepy admission she had made the night before.

As she approached the boiler room, she heard the familiar sounds of a mechanic tinkering, the dulcet tones of a disorganized toolbox and an unruly boiler. She quietly descended the steps and found Alice hunched over one of the secondary boilers, examining a small valve through her goggles.

"You know everyone else has left the ship, yes?" Violet announced. "Aren't you excited to ditch the coveralls and have some fun in the city?"

Alice jumped with surprise and stood up with her goggles still pulled down over her eyes. She was wearing a clean set of coveralls, a navy blue pair with her name emblazoned over the breast pocket.

"Captain," she said with a smile, "you surprised me."

"You look considerably more rested than the last time I saw you." It was true; the color had returned to the mechanic's cheeks, and the deep sags under her eyes had disappeared.

"I don't even remember how I got back to my quarters yesterday," Alice admitted. "When I woke up today, I ran straight to the lab to see how the test went. Kady couldn't believe I slept through it."

Violet considered the possibility that Alice had no memory of what she said the night before, and that it had been nothing more than an example of an exhausted, overworked mind. "Well, I can't believe you went that long without sleeping or eating," she said carefully. "After all, even a great mind needs rest. You know, Napoleon—"

"Tried to go without sleeping, and lasted three days," Alice finished. "I know the story. I guess he had nothing on my ability to keep working, eh?" She grinned and tossed a wrench into the toolbox, where it landed noisily.

"Indeed." Violet cast an eye over Alice, her broad shoulders, ample stomach, wide hips. She shivered, even though she wasn't cold. She never was in the boiler room.

"Did you need something, Captain? I would have thought you'd be in the city celebrating the success of the cloaking device, raising a glass to Kady."

"Well what about you, why aren't you celebrating this evening?"

Alice placed the hammer she was holding back into her toolbox with a soft metallic thud. "Still recovering, I suppose, and even though Ivy is a model student, she's still inexperienced. I wanted to check on things, make sure we'll be ready to go tomorrow." She dusted off her knees and wiped her greasy hands on her thighs.

"And?"

"And yes, everything is fine, save for a few minor adjustments." She turned and tapped the boiler she had been examining. "Old Bessie here just needed some tweaking."

"Old Bessie? You're naming my boilers now?"

Alice raised an eyebrow. "*Your* boilers? Down here, this is my domain, Captain." She leaned against the workbench, her hands braced on either side. "I just don't think Old Bessie would respond to you the same way." She winked and gave the captain a wide grin.

Violet laughed and shook her head. "I suppose that's fair. Old Bessie it is." She paused to search Alice's face for any hint of what she'd said the night before. Alice was busying herself with returning tools to their homes, wiping away grease from the valve she'd been working on, and making a note of pressure gauge readings in her notebook. Violet couldn't help but notice how Alice's coveralls hugged her ample hips and wide thighs. She let out a loud, frustrated sigh.

"Something wrong?" Alice asked distractedly, looking up from her notes through her goggles.

"Yes – I mean, no, it's just – Alice, I think we should talk."

Alice put a hand up to interrupt Violet. "There's no need for that, Captain. I know where we stand."

"Do you, though? I'm concerned we're at different places, here." Violet shuffled her feet and busied her hands with a loose button on the cuff of her shirt. "I'm worried you're looking into this more than I am."

The mechanic pushed up her goggles and laughed. "That's not how I remember it."

"What do you mean, that's not how you remember it?" Violet asked incredulously. She felt annoyed that Alice was being so casual, when just yesterday she had uttered three words that suggested she was far more serious about their relationship, whatever it was.

"I mean, you chased me down the corridor last week." Alice lifted herself onto the workbench and sat, knees wide, her elbows planted on her thighs as she leaned forward. "Seems to me we're even, now."

"I didn't *chase you* down the corridor."

Alice leaned back and shrugged. "However you need to figure it is fine by me," she said nonchalantly. "I understand that you're not comfortable fraternizing with one of your senior officers."

Violet took a step towards the workbench and huffed. "Alice, it's *complicated.*"

Alice shrugged again. "If you say so." She picked up a small wrench and examined it before replacing it in the toolbox. "Was there anything else, Captain? Or did you just want to make sure I'm not falling head over heels in love with you? I have other concerns than my personal life, you know. Like keeping this ship running, staying out of work camps, and not being charged with treason."

The captain recoiled at the word 'love.' She took a step back and glowered at Alice. "Listen, I'm just trying to—"

"Yes, I know," Alice interrupted. "But it's fine. I'll keep out of your way, you keep out of mine. Problem solved."

"It's not as simple as that—"

"Isn't it?" Alice asked, her eyes boring into Violet. "No chance of anything happening if we're never alone together, right?" She hopped off the workbench and dusted of the knees of her coveralls. "Maybe I should head into the city tonight, grab a bite to eat, or—"

Violet lunged forward and kissed Alice hard on the mouth, running her hands up over the mechanic's hips and coming to rest on her soft, wide waist. "Goddamnit, Alice."

Alice grabbed Violet's shoulders and held her at arm's length. "Violet, what's going on?"

The captain wiggled out of her grasp and wrapped her muscular arms around Alice's torso. She kissed the mechanic's neck and reached up to flip open the toggles on her coveralls. "Just be in the moment," she whispered.

Alice pulled away. "If you're going to blame this on me anyway, I might as well make it worth it," she growled. With one fluid motion she grasped Violet with an arm and lifted her onto the workbench, kissing her feverishly and laying hot, fervent kisses on her full lips. With one hand planted next to Violet's hip, Alice snaked her other hand under her shirt. "How long is this going to go on, Captain?" she whispered. "How long will we sneak in the shadows, stealing kisses?" She unbuttoned the captain's vest and blouse, tossing them to the floor. Violet leaned back on her forearms and Alice sidled her way in between her legs.

"Alice—" Violet began.

"Shut up," Alice responded, kissing her again as she opened the front-facing clasp on her lacy black bra and threw it to the ground, leaving her small, dark breasts exposed. "I'm not just a plaything, you know. I'm an actual woman, with feelings."

"I know, I—"

"Take your pants off," Alice ordered.

Violet obeyed, unfastening her large brass buckle and shimmying out of her tight olive green trousers until they fell to the floor. She pulled at her matching black underwear, tugging it over her thighs and throwing them over her shoulder. "So what now, Mechanic?" she teased.

Without a word, Alice knelt on her kneepads in front of the workbench and buried her face between Violet's legs. The captain gasped loudly and tensed, waiting for what was about to happen. Alice traced circles on Violet's most sensitive parts as the captain quietly and quickly breathed words of encouragement, her hands resting comfortably on Violet's muscular thighs. She leaned in closer, pressing her mouth against the captain and exploring her with her tongue.

"Gods, Alice!" the captain groaned, rotating her hips in time with the mechanic. Her breath quickened and became louder and more impatient as Alice continued, as she approached the cusp of climax.

Suddenly, Alice sat back on her haunches and wiped her mouth with the back of her hand.

"What – what are you doing?" Violet asked desperately. "Don't stop!"

Alice smirked and tapped a finger against her chin. "So, *Captain,*" she began, "Are we at different places? Or shall I continue?"

"Continue, continue," Violet begged, widening her legs. "Please."

Without a moment's more hesitation, Alice leaned forward once again, fervently attending to the captain's baser needs with enthusiasm and crimson passion.

Violet felt heat building inside her, a molten, powerful tension she hadn't felt since she was a young woman. She reached out for Alice and laced her fingertips behind the mechanic's head, pulling her closer as she breathed harder than she had in years. Finally, the tension released, and she cried out, echoing around the empty boiler room. When her vision cleared, she looked at Alice, still kneeling on the floor. "Alice."

"No need to thank me, Captain," Alice said in a sultry tone, "just one of my many services aboard the Cricket." She stood up and placed her hands on Violet's taut stomach. "Services only available to you, of course."

The captain, still breathless, replied, "Alice, you're the finest mechanic I've ever met."

Alice threw her head back and laughed. "I should hope so, after that. No boiler is so complicated as a woman."

Violet frowned. "I would hope that a boiler doesn't hold the same allure," she muttered.

"Of course not," Alice replied, kissing the captain's breasts. "But I don't get paid for servicing captains."

· · · ·

VIOLET AWOKE THE NEXT morning, wrapped in nothing but Alice's arms underneath the crisp white bed linen. She blinked blearily and rubbed the sleep from her eyes. Alice was still fast asleep and snoring softly, her braids half undone with stray hairs framing her pale face in the dim light. Violet reached for Alice's goggles and peered through one of the lenses with one eye as she tried to make sense of the display. It was early, almost too early to be awake, but Violet wasn't the kind of woman who could go back to sleep once she awoke. She sighed and gently tried to remove Alice's arm without waking her as she slid out of bed.

"Wha – where are you going?" Alice mumbled drowsily as she stirred. "Don't leave, come back to bed."

"I was going to make us some coffee, and some breakfast. Don't worry, I'll be back," she soothed, realizing she needed to reassure her because the last two times they'd done this, Violet had been gone before Alice woke up. "The rest of the crew won't be back on board for hours yet."

"Mmm, breakfast," the mechanic replied as she turned over and fell back asleep immediately.

Violet bent down and kissed Alice on the cheek, admiring the mechanic's naked body. She dressed lazily, taking her time to lace up her boots and tie her tight curls into a loose bun, smoothing loose curls back behind her ears. She unlatched the lock on the door and quietly sneaked into the corridor, well aware that Ned was still on board. The captain knew her crew well, and didn't expect to see Ned up and about for a few more hours, at least. As she slowly closed the door behind her, she heard something behind her. She reached for her revolver before remembering she had left it holstered in the room. She spun around, ready for a fight.

Barnaby put both hands out, with palms facing towards her. "Easy there, Captain, no threat here."

She glanced towards Ned's quarters and saw the door standing ajar. "What were you doing in Ned's room?" she asked in a hissed whisper.

"Why are you sneaking around?" he countered. He looked at Violet's disheveled appearance. "If I didn't know any better, I'd say you've been spending some quality time with our favorite mechanic."

Violet narrowed her eyes. "None of your business."

"And the same to you, then." He narrowed his eyes and tried to look tough, but he was no match for Violet's confidence and years of experience as a captain.

"Well what are you doing out here so early?" she demanded.

He shrugged. "Couldn't sleep, figured I'd find some coffee and some breakfast. Care to join me?"

"Not really." She sighed, defeated. "Fine, follow me. But no talking. It's too early, and I'm not caffeinated yet."

They walked through the ship in silence for several long minutes before Barnaby could no longer handle the tension of the quiet. "So..." he began, "fraternizing with the crew, eh Captain? Whatever would the rest of them think? Perhaps you're at risk of exhibiting *favoritism.*"

Without a sound, Violet whirled around and pinned Barnaby against the wall with her arm. "Don't you. *Ever.* Say a word about this. To anyone. Not even Ned." She sighed. "Especially not Ned."

He had been taken off guard and there was terror in his eyes for just a second before his charm and charisma took hold once more. "Oh, come now, Captain, Alice is quite a catch, don't you think?"

She leaned onto her arm to put more pressure on him. "I mean it, Barnaby. I will throw you off this ship faster than you can talk me out of it, I don't care who you're fucking."

He swallowed hard. "Okay, okay!"

"I don't care if we're mid-flight in the middle of dark space. I'll open that loading bay door and push you out myself. I know we need you to sort out our current situation, but beyond that? You're just another mouth to feed. So keep it shut." With that, she released him and continued her march towards the mess hall. She made a mental note to make sure Alice installed a rudimentary kitchen the next time they picked up supplies; if spending the night with her was going to be a regular occurrence, she'd rather not have to dodge crew members in the hall to avoid suspicion.

She turned into the mess hall, empty and dark. Without turning the main lights on, she made her way to the galley and began to prepare a large carafe of coffee, pouring scalding hot liquid into the tall enamel container. She stacked two mugs to take, and fished a small bag filled with pastries from underneath the counter. Barnaby stood in the doorway expectantly, his hands outstretched. Violet laughed darkly. "I'm not preparing anything for you. You live on this ship, you fend for yourself."

"I don't know where anything is. And it's dark," he pouted.

Violet hit a switch and the room flooded with light. She squinted involuntarily at the sudden change in brightness, and waited for her eyes to adjust. "Better get started learning where things are, then, shouldn't you?" She nodded towards the walk in pantry. "Coffee is in there. You're on your own for food, though I'm sure Ned ferreted something away, you'll have to ask him. I assume you know how a sink works?"

"*Yes*," he replied, clearly offended.

"Well then, the galley is yours." She turned on her heel and made her way back to her quarters, walking steadily to prevent the coffee from spilling out of the carafe. She could smell the fresh yeast of the pastries, picked up from the local bakery just last night. The captain put the confrontation with Barnaby out of her mind, deciding to instead think about the events of the night before.

She was in an awkward position with Alice now, being too attached with a member of the crew, but still the captain of her ship. What would the others think? They would think she was distracted and vulnerable, especially now that they were fighting off the Coalition at every turn. She had a duty, a responsibility to each of them, not just to keep them alive but to keep them prosperous, fulfilled, and happy. It was a significant burden to bear, but one she had chosen willingly.

She grabbed the pastry bag with her teeth to free a hand to open the door, and quietly entered.

Alice was sitting up in her bed, bright eyed with messy silver braids and her large, full breasts settled on her belly. "Ooh, coffee," she said eagerly as she reached out for the mugs.

"I didn't think you'd be awake yet," Violet said quietly. "You looked dead to the world when I left to hunt down some breakfast. You were even snoring."

Alice looked horrified. "*Snoring*?"

Violet set the carafe and pastries down on the table. "It was endearing."

"I'm sorry, I don't think I snore usually," Alice added. "Thank you for breakfast."

"You do."

"I do what?" she asked, pouring the coffee into the mugs.

"Snore. Usually."

"Oh, gods, how embarrassing," Alice said, unwrapping the pastries. "I'm sorry."

"Don't be. I can sleep through almost anything. I only notice because I'm an early riser."

"Oh, is that why I keep waking up alone?"

"Alice— "

Alice handed her a mug and a pastry. "I told you, Captain, I understand. You can't be seen with a crew member."

Violet's hard stare softened. "You can call me Violet in here, you know." She reached out and traced a scar on Alice's arm, the one she'd gotten when she was first on the ship. It was healed now, nothing more than a shiny pink line.

"I don't want to get into any dangerous habits." Alice took a bite of the pastry and chewed thoughtfully.

"I think it's a little too late for avoiding dangerous habits," Violet laughed. "Aside from sabotaging Coalition equipment, stealing shuttles and confidential data, and aiding rebels, you seem to have picked up quite a knack for secret meetings with pirate captains."

Alice took a sip of the scalding coffee. "What is this, anyway?" she asked.

"Does it really need a label?" Violet asked uncomfortably.

The mechanic looked at her with confusion. Then, "The *pastry*, Captain. What's it called?"

Violet coughed nervously. "Oh right, of course. It's called babka. You've *never* had one?"

"I spent most of my life in the Coalition. Pastries like this would have been seen as an indulgence." She took another bite and smiled. "I'm happy to make up for lost time now, though."

"What about on shore leave? You never ventured into the cities, tried different foods, had some fun?"

"Coalition shore leave is almost always on a Coalition base, and if you're not a new recruit hopped up on adrenaline and youth, there's not actually that much to do. And I didn't have much help on those vessels." She took a long sip of her coffee. "I didn't have enough time to make it into the city and back before I was needed for materials inventory or emergency repairs, so I rarely went anywhere. Shore leave wasn't for the mechanics. Having Ivy as a student is great in many ways: not only do I get more help, but she's bright and promising, too. And..." she trailed off.

"And?"

"And it means I have more time for things like this." Alice placed her mug on the table beside her, turning the handle inwards. She reached over and caressed Violet's scar gently, tracing it down her cheek and over her shoulder. "When did you get this?" she asked gently.

"It's a long story."

Alice snaked an arm around Violet's waist. "I have time."

"It was a long time ago, just after I graduated from the Coalition flight school. My mother was so proud, I was going to be flying the large military transport vessels. I was top of my class, and I set records in the practical exam."

"Impressive."

Violet nodded. "I thought so, too. I felt like I was untouchable. I was traveling the nearby systems before my deployment, eating all the food I could find, drinking until I passed out in strangers' beds. In some way, I thought I was immortal." She sipped the coffee slowly, savoring the warmth.

"And then what happened?"

"The letters from home stopped coming. For awhile I thought that they'd been busy, no time to write. I dismissed it as a fact of getting older, of growing up and becoming an adult. Then, just a few days before I was supposed to report for duty, I decided to return home to see my mother and my sisters. I arrived at the house, I burst through the door to surprise them, and I found them all gaunt, sick. Emaciated. Starving."

"Oh, no," Alice whispered softly.

"The Coalition had heard of a rebel community in the area that hadn't been wiped out in the aftermath of the first rebellion. They stopped allowing supplies in, they tried to starve them out. My sister Rose died a few days after I returned home. Her immune system had been overworked, damaged by a lack of nutrients. We buried her in the local graveyard."

"Violet, I'm so sorry."

"I was young, and I was sick with grief. I didn't show up for my deployment. Coalition members came looking for me, to drag me off to pilot their ships. After all, I had signed on the dotted line, hadn't I? Signed my life away. I tried to fight them off, failed."

"How did you get out of service, then?"

"They threw me in the brig while they figured out what to do with me. I seduced a guard and she set me free. The first town I got to, I cut out my Coalition chip so they wouldn't find me." She traced the scar on her arm where the chip once was, a long time ago. The scar was so faded now, like it had never even happened.

"You cut your own chip out?" Alice asked in horror, her face drained of color at the mere thought.

Violet shrugged. "What else could I do? There were no fancy EMP guns then. Those didn't exist until Kady developed them a few years ago. You should be grateful, without those you'd be sporting a scar on your arm, too." Violet reached out and caressed Alice's arm.

"So then what? You still haven't said where you got your scar from."

The captain sighed sadly. "I went back home. I convinced my other sister, Acacia, to raid the local Coalition depot with me, to steal supplies and distribute them to the community. My mother, she begged us not to go. But we were young, and headstrong, and angry. We didn't want Rose's death to be in vain. So we went, we broke into the depot. We stole medicine and food, mostly. The alarms got triggered, and we had to run." Her eyes began to well up with tears. "A bullet from a Coalition soldier grazed my face. I couldn't see, there was blood everywhere, it ran into my eyes. I just kept running. By the time I looked back, I realized Acacia wasn't with me anymore. They had killed her, and left her body in the middle of the courtyard of the depot. My mother and I, we had to flee after that. We moved a few times. She started working with rebel sympathizers as part of the rebellion. We grew distant, I knew that she had blamed me for Acacia's death. One day, I jumped on the first ship I saw leaving the port, and I never looked back." She wiped an angry tear from her cheek. "That was a long time ago."

Alice wrapped the captain in her arms and rocked her softly. "I'm so sorry that happened to you. You didn't deserve that, and neither did your family."

Violet buried her face in Alice's neck. "It still hurts, even all these years later."

"I know."

They stayed like that for a long while, and Alice held and rocked the captain until the sounds of mid-morning crept upon them. They heard ships landing and leaving the port, and sounds from the dock workers, and the footsteps of crew members who had returned early to prepare for their departure. Finally, Violet broke away from their embrace and wiped her cheeks.

"I've never told anyone that," she said quietly.

"Not even Kady? Or Ned?"

"They know my sisters died, but not that I was involved. They just know that it was largely the fault of the Coalition."

"You can always talk to me. About anything," Alice reassured her.

Violet closed her eyes, willing the memory of her starving family to fade. It never did, and that was why she kept fighting, all these years later. She saw her sisters in the face of every desperate rebel. "We need to start planning our departure, don't you think?" Violet asked quietly, still visibly shaken from her admission. "It's getting late, and we shouldn't hang around too long."

Alice pushed her long, silvery braid over her shoulder. "Are you sure you're alright?" The mechanic reached for Violet's shoulder. "We could stay awhile longer, just until you're feeling better," she offered. "What things make you feel calm? What can I do?"

"I could use a bath," Violet admitted, catching sight of herself in the mirror. "A long, hot bath."

"Well then, I'll leave you to it," Alice declared. "I should probably clean up too, before we head out." She stood and scanned the room for her clothes. "I'll be out of your way just as soon as I find my boots. "

Violet wrapped her arms around Alice's ample waist from behind. "You could just bathe with me. To save water."

Alice looked over her shoulder at the petite captain, her tight curls framing her face. "To save water, of course," she replied with a wink. "I thought that would be too intimate. For you. With a crew member."

Violet snorted. "I've already slept with you, Alice, I think we're past that now."

"You know what I mean. Sleeping together is one thing, bathing together is another." Alice was standing at the door to the bath, in full view of the mirror. Violet saw her reflected in the glass, a tall, naked, round woman. Her pale skin, littered with scars of old burns and injuries, was juxtaposed with the black of her own dark arms clasped around her waist. She wanted to remember this moment. She closed her eyes as if to burn the image into her memory.

"I do enjoy you, Alice," Violet said softly, hugging her tightly. "In another life, maybe it could have been different. Maybe we could have been together, properly."

Alice opened her eyes and turned to face the captain. "I'd rather midnight meetings and secrets than nothing at all."

"I can do that, at least." Violet began to undress, kicking off her unlaced boots towards the door and unbuttoning her shirt, pulling her hair into a tight bun and smoothing it back gracefully. "Alright well get in then," Violet said with a laugh. "What are you even looking at?"

"You."

Violet's cheeks burned and she glanced away. "I look the same as I did last night," she mumbled.

Alice tilted her head. "Yes. But it was dark then." She reached out and took Violet's hands in her own. "I just want to remember the moment, that's all."

The captain looked up into Alice's wide ice blue eyes and exhaled softly. "You make it hard to say no to you."

"Then don't say no," Alice laughed as she unbraided her hair and let it fall loose over her breasts. "Come on, it won't be long before you start to worry that someone will see me leaving your quarters," she continued as she reached across the deep, cast iron and claw foot tub to turn the tap.

Hot, steaming water cascaded into the tub, and condensation began to collect on the unframed mirror that was propped behind the sink. Soft sunlight leaked into the room from a frosted glass window high on the opposite wall, the sunbeams diffused into a vague, gentle orange glow. The tub filled quickly. Alice gingerly stepped into the tub, testing the water. Satisfied by the temperature, she climbed in and folded her legs beneath her, her long silver hair draped over the edge of the tub. She nodded to Violet, who followed suit and sank into the deep tub with a heavy sigh. She stretched a leg out and rested it in Alice's lap.

"This is nice," the captain murmured, her eyes closed as she relaxed into the hot water. "Good idea."

Alice didn't say anything, she sat silently in the tub and absent-mindedly massaged Violet's calf. She reached out for a bar of soap and dunked it briefly to lather it. The soap was a pale yellow and smelled like a pine forest, of tight pine cones and crisp autumn air, a scent that reminded Violet of home. Alice lathered the soap in her hands, the bubbles spilling over her palm into the water. The steam rose to the ceiling in curled tendrils and settled on the mirror's glass, dripping down into the sink.

The captain breathed softly, enjoying the attention and soft care. She never wanted this moment to end. She wanted to live in the moment forever, uncomplicated by the messy politics. Here, soaking in the hot soapy water, being gently caressed by a woman who cared for her, life seemed easier and manageable. She pushed away thoughts of her responsibilities as a captain and to others who depended on her for their survival. The tap dripped lazily, splashing into the full tub. Violet opened an eye and saw a tear roll silently down Alice's face.

"Alice, what's wrong?" she asked urgently, propping herself up by her elbows on the edge of the tub.

The mechanic quickly brushed the tear away and shook her head. "Nothing, I don't know. The smell of the soap, it just, it reminded me of something. A memory, I guess. It's more of a hazy feeling."

"It must be hard not remembering much of your family," Violet said gently.

"It's not even about that, really." She reached forward and dragged the soap across the captain's shoulders. "I've not been with anyone in quite some time. I didn't realize how much I missed it."

Violet nodded slowly. "I guess I know what you mean. I don't generally get this attached."

"So you're attached to me, eh?" Alice asked playfully, her voice echoing across the bathroom.

"Shush," Violet smiled. "You know what I'm trying to say."

"I do." Alice cupped water with her hand and rinsed the suds from Violet's shoulders. "I would have thought with all that black lace that you'd have a more floral scented soap."

Violet wrinkled her nose. "No thank you," she said and shook her head. "I like deeper, more complicated scents." She took the soap from Alice and leaned forward to wash a streak of grease from the mechanic's elbow. "How do you even manage to get grease under your boiler suit?" she asked with a snort.

Alice shrugged. "Sign of a good mechanic?"

"The best mechanic," Violet replied softly as she dragged the soap across Alice's stomach. "The best I've ever had."

"Are you referring to my skills with a boiler, or with you?" Alice asked with a smirk.

"Both."

"Well that's a kind of job security, I suppose." Alice leaned back against the tub and unfolded her legs, stretching a leg along the rim of either side of the tub.

Violet washed the mechanic's calves and thighs, scrubbing at the odd spot of stubborn grease and dirt. Blonde hairs shone in the dim sunlight of the room, droplets of soapy water glistening. She worked silently, the only sounds the slow drip of water and faraway, unimportant footsteps.

"I can fix that tap for you," Alice said absent-mindedly. "Would only take a few moments."

"It's not important," Violet replied, "not when there's so much other maintenance to be done."

Alice dunked her legs beneath the cooling water to rinse the suds away. She gazed intently at Violet, who had replaced the soap into its dish. "Violet..."

"Mm?"

"Thank you."

The captain leaned forward and kissed Alice gently. "There's nothing you need to thank me for." She shivered. "The water is getting cold, though, and we have places to be."

Alice nodded and climbed out of the tub onto a thick green mat, and wrapped herself in a huge towel. Violet drained the tub and held her hand out for Alice to deliver a towel. They dried and dressed quietly, moving around each other like an impromptu dance. Alice sat on the bed to lace up her boots.

"So, Mechanic, are all systems go for our departure?"

"Aye, Captain," Alice replied with a mock salute. "Just a few checks to complete before takeoff."

"Then I'll see you on the bridge when you're ready to give me your report." Violet bent down and kissed Alice, tucking a stray silver hair behind her ear. "Don't let anyone see you leave my room."

CHAPTER TWENTY-THREE

VIOLET WALKED THE CORRIDORS of the ship and ticked off the final checks for a pre-flight examination. As always, everything had been properly secured, the crew had all returned from their night in the city, and the cloaking device had held. It had its limitations in that she had to set the vessel down in a secluded area so as not to draw attention to people appearing from thin air. They had parked on the far end of the port, usually reserved for dignitaries and celebrities, and so these spaces had the benefit of privacy.

She thought about her relationship with Alice, and how it would only continue to grow more complicated. The mechanic had some kind of hold over her, and she hadn't felt like this about someone in many years, maybe ever. She felt a pull towards Alice, and caught herself daydreaming about sleepy mornings and walks in the park. Still, she had an obligation to her crew and to the rebel communities she had promised to help, and building a happy home with Alice didn't fit into that agenda. Violet shook her head to clear her thoughts. She focused on the dull thud of her boots on the metal grate and the smell of fresh bread from the mess hall, no doubt a fresh batch baked by Ned. She could almost taste the hot, yeasty sourdough, and her stomach growled angrily in protest. Without a second thought, Violet took a detour towards the promise of a satisfying lunch.

Crew members were scattered around the mess hall, ripping at loaves of bread and sitting with their scuffed boots propped up on unoccupied seats. Ned, or at least she assumed it had been Ned, had left a pile of bread in the galley, covered with cotton cloth to retain the warmth of the oven. Violet piled a plate high with bread, butter, and fresh jam, the latter of which had been given to them by the rebels they had helped. Her stomach rumbled again, eager from the promise of food.

Alice and Ivy were sitting at a table in the far corner, engrossed in conversation and poring over a stack of blueprints in front of them. As Violet approached, she saw that the schematics were covered in crumbs from their lunch, and there was a smudge of deep red jam on the corner of a page halfway down the stack. Ivy's brow was furrowed as she scribbled calculations into the margins of a page while Alice checked her work in another margin. Alice also had a smudge of graphite on her nose from the pencil lead.

"Good afternoon, Ivy," Violet said cheerily.

"Morning, Captain," Ivy mumbled as she wrote, not even bothering to look up. "Just need to finish this calculation..." she trailed off.

"Afternoon, Alice," Violet said, as though she hadn't woken up in bed with her just hours before.

Alice coughed nervously. "Uh, afternoon, Captain. Something we can help you with?"

"Just wanted to ask about final checks before we lift off in awhile. Anything of note?" She looked at the schematics over Alice's shoulder and nodded. She was no mechanic, but she could see they were planning something important.

"No, everything is in order, just like I said this morn – I mean, yes, everything is in order." Alice cleared her throat and stared back at the pages in front of her.

Violet coughed and looked at the papers on the table. If she wasn't careful, she would blow their cover and it would be weeks before they'd be able to sneak off together again.

Ivy looked up from her calculations and glanced back and forth between Alice and the captain, but said nothing and returned to her work.

"And I've already submitted my report to Ned up on the bridge," Alice added quickly. "We're all set, everything has been tested and given routine maintenance."

"What's all this, then?" Violet asked, gesturing at the piles of schematics.

"We're working on some prototype ideas to improve performance of the core systems," Ivy answered. "Take a seat, Captain, and I'll show you."

Violet dragged a chair from a nearby table and took a seat, balancing her plate of steaming bread on her lap as she ate. "Show me," she said between huge bites of hot, buttery bread.

"We were brainstorming how to kick up the speed from the thrusters," Alice continued, "and Ivy had some ideas about re-routing power supplies to better reflect how we use the ship. We're just working out some equations to see how feasible it is."

"Impressive," Violet replied, swallowing a mouthful of sourdough. "And will it be feasible? Can I look forward to a faster, sleeker ship?"

Alice glanced down at Ivy's calculations and nodded. "Eventually. This ship is older, and the systems will need updating, some of the electronics will need significant overhauls. But assuming we have no major repairs to prioritize over the next few months, I'd say we can pick up all the supplies in Bradach and have a faster, more efficient ship by the end of the year. Assuming Ivy is here to help me, of course. I can't do it by myself."

"You won't get rid of me now," Ivy mumbled as she checked her work for the third time. Alice smiled at her trainee proudly, obviously impressed with how much she had learned in so short a time.

"How come the Coalition never asked you to update their older models, then? Surely if it's as easy as you suggest, improving their existing fleet would be much cheaper than building new ships every couple of years."

Alice rolled her eyes. "Because the ones who own the shipyards are the ones who make the laws on declaring existing vessels defunct. They make money from government spending, the older models get scrapped for cash and new models get built. There's not much wrong with this ship, for example. Newer models are more efficient, with better dark space scanning equipment and more powerful thrusters, but most of that can be manually upgraded using spare parts on the black market."

"Well aren't you becoming the shrewd pirate?" Violet asked with a grin. She cocked an eyebrow appreciatively, before shoving another hunk of bread into her mouth.

"Er, I suppose so," Alice replied, blushing with pride.

"And Ivy, you're enjoying your new role on the ship?" Violet asked as she swallowed. "You could always ask to be reassigned," she added, mostly as a joke.

"Don't you dare take my apprentice from me, Captain," Alice said with a laugh. "Without her, you won't get your fancy updated ship."

"I feel like I'm in my element working with Alice," Ivy said confidently. "I've never known what I was good at, other than hustling tourists at card games. But I've already learned so much from Alice, and I think I can be a real asset to the crew if I can stay her apprentice."

Violet sat back in her seat and smiled. "I've certainly never regretted saving your ass from that pissed off casino owner," she laughed. "You're already an asset, Ivy. And of course you can stay a mechanic apprentice, you've both managed to accomplish so much already. I don't know how Alice managed a huge ship like the Stronghold without a team."

"I don't know, either," Alice replied as she looked at her apprentice warmly. "In any case, aren't we scheduled to be leaving soon?"

"You're right about that, Mechanic. I'll see you on the bridge after take-off for a briefing on the next drop zone."

"Aye Captain," Alice said, carefully brushing the crumbs from the schematics into her cupped hand.

Violet slathered the last remaining chunk of bread with butter and jam, and stuffed it into her mouth as she stood. She chewed slowly, savoring the taste, and waved wordlessly at the mechanics, who had already returned to their calculations.

• • • •

ALICE TRANSFERRED THE crumbs from their lunch onto a plate and set it on the table behind her. She furrowed her brow at the improvement plan in front of them, envisioning how they would carry out the proposed updates.

"So," Ivy whispered after Violet had left the room, "what was that all about?"

"What was what all about?" Alice asked innocently, staring hard at the schematics. She knew if she met Ivy's gaze, her apprentice would know about what was going on with the captain, or at the very least, suspect something.

Ivy crossed out an incorrect calculation in the margin and made a note of an inconsistency. "I don't know, just seems like maybe there was something there. With the captain."

Alice didn't reply. She was expending all her concentration to hide the scarlet blush in her pale cheeks. She pretended to be engrossed in the blueprints of the ship, as if she hadn't heard Ivy at all.

"I'm sorry, Alice, I shouldn't have said anything. It's not my place, and you're my mentor, and we all have secrets we want to stay hidden. Some things aren't meant for the light of day. Some things are better left in the past, so we can build a new future for ourselves."

Alice looked up and sighed. "Just don't say anything to anyone, Ivy, please," she whispered with a resigned sigh, "if Violet – er, the captain – knew that you suspected anything, she wouldn't want to see me any more."

"Of course I'd never say anything," Ivy said with an impish grin, "I was absolutely right, though." Ivy sat back in her seat, clearly impressed with her own intuition.

Alice shook her head with a laugh. "Ivy, the card sharp. Has a nice ring to it." She smoothed the edge of a page. "That's a back story you don't hear every day."

"I much prefer my job here on the Cricket. Less likely I'll need to hide from the pissed off folks I hustled."

"Somehow I'm not surprised that an excellent card player is adept at reading faces," Alice said with a wry smile. "Just try not to read mine too much. I have a terrible poker face."

"Yes, you do," Ivy laughed. "You'd have been my first mark if I was still hustling poker games."

"Good thing I don't play poker, then." Alice erased smudges on one of the pages, the result of smeared graphite.

Though she trusted Ivy to keep her secret, Alice couldn't help but feel irritated that her trainee had figured things out so easily. Sure, she was trained in the art of detecting a lie, but if Violet ever found out that anyone else on the ship knew about their...well, whatever it was, she would freeze Alice out.

"Have you finished with those preliminary calculations?" Alice asked tersely, keen to shift the conversation away from her tryst with the captain.

Ivy widened her eyes in surprise and pushed pages across the table. "Er, uh, yes, I think they are correct. You'll want to double check, I imagine."

Alice examined the pages and nodded. "These look good. And I double check everything, you always should. No matter how skilled a mechanic you are."

Ivy nodded silently and made a note in her notebook.

The ship's engines roared into life, and the familiar low hum returned to the soundscape of the vessel. Crew members cleaned their places and filtered out of the room to return to their duties. The Cricket lifted off and left the bustling port behind, fading into a small dot on the surface of the moon as they rose through the artificially generated atmosphere and cast into the dark space between them and their next drop site.

"You can file these in the boiler room," Alice said, stretching her arms up over her head and yawning. "I have to get up to the bridge for the senior officer briefing."

Ivy nodded again and stashed her notebook inside the wide front pocket of her overalls. She stuffed a tuft of green hair back under her flat cap and sprang up from her seat eagerly.

"And if you get a moment, please check the pressure gauge on the tertiary boiler again. It looks fine, but I suspect there are some small fluctuations that might imply we need to replace a seal in the next few weeks."

"Sure thing, I can do that." Ivy scooped up the loose schematics from the table and stacked them neatly together, sending a rain of leftover crumbs onto the floor.

"Don't worry, I'll clean that up," Alice reassured her.

Ivy nodded once more and traipsed heavily out of the room, her lanky legs dragging her back towards the boiler room.

Alice brushed the crumbs off the rough wood planked flooring and cleared her place. The mess hall was empty now, and she savored the relative silence. The whirr of the air filtration systems and the deep bass of the engines was a pleasing white noise, and it blocked out the chatter and footsteps of faraway crew members. Her thoughts drifted back to the morning, waking up with Violet, sharing breakfast and a part of herself she had locked away for a decade at least. She could feel herself falling for Violet, and with every passing day it became more difficult to remain on her feet.

Her radio crackled and yanked her thoughts away from the captain.

"Alice? Alice, we need you on the bridge. Immediately."

"Aye, on my way." She checked the time on her goggles, thinking she had been lost in thought longer than she realized. Maybe she was late for the officer's meeting, and that's why Ned sounded so upset on the radio. But, no, time hadn't run away from her. It was less than fifteen minutes since they had lifted off from the port.

Worried, Alice picked up her pace towards the bridge. Whatever had upset Ned, it couldn't be good. No, it wouldn't be good at all. Her tall, muscular legs propelled her towards the bridge, taking steps two at a time and outpacing other crew members in the corridors. She arrived on the bridge and was met with a pale faced Ned and a worried Kady. Violet stood at the front of the ship, facing the transmission display. Alice looked at Ned, and then to Kady, and then to the transmission. It looked to be the same as before, cycling through all their photos with WANTED stamped across them. There was more text below their pictures. She squinted and tried to read what it said.

WARNING:

THIS CREW IS HEAVILY ARMED, AND DANGEROUS.

WANTED FOR THE MURDER OF INNOCENT CIVILIANS.

5 MILLION CREDIT REWARD FOR THEIR RETURN, DEAD OR ALIVE.

By order of Corporal Allemande

Alice felt her blood run cold. Her stomach immediately twisted into an angry knot, pulsing with each accelerated heart beat. "Murder," she whispered softly.

"We're not safe anywhere now," Kady said angrily, "not with that kind of price on our heads. Every civilian, pirate, and off-duty Coalition soldier will be looking for us."

"Why does it say murder?" Alice asked incredulously. "We didn't murder anyone!"

"Why is it always a surprise to you, Alice?" Violet spat as she turned and faced her officers. "Why are you always shocked to discover that the Coalition lies? Haven't you learned by now? Don't you *know*?"

Alice fell silent and stared at her scuffed brown leather boots on the threadbare navy blue carpet of the bridge.

Violet sighed angrily as she looked back at the transmission. "Ned, how long do you think they've been transmitting this?"

"Not long. A few hours, maybe. Perhaps less."

"Well that's something, at least. Kady, what about your cloaking technology, can that run full time?"

"Not unless we can divert power from somewhere else, it requires significant juice."

Violet looked back at Alice, who continued to stare at the floor, stunned by the new developments. "Alice. Weren't you just telling me you can improve efficiency of the thrusters? That would free up some power, wouldn't it?"

Alice looked up from her boots. "I told you, even with Ivy and I both working on it, those improvements would take a few months. Not to mention we wouldn't be hurtling through dark space during those upgrades, either."

"Well, you'll have to figure something out, and fast. Otherwise the vultures will circle, and that will be it."

Alice scoffed. "I can't just magic up parts, *Violet*. It doesn't work like that!"

Kady and Ned exchanged a confused glance.

"I brought you on board because you're the best goddamn mechanic in the nearby systems, and probably more. Figure it out!"

"Okay but if we explode mid-flight, then that's on you!" Alice shouted, much to the surprise of everyone else in the room. Ned flinched and Kady's eyes widened in surprise. Violet squared her shoulders, ready for a fight; her eyes were full of fire.

"Well if we all get arrested, tortured, and killed, then that's on you!" the captain roared.

"*FINE*!" Alice yelled as she turned on her heel and stalked off the bridge. The three remaining crew members were silent as they heard Alice shout into her radio for Ivy to meet her in the boiler room.

• • • •

"ER, BOSS?" NED SAID quietly. "I can head further out, to mask us until Alice can find some extra power to run the cloaking shields."

"If you head too far out, then we'll never make our next drop in time," Violet stated with an edge to her voice. "Alice will just have to figure it out." She knew that even considering making the drops was almost guaranteed to put them all into grave danger, but she felt an inescapable need to cling to anything that felt normal.

"Is the supply drop really a priority right now?" Kady asked incredulously. "We're about to have half the system on our asses, and you're worried that the rebels will have to wait a few extra days for supplies?"

"If we don't get them that food, and those medical supplies, then they die. The situation is critical, Kady, you know that. I thought your priorities would be with the resistance, not with saving your own skin," Violet hissed, her tone sharp and accusatory.

"I can't help anyone if I'm *dead*," Kady said, challenging her captain. "I say we act cautiously, get the supplies once we know how to deal with this."

"We're doing the damned drop," Violet said evenly, as if daring Kady to defy her again, "regardless of the circumstances." At least if they made the drops on time, she and her crew wouldn't be the reason that people starved. She couldn't have one more innocent death on her conscience.

"Er, Boss?" Ned interjected softly, nodding towards the transmission. Now under the previous text, was a new additional message.

ALL PLANETS, MOONS, AND TRADING BEACONS CLOSED TO ALL NON-COALITION VESSELS. RETURN HOME, AND YOUR SHIP WILL BE PROCESSED BY COALITION EMPLOYEES. NO ADMITTANCE, NO EXCEPTIONS.

Violet stared in wide-eyed horror. Their options were disappearing quickly, and she began to imagine all their bodies in a pile, stacked in the courtyard of a cold Coalition base.

"Looks like that supply drop is off the table for now," Kady murmured.

"What about your cloaking shield?" Violet asked quickly, coming to her senses. "That would get us through, no one would even know we were there!"

Kady shook her head slowly. "The cloaking shield can hide us from view, but it can't hide us from the Coalition's lockdown sensors. They'd know we were there immediately."

"What about a different kind of shield? What about some way to mask our heat signature?"

"I would need a team of scientists and at least eighteen months to develop that," Kady replied sadly, mesmerized by the transmission screen, "and even then, there's no guarantee that the Coalition won't upgrade their sensors."

"Fuck!" Violet yelled at the screen. "Fuck." She squeezed her eyes closed and tapped her temple, willing an idea to present itself. Her heart raced, pumping adrenaline through her veins. Fight or flight, indeed. She opened her eyes and watched Ned plot a course towards an asteroid belt, a section of space filled with cold, burned out meteors, rocks, and debris from early space exploration. The readings in there were always too frenetic that it was difficult to tell a ship from a rock from far away. Kady stood over his shoulder, her brow furrowed as she studied the plan he had mapped out.

Violet collapsed into her captain's chair and stared through the large front window, clean but scuffed from brushes with space junk. A small asteroid lightly scraped against the exterior of the ship with a soft metallic hiss. She sat, head in her hands, running through scenarios in her mind. In every one of them, they all ended up dead. And then, she had a brilliant, daring plan. She sat upright in her seat.

"Ivy," she said aloud to her senior officers, "we need Ivy."

· · · ·

ALICE ANGRILY SPREAD the schematics out onto the workbench, tearing the corner of one and sending another to lazily float towards the rusted floor, where it wedged itself under the corner of the table. She unfurled the last schematic, and it rolled up on itself. She impatiently slammed her large rusted wrench onto the workbench to weigh down the creased page and smoothed it out to the edges of the bench with her hand.

"Er, Alice? What's going on?" Ivy asked as she carefully descended the steps into the boiler room, keenly aware of Alice's shortened temper. "How can I help?"

"We have to make a miracle happen, that's what," Alice replied angrily. "The Coalition is looking for us, and there's a 5 million credit price on our heads. For murder." She looked up at Ivy. "Except you. You're not on the wanted list. It's like the Coalition has no idea who you are."

Ivy took a deep breath and let it out with a sigh. "There's a simple explanation for that," she said. "I've never told anyone."

Alice straightened and looked down at her young, petite apprentice. "Ivy, what's wrong?"

"Nothing, well, not anymore," Ivy said in a rush. "It's just...I was born as someone else. The Coalition has no record of an Ivy Hill in their database."

Alice raised her eyebrows and nodded slowly. "Well, it's to your advantage now. You're basically untraceable." She sighed again and looked down at the schematics. "You and I have to figure this out, or the rest of us won't live to see next week."

The color drained from Ivy's face as she digested the situation. "Now what?" she asked quietly.

"Violet and Kady need us to figure out how to reroute power for the cloaking shield to hide us while we figure out what to do. Those plans we were considering this morning, that we told Violet would take months to complete? Well, we have about two hours, maximum."

Ivy stood for a moment and considered what Alice had told her. She squared her shoulders and nodded definitively. "Well, then, that's what we'll do. Tell me what needs to be done."

Alice sighed. "We don't have time to complete these upgrades properly, so any way to shorten the process or circumvent normal protocols will be necessary. And hopefully, we'll be able to do it without blowing up the ship." She smiled wryly. "I never thought it would end like this, you know."

Ivy straightened her posture. "If I've learned anything in my years of hustling Coalition soldiers at cards, it's that nothing is over until all the cards are off the table." Ivy frowned at the schematic on the table. "Well what if we started by disabling all power to private quarters and rerouting that up to the bridge?"

"Yes, that was my initial thought too. It's certainly the most logical first place to cut power, but it's not nearly enough for the cloaking shields." Alice pulled a pencil from behind her ear and scribbled notes into the margins of the page, leaving shavings of graphite that smeared across her hand. "If we can get into the main electrical interchange here," she said, circling an area of the schematic, "we could possibly splice power into the main grid from tertiary sources, like the backup solar reserves and power from the automatic override protocols. It means someone will have to pilot the ship at all times, but—"

"Captain Violet is a pilot, isn't she?"

"Yes."

Ivy nodded slowly. "Well let's do it, then. Tell me what I can do."

"Dig out every kind of bonding agent we have, so long as it conducts electricity. Grab the amperage meter from my toolbox, third drawer down." Alice shuffled through the pages, looking for the detailed schematic of the main grid. She was an accomplished electrician, to be sure, but every ship had its small differences, and she didn't relish the idea of electrocuting herself. Though at least then she wouldn't have to endure torture or work camps, if she was already dead. As she searched for the page, Ivy noisily searched through drawers and boxes for bonding agents, tossing acceptable rolls of tape and tubes of glue into a pile in the center of the room.

Alice spied the missing schematic tucked underneath the workbench and bent to retrieve it, dusting off the greasy cobwebs it had attained on the floor. Ivy had amassed a sizable pile in the center of the room, and she rattled in the toolbox against the wall, searching for the amperage meter.

"Okay, Ivy," Alice called to her assistant, "I've got the plans here." Ivy pulled the meter from the back of a drawer, victorious, and placed it on the corner of the workbench, on top of the page to keep it from curling in.

"You see here, in this cross section?" Alice asked, gesturing at an exploded view of the main circuitry. "We need to splice these together, and reroute power from here." She circled fuses and wires as she spoke, and Ivy nodded.

"Yes, I see." The trainee tilted her head as if memorizing the schematic.

"We'll need to shut down power to that grid while we work, which means we'll need all the kinetic flashlights we can get. You'll need to ask the crew to temporarily donate their personal ones, too."

As Ivy scribbled in her notebook, Alice heard familiar sharp footsteps approaching the boiler room stairs, and her chest tightened in anticipation of another tense argument. She didn't have time to spar with Violet, not now.

"Ivy?" Violet asked as she descended the metal stairs, her boots noisily punctuating her arrival. "I need to discuss something with you."

"Whatever you need to discuss with my apprentice, you can discuss with me," Alice interjected defensively.

"This doesn't concern you, Mechanic," Violet replied without even glancing towards Alice, "I need to speak with Ivy."

The apprentice recoiled from the thick tension in the room and squinted. "What do you need, Captain?" she asked.

Violet placed her palms on the workbench and took a deep breath. Alice, noticing that the captain's hands had smeared her notes, sighed dramatically to emphasize her annoyance.

"Ivy, as you know, you're the only one the Coalition hasn't released photos of."

"Er..." Ivy mumbled, visibly nervous about where the conversation was headed. "I, uh..."

"We need you to do something very important, but very dangerous. It's a matter of—"

Alice felt a fiercely protective instinct grab hold inside her. Ivy shouldn't have to explain her entire history to the crew, nor should Violet be putting her in harm's way. She was just a *kid*, after all. "All due respect here, *Captain*, but you can't just yank my apprentice out from under me after dumping an impossible task in my lap—"

"I'll do it," Ivy said quickly. She stood straight and confident now, and Alice closed her mouth. She wanted to support her apprentice in whatever decision she made.

"You don't even know what it is yet!" Violet said with almost a laugh. "It's a matter of deleting files at a Coalition headquarters. If we can remove all traces of us, then we might be able to buy some more time. We might just be able to get out of this mess."

"I thought everything was on lockdown? How would I get past the checkpoints?"

"Well, thanks to *Alice*, we have a small Coalition shuttle in the loading bay, remember? And Kady is currently working on reinitializing the interface with a false Coalition identification code: one that will get you past all the checkpoints. She has cautioned me that this identification number will only be viable for a few hours after creation before the Coalition servers sync and it gets purged from the system."

"What about getting into the security plant?" Alice interjected spikily. "She can't just waltz into highly classified zones without raising a few eyebrows."

"We're still working on that," Violet admitted. "Kady is hopeful that she can create a temporary passcode that would make it seem like you're a member of the security team at that location."

"If it's a passcode you need, I might be able to help," Alice said.

"Your passcode will have been deactivated!"

"I'm not talking about *mine*." Alice rolled her eyes and sighed. "I know someone who can get us in."

Violet narrowed her eyes. "Who is this secret helpful soul, then?" she demanded. "We can't take any more risks than necessary. We can't be involving half the nearby systems, someone is bound to sell us out."

"I can guarantee this is less risky than sending Ivy in there with a fake passcode and hoping that it works. It's Jhanvi. She works in the security detail monitoring rebel clusters in the nearby systems."

"If she monitors rebel movements, why the hell would she help us?" Violet asked incredulously.

Alice shrugged. "She's sympathetic to the cause. Knows how to cover her tracks, and does it well. She's been assisting the resistance for years. She's been helping me track down information about my parents and that old map."

"And you learned all this about her in one evening on Delta-4?"

Alice looked at the captain quizzically. "I never said I'd only met her that night. We've known each other for years, almost a decade, even."

"And you never reported her to the Coalition before you ended up here? Are you telling me that you knew about her dealings for years and never said anything?"

"I didn't know about that until I ran into her in town that night. I was shocked to see her there and started to panic that she would recognize me and turn me in, until she pulled me aside and explained what she was doing. She'd heard that I went rogue, so we caught up."

Violet scoffed. "And you're sure that she wasn't just undercover? That she wasn't just observing rebel movements to report back to her superiors?"

"Well we didn't get arrested there, did we? She knew where we were docked and could have turned us in, but she didn't. Like I said, she's been trying to help me track down information about my family. I think if you let me contact her, we could use her passcode to get Ivy into that building."

"What do I need to do once I'm in?" Ivy asked persistently, reminding her mentor and the captain that she was still in the room. "I'll need to know exactly what files to delete."

Violet turned towards the young apprentice. "Kady has a list for you, don't worry about that. Now, are you sure – in fact, absolutely *positive* that you want to do this?"

Ivy nodded resolutely. "This crew is my family, and I'll do whatever it takes to protect them."

"Alice, head to the bridge and contact Jhanvi for that passcode. Ivy, go to Kady's lab and she will brief you on the I.D. code for the shuttle. Are you okay to fly a shuttle?"

"Learned to fly shuttles when I was eight," she said with a grin.

CHAPTER TWENTY-FOUR

ALICE HAD OBTAINED the passcode from Jhanvi, and they had bundled Ivy into the shuttle. They sent her to the Coalition base less than an hour before, and now they were deep into the waiting game. The senior officers of the Cricket crowded around Ned's desk on the bridge. Hyun leaned against the wall that was covered in faded star maps, her face pale and worried.

"How long before she reaches the base?" Hyun asked nervously. "What if she gets lost, or the shuttle I.D. code doesn't work?"

Kady reached out and rested her hand comfortingly on the medic's shoulder. "We won't be able to hear anything from her monitor until she's near an amplifier tower. The closest one is on the base. The code will work." Kady frowned. "It has to work."

Hyun nodded and fiddled with the large blue buttons on her tailored green jacket. She looked at the large time display that Ned had set to count down until the time that the servers would sync and purge the fake I.D. code that Kady had created. 70 minutes. 69. 68. Minutes passed in nervous silence as the crew waited for news. Ned raked his huge fingers through his long ginger hair, compulsively combing out imaginary tangles. Alice shuffled her worn boots against the tattered carpet, making a strangely satisfying scraping noise.

"She should be there by now," Hyun mumbled as the clock ticked down to 65 minutes remaining. "What's taking so long?"

"Maybe she decided to give us up to the Coalition," Kady said wryly. "It would serve us right for sending her on this mission in the first place."

"Ivy would never betray us," Alice said with a hint of defensiveness. After all, Ivy was her trainee, and worked with her on projects they planned together. Alice had grown close to the young woman, who had proven herself as an asset to the crew and the maintenance team time and time again. She was worried for her safety on this mission, a dangerous task for any of them, much less a 19 year old trainee mechanic and ex-card shark.

"She'll get there," Violet reassured her crew. "We'll get out of this mess." The captain crossed the bridge and sat in her chair, her perfect posture suggesting that she wasn't as calm as she seemed. "She probably had to take a detour."

Kady hoisted herself up to sit atop Ned's desk and crossed her legs, the long black fabric of her hooded cape draping across the surface and covering a stack of well worn notebooks.

Alice squinted at the clock, willing it to move slower. 64 minutes. 63.

"At this rate she won't even have an hour to get in and get out," Hyun said, her voice cracking with worry. "Can this even be done in that much time?"

"It would be a tight squeeze, that's for sure," Alice said with a worried tone. She looked again at the clock and tried not to think about how the odds of their success ticked away with each second.

62 minutes remained.

Alice began to pace across the bridge, from the captain's chair to the doorway and back again. The soft metallic thuds of her footsteps seemed to punctuate each second. She thought about everything she had given up to be here and swallowed hard. Would the Coalition have rewarded her in earnest if she had given up the crew of the Cricket the second she returned to the Stronghold? Maybe, but maybe not. She had given them decades of her life and only been told half truths and given broken promises. Still, a dull, lonely life on a Coalition rig was better than certain death, wasn't it? Maybe. Maybe not. She was shaken from her deep thoughts when Violet gently caught her hand and shook her head. Alice looked around at her scared crew members, and it became clear that her pacing had set them all even more on edge. She huffed quietly and pulled away to lean against the wall opposite from Ned's desk.

58 minutes.

Hyun was crying softly, her head buried in Ned's shoulder as he gently patted her back. Kady began to fidget as she stared at the clock, a little more hopeless with each moment spent. Alice knew that if Ivy couldn't wipe their information from the servers, they'd never make it out of this situation alive. The broadcasts would continue and the price on their heads would increase. Eventually, someone would find them and turn them in. They were no match for the Coalition military, so they'd either surrender or die fighting. If Ivy deleted any trace of them, hopefully the heat would die down while the Coalition scrambled to reinstate the broadcasts, but then they would have no photos, no information about their ship, and no record that any of them had ever existed. Still, that would only buy them time. Kady squeezed her eyes shut, her hands clenched into tight fists. They were gambling Ivy's life, all of their lives, on a hopeless plan that would only buy them time and some anonymity at best.

56 minutes.

• • • •

VIOLET LEANED FORWARD in her chair, the springs creaking as she shifted her weight. She stared into the dark abyss and tried not to think about their odds of success, which would now start to decline exponentially. She smoothed a stray hair into place and tucked it into her bun. She tugged at her waistcoat to straighten the hem, and checked her holster for the hundredth time. Her revolver was laying in wait for the next threat: a rival pirate, a Coalition scout, a rowdy drunk at the Purple Pig tavern. It couldn't do anything for her now, but she still felt a little bit safer with it strapped safely under her arm.

"Should we be thinking of a contingency plan, Captain?" Kady asked softly. "It's seeming unlikely that she will be able to delete the information and get out before the servers sync. Maybe she was caught on her way in."

The captain stood and clasped her hands behind her back as she stared into the deep black of empty space. "Unless we can delete that information, we'll be swarmed the second we move. Let's give her a few more moments before we abandon her, shall we?"

Kady clenched her jaw and nodded tersely. Her eyes flicked to the time display just as the minutes dropped to 50.

Violet scanned the horizon, staring into the abyss and praying that they wouldn't be found. Most pirate captains were a chaotic neutral and took no sides in the rebellions and revolutions. They'd have no moral quandary in turning the crew in, they would accept their payday, upgrade their ships, and go on with their lives. She thought briefly about whether they'd be able to pay off the pirates, or blackmail them. Maybe some, if they were lucky. But she couldn't protect her crew from all the pirates in the near systems, and she certainly couldn't shield them from the almighty over-weaponized Coalition military.

48 minutes.

The captain knew success was almost an impossibility at this point. If Ivy hadn't even approached the base yet, she'd never be able to complete the mission and get out before the systems synced. They were all but blind, with no functional tracers on Ivy's shuttle. Any non-Coalition technology on the shuttle would be immediately detected in a lockdown like this one. They just had to hope that Ivy got within range of a signal amplifier and would be able to communicate. Violet pressed her hand against the glass and watched it fog up around her fingers. The glass was cold, even though it was insulated with isothermic materials to protect it from the rapid and dramatic temperature changes between space and terraformed planets.

44 minutes now.

As Violet stared into the vast deep space, a glint of something in the far distance caught her eye, and her stomach leapt into her throat. "Ned," she said with a strangled voice, "scan the northwestern field for vessels."

Hyun was still sobbing. Kady slid off the desk and stared into space, her eyes wide with fear. Alice didn't move from the wall, and Violet could see the color drain from the mechanic's face minute by minute.

"One vessel in the northwestern field, Boss," Ned said quietly. "If it continues on its course, it would most likely become aware of our position in about fifteen minutes."

"Any other information?" Violet asked, controlling her voice to make it sound even and calm, even as her stomach tied itself into knots.

"It's a Coalition patrol vessel."

Kady gasped, but the gasp became tangled in her throat and made an odd, primal sound of terror. Violet wondered if this is what cornered animals feel like before they're trapped, caged, and killed for their flesh or pelts. She wondered what the Coalition would do with her own meat, once they killed her. Burn it, or shoot her corpse into space, she mused darkly.

"Alice." Violet turned slowly to face the mechanic, who was staring at the floor. "Alice, how can we power up that cloaking shield? We need it. We need it right now."

The mechanic slowly looked up and stared at Violet as if she didn't understand. The captain wondered if she was in shock.

"The cloaki—" Violet started to repeat herself.

"I heard you. I'm thinking."

"Well think faster, will you? Otherwise we're all fucked!" Kady shouted, tears streaming down her cheeks. She wasn't the only one – Ned's beard was glistening with tears as well.

Alice nodded slowly, her eyes squeezed shut. Violet watched the mechanic's face intently, trying to read what she was thinking, almost daring to hope she would find a way out of this mess.

"I can do it," she said, "but it means disabling the air filtration system. We'll only have about twenty minutes of air, maybe thirty if we can pull the rest of the crew into one room and shut off the rest of the ship."

"Do it." Violet squared her shoulders and lifted her chin. "Do you need any assistance?"

"I'll need light to see what I'm doing. Send Jasper, he's got a steady hand and he'll be able to help me readjust the modules."

Violet brought her radio to her mouth and spoke. "Calling all crew: convene in the mess hall. Air filtration will be temporarily disabled. Jasper, meet Alice in the main atrium for your assignment. Captain out."

• • • •

37 MINUTES.

She felt a pang in her chest as she realized that Ivy couldn't save them now, and if she was still that far from an amplifying tower, she was likely lost, or the shuttle had broken down somewhere they'd never find it. In less than an hour, they'd gone from worried Ivy wouldn't be able to save them, to worried they wouldn't be able to save *her*. Hot, angry tears welled up in Alice's eyes. Anger at herself for putting Ivy in this situation to begin with. Angry that the plan hadn't worked, angry that her life was about to take a dramatic turn for the worse. She furiously wiped the tears away and clenched her fist around her favorite wrench in her tool belt, her knuckles white with the pressure.

She reached the atrium in record time, and was relieved to discover Jasper was already there, his huge muscular mass casting a long shadow across the floor. He cracked his knuckles in anticipation.

"Just tell me what to do, Alice," he said with a quiet confidence that bolstered Alice's own.

"I need you to lift off that door to give me access to the main power exchange, and then shine light into the space while I reroute power and try not to electrocute myself in the process. There's no time to power down the ship first, so this is a little risky."

Jasper nodded and heaved the door from the wall effortlessly, as if it was a sheet of aluminum and not several layers of steel. Alice was glad she had requested him to assist her. He leaned the huge access door against the opposite wall, gently setting it down with barely a sound. He reached into his deep pocket and pulled out a large kinetic torch. He wound the small yellow crank thirteen times, the same way he always did, and clicked the switch, flooding the space with cold blue light.

Alice stepped into the dark space and brushed away a cobweb that was covering the circuit box that hung on the wall. She would have to trip the circuits first before re-routing power, and hope it was enough to prevent electrocution or short circuiting critical ship systems. She carefully pried off the face of the circuit box and began disabling the systems she was about to reroute. First the power supply to the cloaking shield, which wasn't currently in use but still receiving power, and then the air filtration system. As she toggled the switch, the ship became quieter, and took on a deathly stillness. The back of her neck prickled with anxiety.

"Okay Jasper I'm about to begin re-routing the electrical relays. If you could just shine the light into the far right corner for me?"

Without a word Jasper adjusted the position of the light, balancing the kinetic torch on his right shoulder. As Alice's eyes adjusted to the change in light, she wondered how he could stand so still and motionless. Sure, she was tall and broad too, but she always felt like she was one wrong twist away from tripping over her own feet.

She squatted down next to the tangle of wires, the green canvas fabric of her boiler suit taut over her thick thighs. She began to mentally label each wire: navigation, lighting, loading bay door, mess hall. Cloaking shield. Air filtration. She separated those wires from the rest and put a piece of tape on each so they wouldn't get lost in the tangle again. She took out wire cutters, pliers, and conductive glue from her tool belt. She lingered on the glue, remembering it was less than two hours ago when Ivy was helping her prepare for a risky, but not quite *this* risky, plan.

"Alice to the bridge: any word from Ivy? Anything on the sensors yet?" She set the radio down on the floor next to her.

"No, nothing," came the muffled reply.

She followed the air filtration wire up to where it disappeared into the wall, providing power to the system that let them breathe. She instinctively took a deep breath before snipping the wire cleanly. She stripped it and the cloaking shield of their protective casing and held them together. She used her free hand and her teeth to pry the lid from the conductive glue and coated both wires. She would be able to reinstate the air filtration power, but it would take longer. Whatever plan Violet was cooking up, she hoped it was enough to save them and save Ivy, too. Alice waited a moment for the glue to set and sat back on her haunches. For a last ditch attempt, she felt surprisingly calm. She wondered if that was the influence of Jasper's quiet strength, or the fact that she was most useful when working on a ship. Either way, she was relieved that her hands were steady and her breaths regular and measured. She picked up the radio from the floor and dusted it off.

"Alice to bridge: it's done. Engage the cloaking shield. We have 30 minutes to save our own asses or die trying."

"Aye Alice, we hear you. Boss says return to the bridge for an officer meeting and send Jasper to be with the rest of the crew in the mess hall."

She clipped the radio to her tool belt and stood up slowly so as not to crack her skull on the low ceiling of the space. Turning, she saw that Jasper was preparing to replace the heavy door.

"No, don't," she said quickly, "if I have to get back in there to reinstate the air, I won't have much time."

He nodded and switched off the torch. "Happy to help, Alice," he said, "I'll go meet the others."

Alice reached up and clapped Jasper on the shoulder with a smile. "We'll get out of this one way or another," she said reassuringly, relieved that

Jasper couldn't hear her internal monologue. Death was one way out of this, after all.

She made her way back to the bridge, walking quickly and purposefully. With only 30 minutes before the air ran out, there wasn't a single second to spare. As she walked, she set her tools back in her belt in the order she preferred most: most used tools like adjustable pliers and three different screw drivers in the front for easy access, and other tools like a rubber mallet, a small welding torch, and her favorite large wrench sat near the sides of the belt on her hips. The weight of the belt hung around her middle and made her feel secure and confident, as if she could repair her way out of any situation. She hoped that was the case now, as the strange whine of the cloaking shield kicked into gear. She couldn't hear the sound of the shield the last time it was used, because the noise was masked by the low hum of the air filtration system.

The mechanic stepped onto the bridge and looked at the countdown timer. 15 minutes remaining. Her chest tightened with worry, and suddenly her lungs felt too big for her ribcage. Breathing felt difficult, as if some invisible force had her in vice grips, squeezing the air out of her. Where was Ivy?

"Well done, Alice," Kady said quietly, her face gray and devoid of emotion. "The patrol shuttle didn't see us."

"So are we going to disengage the shield and give power back to the air filtration now?" Alice asked. "We don't have long to make a decision."

Violet stared out the wide window, her hands on her hips. Alice knew that she was searching for a solution that wouldn't doom her entire crew to capture and death.

"We keep the shields, for now. We can't risk being seen and reported." The captain turned to face her senior officers. "At this point, we have to assume that Ivy was not able to delete the data. We don't even know if she made it onto the base, and if she did, it's likely she was already captured."

"So what, we just leave her to die?" Alice asked in a small voice.

The captain raised an eyebrow. "Do I seem like the kind of captain that would abandon the crew member who willingly risked her life to save our asses?"

"But Captain, the air!" Hyun interjected.

Violet raised a hand to acknowledge her medical technician. "Yes, Hyun, I know. But we can't even be sure that patrol shuttle is out of range yet. For all we know, it's using the same kind of cloaking technology we are, trying to lure us out of the shadows. It's Coalition tech, after all."

"What do we do when the air runs out?" Ned asked. "We'll have to make a decision well before that moment."

"We wait for Ivy. If she's not back when the counter hits zero, then...well, then we reinstate the air filtration system and get the hell out of here, head for the drop zone and hope we're not spotted. Then we'll re-group, and Alice can work on a more permanent solution to keep the cloaking device functional."

"But Captain, the lockdown is still in place whether or not Ivy was successful in deleting the data. How would we get through the checkpoints to the drop zone anyway?" Kady questioned. "We'd be spotted immediately upon approach, especially without the cloaking shield in use."

Violet gave a frustrated sigh. "We don't have many options at this point, Kady. We can't drift in space forever, and we'd run out of power in a few days anyway. Alice, what would happen if we kept cycling the power reserves between the air filtration system and the cloaking shield?"

Alice shook her head. "The wiring would start to disintegrate. One switch or two is possible, but beyond that the risk of failure increases exponentially."

11 minutes ticked down to 10 in the blink of an eye.

"Ned, add a secondary countdown to reflect the air supply, please." Violet eyed the countdown with contempt, as if it was the sole reason for their current misfortune. A second countdown appeared alongside the first. 10 minutes to wait for Ivy. 25 minutes of air.

"What if we headed back to Bradach?" Alice asked. "Surely there are no Coalition checkpoints there."

Violet shook her head. "We've got too much heat on us, it's part of the etiquette we all agree to follow for access to Bradach. We can never knowingly lead Coalition there, never give them a reason to land and investigate what goes on there. Besides, there would still be a risk that someone could inform on us, even though it's technically against the town law. That price on our heads would be too much for some to resist."

"I think it's important to think about all the possibilities here," Kady said. "If Ivy made it to the base, and if she was captured, we have to realize there's a chance that she will give us up."

Alice shot Kady a look across the room. Though she hadn't known Ivy long, she knew her trainee would never willingly give them up. "I told you before, Ivy would never betray us."

"You've never seen what they do to rebels or pirates," Kady shot back. "No one in this room would be able to withstand the kinds of torture they put people through in the name of protecting the Coalition." She fidgeted with her hair. "I hear they continue the torture even after they get a confession."

Alice felt the bottom drop out of her stomach as her mind flashed with images of Ivy being tormented by Coalition officers. Kady was right in that she had never seen these interrogations first hand, but she'd heard stories through the years. She'd never believed them, chalking them up to tales told to discourage dissent.

"We have no evidence she even made it to the base," Violet interjected softly, "but you're right, Kady. It's not out of the realm of possibility."

"So what now? If we leave, try to hide somewhere else, Ivy would never find us if she's on her way back, or if she's been stranded somewhere. She wouldn't even know where to look." Alice's chest felt tight, like her ribcage was shrinking around her lungs. "But if we stay, there's a chance that she could lead them straight to us?"

Violet nodded grimly. "It would seem that's the situation. Not many options with happy endings, I admit. Still, we have to do something, we can't just sit here and wait to be captured or blown apart."

The last few seconds of Ivy's timer ticked down to zero. They had a decision to make.

CHAPTER TWENTY-FIVE

"I THINK WE HAVE TO assume now, that Ivy's shuttle failed. She's stranded somewhere, she must be, but we can't risk getting close to that base to try and find her. Or, she made it to the base and didn't check in with us for some reason, and she's been captured. If she had been successful, she would have returned by now." Violet stood and faced out the window, arms folded across her chest.

Hyun stifled a sob as she leaned against the wall near Ned's desk. She covered her mouth with her hand and squeezed her eyes shut as a tear slipped down her cheek.

Violet's breathing was shallow and quick. "We also have to assume that the information hasn't been deleted, and that the broadcasts will continue to air every few hours on all signals. They already lied and blamed us for murders that they likely committed, so who knows what else they'll add to that fictitious rap sheet."

"Boss, we've got a non-branded vessel headed this way. Definitely not Coalition, but they have no call sign and they won't be in visual range for 30 more seconds. Stand by." Ned tapped at the screen in front of him and frowned.

Violet looked to Kady. "The cloaking shield is at full strength?"

Kady nodded. "Unless they slam right into us, they won't even know we're here."

"Is collision a possibility?" Violet asked Ned, who furrowed his brow at the screen above his mahogany desk.

"Unlikely, but they appear to be slowing their craft. Visual confirmation in 14 seconds. Boss, I think we should prepare for evasive maneuvers , just in case."

The captain nodded and threw herself into the pilot's seat against the wall, which sat in front of a panel of hundreds of flashing buttons. She grasped the ship's tiller and breathed deep, releasing tension from her shoulders. Though the Cricket was frequently on autopilot with the more recent course plotting technology, nothing could match the reflexes of a trained pilot when performing evasive maneuvers. She glanced out the window and cast her eye over the hull of the ship, and saw a tiny blue spark shimmer over the surface.

"Kady, is the cloaking shield electromagnetic?"

Before the scientist could reply, a ship came into view and stopped dead in front of them. It was dead Captain Leo's ship, with Captain Josie at the helm.

Violet's blood ran cold. "Kady, can they see us?" She glanced back at the hull and saw more blue sparks dancing on the surface.

"They shouldn't be able to..." Kady said, fumbling with the cloaking shield control. "There's not enough power," she said with a panicked edge to her voice. "Alice, there's not enough power!"

Alice made it to the doorway of the bridge in two huge steps. "I'm going to splice in more power, but it means no auto-pilot!" she yelled.

"Go!" Violet yelled back, and watched Alice disappear down the hall. A bead of sweat dripped down her face, and she wiped it away with her sleeve. Things were only getting worse, now. Ivy was missing, they were running out of air, the cloaking shield was failing right in front of the crew that held the biggest grudge against them, and it seemed like there was no way out of this mess that didn't end with all of them dead.

Her radio crackled to life. "I know you're there, Violet," came Josie's voice. "I saw you for just a second on the radar. It was long enough. You're using our technology. You can't fool me."

Violet dared not even breathe. Josie wouldn't be able to hear her unless she depressed the radio's transmission button, but she felt so seen, so vulnerable and trapped. The bridge was completely silent.

"Don't bother reinitializing your shield, I've already called in your position. For a full pardon for me and all my crew, of course, and a *significant* reward." Josie laughed a cold, icy laugh before ending the transmission.

Half the screens went dead, and Violet knew Alice had cut the power to the autopilot, radar, and navigation systems. From here on in, she was flying blind, and it didn't even matter. They'd been caught anyway, and it was all over. Images of her crew's dead corpses flashed again through her mind, and she felt heat spread throughout her body. She was angry, livid that this was how they were going to go out. Called out by an inferior vessel, dependent on the power of the Coalition military to get their way. Every muscle in Violet's body tensed as she prepared for the worst.

Suddenly, the ship was rocked by a huge explosion, or a collision. Violet didn't know what, she just knew that the rest of her senior officers had gone flying across the bridge. She would have, too, if she hadn't been grasping the tiller with all her strength.

She grabbed her radio. "Report!" she yelled, hoping another member of the crew would know what had just happened. Without internal diagnostics, she had no idea what was going on. There was no response from the crew.

Violet looked out the window and saw that the cloaking shield had reinitialized. Too little, too late. Alice's valiant, impossible efforts had been for nothing. All of this had been for nothing.

"Report!" she yelled into the radio again. Had the Coalition arrived? Was another ship attacking them from the rear of the ship? She couldn't see anything other than the hull from here, and with navigation and auto-pilot offline, she wouldn't dare leave the pilot's seat. Still, there was no response from any member of the crew. Ned and Kady lay in a heap on the floor, after being thrown across the bridge with the impact. Hyun was clutching to Ned's desk for stability.

"Yes, it won't be long now," the radio teased. "The Coalition will arrive any moment."

Violet furrowed her brow in confusion. If Captain Josie was unaware of the explosion, then what the hell had that been? "Repo—" she started to say again, but was cut off.

"Violet, bridge, are you there?" came a panicked, breathless radio call from Alice. "Collision, it's—" she gasped for breath. "It's Ivy, she crashed into the loading bay! But they're right on our tail and—"

Another explosion rocked the ship, and the power went out. All they had left were the main thrusters. No lights, no cloaking shield, no failsafe for when the air ran out. When was it going to run out, anyway? The countdown clocks were blank. Violet racked her mind: had they said five minutes remaining? Whatever they had said, there was no time to lose.

The ship's thrusters roared into life, but the familiar glow of the navigation panel was absent from the lack of power. They didn't even have any reserves left, all they had was what was left in the thrusters' storage generator, and whatever the boilers could produce. While they worked miracles providing energy for the rest of the ship, the thrusters needed their own power source, separate from the rest of the systems in case of situations just like this.

Violet inhaled deeply and pulled the tiller towards her body, pushing the ship forward and into flight. They began to pick up speed quickly, and Violet led the ship through a complex course, weaving in and out to try and avoid taking any more fire. She wasn't sure the ship could take another hit like that one.

"Hyun! We need help!" Alice screamed from the corridor outside of the bridge. Hyun instinctively pulled the emergency medical kit from underneath Ned's desk and snapped into action. Though Violet had her sights set firmly into space, she could hear Hyun's authoritative, medical training take over, and it gave her courage to carry on.

* * * *

JASPER AND ALICE DRAGGED an unconscious Ivy onto the bridge, a huge purple bruise spreading over her left cheekbone and up over her eye socket. Something had hit her in the face, and hard. Alice knew that Ivy's cheekbone was likely broken, and she probably had a concussion, too. When she had dragged her from the shuttle, she was still conscious.

Hyun looked over Ivy with an efficient, careful eye. "Ivy? Can you hear me?" She examined the bruise and shook her head. "What hit her?"

"I'm not sure," Alice replied, "she was like this when I pulled her off the shuttle. She was awake then, though."

The medical technician nodded with a stern brow. "Yes, it's possible she passed out from the pain. We can only hope it's not because her brain is bleeding." She lifted Ivy's eyelid and shone a small light, and Ivy's pupil contracted. A good sign, and Alice knew it. Hyun's intent gaze shifted across Ivy's body, scanning for injuries that needed to be treated. She spotted a small patch of slick red on Ivy's thigh that was spreading fast. "And this?" she gestured at the hidden wound.

Alice' stomach churned at the sight of the blood. "I don't know, I didn't see that!"

Before Alice was even finished speaking, Hyun was already preparing a tourniquet to stem the flow. "It's possible she nicked an artery, but I can't be sure until I can get a proper look." She tied a strip of white cloth around Ivy's leg, just above the wound. She pulled the knot tight and leaned over Ivy, putting her ear close to her chest to make sure she was still breathing regularly.

"What the hell happened?" Violet shouted from the pilot seat, over the roar of the thrusters. "What kind of damage are we looking at?"

Suddenly, Violet yanked the tiller to the left and the ship creaked and groaned as it jerked to the right. The thrusters shuddered for a moment before bursting back into gear as they changed course. Alice braced herself against the door frame, and Hyun had thrown herself over Ivy's unconscious body to protect her from any potential falling debris. Ned and Kady grasped the desk so hard that the drawer hinge snapped. Violet was flying blind, and Alice knew how dangerous that was in normal circumstances, much less being pursued by a rival pirate ship and the Coalition.

"Alice! What happened?" Violet yelled again, pulling hard on the tiller to bank left.

"I don't know!" Alice shouted back, raising her voice over the strained huff of the thrusters. Without all the other systems online, the ship was louder, and it was almost impossible to hear Violet over the din. "I heard an explosion in the loading bay so I ran towards it. When I got there, Ivy was slumped over in the shuttle!"

The ship pulled left and right, and the metal screeched in protest. Hard turns weren't meant to be made at such high speeds, and certainly not on a craft this out of date. The structural integrity wouldn't be able to withstand this kind of abuse for much longer, and Alice knew it. One look at the captain showed that she knew it, too.

Violet's radio blinked on her belt, but no one could hear it above the roar. Alice stumbled across the bridge to retrieve it, and unclipped it from the captain's belt. Alice held the radio close between her ear and Violet's to try and make out the message.

"There's no use...running," said Captain Josie's voice, from the radio, thick with static and interference. "We got you this time, Violet."

Violet pulled the ship to the left, and Alice stumbled backward. She pulled herself to her feet and brought the radio back up to their ears just as the thrusters fell unexpectedly silent. Josie's voice rang clear around the bridge.

"What do you mean, *we're being boarded*? We were promised clemency! Hey, who the hell do you think you are—" The radio fell silent.

"She was a fool to trust them," Violet said under her breath. She pulled back on the tiller and tried to re-engage the thrusters, but the ship was silent and the engines dead. They were coasting through space, but without the ability to accelerate or change direction, it would be a matter of minutes before they were caught and arrested. "Alice!" Violet yelled.

Alice jumped to her feet without a word and sprinted from the bridge, giving Ivy a concerned backward glance as she disappeared down the hall. She was running to the boiler room to try and generate power for the thrusters. Air would have to wait. The only question was would it be too late? Was there even any more power to reroute?

• • • •

THE CAPTAIN PULLED on the tiller over and over, desperate to escape the Coalition's grasp. The thrusters remained silent as the grave, like their very own cemetery. She pounded on the controls, willing them to show a flicker of life. She looked out over the hull and realized it might be the last time she flew as a free woman. She was old enough that she'd spend the rest of her life in a Coalition work camp, and that's if she even survived being arrested. The military wasn't known for being particularly gentle when taking known pirates into custody, much less pirates with a five million credits price on their heads.

Far in the distance, she saw a speck of land that was dwarfed by Zeta-6, the nearest planet. Suddenly, the old maps that she kept in the corridors flashed through her mind. Wasn't there an old rebel base on one of these old small moons? They were running out of time, and air, and if they didn't land soon they'd either suffocate on the ship or die in work camps.

Another explosion rocked the ship, and Violet knew that they had taken another serious hit. She turned and saw Hyun crouched over Ivy, applying pressure to her wound and checking her vitals every few seconds. Ned and Kady looked lost without their normal roles on the bridge, nervously staring at Hyun and Violet in turns. Violet nodded at Ned and took a deep breath. Once more she turned to the tiller and wrenched hard as she kicked the console under her feet. Much to her surprise, the thrusters roared into life and the Cricket shot forward. Ned and Kady tumbled against the desk behind her, but her focus was sharpened now. Adrenaline coursed through her as she gripped the tiller. She visually calculated the path towards the speck of land and pointed the ship towards it. She felt the warm brass of the tiller beneath her hands, and heard the thundering of the thrusters. She tasted the burnt air from the explosions elsewhere on the ship, and felt tightness in her chest as the air supply began to dwindle. It smelled like burned rubber and electrical fires.

The radio flashed and crackled with static. Any message that faint could only be the Coalition ship that was pursuing them, so Violet switched it off. They would just be telling her to surrender or they would begin to resume fire. She wasn't about to give up and let her crew be arrested, not when they had a chance. Violet had no idea what they would do when they landed, but at least they would be alive. Maybe they could run. Maybe they would lose the Coalition tail, though at this speed that seemed unlikely. Maybe they could bargain for their lives, pay off the mercenaries. She leaned into the ship and dropped her shoulders, exhaling onto the window in front of her and fogging a small patch with her breath. Where was Alice?

"She's losing blood," Hyun yelled, tightening the tourniquet. She had to be careful not to cause nerve damage to Ivy's leg with a bandage this tight. She couldn't stem the flow, and Ivy's borrowed coveralls were dark with blood. She looked so small in the mechanic uniform she'd borrowed from Alice, so fragile.

"Hold tight, we're going to land in a few minutes!" Violet responded, willing the ship to move faster. The small spit of land was growing larger as they approached, and the captain was starting to worry about the lockdown. What if they couldn't land at all?

"She needs proper medical attention!" Hyun shouted. "She needs surgery, and she needs it now!"

"Jasper, help Hyun take Ivy to the medical bay so she can perform the procedure as soon as we land. I don't know how long we'll have, no longer than a few minutes."

The muscled man easily and gently lifted Ivy, nodding towards Hyun. He carried the limp girl through the door and down the corridor, and the medical technician followed him, tying back her long dark hair in preparation as she went.

"Ned, Kady, we need a plan for when we land," Violet told her senior officers. "It's likely the Coalition will be right behind us, hoping for arrests. I imagine with the falsified reports, they won't hesitate to shoot."

"We'll need to vent the ship when we land or we'll all suffocate," Kady said matter of factly. "So we can't seal the ship and hole up and hope for the best. They'd probably just shoot the doors off, anyway."

"I'll head to the loading bay to vent the ship," Ned offered. "If we can get navigation and radar systems back on line then I might be able to plot a course. That's assuming we have enough power, of course."

"If we can stall them for an hour, maybe we could use the solar power storage to refill the reserves. Of course, they'd just be right on our tails again," Kady countered. "And then we'd be right back where we started."

Violet wove the ship back and forth gently now, knowing that any jerky movements would make Hyun's task of preparing to perform surgery almost impossible. They were nearing the small moon, and she began to prepare the ship to descend through the artificial atmosphere.

"We just need to buy time for Hyun to patch up Ivy. She's quick, but she'll need the medical bay to be uninterrupted for at least a little while. We'll have to stall them, give her time to perform the procedure and give the solar tanks time to refill. Give Alice time to rework the wiring and perform emergency repairs."

"How will we stall them? Like you said, they're likely to shoot us all on sight," Ned said worriedly as the Cricket began to descend.

"We'll just have to be creative then," Violet said with confidence. There was something about manually piloting a ship that made her feel almost invincible, even under the current circumstances.

• • • •

VIOLET SCANNED THE horizon for a place to land the Cricket. This was an incredibly small moon, and she could probably fly around the whole thing in less than ten minutes if they had the time. The tall communication tower that was on every planet, moon, and trading beacon came into view, and Violet let out a small gasp. The tower had been partially dismantled, huge pieces of the structure dangling and nonfunctional. No wonder the lockdown didn't apply here, there was no form of communication in or out. No doubt the Coalition felt there was no point in monitoring such a tiny, insignificant moon. She engaged the landing gear and aimed the ship towards a derelict settlement that looked long abandoned. She had been right about a rebel community existing here, but it was clear that it hadn't been occupied for years, maybe even decades. Still, the old buildings could give them some cover, offer some kind of opportunity to stall them enough. And then what? Lead them on a chase across the near systems until they ran out of fuel reserves again?

"Prepare for landing," she said as the thrusters disengaged and the ship used existing momentum to coast towards a flat piece of land next to the settlement.

Kady checked the holsters under her arms and bent down to loosen the dagger that was lodged in a belt around her thigh, under her long black flowing cloak. Ned heaved a heat gun free from under his desk and powered it on.

"Why was that even under there?" Kady asked with a nervous laugh.

Ned shrugged. "Dunno, but it's useful, aye?"

Violet set the ship down as gently as she was able and leapt out of the pilot's seat. She switched her radio on and spoke quickly and confidently into it.

"Attention all crew: the ship will be vented in just a few moments. We need to stall the Coalition as long as possible. There's a nearby settlement where you might find supplies. Grab any generators and power tanks that you can, but do not engage the Coalition forces unless absolutely necessary. Don't get shot. Don't get captured. Captain out." She nodded to Ned, who exited the bridge with Kady to vent the ship and give them the air they needed to survive, air that was quickly dwindling. She was shocked they even managed to get this far without the air filtration system, if she was honest with herself.

She raised the radio to her mouth again. "Alice, come in Alice. We need a damage report and an ETA on emergency repairs."

"Alice here, a boiler threw a gasket and another got punctured by debris. I'm down in the boiler room. Patching will take at least twenty minutes, and I also have to rewire the main console before lift off. I'm fine here, go see to Ivy!"

Violet nodded to herself and headed towards the medical bay. The ship hissed as it decompressed the moment Ned vented the ship, and she felt herself instinctively take a deep breath. She didn't realize she had been breathing so shallowly. She inhaled slow and long as she walked the corridor, hoping that against all odds they'd have a decent lead on the Coalition ship that had been tailing them. There was no way they hadn't been tracked here, so their best hope was any kind of delay. And then what? She didn't know yet, but she was mentally tracing each outcome from start to finish. She rounded the corner into the medical bay, and Hyun was already hard at work fixing up Ivy's leg. Jasper stood nearby, handing her medical instruments as she asked for them. If they all managed to get out of this alive, he might make an excellent medical assistant, if he was interested.

"Scissors." Hyun was hunched over Ivy's limp body, working to stem the flow of deep red blood that pooled on the table.

"What's the prognosis?" Violet asked. "We don't have much time, but—"

"She was shot," Hyun interjected. "I don't know what happened, it must have been before she got back on board, before Alice found her. Or maybe shrapnel, I don't know." She snipped a long black thread and tossed the tiny silver scissors onto a black tray to her left. "Good news is, whatever it was, it was a clean exit. Barely missed her femoral artery, if it had caught her, she'd be dead by now, especially with that whiplash chase." She looked up at Violet over a pair of yellow tinted medical goggles. "She's still unconscious, though. I can't do anything except hope it's not a brain bleed. I can't do anything about that under current conditions."

Violet nodded gravely. "I understand. You'll update me if there's any news?"

Hyun nodded. "Of course. Do we have a timescale to departure?"

"Unfortunately not. We're going to try and stall them, once they land, long enough for emergency repairs and solar refuelling. And then we'll just have to see what happens." Violet looked down at Ivy's body and was hopeful when she noticed color returning to her cheeks. Maybe she'd be okay after all, and could tell them all what had happened, and why she'd never made it to the Coalition base to delete their data.

Violet's radio fuzzed with an incoming message. "Boss – BOSS!"

The captain quickly unhooked the radio from her belt. "What is it, Ned?" she responded.

"Coalition ship about to land right on top of us – er, next to us. What should we do?"

"Gather the rest of the crew members and get them inside the ship, right away." She looked at Hyun and Jasper, forming a plan in her mind. "Stay hidden here in the med bay. We'll try to stall them long enough for repairs, and then....and then we'll see." She looked at Jasper. "Barricade the door, and stay quiet. Keep Ivy safe."

Jasper nodded. "I will, Captain." He put a hand on Hyun's shoulder. "We both will."

Violet backed out of the room and closed the heavy metal door. She heard the deadbolt slide into place, and Jasper shoving something up against the door. She hoped that would keep them safe a little longer, at least. Her mind raced as the Coalition ship began to land, the roar of the engines echoing around the silent Cricket. The lights flickered weakly in the corridor, and Violet knew that the solar storage tanks were beginning to fill. With her crew inside the ship, she began to consider the possibility of sacrificing herself for them. Would the Coalition even go for it? Was she really willing to spend the rest of her life in a work camp, waiting to die of exhaustion or old age?

The loading bay doors and air lock were open to vent the ship, and Violet walked right through. She glanced around the bay, the totaled shuttle as the centerpiece of the wreckage. Supply crates were overturned, with produce and medical supplies spilling out across the floor. The shuttle door was hanging by one hinge, and the back half crushed by an unknown impact. The loading bay door itself was partially caved in, though, she assumed, still functional. It must be, if Alice had been able to pull Ivy out of the shuttle and into the ship to safety. A heap of spare parts had come loose from their box and was now piled on top of a crate full of scrap metal they had planned to sell when they returned to Bradach in a couple weeks' time. It was odd, how fast things could change. They had planned to split the profits as usual, take an extra long shore leave there and give Alice and Ivy time to work on the planned upgrades. She had planned to take Alice out to dinner, a nice place. Nicer than the Purple Pig, anyway.

She kicked a piece of debris and it went skittering across the floor. She stepped over a broken crate, and the raw wood snagged her tight fitting trousers, tearing a small hole on the outside of her thigh. She frowned at the tear, snapped off the jagged piece of wood, and tossed it into a corner. The loading bay door was wide open, and she could see the Coalition ship land a short distance away. She wasn't even surprised to see that it was the Stronghold: after all, they had a vendetta to equalize. Military members streamed from the ship and Violet smirked; they'd sent an entire army just for them. If nothing else, it was proof of her reputation in these parts, and proof of what her crew had accomplished. No doubt the top brass in the Coalition were infuriated that they had undermined their siege of rebel camps all across the near systems.

Captain Augustus Allen shouted across the derelict camp, his hands cupped around his mouth. "Surrender now, Violet, and your crew might make it to the work camps alive." Even at this distance, he looked smug, the power of the Coalition military bolstering his confidence. He certainly hadn't looked that sure of himself when Violet was pillaging his ship and stealing his mechanic away, that was for sure.

Violet tossed her revolver to the ground and kicked it away to show she didn't intend to shoot first. She held her hands out at hip length, palms out. "I think we can come to an agreement," she said loudly as she neared the Stronghold and the battalion of military crew members. "I'll happily surrender, so long as my crew goes free. We have injured members that need medical attention."

Captain Allen laughed a cold, hollow laugh. "You know I can't do that. You're all wanted for murder, piracy, and theft. And that goddamn mechanic is wanted for treason. The scientist, too."

"We don't want this to end in a bloody mess," Violet said coolly. "Just arrest me, and say the rest escaped. They'll never be a problem for you again."

He raised an eyebrow. "Somehow I doubt that." He nodded to a short, muscular woman on his right and motioned for her to search Violet. "We'll be arresting all of you, and you'll have the pleasure of dealing with our honorable court system."

The short woman ran her hands across Violet's back, searching for hidden weapons. "You could at least ask me out for dinner first," she said sarcastically. She just needed to stall enough time, and then figure out how to get away, back on the ship, and take off...somehow. It was an evolving plan, to be sure.

"I'll do you a captain's courtesy of not clapping you in irons," Allen said, "but I can't extend that to the rest of your crew." He nodded towards the open loading bay door, and a small group of the military crew members advanced on the ship, weapons holstered. "Search the ship, arrest everyone. Take anything valuable, but we'll be leaving that piece of shit ship here." He turned to Violet and smirked. "Is a several decades outdated, stolen ship the best you can do? Pitiful, really."

Violet stuck her chin out. "Managed to best you though, didn't it?" She winked at Captain Allen, and fury flashed across his weathered face.

He gestured around at the rest of his crew. "I'll agree you won the battle, and I didn't expect Alice to defect, but I've won the war. We'll always win the war."

"Wait! Stop!" Alice screamed as she ran off the Cricket and towards the military crew. Startled, they fumbled for their weapons as she flew towards them.

"No!" Violet shouted at Alice. "Get back on the ship!"

"You're not taking her!" Alice shouted as she bodychecked a stunned crew member and threw him to the ground.

"Alice, what the hell are you doing?" Violet yelled across the camp. Her voice echoed across the crumbling brick buildings.

The mechanic wrestled a wrench from her tool belt and smacked one of the crew in the gut. He made a soft grunting noise and fell to the ground clutching his stomach and gasping for air. Alice had stunned his phrenic nerve, knocking the wind out of him. Another came up behind her and hit her in the jaw with the butt of his rifle. He grabbed her arm, pulling it behind her and twisting upward. Alice crumpled, defeated.

Captain Allen approached her as she knelt on the ground. "You could have had early retirement, Alice. Instead you aligned yourselves with this...scum." He bent down to look her in the eyes. "Shame. You were a talented mechanic. Now, you're just a treasonous dead woman walking."

Alice's eye glinted with fire, and she spat in his face. "Rot in hell, you filthy liar. You never would have let me have early retirement, you never would have even let me off that ship. You suspected me from the moment I came back."

He scowled as he wiped off Alice's spit with the cuff of his crisp white Coalition captain's uniform. "Yes, well that suspicion was warranted, wasn't it?" He straightened and waved his hand nonchalantly to the military crew member who was restraining Alice. "Take her to the brig. We'll let Asset Protection deal with her first thing in the morning."

Violet swallowed hard. Asset Protection was the secretive branch of the Coalition tasked with extracting information though any means necessary, usually torture. They'd be wanting information about their contacts, the rebel bases, Bradach, and their technological advances, courtesy of Kady. Violet's stomach tied itself into a tight knot and she dry heaved with the thought of Alice being tortured. She clasped her hands over her stomach and bent double with the pain.

Allen raised an eyebrow. "And thus, it becomes clear, why a loyal Coalition mechanic would defect to a second rate pirate ship. Did she *love* you, Violet?"

She felt like someone was strangling her. They were outnumbered. The Coalition had Alice, and she'd be tortured and killed, her body dumped in dark space like it was nothing but debris. Her entire crew was going to be captured and imprisoned. Kady would probably be tortured, too, as a treasonous Coalition scientist. She felt like her spine was detaching itself from her limbs, like her bones were melting into red gelatinous ooze inside her skin.

Alice and her captor disappeared into the Stronghold, and the group of military crew continued to advance towards the Cricket, weapons now drawn as they approached. Violet thought of Ivy, laying on a stretcher in the medical bay, limp and weak from blood loss. She hoped the Ned and Kady had barricaded the rest of the crew in the mess hall, but it probably wouldn't do much good. They were outgunned, and they would need something like divine interference to get out of this alive and free.

The Stronghold captain clasped his hands behind his back and cocked his head. "Was it worth it, Violet?" He walked in a circle around her, stalking his prey. "You couldn't think you'd get away with it forever. I'm not a man to be trifled with, and the Coalition is more powerful than all the pirate vessels in the galaxy, much less the near systems." He paused and took off his cap to scratch his temple casually, as if they were having an unimportant conversation about the weather, or the price of wheat. "Even if your friends hadn't called in your position, we'd have caught up with you eventually. It's not hard to track pirates who travel space, delivering groceries to rebel camps. Why even bother with them, anyway? That alliance certainly hasn't helped you in your time of need."

"Because it was the right thing to do," Violet whispered as a tear dripped to the ground. She felt utterly defeated, a failure to her crew and to Alice. "Because someone has to fight against a system of unjust laws and corruption."

He laughed again, a cold, unfeeling laugh. The smile did not reach his eyes, and his glare bore into Violet's soul. "You forget, Violet. We'll always win the war."

At that precise moment, the C.S. Stronghold erupted into flames with a huge blast. The windows of the ship shattered, the glass flying in every direction. The heavy metal doors bowed outward and blew off their hinges, sending the doors flying across the camp. Flames escaped from the empty windows, licking up the side of the ship. There was a muffled secondary thundering that she knew would be the artillery and weapons hold. The reverberations of the detonation shook Violet's bones, and the heat burned her face. She stared into the fire, tears streaming from her eyes. No one would have been able to survive that kind of explosion.

"Alice!" she screamed into the flames, falling to her knees in defeat.

CHAPTER TWENTY-SIX

ALICE AND VIOLET WALKED the brick streets of Bradach with their hands intertwined. They had just finished a rich, sumptuous meal at one of the port's finest restaurants, and they'd dressed for the occasion in tailored, brocade waistcoats. Violet wore green, and Alice wore a deep blue that brought out her eyes. They'd met with Jhanvi, who delivered the disappointing news that there was no further information on Alice's parents, not unless they found someone who could break the code on the map. It didn't matter as much as it once would have, now that Alice had found a new family aboard the Cricket.

The ship was nearing completion of the upgrades, with the help of Ivy, and soon they'd be back in the sky, performing daring heists and delivering supplies to rebel communities. But for tonight, they were taking a few hours out to just be together, and be grateful for each other's company. They stopped in the hidden garden and sat on the tree stump in the far corner. They had returned to this garden several times during this shore leave, and it had become a place of respite for them. Alice curled her arm around the captain and pulled her close as they watched the sun dip in the sky.

Much to Violet's surprise, the rest of the crew didn't care at all that she and Alice had begun seeing each other in secret. In fact, when she made the official announcement, after they dropped off the last of the defectors, most of them laughed. They already knew. So Alice had moved into her room, and Barnaby into Ned's, and the empty rooms were used for storage. No one had protested. Hyun took on Jasper as a medical trainee, and he seemed cut out for the role. He was more confident, and Violet sometimes saw him studying anatomy books even in his free time. Hyun was happy for the help: with their data deleted from the system; she was free to return to Banríon tournaments. She won the biggest tournament Bradach had to offer, and donated the winnings to pay for medical supplies for more rebel camps – but first, she bought her mother a house, in cash.

Alice took in the sights of the garden, with its lush, brightly colored flowers that hung from baskets and climbed the trellis along the walls. She breathed deep the thick scent of Bradach, her lungs nearly healed from the smoke that had almost killed her. She swallowed back a cough.

"I thought I was going to lose you," Violet said quietly.

"You didn't," Alice reassured her. "You won't get rid of me that easily." She squeezed Violet's hand gently.

"I know I should have said it sooner, I just—"

"It's okay."

"No, Alice, I...I love you."

Alice's cheeks flushed and she smiled. "I love you too, Violet." She kissed her captain, and she tasted of sweet red wine, and she felt like home.

CHAPTER TWENTY-SEVEN

CAPTAIN AUGUSTUS ALLEN dropped his cap to the ground, his mouth hanging wide with surprise. A few of the military crew that had been standing closer to the Stronghold stumbled backward as they tried to escape the heat of the explosion.

"What the fuck happened?" he bellowed to his crew. No one responded to him, too concerned with escaping the heat and choking smoke emitted from the unexpected explosion.

The crew of the Cricket appeared in the loading bay doorway across the courtyard of the derelict camp. The Coalition crew members that had been advancing on the ship, weapons drawn, shouted at them to stop and relinquish any weapons. Captain Allen stared at his ruined, state of the art vessel as bits of flaming metal fell to the ground and smoldered. The air was thick with black smoke from the blaze, and many of the military crew pulled their crisp, soot stained shirts over their faces to act as a makeshift mask.

Violet sobbed violently, choking on the acrid smoke that rose like a feathered plume into the sky. She wrapped her arms around herself and rocked back and forth on her knees as she cried. No one moved to arrest her or contain her; it was clear that she was no threat now.

The smoke flooded the empty camp, bringing stinging tears to the eyes of both crews. There seemed to be no end to the flames, or the smoke, or the suffocating fumes the fiery ship emitted. A series of small explosions punctuated the moment as the blaze reached the secondary generators, and the flames shot out of the scarred windows anew.

Violet stood, shakily, and faced Captain Allen with red rimmed, blood-shot eyes and clenched fists. She took a step towards him, and he recoiled, afraid she would hit him. He motioned for one of the shocked Coalition crew to restrain her, the same short, muscular woman as before. The woman took a tentative step towards Violet, who roared, "Don't you *dare* fucking touch me!"

The woman hesitated and looked at Captain Allen, who seemed just as shocked and unsure as every other crew member, pirate and Coalition, on this small, deserted moon. He leaned away from Violet, whose fury and despair changed the structure of her face. She was wracked with grief, her eyes bloodshot, and it was clear to his crew that he was intimidated. He motioned for his crew member to stand down.

Violet slowly turned towards the opposite end of the courtyard, where her own crew stood in the loading bay door facing their inevitable captors. They were scared, as scared as she was. Ned leaned against the door of the ship, unstable without his cane. He rested a hand on Barnaby's shoulder, who was covering his face with his hands and crying softly. Kady stood off to the side by herself, her hands clasped behind her back and her eyes cast to the floor. The rest of the crew shifted their weight and shuffled their feet, waiting for whatever was about to come next.

Capture or death. Maybe both. Violet knew they were thinking of their families, of people they loved. She hoped that Jasper and Hyun had kept Ivy safe, at least for now. Her chest tightened when she thought of Alice, and she retched again in agony. Alice was gone. Alice was dead.

She watched as Barnaby took a step towards the advancing Coalition troops, his hands held high to show he had no weapons.

"I just want to talk," he said to them in a choked voice, his eyes fixed on Captain Allen. "I want to ask him what his plan is now. Maybe we can all work something out."

Violet didn't care what happened now, not really. They'd all be imprisoned or killed. Alice was dead, and she felt hollow and empty. A husk, a shell of a person. Even if they got out of this alive, they'd be tortured, spend the rest of their days in Coalition work camps. Alice was dead.

"Barnaby, I should have known," Captain Allen said, his voice wavering with faux confidence. "Though I'll admit, I didn't suspect you'd end up with the same crew. Interesting how that panned out. I'll have to write it in my report when I send you to Asset Protection for treason."

Barnaby cocked his head and stared quizzically. "And how do you plan on sending that report? Your ship is gone. The communications tower was dismantled years ago. No messages in or out."

Allen stared across the ruins of the camp at a man he'd known for years to be the best negotiator in the near systems. "We'll be commandeering your ship, of course."

"How? You have no mechanic. You traded mechanics for military crew, and none of them are equipped to handle the kinds of repairs the Cricket needs to fly again. We're all here in the same boat, Captain." Barnaby grew more confident and advanced on his old captain, his hands still held in the air.

Violet's gaze slid across the camp, watching the Coalition crew begin to lower their weapons and cast glances to each other. She could sense the dissension in their ranks, she knew Barnaby had deliberately planted a seed of doubt in their minds. She looked to her senior officers, Ned still leaning against the door. Kady's position had shifted almost imperceptibly, but Violet noticed that the revolvers she had thrown down after exiting the ship had disappeared from the ground. Had Kady picked them up?

"I'm sure we'll manage," Captain Allen snarled, "even if we have to dismantle your entire crew to do it. I have every confidence that you'll be able to figure out how to repair this ship when the alternative is being taken apart, piece by piece."

Barnaby shook his head and pursed his lips in frustration. "I respected you, Captain Allen. But your mechanic of three decades just died, and your ship has exploded, and your crew doesn't know what to do." He took a step forward. "Alice is dead, Augustus. Doesn't that mean anything to you?"

"Captain Allen," he replied icily. "And she means nothing within the scope of what the Coalition means to every settlement across near systems. She was a traitor. She committed treason. I have no time for liars and thieves." He moved to unholster his revolver. "And that goes for you, too."

Before Captain Allen could take his revenge on Barnaby for making a fool of him, there was a loud, strange dragging sound from the open loading bay door of the Stronghold. The flames had begun to subside, leaving behind the charred metal skeleton that had once been the pride of the Coalition trade fleet. Bits of flaming debris littered the crumbling brick buildings and cracked, mossy cobblestone paths. Violet turned slowly to the Stronghold, and every eye was fixed to the ship.

Alice emerged from the lingering flames, the end of her silver braid smoldering and covered in ash. She was bent, dragging the body of the Coalition crew member who had escorted her onto the ship. Exhausted, her lungs were filled with the acrid, toxic smoke. She collapsed in the doorway and fell back into the ship, behind the unconscious Coalition captor.

Violet stumbled over her own feet as she scrambled to reach the door of the Stronghold. "Alice!" she yelled into the thick smoke. "Alice, I'm coming!"

The other Coalition crew members stood transfixed by the unexpected resurrection. A few near the ship pushed Violet out of the way to drag their friend to safety, grabbing his ankles and pulling him down the ramp and off the Stronghold. Violet shoved the Coalition crew member who tried to restrain her. He tripped backwards off the ramp, and by the time he recovered his balance, Violet had run into the still burning ship.

"Alice!" she shouted. Her eyes burned, she couldn't see. She reached out, and Alice grasped her hand. She pulled hard, yanking Alice upright and dragging her back towards the door and out of the ship. They fell in a heap off the ramp, and Violet leapt up and yelled back to someone, anyone who would listen. "She needs medical attention! Get Hyun!" She wasn't about to trust Alice's life to someone who wanted her dead.

Alice's distraction of emerging from the flames alive had allowed the Cricket's crew to capitalize on the inattention of the Coalition crew. They now had weapons drawn, pointed at the backs of their would-be captors. But Captain Augustus Allen had also taken advantage of the distraction, and was now pointing a large revolver at Barnaby.

"How do you think this is going to end, Violet?" he asked, cocking the revolver. "You're outgunned."

Violet cradled Alice's head in her hands and stroked her singed silvery hair. "That may be true," she said softly, the roar of the flames now just a quiet hiss of steam escaping from the external vents. "But we're a family, and I'm not going to let you harm a single one of them."

"Give it up, Violet," he laughed. "You're not going to come out of this alive unless you stand down."

"And what of your crew?" Kady asked loudly. "How will you keep them fed while you tear us apart in hopes that our ship can be repaired?" She glanced sideways at her captain and nodded confidently, showing that she, too, had noticed the quiet questioning from the Coalition crew. "All of our food and supplies were damaged. We have nothing left."

Allen wavered almost imperceptibly. "Alice can repair your ship, and we'll be on our way in no more than a few days."

"I don't know if you've noticed, Captain Allen, but Alice isn't fit for duty," Hyun retorted as she gently pushed her way through the crew of the Cricket, holding a medical bag in one hand and holding the other out to show she was no threat. She was wearing her worn white medical coat, which was now covered in Ivy's blood, splattered across the front. "She needs immediate medical attention, and so does your crew member. Where is your medical staff?"

He looked around at his crew. "Medical staff was left behind on the base." He squared his shoulders and held the revolver out, with his elbows locked. "We know what we're signing up for, sometimes that means an unfortunate, unexpected injury."

"He'll die if no one sees to him," Hyun clarified as she crossed the ruins. "I'll see to Alice first, and then I'll see to your crew member. But you have to put the guns down."

Several of the Coalition crew members immediately laid their weapons down, wanting their unconscious friend and compatriot to get the necessary medical attention. But Captain Allen kept his revolver trained on Barnaby. "I'm not going to negotiate with pirates."

The short, muscular woman quietly set her rifle down on the ground and stepped back from it. "Captain Allen, aren't we bound by Coalition law to do whatever it takes to preserve a colleague's life?" She spoke softly but surely, a steely glint in her eyes. "Are you just going to let him die?"

Hyun knelt down next to Alice and strapped a small respirator over her nose and mouth. Violet gently laid Alice's head down and stood to face the rest of her crew and Captain Allen's, giving Hyun the space she needed to see to Alice's injuries.

Violet was bolstered by Alice's survival, and felt stronger than ever. She cleared her throat and addressed the Coalition crew with a clear, steady voice. "Any of you who want to come with us, lay down your weapons. We'll ensure your safe passage to a neutral base, where you can join another crew. I'm sure you'll all understand that given the circumstances, I can't take you on staff myself." She looked down at Alice and smiled with relief. "This is a one time only offer. Lay your weapons down, or face potential starvation on this desolate moon, or injury, or whatever else the Coalition has in store for you."

Allen laughed. "These are some of the finest Coalition members, some have served for years. They'll never join you. And they also know that you would kill them the moment they step on board."

"I'm a woman of my word, pirate or not," Violet said, her voice calm and firm. "The Coalition may not keep their promises, but I always do."

Quietly, a few Coalition crew members set their weapons on the cold, mossy ground. They kicked away their rifles, their heat guns, and their revolvers. Other crew members stared at their fellow crew mates in shock, but they didn't raise their weapons to the defectors.

Violet looked to her crew and noticed a hole in the crowd: Kady was missing. She cracked a small smile in the corners of her mouth. She was starting to see a way out of this mess, if Kady was doing what she thought she might be. "Last chance, everyone: lay down your weapons. I promise, our brig is very comfortable, and you'll be set free at the first opportunity."

She watched as nervous glances were exchanged, and weapons set down. Some of the Coalition crew, if you could still call them that, had begun to strip off their uniforms, leaving them in standard issue gray pants and ash covered white cotton undershirts.

Captain Allen was left with a small group of uniformed officers, who had begun to back into a tight circle.

"Cricket crew, kindly collect the weapons and store them in the armory under lock and key. Escort these good people to the brig, and ensure they have plenty of water, blankets, and supplies. Their weapons will be returned to them when they leave our ship."

Allen stepped towards Barnaby, who still held his hands up in surrender. "I can still kill this one if you even think about it," he shouted, his voice becoming unhinged and unstable. "The rest of you, you'll be court-martialed the second we return to base if you so much as set foot on that ship!" he roared.

"You'd have let Roberts die," one retorted loudly, gesturing to the unconscious Coalition crew member that Alice had dragged from the wreckage, now being tended by Hyun. "And you'd have let us starve, too." The defectors quietly boarded the Cricket, led by Ned.

One of the last defectors turned to Captain Allen as she stepped onto the Cricket. "Fuck you, Allen!" she yelled, and several of her crew members laughed.

"It seems like loyalty to your crew counts for a lot these days," Violet mused. "And you're not going to shoot poor Barnaby, either."

"And why is that?" he retorted.

Kady jumped down from the Cricket, holding one of the droids in the palm of her hand. Her cloak swirled around her legs, and she pushed the hood down off of her head. "I think you may remember these, Allen?"

"I remember you," he said, "you're that scientist who defected a couple years back. Imagine if they found you. Imagine the mountain of credits I'll get when I turn you in. Imagine the front page of the papers after I tell the reporters that I saved the near systems from a dangerous terrorist who had stolen Coalition technology."

She held the droid aloft. "I don't think that's going to be happening."

"You can't detonate that, or all those new friends you have will also die. So will Alice, and Barnaby."

Barnaby moved now, showing his arm where the chip was implanted. "It's been deactivated, Augustus. Why do you think they've never been able to track some defectors? Kady was waiting inside the Cricket to deactivate their chips. It's quite ingenious, really, only takes a second." He dropped his hands to his sides. "They're free to go and do as they please."

The color drained from Allen's face. "That can't be true."

"I assure you, it is true. Now drop the weapon." Kady gestured to Allen's revolver.

One of his remaining officers laid his weapon down and looked pleadingly at Violet. "I've changed my mind, can I come with you?"

Violet shook her head slowly. "I did say it was a one time offer. You'll have to stay here."

"You're going to leave us here to die!" the officer shouted, sharp panic in his voice. "You have to let us come with you!"

"We'll make sure someone drops by to pick you up in a few days. I'm not a monster, but I am practical and fair. We'll send an anonymous tip to the Coalition when we get to a neutral trading beacon in a day or two." Violet stood guard over Alice, who was now sitting upright and taking everything in silently.

"You!" Allen yelled at Alice, brandishing his revolver. "What did you do to my ship, you treasonous brigand? I'll see you killed for your crimes, I swear it!"

Still wearing the respirator, she wordlessly pulled one of the detonation droids from her sooty coverall pockets. She set it on the mossy ground beside her, and gave Captain Augustus Allen a mock salute.

"It's important to remember that Coalition technology always leaks out," Kady said. "Best not to make weapons you have no defense for. We found another pirate ship with these on board before Alice stole a box from your ship. They're out there, Allen."

"You still can't go anywhere, your ship is inoperative!" Allen screeched in desperation.

"Oh, we lied." Kady shrugged her shoulders. "We just needed some extra power reserves, which we've got now. Plenty to get us somewhere safe, right Captain?"

Violet nodded. "The Cricket is beat up, but she'll survive. I guess that's it for us, isn't it, Augustus?" She stepped towards him and smirked. "Looks like we won the war, doesn't it? You're out of options."

Resigned, he lowered his revolver and holstered it. "You'll never get away with this. They'll catch you the second you make contact with anyone."

"We'll see about that," Violet replied confidently. "We have a lot of friends across the near systems that would do anything to help us out. Seems that's not the case for you. Not anymore."

· · · ·

WITH THE CREW AND THE defectors safe on board, and the power restored to the appropriate systems, Ned plotted a course to the nearest neutral trading beacon, and the ship lifted off. Violet watched the Coalition loyalists grow smaller as the ship rose higher and into the atmosphere, until they were obscured by clouds and lingering plumes of smoke from the explosion.

She walked the corridors to the crowded med bay, where Alice, Ivy, and the injured defector were receiving treatment. As she entered the room, Hyun and Jasper were hard at work tending to the injured parties. Alice sat up in bed, her eyes closed as Hyun dressed her burns. She was wearing a medical gown, her Coalition issues coveralls cut and discarded at the foot of the bed, singed and torn. Violet smiled at the mechanic and took her hand. "You scared me, Alice."

"Sorry," Alice rasped, her voice burned from the smoke. She interlaced her fingers with Violet's and nodded towards Ivy's bed. "Ivy."

"Hush now," Hyun said sternly with a smile. "Let your throat and lungs heal." She busied herself propping Ivy up with a plethora of cushions.

Ivy blinked blearily. "Cap," she said softly. "Did we win?"

Violet gave a wry smile. "Well, in a way, but we still have to worry about the lockdown, and being called in. But we're safe, for now. We scavenged some generators, so we can keep the cloaking shield on permanently."

"But Captain, the data..." Ivy cocked her head in confusion and winced in pain as Hyun checked her bandages.

"It's okay, you did your best," Violet reassured her. "We were wrong to even put you in that position."

"No, Captain, I—" she winced again as Hyun checked the wound on her head. "I got rid of the data. I purged it from the system."

Violet blinked and looked at Hyun quizzically. "Ivy, I think you might be confused, you never made it to the base."

"No, I did," Ivy insisted. "The microphone got damaged somehow. I could hear all of you, but you couldn't hear me."

"You deleted the data?" Violet asked again, her eyes wide.

Ivy gave a tiny nod. "It's cleared from the system. As far as Coalition is concerned, we never existed. There may be stories about us, but that's all." She grinned impishly. "It's like we never existed. You're all ghosts, just like me."

Violet began to laugh a deep, raucous, belly aching laugh, even as Hyun tried to shush her. She bent double with laughter, as tears streamed down her cheeks. "So what happened to the shuttle?" she asked in between gasps of air.

"I was a little late getting back, and the Stronghold saw me flying in. They caught me as I was trying to land in the loading bay, if they'd got me any sooner I wouldn't have been able to make it back." Ivy shifted against the cushions propping her up. "Hyun says I'll make a full recovery, I'm just not allowed to sleep tonight, in case of concussion."

Hyun sat in a squashy chair near the door. "Yes, but I'll stay here with you. I'll need to monitor you all. Jasper has agreed to take shifts with me, Captain."

Violet nodded. "I thought he might ask for that. And the unconscious crew member?"

"We've loosely restrained him for now, but I don't think he'll be a problem. It's my understanding that one of the defectors is in fact his lover." Hyun looked at Violet from the corner of her eye. "Seems maybe he's not the only one fraternizing with coworkers?"

The captain cleared her throat. "I, uh..." she started, "it's complicated, and— "

Alice leaned forward and kissed Violet, squeezing her hand. "Shh."

Violet smiled and kissed her back. "I guess it's not that complicated after all."

END OF BOOK ONE

Keep reading for a sneak peek into the next novel in the series, Imperfect Shot.

Sign up for my newsletter and get information about convention appearances, book launch parties, new releases, and more! Get bonus content for the Cricket Chronicles series like deleted scenes and extended cuts. You can unsubscribe at any time with no obligation.

http://eepurl.com/gOQBaP

• • • •

FOLLOW ME

You can follow me on Twitter at @IMRyannFletcher, on Facebook @RyannFletcherWrites, or email at RyannFletcherBooks@Gmail.com. It's always great to hear from you!

IMPERFECT SHOT PREVIEW

Evie scrubbed at a sticky patch on the worn wooden bar, watching the slight sheen of the dried ale disappear. She rubbed her shoulder, prodding at the knot in the muscle from a long day of hefting heavy boxes of ale, whiskey, and wine all the way from the port back to the Purple Pig Tavern where she had worked for the better part of five years. She didn't mind the work, but preferred it when people left her alone to do her job. Pull a pint, serve the liquor, wipe the bar. Her boss, Tansy, was trusting her to make fair trades, goods for booze, and log it all at the end of her shift.

The gold clock on the wall ticked slowly, in spite of the glare she gave it. She could swear it was moving backwards. Her girlfriend was coming back from a salvage mission today, after three weeks drifting in the Near Systems looking for scrap they could sell at a profit. Holly was the most beautiful woman Evie had ever seen, tall and curvy with long, wavy locks of brunette hair and eyes so blue, you could almost see straight into space when you looked into them. In fact, Evie wasn't sure how she managed to end up with someone as perfect as Holly anyway, not with her dead end job. When she met Holly in the Purple Pig six months ago, her heart nearly pounded out of her chest. She'd almost choked on the dregs of her ale when Holly gently caressed her cheek and asked her on a date.

"Hello Babes!" Holly shouted as she burst through the swinging doors of the tavern. She swung her long, shapely legs over a bronze stool and leaned seductively over the bar in front of Evie. "Did you miss me?"

"Of *course* I missed you," Evie said, unable to contain her enthusiasm. "I've been counting the days until you came back."

"I'll bet you have," Holly said with a wink. "When are you off? I can't wait to tell you my surprise!"

"A surprise?" Evie hadn't been expecting a gift. In fact, just seeing Holly's perfect face was gift enough for her. She'd missed her desperately, and being in Holly's presence was like raising your face to the sun after a long, cold night.

"Mhmm," Holly nodded absent-mindedly. "So when are you finished?"

"Another few minutes yet," Evie admitted, a sullen, petulant tone to her voice. She couldn't leave until her replacement, Eli, arrived, and he was never early. Even if he was, she doubted he'd let her leave even a few seconds before the end of her scheduled shift. "Why don't you grab a seat and some food, and I'll join you when I'm finished?"

Holly wrinkled her nose. "I don't want to eat *here*."

Before Evie could argue, a group of scrappers wandered in, laughing and shoving each other playfully. Holly waved to them and grinned, her pearl white teeth nearly blinding in the relaxed, dim light of the tavern. "Hey!" she shouted, beckoning to them loudly over the din of the other tavern patrons. She turned back to Evie. "Babes, say hi to my team." Her sparkly eyes glimmered and melted Evie's heart. How could one person be so beautiful, so intelligent and perfect, and be interested in her? Evie gazed at Holly's face, and couldn't wait to feel the weight of the woman in her arms. "Babes?" Holly prompted.

Evie waved and squeaked out a quiet "hello" before they, and Holly, left the bar to crowd around a table in the center of the room, but not before placing a sizable drinks order. She bustled about, preparing their drinks one by one. Two pints of ale, seven shots of whiskey, four glasses of fortified red wine so strong it would eat through the lush purple velvet that covered the walls. The group was chatty and loud, and Evie watched their interactions with interest. Holly had told her that the crew had all known each other for years, hopping from ship to ship to get the most lucrative salvage missions, but the way they all looked at her told Evie they were just as dazzled by Holly's presence as she was.

"Hey, Holly," said a sultry voice from the entrance. When Evie looked, she saw a tall, broad shouldered woman with features almost more striking than Holly's. She was dressed in the same navy blue jumpsuits as the others, with their salvage team name represented by an embroidered gold snake on the collar. The woman glided over to the table and leaned gracefully on the back of Holly's chair. "I looked everywhere for you at the port, I didn't realize you'd be coming here."

Holly beamed up at the woman with wide, innocent eyes. "I just assumed you'd head up this way, Babes," she said sweetly, and Evie flushed with jealousy. "Anyway you're here now, but we aren't staying long, the food here sucks."

"We have a new cook since you were last here," Evie interjected helpfully, and punctuated her suggestion with a nervous cough. Holly's team intimidated her; they were brazen, successful salvagers with plenty of credits to spend and none of the insecurities that plagued Evie.

"Oh, don't worry Babes, we have plans to eat at that new place on the other side of the port."

This was the first Evie was hearing about it, and in fact she had assumed that she and Holly were going to go back to her room and have a quiet night in. Maybe Holly wanted her to become more friendly with her team? "Oh, okay, I'll run home and change my clothes," Evie said, untying the strings of her dirty, ale soaked apron. She heard Eli come in through the back door of the tavern, and the clock finally proved that her shift was over.

"Oh, Babes..." Holly said, looking guilty. She walked to the bar and leaned over it to kiss Evie on the cheek. "We only got reservations for team members." She made an apologetic face that made Evie giggle. "I can't wait to tell you about your surprise, though...meet you later, at yours?"

Evie nodded enthusiastically. "Of course." She was disappointed that they weren't going to have dinner together, but this is just how things were with Holly. She had important clients to meet and impress with her charm and prowess in salvage, and Evie with her shabby dungarees and messy tuft of hair just didn't fit into that world. It was understandable, and in fact, necessary, that she wasn't a part of that scene. She would only hurt Holly's chances at the more profitable contracts, and she'd never want to do that. Her pride wasn't worth her girlfriend's career, that was for sure.

"We're heading off, Babes," Holly called from the table. "I'll see you later, yeah?"

"Yeah, see you later," Evie agreed, though she couldn't quite swallow back the disappointment that she wasn't going with them. At least she had time to go back home and get cleaned up before Holly came over; she hated the way that Evie's clothes smelled after working a shift. Grease, booze, and on particularly unfortunate days, vomit. She watched the group gather their things and leave half empty glasses on their table, waving over their shoulders as they piled out onto the cobblestone street. It would have been nice if they had returned their dirty cups to her at the bar, but it was okay, they had reservations at the swanky place across town. She collected the dishes and piled them on top of a sticky tray, and looked up just in time to see the new woman drape an arm around Holly's shoulder. Envy burned in her stomach, but she swallowed it down. Holly would never betray her, that woman must just be a close friend.

A woman dressed in black pushed her way past Holly's group into the tavern, rolling her eyes. She sat down at the bar and pushed a wide, heavy hood off her head. It flopped onto her shoulders and she looked up at Evie. "Rum. Make it a double." She had a confident, disarming smile that Evie liked, even though she'd never seen the woman in the Purple Pig before.

"Sure thing, coming right up," Evie said, pouring thick, amber liquid into a small glass. "I've not seen you in here before," she offered, setting the glass in front of the woman.

"I'm finishing up an assignment," the woman said bluntly. "I've been in here once or twice before, though."

Evie glanced over her shoulder into the kitchen area of the tavern, but she still couldn't see Eli. Odd, but she shrugged it off. "Well, welcome back, then," Evie said, trying to put the thought of Holly and the woman out of her mind. "Staying long?"

"No," the woman replied. "My line of work is very fast paced, you could say."

"And what do you do for work?" Evie asked. But before the woman could answer, Eli stumbled into the bar.

"Evie," he said in a pleading voice. "Can you take my shift? I'm a little, uh—"

"Hungover?" Evie interjected. "I can tell. You look like you're about to keel over." She sighed angrily. "Eli, I told you, Holly is back tonight, I can't work late. She's been gone for weeks, and once she gets back from dinner with her team, I—"

"She went to dinner without you?" the woman asked. "After weeks away?"

Evie stared. "Yes, but it's for work, she had no choice."

The woman shrugged. "Sounds like bullshit to me."

Evie turned back to Eli, deciding to ignore the woman. "Eli, are you sure you can't just suck it up and work the shift?"

Eli covered his mouth and retched. "No, Evie, I don't think I can. Can't Tansy cover for me?"

"I don't know, did you ask her?"

Eli shook his head but wandered away to drag himself up the stairs to Tansy's office and room where she lived, ever since she bought the Purple Pig over a decade earlier. Tansy was no stranger to piracy, even though she hadn't grown up in Bradach like Evie had. She'd gotten injured on an illegal salvage mission over ten years ago, and dumped her life savings into the tavern when she realized she couldn't go on salvage missions forever. She'd turned the tavern from a grubby, dank hole into a borderline opulent tavern for pirates and scavengers of all kinds to have a drink and a meal before they set off into space again.

"Did you want anything else?" Evie asked the woman in a steely tone, turning back to face her.

"Another."

"It's not her choice you know," Evie said as she poured rum into the glass. "If Holly had her say, I'd be eating dinner with the rest of them tonight. Or we'd be at my place, and I'd make her dinner. She's beautiful, and kind, and she cares about me."

The woman stared at her for a moment before taking a sip of the rum. "Are you trying to convince me, or yourself?" she asked.

"You!" Evie said, a little louder than she had intended. She felt flustered that this stranger could just insert herself into her life and make assumptions about her relationship. "It's actually rather rude for you to say these things, and I—"

The woman put her hands up to silence Evie. "Look, lady, what's your name again?"

"Evie."

"Look, Evie, I'm not trying to make waves for you and your girl, alright?" she drained her glass and set it down noisily on the bar. "I'm just saying, it seems real inconsiderate. If some asshole said I couldn't bring my girl to dinner, I'd sock him one, right in the nose." She winked at Evie and slammed down a chunk of metal on the bar that looked like a part for an appliance or a ship. "This enough to get me another?"

"I don't know what that is."

"It's some kind of rare ship part, I don't know, some mechanic gave it to me."

Rolling the part around in her palm, Evie examined the piece of metal. It was cold and smooth, a long empty cylinder with jagged edges that suggested it had, until recently, been attached to something. "I don't know, my boss..." Evie mumbled, wishing the woman had something normal to trade for her drinks. Some gold, or stolen scrap metal, or even outdated tech would be preferable to hunks of metal.

"Come on, Blue, I promise it's worth more credits than you get paid in a month." The woman leaned forward across the bar. "Nice hair, by the way."

Evie pushed a stray tuft of blue hair off her forehead and huffed. "Don't call me that," Evie said. Something about the woman's unapologetic confidence and charm was disarming, and made her feel off balance and irritated. She sighed again and logged the odd part into the trade book under the counter before pouring the woman another glass of rum.

"Thank you," the woman said, running her fingers around the rim of the glass. "It's much appreciated, and your kindness won't go unrewarded."

Evie snorted a laugh. "Oh yeah? What are you going to do, waltz in here in a few months and dump a pile of rare ore into my lap?"

The woman shrugged. "Maybe. Or maybe your luck will improve, and you'll end up an heiress to some mining fortune." She held the rum close to her face and inhaled the scent of the amber liquid. "Maybe your girl will take you out for dinner at that fancy restaurant next time." Before Evie could reply, the woman squinted at her and leaned over onto the bar. "You know, I never could see why anyone would want a restaurant like that in a port like this. Pirates, scavengers, nobility, Coalition, it doesn't matter. Give someone a little money and all of a sudden they think they're better than anyone else."

"Mm," Evie nodded, aware that the rum was loosening the woman's tongue. "Yes, I'd agree. But there's no feasible alternative, not while the Coalition still holds most of the Near Systems in its grip."

"See, there's where you're wrong, Evie," the woman said, pointing at her. "Sometimes, you just gotta pry up some planks and see what's underneath. If it's rotten, it's rotten. And rot needs to be gotten rid of, don't ya think?"

"I think you should take a breather on that rum," Evie laughed, taking the empty glass from the woman. "What are you in here running from, anyway?"

The woman stared for a moment. "Nah. Nothin'. Just wanted a good time."

Evie turned to serve another patron of the tavern, and paused to wipe down the bar again. Where the hell was Eli? The clock chimed, and Evie wondered if Holly was enjoying her meal at the upscale restaurant. She wished she could go there someday, but unless things changed for her, it was unlikely that dream would come true. Tansy paid her a fair wage, but there were limits to her generosity. Bradach assured that every citizen had shelter, food, and care, but Evie had always wanted more for herself than to stay where she'd been planted, infamous pirate port or no. What else was out there for her? Maybe nothing. Maybe an adventure, or at least an experience to remember that wasn't the same old routine of working at the tavern, and going home to her small room in a shared house.

"Eli?" she called up the winding staircase, her voice lost among the noise of the tavern. "Eli, come on!" she said, getting frustrated. She turned back to the bar and cleared the empty glasses, setting them noisily into a damp wooden crate.

"You should stop being a doormat," the woman said, her head propped up on one hand.

"I'm not a doormat," Evie replied, her tone with more of an edge than she had intended. "What else am I supposed to do, just leave?"

The woman laughed. "You could do that. You could also march up those stairs and drag his hungover ass back down to the bar and leave him to nurse his headache and his sore stomach while you go home to the girlfriend who definitely respects you enough to not get cuddly with her new recruit right in front of your place of work." She tilted her head to the side in an appraising way as she looked at Evie. "But that's just me."

"You know, I'm surprised you've not been thrown out of more taverns with this kind of attitude. Most barkeeps wouldn't tolerate it, you're lucky I'm nice."

"Alright, prove me wrong. Throw me out, then." The woman raised an eyebrow and sat up straight, like she was challenging Evie to toss her out of the tavern for her comments about Holly. A moment passed, and Evie went back to wiping down the bar. "That's what I thought," the woman said, a smile playing at her lips.

"Hey, Evie," Tansy said apologetically as she descended the stairs outside her office. "Eli's not in good shape. Certainly not in any condition to work tonight." Tansy's tweed shorts brushed against dark skin and alloy; her time as a scavenger had left her with one top of the line, expertly crafted cybernetic prosthetic leg that she was proud of showing off. "If you could just stay on for another couple of hours..."

"I told Eli that I have plans tonight," Evie complained. "Holly is back, and I was going to spend time with her."

"Holly, who went to dinner *without* her," the woman snorted.

Evie whirled around and glared at the woman. "Keep out of this," she hissed.

"Alright, let's just take a breath, Evie," Tansy said, stepping behind the bar and tying an apron around her waist. "I'll cover for Eli until the next shift starts. Go see your girl. I'll see you back here tomorrow."

"Thank you," Evie said, heaving a sigh of relief. "You don't know how much this means to me." She wiped her hands off on her worn canvas dungarees and lifted the bar counter to slide out from behind it. "I'll be here for my shift, don't worry."

"Yeah, you'd better be," Tansy laughed. "Next time I'll be the one with plans. Don't let me down like Eli did tonight."

Evie rolled her eyes. "Definitely not." She yanked her cap from a hook on the wall and gestured towards the woman at the bar. "And no more for her, she's had enough." She smirked at the woman's incredulous face and clapped her on the back. "Not so much a doormat as you thought, am I?" she said, low enough so only the woman could hear.

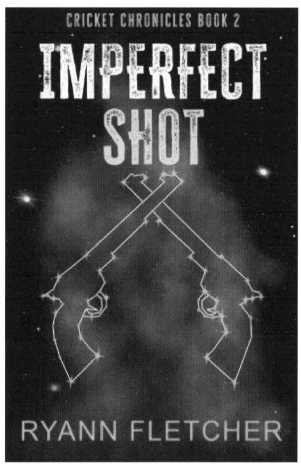

Coming soon in paperback and ebook! Pre-order your copy at
https://books2read.com/imperfectshot

Thank you

DEUS EX MECHANIC WAS my first novel, and wouldn't exist without a long train ride without wi-fi, too many notebooks, and the absolute, unwavering support of my wife, without whom this book wouldn't exist. Her constant enthusiasm is what pushed this book from idea to first draft to final, even in the face of several setbacks.

Another huge thanks to all beta readers and advance copy readers and their honest feedback. Your patience with me is noted and appreciated, and your cheerleading helped this book overcome the last few hurdles between finished draft and published copy.

And finally, I want to thank YOU for reading this book, and putting your faith in me as an author to purchase this book. I hope that you will stick with me and the crew of the Cricket and join us again in book two: Imperfect Shot.

Printed in Great Britain
by Amazon